RUNAWAY

Also by Peter May

FICTION

The Lewis Trilogy

The Blackhouse

The Lewis Man

The Chessmen

The China Thrillers

The Firemaker

The Fourth Sacrifice

The Killing Room

Snakehead

The Runner

Chinese Whispers

The Enzo Files

Extraordinary People

The Critic

Blacklight Blue

Freeze Frame

Blowback

Standalone Novels

Entry Island

Virtually Dead

NON-FICTION

Hebrides (with David Wilson)

PETER MAY

RUNAWAY

Quercus

First published in Great Britain in 2015 by

Quercus Editions Ltd
55 Baker Street
7th Floor, South Block
London
W1U 8EW

A CIP catalogue record for this book is available from the British Library

ISBN 978 1 78087 455 5 (HB)
ISBN 978 1 78429 982 8 (TPB)
ISBN 978 1 78429 995 8 (EBOOK)

10 9 8 7 6 5 4 3 2 1

Typeset by CC Book Production

Printed and bound in Great Britain by Clays Ltd, St Ives plc

For Janis

The Moving Finger writes; and, having writ,
Moves on: nor all thy Piety nor Wit
Shall lure it back to cancel half a Line,
Nor all thy Tears wash out a Word of it.

The Rubáiyát of Omar Khayyám

PROLOGUE

London

He wakes in a cold sweat from a dream pervaded by darkness and blood. And after a lifetime of being someone else in another land, he wonders who he is now. This man who, he knows, is fading all too soon. A life squandered for a love lost. A life that seems to have passed in the blink of an eye.

The three weeks since he has returned to these shores have somehow felt the longest of that life. Strange how pain and fear stretch time beyond limits undreamed, while the search for happiness is over almost before it begins. And from some long-forgotten past, lost in chalk dust and warm milk, comes a recollection of relativity. Put your hand on a hot stove for a minute, and it seems like an hour. Sit with a pretty girl for an hour, and it seems like a minute.

He came by boat. A ferry crossing from Calais. Symbolic of that day so long ago when he had steered his boat through a spring haar to a foreign shore. There had been a moment at passport control. His heart almost stopping as the immigration officer opened his passport. But he had given it the most cursory of glances. Because, of course, no one was looking for him any more. Not after all these years. An old man, pale and perspiring, he had been waved through without a second look. That's who he is. A stranger here now.

It is dark and hot in this squalid little bedsit, curtains drawn against the lights of the city and the constant thrum of night traffic invading his dreams. What little light there is gradually forms shadows around the room, and for the first time he realizes that something has wakened him. Some sixth sense that warns him suddenly that there is someone else in the room.

He sits up, startled. 'Who's there?'

For a moment there is silence.

Then a voice swings out of the dark, words like boxing gloves landing soft blows about his head. 'Relax, old friend. It is time we talked.' Gentle and almost reassuring.

He knows immediately who it is. 'How did you find me?'

He hears the other smile.

Then the voice again, condescending, almost chiding. 'Simon, Simon. It was a simple matter to follow you from the café.' A breath. 'How on earth did you manage to stay undetected all this time?'

'What do you want? Did I not make myself clear?'

'Crystal.'

'Then what is there to talk about?'

The shape of a man detaches itself from the shadows and looms suddenly over him. 'Death, of course.'

Simon hears, more than sees, the movement. The rustle of cotton on silk. And then the soft, cool texture of the cord as it loops around his neck. It tightens with unexpected speed and ferocity. There is no time to cry out. His hands grasp his attacker's wrists, but the realization comes quickly that he is not strong enough to stop this. Still, he won't give up the struggle. This is not what he came back for. But what strength he has ebbs quickly, and he becomes aware of a face just inches from his. The little light there is in the room gathering itself into reflections in once familiar eyes. Cruel now, and filled with hate. He feels the other's breath on his face, like the breath of eternity. Before blackness comes to extinguish light and life for ever.

Slowly his killer releases his lifeless form to fall back on the bed, frail with age but heavier now in death. The click in the dark seems deafening and the light that falls upon the bed, like the dead man, almost shocking.

Hands in latex gloves untie a canvas roll, and open it out on still warm sheets. Light reflects on a choice of five glinting, sterile scalpels. Simon's nightshirt is rolled back from his left forearm, and one of the scalpels is selected. All performed with the unerring certainty of a man who knows he has all the time in the world for this.

Carefully, and with a well-honed and dextrous skill, the killer starts to cut away the skin of the forearm, effectively flaying it. There is very little blood to stain the bed. For the heart has long since given up any attempt at pumping it around Simon's rapidly cooling body.

2015

CHAPTER ONE

Glasgow

I

Jack stepped down from the bus almost at the end of Battlefield Road and raised his head towards the darkening sky with a sense of foreboding. He took in the brooding silhouette of the smoke-stained Victoria Infirmary that climbed the hill above the field of battle where Mary, Queen of Scots, was once defeated by James VI, and felt as if someone had just walked over his grave.

He knew, in truth, that he no longer needed his stick. Most of his strength had returned, and the prognosis following his minor myocardial infarction was good. The diet they put him on had successfully lowered his cholesterol and the daily walking, they said, would do him more good than an hour in the gym.

Still, he had grown to depend upon it, like an old friend. He enjoyed the feel of the brass owl curled into the palm of his hand, steadying, reliable. Unchanging, unlike everything else around him.

Gone was the old Queen's Park School, abandoned, then damaged by fire, and finally demolished. The Battlefield Rest, with its green and cream tiles and clock tower, once a news kiosk and waiting room for city trams, now an Italian restaurant. The red sandstone Langside Library was still there, a final gift from Carnegie, but the infirmary itself, filled for Jack with both formative and final memories, was due for closure, its functions to be replaced by the new Southern General.

His tonsils and adenoids had been removed here as a child. He could still remember the smell of rubber as they put the mask over his face to send him to sleep in the operating theatre, and the line of light beneath the door of his two-bed ward that night, mysterious shadows passing back and forth in the corridor beyond, like dark demons stalking his young imagination.

But as he stepped into the shabby green-painted foyer and breathed in that depressing antiseptic hospital smell, the memory that almost overwhelmed him was of the death of his mother.

Those dark winter evenings he had spent at her bedside, finding her sometimes distressed, at other times almost comatose, and once lying in her own filth. And then, finally, the night he had arrived to find her bed empty. Moved, the ward sister told him, to another building.

It had taken him some time to find her. And when he did, he felt as if he had stepped on to a stage set for some dreadful denouement. A cavernous Victorian ward, chaotic in its arrangement of beds and screens, light in pools barely permeating the darkness. She had gripped his hand, scared by the moans and occasional cries of unseen patients, and whispered, 'They've brought me here to die.' And then, 'I don't want to go alone.'

He had sat with her as long as they would let him. Then visiting time was done, and they told him he must leave. She hadn't wanted him to go, and his last sight of her was glancing back to see the fear in her eyes.

The next morning a police officer came to his door. The hospital had lost his number – as they always had, no matter how many times he gave them it. His mother had died during the night. Alone, as she had feared, and it had filled Jack with a lingering sense of guilt that had never quite left him.

He had heard that Maurie was suffering from cancer, although he hadn't actually seen him in years. And when his rabbi called to say that Maurie wanted to see him, it had come as news that his old friend had also suffered a major heart attack. Still, neither piece of news had prepared him for the shadow of a man who lay propped against the pillows of his hospital bed.

Maurie had always been inclined to plumpness, even in his teens. Then the good life that followed his elevation to the Glasgow Bar – and a solicitor's property business that earned him a small fortune – had turned plump into corpulent.

Now only loose skin hung on his bones, a once full face cadaverous, his age-spattered skull almost bereft of hair following the chemo. He looked twenty years older than Jack's sixty-seven. Of another generation.

Yet those dark brown eyes of his still burned with an intensity that belied appearances. There were tubes attached to his arms and face, but he seemed oblivious of them as he pulled himself into a seated position, animated suddenly by Jack's arrival. And in his smile, Jack saw the old Maurie. Mischievous, knowing, superior. The ultimate showman, self-confident and full of himself onstage, knowing that he had a great voice, and that no matter how many of them there were in the band, all eyes were on him.

Two nurses sat on the end of the bed watching *Coronation Street* on his television.

'Go, go,' he urged them. 'We have things to discuss in private here.'

And Jack was struck by how feeble that once powerful voice had become.

'Shut the door,' he said to Jack, when they had gone. Then, 'I pay for that bloody TV, you know, and they watch it more than I do.'

Jewish was a part he enjoyed playing but never took too seriously. Or so Jack had thought. 'My people,' he had always talked about with a twinkle. But nearly four thousand years of history ran deep. Jack had grown up in a Conservative, south-side Protestant household, and so when he first started going to Maurie's house it had seemed strange and exotic. Gefilte fish and matzo bread. Shul after school, synagogue on the sabbath, and the bar mitzvah, that coming of a Jewish boy's age. Candles burning in the Menorah, two in the window on the eve of the sabbath and nine at Hanukkah. The mezuzah affixed to all the door jambs.

Maurie's relationship with his parents had been conducted *à haute voix*, at first shocking to Jack, as if they were constantly at war with one another. Always shouting. Before he had come to realize that it was simply their way.

Maurie grinned at Jack. 'You haven't changed a bit.'

'Liar!'

Maurie's smile faded and he lowered his voice, grabbing Jack's wrist with surprisingly strong fingers. 'We've got to go back.'

Jack frowned. 'Back where?'

'To London.'

'London?' Jack had no idea what he was talking about.

'Just like we did when we were boys.'

It was several long moments before understanding finally penetrated Jack's confusion. 'Maurie, it's fifty bloody years since we ran away to London.'

If anything, Maurie's bony fingers tightened around Jack's wrist in a grip that was almost painful. His eyes were focused and fixed Jack in their gaze, and there was an imperative in his voice. 'Flet's dead.'

Which only plunged Jack back into confusion. Was it an effect of the drugs that Maurie was on? 'Who's Flet?'

'You know!' Maurie insisted. 'Of course you know. Think, for Christ's sake. You remember. Simon Flet. The actor.'

And recollection washed over Jack, cold and depressing. Memories buried for so long that their sudden disinterment was almost startling. He took a moment to recover. 'But Flet must have been dead for years.'

Maurie shook his head. 'Three weeks ago.' He reached over with difficulty to pull a folded Scottish *Herald* from his bedside cabinet. And he pushed it into Jack's chest. 'Murdered. Strangled in some seedy bedsit in the East End of London.'

Like opening the grave of some long-buried corpse, the odour of sudden, unpleasant recollection caused Jack to clench his teeth, as if fighting hard not to breathe in for fear it might contain contaminants.

Maurie's voice fell to barely a whisper as he leaned towards Jack. 'It wasn't Flet who killed that young thug.'

Now Jack was startled. 'Yes, it was.'

'It wasn't! It was only me that saw what happened. So it's only me that knows.'

'But . . . but, Maurie, if that's true why didn't you ever say so before?'

'Because there was no need. It was a secret I meant to take with me to the grave.' He jabbed a finger at the newspaper. 'But this changes everything. I know who committed that murder in 1965. And I'm damned sure I know who killed poor Simon Flet.' He drew a deep breath that seemed to tremble in his throat, as if there might be a butterfly trapped there. 'Which means I've got to go back again, Jack. No choice.' And for a moment he gazed beyond his old friend, lost in some sad recollection. Then he returned his regret in Jack's direction. 'I don't have much time left . . . and you're going to have to get me there.'

II

An acoustic guitar leaned against a wall in the corner of the room. A Gibson. But Jack could tell from the dust gathered on its shoulders that it was a long time since Dave had played it. It just sat there, like the reminder of a lost youth, and all the failed ambitions born in an age of dreams.

Dave had lost weight, and Jack assumed he wasn't eating. Although he claimed to be off the drink, Jack could smell it on him. The whole room reeked of stale alcohol.

Dave followed his gaze towards the guitar. 'She's got more mellow with the years,' he said. 'Ageing like a good wine.'

'When was the last time you played?'

'Ohhh . . .'

Jack could tell that he was about to lie, but then he seemed to think better of it.

'Been a while,' he said instead, and he ran a rueful thumb over the uncalloused fingertips of his left hand. 'Amazing how quickly they soften up.' He glanced at Jack, a wry smile creasing his unshaven face. 'And how painful they get so quickly, when you start again.'

Jack looked around the room. Curtains half drawn across the

nets. A single bed pushed against one wall. A TV in the corner. A couple of well-worn armchairs gathered around the old tile fireplace. This had been Dave's parents' bedroom back in the day. A house inherited on the death of his widowed mother, and chosen to be the home in which he would raise his own family. A home full of dark, brutal memories that not even the bringing of new life into the world could erase. A home that seemed destined for sorrow. A wife gone in search of happiness elsewhere, a son returned like a cuckoo to the nest. Dave struggling with drink, confined now to a single room and soon, Jack had no doubt, displaced altogether. A care home perhaps, or sheltered housing like Jack.

Dave pushed himself back in his armchair and regarded Jack thoughtfully. 'So Maurie's no' long for this world?'

'I shouldn't think so. He looked terrible, Dave. Really awful.'

'And how does he think he can make the trip tae London?'

Jack said, 'He wants us to take him.'

Dave's chuckle was mirthless. 'Aye, like we're fit for it.' His pale, dry lips shook off their attempt at a smile. 'But I dinnae understand why he's only telling us noo that it wisnae Flet that killed the guy.'

Jack pulled out the folded copy of the *Herald*. 'It's the story of Flet's murder that sparked it.'

They heard the front door open and close, then heavy footsteps in the hall. The door of Dave's room swung open and a middle-aged woman stood breathing heavily, glaring at them both. She might have been attractive once, Jack thought, if it wasn't for the downturned mouth, an outward reflection of the inner person. But then, he mused, who else would have married Dave's boy? She wore neatly pressed black slacks, a short grey jacket over a white blouse, and a face like milk left out in the sun.

Her focus fell on Dave. She said, dryly, 'You're back.'

'Observation always was your strong suit.'

Her mean mouth tightened. 'I found your stash.'

And Jack could see how disappointing this news was to his friend.

But Dave tried not to show it. 'How'd you know it wisnae Donnie's?'

'I don't care whose it was. It's all gone down the sink.' The hint of a smile lifted the corners of her mouth, and she glanced at Jack. 'And I'd be pleased if you didn't bring your drinking buddies round to the house.'

Jack bristled and stood up. He shoved the *Herald* back in his pocket. 'Maybe we should continue this conversation somewhere else, Dave. There's a nasty odour in here.'

Dave pushed himself to his feet. 'Aye, you're right. Somebody should tell her no' tae wear nylon.' He pulled a grimace in the direction of his daughter-in-law. 'And the next time you want tae come intae my room, fuckin' knock, alright?'

They took the bus to Queen's Park. Jack had a dental appointment later and didn't want to risk being late.

'Long way tae go tae the dentist,' Dave said.

'It's a family association that goes back a generation. His father was my father's dentist. And anyway, his name always tickled me. Gummers.'

'Ha!' Dave guffawed. 'That's like Spark the electrician.'

They got off the bus at Shawlands Cross, and Dave suggested they go into the Corona Bar. But Jack steered him over the road to the park and proposed instead that they sit by the pond. No one would disturb them there.

They found an empty bench at the foot of a sweep of path that led down to the stretch of slate-grey water where Jack's father had played as a boy. Sometimes there were ducks on the pond, but strangely today it was mostly seagulls. Harbingers, perhaps, of a coming storm.

It was early April, but the wind was still cold, and both men were wrapped up warm in winter coats and scarves. Dave wore a flat cap pulled down over once chiselled features that had lost their definition to become lugubrious. Loose flesh on a thin face. Jack's hair, although pure silver, was luxuriant and carefully styled, and vanity prevented him from wearing a hat to spoil it. Dave was tall, a good three inches taller than his friend, and they made an odd pair sitting side by side on the park bench. Like bookends, Jack thought, and a refrain from the song played itself briefly in his memory.

'Let me see,' Dave said, and he slipped on a pair of tortoiseshell reading glasses as he unfolded the paper.

Jack jabbed a finger at the article on the lower half of the facing page, and Dave read aloud. Just as they had been made to do in class, sitting in rows, and reading a paragraph in turn from some dull history book, as if that somehow constituted learning.

'*Murdered after fifty years on the run.*' Dave looked up from the headline. 'Fifty years, eh? Say it fast and it disnae seem like anything at all.'

He turned back to the paper.

'*Sixties film star Simon Flet, who vanished in 1965 after bludgeoning a man to death during a drug-crazed party in London's West End, has been found dead in a bedsit in Stepney.*

'*The body of the 74-year-old man, missing for half a century, was found strangled in his bed two weeks ago, after his landlord was forced to break into his room. Police believe he had been dead for a week.*

'*His identity, however, was not confirmed until yesterday following the results of DNA testing.*

'*After the killing in 1965, Flet fled from the Kensington home, then and now, of Dr Cliff Robert, whose knighthood for services to medicine was recently announced in the New Year's Honours list.*

'*Although Flet was presumed drowned while trying to escape to France in a small yacht he kept anchored at a marina near Portsmouth, neither his boat nor his body was ever found. Rumours that he was still alive have persisted over the decades, with numerous "sightings" reported from around the world. The mystery of the missing actor was even more enduring than the disappearance nearly ten years later of Lord Lucan, and has been written about many times over the years.*'

Dave inclined his head towards Jack, his face sculpted from doubt. 'How's that possible, then?'

'What?'

'DNA. They didnae have DNA back then. How would they get a sample of Flet's, even if they knew who tae test for?' He paused. 'And how the hell would they know that?'

Jack reached over and took the paper back. For a moment he fumbled in his pockets, then tutted his irritation. 'Give me your glasses.'

Dave slipped them from his nose but then held them back. 'Wait a minute. Your heid's bigger than mine. You'll bend the legs oot.'

Jack snatched the glasses from him and pushed them on to his face. He scanned the article in front of him then started reading.

'*Police initially drew a blank in their attempts to identify the dead man. But investigating officers were intrigued by a patch of skin cut away from the left forearm, concluding that the killer had tried to remove some distinguishing mark. Questioning of the landlord and fellow tenants revealed that the victim had sported a small tattoo of a bluebird on that forearm. This led to an extensive search of both active files and so-called cold cases. But in the end it was a simple internet search which turned up mention of a similar tattoo in an article written ten years before about the mysterious disappearance of the actor Simon Flet.*'

He glanced at Dave.

'Do you ever remember seeing that? The tattoo, I mean?'

Dave's face set in grim recollection and he nodded.

Jack read on.

'This took police to the home of Flet's surviving younger sister, Jean. She still possessed a lock of Flet's hair cut from his head by his mother when he was a baby and kept for posterity, which was the fashion at the time. A DNA comparison confirmed the identity of the dead man.'

He removed his friend's reading glasses and Dave grabbed them back, trying them on and testing them for size.

'You have! You've bent the legs oot.'

But Jack wasn't listening. He was gazing out across the water, beyond the traffic in Pollokshaws Road, towards a terrace of stone-cleaned sandstone houses.

'I was born just over there, you know.'

Dave followed his eyeline. 'Eh?'

'Marywood Square. In a nursing home. That's how they did it back then. Just a few hundred yards away from where my dad grew up in Springhill Gardens.' He glanced back along the road towards the square of red sandstone tenements gathered around an overgrown patch of garden. 'It's funny. When I went to see Maurie last night, I remembered getting my tonsils out at the Victoria.' He looked at Dave. 'But I also remember my dad telling me the doctor came to the house and took his tonsils out on the kitchen table. Can you imagine? Seems medieval now.'

Dave breathed his exasperation. 'Whit's that got tae dae with this?' And he poked a finger at the article.

Jack shrugged. 'Nothing. Just . . . where did they all go, Dave?'

'Where did what go?'

'The years. The dreams.' He turned a pale smile towards the other man. 'I never thought I'd be old, Dave. Never felt old. Not really. Always just a boy in my head. Until now.' Then focus returned to Jack's washed-out blue eyes. 'What are we going to do?'

'About Maurie?'

Jack nodded.

'Maybe we should both go tae see him, Jack. I mean, he cannae really expect us tae go off on a daft goose chase just because of some dying whim of his.'

Jack smiled. 'No. That wouldn't be at all responsible, would it?'

A nearby primary school had spewed children out into the cold afternoon, their shrieks and laughter rising above the rumble of traffic on Pollokshaws Road. Pigeons fluttered around a clutch of youngsters gathered at the water's edge trying to catch something in a net. Mothers with prams stood around a play area beneath still naked trees, and the red of the sandstone tenements stood sharp and clear against a chill blue sky.

Jack and Dave walked together towards the park gate on the corner. Two elderly men, shadow people with spent lives and nothing much to show for them, invisible to the children and their young mothers. At the junction of Pollokshaws Road and Balvicar Street they shook hands and Dave headed off to get a bus home. Jack's appointment with the dentist was imminent, but he stood for a moment watching Dave amble past the bus stop and cross the road towards the New Regent Bar, before he turned wearily away towards Victoria Road.

III

Jack got off the bus just past the Derby Café at Netherlee. The 'Tallie', they called it when they were kids, some corruption of 'Italian', because all the cafés then were Italian-owned. The Derby, Boni's at Clarkston, and another at Busby, whose name he had forgotten. They all made the best ice cream. Single nuggets and double nuggets, and wafers and cones. Fleetingly, he wondered if 'Tallie' would be considered politically incorrect these days.

The road at the end of the block of shops took him down past the primary school. The car park there was almost empty, but there was a group of kids playing football on the grass, their raised voices drifting through the branches of winter trees barely in bud. By contrast the car park for the sheltered housing was almost full. Not that many of the residents had cars, but there were always staff in the building, and visiting relatives.

Jack's heart sank as he saw his daughter and son-in-law emerging from the block of brick-red flats. They were looking less than pleased, and had nearly reached their Mondeo before they saw him coming. Their son – Jack's grandson, Ricky – had his backside propped against the boot of the car, face buried in his Nintendo 3D gaming device as it habitually was, thumbs furiously working the buttons. Even at this distance Jack could hear the inane sounds of an animated game floating across the car park.

Susan was a sweet girl but, like her mother before her, less than assertive. Malcolm was most definitely the dominant half of the partnership. He and Jack had never been fond of each other.

Jack was not at all sure who it was that Ricky took after. From somewhere in his genetic history he had inherited the fat gene. It had not come from his parents or grandparents, but it left him constantly fighting and losing the battle of the scales. He was substantially overweight, and wore the largest and baggiest jog pants and shirts that he could find, which only ever fitted where they touched. But by way of compensation, he had been blessed with an IQ that was quite simply off a very different kind of scale. He had sailed effortlessly through school, and then university, achieving an honours degree in mathematics and computer science a year earlier than he should have. Only to find himself unemployed and, because his weight had stolen his confidence, almost unemployable. Which had led him to retreat into a nocturnal world of computer games, and to sleep away most of his daylight hours.

'Where the hell have you been?' Malcolm had never been one to mince his words.

Jack smiled. 'Nice to see you, too.'

'Dad, you know we always come to see you on a Friday

afternoon.' Susan was more conciliatory, but her words still carried accusation.

'I had a dental appointment. I forgot. I'm sorry.'

'Hi, Grampa.' Ricky didn't even look up.

'Well, you're here now,' Susan said, and she glanced a little nervously towards Malcolm. 'We've got time at least for a cup of tea.'

'That'll be nice,' Jack said. But no matter how hard he tried, he couldn't keep the sarcasm out of his voice.

He took the lift to the first floor on his own while the family took the stairs. Had he been alone he would have taken the stairs himself, but this provided some moments of respite before what he knew was the coming storm. Maybe, he reflected, that was why there had been seagulls on the Queen's Park pond. Anyway, in the end, it was why he was here. In the months after his heart attack the stairs at home had been a problem. Malcolm and Susan had put his name on the waiting list for sheltered housing. Installing a stair lift in the house would be far too expensive, Malcolm had said, and would reduce the resale value of the property.

The family had been living with Jack ever since their house had been repossessed by the bank during Malcolm's brief period of unemployment when he was laid off by one of the major insurance companies. It was to have been a temporary arrangement. But two years on they were still there, despite Malcolm having found another position. A flat had come up in this sheltered housing complex at Netherlee sooner than any of them expected, and Jack had moved out of the downstairs lounge, where he had been sleeping, and into his own flat. Now his family were just counting the days, he was sure, until they could claim their inheritance. It made Jack uncomfortable to feel that they were just waiting for him to die, and he was damned if he was going to oblige. At least, not in the short term.

They stood waiting for him outside the door of his flat at the far end of the corridor, and Jack could hear the bloops and bleeps of Ricky's Nintendo drifting along it.

'Maybe you should turn the sound down, son,' he said. 'Some of the old folk in here are a bit sensitive to noise.'

Ricky glanced at him with irritation and began plugging in his headset.

Inside, Jack put the kettle on, delaying for as long as possible the moment when he would have to go out and face them. When finally he did, Susan was perched anxiously on the edge of the recliner and Malcolm was standing by the window staring morosely out across the lawn below to another block of sheltered housing beyond it. Ricky was sprawled on the settee, still engrossed in his game.

Malcolm turned and glanced at Susan. Her cue to speak.

'Dad, Mrs Rodgers' folks have been on the phone again.'

Jack knew, because Fiona had told him.

'They say they're going to have to insist that you stay away from their mother. If you don't, they're going to make a formal complaint and ask to have you removed from the complex.'

'That's jolly Christian of them,' Jack said. He knew that Fiona's family were church folk, even although Fiona described herself as 'lapsed'.

Susan said, 'Fiona's told them that you're thinking of giving up your single flats in exchange for a double.'

'It's disgusting, Jack.' Malcolm pulled an appropriate face to illustrate his point.

'Is it?' Jack felt his hackles rising. 'And at what age, exactly, does sex between consenting adults stop being natural and become disgusting?'

'Dad . . .' Susan was embarrassed.

'No, tell me. When? At forty, fifty, sixty? What age are you, Malcolm, forty-five? Are you still fucking my daughter?'

'Dad!' This time Susan was shocked, and was on her feet in an instant.

Malcolm said, 'That's enough, Jack.'

'No, it's not! How dare you come in here and tell me who I can and can't sleep with. Fiona and I are not a couple of teenagers. And *you* are not my fucking parents.'

'Dad, for heaven's sake watch your language in front of the boy.'

Jack nearly exploded. 'The boy? The boy's not even fucking listening!'

And they all turned to look at Ricky.

It took a moment before awareness invaded his game and he swung his head towards them, perplexed. 'What?' he said.

CHAPTER TWO

I

Two successive nights at the Victoria Infirmary and Jack was starting to feel like an outpatient. Being an inpatient following his heart scare, albeit briefly, had been bad enough. Beyond those critical first few hours they had moved him to a geriatric ward to complete the rest of his recovery. That was the first time it had ever occurred to him that he was 'old'. The first time he had stood back to see himself as others saw him. An elderly, silver-haired gentleman, robust enough, but clearly past his sell-by. The all-pervading smell of urine in the ward, and a sleepless night spent listening to the wails and caterwauling of dementia patients, had persuaded him to check himself out first thing the next morning. He was damn well going to convalesce at home.

He smelled drink on Dave's breath when they met outside the Battlefield Rest, breath that billowed around his head like smoke in the cool, still night air. Hard to believe it was April.

He said, 'You know, I just realized on the bus tonight that it was exactly fifty years ago this month.'

Dave was puzzled. 'What was?'

'That we ran away to London.'

'Really?' He took off his cap to scratch his head. 'Jesus. If I'd known then what I know noo . . .' He caught Jack's eye and a smile came briefly, sad and funny at the same time. 'I'd probably still be a drunk.'

'Aye, very likely.' Jack took Dave's arm. 'Come on, let's go see what Maurie has to say for himself.'

If anything, Maurie seemed worse than he had the previous evening. He lay with his eyes half closed, skin the colour and texture of putty, his arms lying outside the sheets, giant knuckles on withered hands. There were three nurses sitting on the end of his bed watching *The Street* tonight, more interested in idle chatter than anything on-screen.

'Jesus!' Jack said. 'He's foaming at the mouth!'

And the three of them jumped off the bed, turning in alarm as Maurie opened his eyes and looked confused.

'He's not!' The senior nurse turned an accusatory look towards Jack, who just shrugged.

'Aye, well, he might have been, and you wouldn't have been any the wiser, would you?' He held the door open. 'Would you mind, ladies? We've got things to discuss here with Mr Cohen.'

All three glared at him and made their exit with a bad grace. Jack closed the door. Dave gazed at Maurie in shocked disbelief.

'Bloody hell, mate, what have you been drinking? You look worse than me.'

Which forced a smile to Maurie's lips. 'Aye, well . . .' he said. 'I think my liver's about the only thing left functioning.' He heaved himself into a seated position. 'Good to see you, Dave. You still playing?'

Dave flicked a glance at Jack. 'No' as much as I'd like, Maurie. You still singing?'

'Like a lintie.' Which made him laugh, which turned into a cough, and they heard phlegm and God knows what else rattling in his chest.

'You're in no fit state tae go tae London, boy,' Dave said.

'I'm as fit as I'll ever be.'

'Aye, well, that's probably true.' Dave pulled up a chair and leaned in towards Maurie. 'Yer aff yer fucking heid, man. We cannae go tae London.' Dave's accent had always broadened when he got emotional. 'We've nae money, nae transport, and you cannae walk. So we're gonnae get far, eh?'

'I've got money,' Maurie said.

'Good for you. I huvnae.' He looked at Jack, who was watching them from the end of the bed. Then he turned sad eyes back to Maurie. 'It's a crazy idea, man. Give it up.'

But Maurie shook his head. 'No.' He looked from one to the other. 'And if you won't go with me, I'll pay someone to take me.'

'Give us one good reason why we should,' Dave said.

'Because it's the right thing to do. Even if it has taken me fifty years to realize it.'

'Jack says you're saying it wisnae Flet who killed that guy, after all.'

Maurie nodded.

'So who did?'

Maurie drew a deep breath. 'You're going to have to trust me on that.'

Dave blew air through his teeth. 'Why?'

Maurie seemed wounded by Dave's doubt. 'Because we have more than fifty years of friendship between us.' He fought to draw in another breath. 'And what have any of us got to lose now? How long before you're in a home, like Jack here? Or in a recovery ward. How long before we're all bloody dead?'

Giving voice to things that none of them had dared even to think about brought a sudden reflective silence to the group. But Maurie wasn't finished.

'And I'll be gone before any of you. All the regrets of my life piled up like overdrafts in a bankrupt account. Only blessing is that I've no kids to be ashamed of me. To cover up the legacy of a disgraced father. Disbarred for fraud and eighteen months in the Bar-L. Christ, my own family'll hardly talk to me.'

The sudden colour in his face was unhealthy. A damaged heart working too hard to pump blood to his head.

'Take it easy, Maurie,' Jack said.

Maurie turned fiery eyes in his direction. 'And what do you have to show for it all, Jack? Forty years counting other people's money? You were talented once.'

Jack tried not to let Maurie's words hurt him. He had built his own defences against failure long ago. 'Lots of people are talented, Maurie. But it's not enough on its own. You should know that better than anyone.'

Maurie couldn't hold his gaze, and his eyes drifted off into some distant past existing now only in his memory. 'Voice of an angel, they said.' Then he snapped back to the present, looking from one to the other defiantly. 'But no point regretting what you can't change. And as long as I'm breathing, there are some things I still can.'

'Like what?' Dave said.

'Well, for one thing, I'm stopping the damned chemo. The cure's worse than the fucking ill, and it's not curing me. So I'll spend the rest of my days on painkillers, and I'll not miss throwing up every five minutes.' He paused. 'And I'll do what I should have done fifty years ago. Even if I can't change it, I can put it right. I'm going, whether you come with me or not.' He glared at them defiantly. 'Well? We weren't scared to run away when we were seventeen. And we had everything to lose then.' He chuckled mirthlessly. 'Blew it, too.' Then he refocused. 'Could be this is our last chance to do anything. Anything!' He raised his eyes expectantly, shifting his gaze from one friend to the other.

The cold night air in the car park came as a shock after the stuffy heat of the hospital.

Jack breathed in deeply. 'This is insane, Dave.'

Dave shook his head. 'Naw. Running away tae the Big Smoke when we were seventeen, that was insane. This is much worse.'

He turned a serious face towards his co-conspirator, before a big smile wiped years off it.

Jack said, 'We're going to need transport. And someone to drive. I'm still not allowed.' He glanced at Dave.

'Aye, I know. And I'm no' to be trusted.'

The sky above them was a sparkling black velvet, a gibbous moon rising into view above Langside College. The sound of traffic filled the air. 'Dave . . . I'm only going to do this if you promise to stay off the drink. At least until it's all over.'

Dave grinned. 'Nae problem. Man of steel, me. Iron willpower.'

Jack looked at him sceptically and sighed, then turned to look up at the ugly black edifice of the infirmary towering above them. 'And we're going to have to figure out some way of getting Maurie out of there.'

II

He sat for a long time in the dark. Light from the street lamps in the car park fell through his window in long, dissected slabs that lay across the floor. He had not brought much with him from the home he had shared with Jenny for nearly thirty-seven years. A leather recliner and footstool. A two-seater settee that folded down into a bed for guests who never came. There was a bookcase full of the books he had read as a young man, when ideas were fresh and new and a whole generation believed they could change the world. How naive had they been?

A signed Russell Flint watercolour hung on the wall facing the window. A girl on a beach with a headscarf and a large fishing net on a pole. Wonderful light on sands recently uncovered by the receding tide. It had come from his parents' house, one of two that had been his mother's pride and joy. And yet, they could only, surely, have been a constant reminder of her own thwarted ambition?

A large flat-screen TV, bought for the flat, simmered silently in a shadowed corner, only the red standby light betraying its presence. A drop-leaf table was pushed against the wall by the door to a tiny kitchen that was little more than a scullery.

This was his space. These were his things. This was his life. Everything diminished to fit within the confines of these four walls.

He hated to admit it to himself. But he was lonely. He missed Jenny. Even though she had never been the love of his life, she was the one he had settled for. And they had always been friends, sharing a life of extraordinary ordinariness together. A life like so many others, treading water in a sea of mediocrity, until sinking without trace. Which she had done nine years ago, stolen away by her cancer.

He pushed himself up out of the recliner and crossed stiffly to the bookcase below the window. Why did everything hurt, these days? Her photograph stood in an elaborately worked pewter frame, a gift from Susan. He lifted it and tilted it towards the light, and her smile filled him with sadness. He ran his fingertips lightly over the glass, as if maybe he could still touch her. But the feel of it beneath his fingers was cold and hard.

She was, perhaps, in her early forties here. She had probably been dyeing her hair even then, but the illusion of youth was successful enough. It was a photograph he had taken himself, and it was something about the love in her eyes that had always touched him. And he wondered if she had ever realized that he didn't love her back. Not really. And yet, what was love? For hadn't he been devastated in the losing of her?

He replaced the frame carefully on the bookcase and turned his watch towards the light from the window. Time to tell her.

He double-checked that his keys were in his pocket before he pulled the door shut, and slipped as quietly as he could along the hall. His footsteps echoed faintly back at him from the walls and glass of the stairwell as he climbed slowly to the second floor. The door of her flat was at the end of the corridor, large windows facing out towards the school.

He knocked softly and waited in the thick silence of the night, breathing deeply to catch his breath. He didn't hear her approach before the door opened and she peered out anxiously into the hall. Her smile lit the darkness when she saw him, and the door opened wider to let him in. He saw immediately that she'd had her hair done. A sheer silk nightdress tumbled almost to the floor beneath her open gown. He smelled her perfume and felt the familiar stirrings of desire. Feelings that never went away. Along with the need for someone to share a shrinking life.

She closed the door and turned to face him expectantly. He slipped his arms around her, drawing her to him, and felt her warmth and her softness. He lay his head on her shoulder for a moment, before kissing her neck and then stepping back to look at her. Something in his eyes or his demeanour said more than he ever could, and her smile faded. A woman's instinct.

'What's wrong?'

He steeled himself. 'Fiona, I've got to go away for a while.'

And it struck him that this was really just history repeating itself.

Half a century later.

1965

CHAPTER THREE

I

It's hard to remember now all the various things that came together to make me want to run away. But the tipping point was my expulsion from school. And, of course, I was always blamed for leading the others astray. But it really wasn't like that.

I was born just after the war, into what they later called the 'baby boomer' generation. And I grew up in Glasgow in the fifties and sixties, two decades that morphed from sepia to psychedelic before my very eyes as I segued from childhood to adolescence.

We lived in the south-side suburb of Clarkston, once a village in the Eastwood district of East Renfrewshire, but subsumed already into the creeping urban sprawl of Scotland's industrial heartland. I remember the trams, and the cranes on the Clyde when they still built ships there. I remember the smoke-blackened sandstone tenements that they knocked down in the post-war years before discovering sandblasting, and the marvellous red and honeyed stone that lay beneath the grime. Flats that, once renovated, are still lived in today, while those they built to replace them have long since been demolished.

I sometimes wish I could get hold of those planners and architects and wring them by the neck.

My father taught English and maths at a school in the east end. He was raised in tenement flats on the south side, opposite Queen's Park. His father had been a street artist before the First World War, but joined the Royal Flying Corps during the war years and trained as a photographer. Somewhere I still have an album of his photographs, taken while lying along the length of some flimsy fuselage and pointing a clumsy camera at the trenches below. Early aerial surveillance. The trenches just looked like cracks in dried mud. Hard to believe there were people in them. After the war he opened his own photographic studio in Great Western Road.

I suppose my dad must have got his religion and his politics from *his* dad. My father was an atheist, and a socialist in a constituency that was then a Conservative stronghold. By a process of osmosis, I guess I must have acquired both from him.

My mother, by contrast, was devout Church of Scotland. And although she never admitted it, I always suspected she was a closet Tory. Her favourite rag was the Scottish *Daily Express*, so I suppose it was only to be expected.

I always felt sorry for my mum, though. She had a marvellous talent for drawing and painting. But her father refused to let her go to art school, despite the impassioned pleas of her art teacher. It simply wasn't the done thing in those days for a woman to pursue a career in art.

So she applied instead to join the civil service. In the entry examination she came out top for the whole of Glasgow. But naturally, since she was a woman, was rewarded with a job as a telephonist. As if that wasn't frustrating enough for her, when she married my dad she was handed her jotters. Married women were not allowed to work in the civil service.

She continued to draw and paint, of course, wonderful shaded portraits and watercolour landscapes. But less and less as the years went by. I always perceived in her a feeling that life had somehow passed her by. And while much was passed on to me by my father, perhaps a sense of failure was the one thing I inherited from her. If she had hoped for success vicariously, through me, then I must have been a source of further disappointment.

In 1965, of course, there was no hint of any of that. I was just exploring my talents and, like my contemporaries, being swept along by the sea of change that was washing over the whole country. And music was what drove it, like the moon and the tides. The Stones, the Beatles, the Who, the Kinks. Exciting, violent, romantic, ground-breaking music that fired the imagination and made everything seem possible.

All remnants of the war were swept away by it, too. Rationing, national service (although the draft was still in force across the Atlantic), the stuffy old BBC Light Programme, short hair, collars and ties. There were pirates out in the North Sea playing rock and roll. Anyone with any spark of musical talent wanted to pick up a guitar and play.

I was desperate to be in a group. To stand up onstage and play guitar and sing about love and loss, and this world that shifted beneath my feet. I had music in my head all the time, and it wasn't long before I found like minds and like talents among my peers.

But I hadn't always been in love with music. When I was six my parents sent me to piano lessons, taught by a spinster lady called Miss Hale who lived in a semi near Tinker's Field, just five minutes from our house. I hated it. I remember sitting in her semi-darkened front room, playing scales on an upright piano, the sound of kids on the swings coming from across the road. C, D, E, F. And now chromatics. And if I made a mistake, having my knuckles rapped with a twelve-inch ruler, even as I was still playing.

I didn't last long there.

Next, I was sent to the Ommer School of Music in Dixon Avenue, which was a good twenty-five-minute bus ride into town. Such was my parents' determination that I should play. I spent four years travelling back and forth every Tuesday night for lessons. In the dark, in all weathers, and on my own. Kids would never be allowed to do that, these days. I remember very clearly sitting in a café in Victoria Road waiting for my bus home one winter's night, drinking an American Cream Soda ice-cream float and watching *Mr Magoo* on a black and white TV set high up on the wall. A man came to sit beside me, and when I told him my bus wasn't due for a while he suggested that he might give me a lift home. But I had been well warned. So I told the owner of the café, an Italian gentleman, who informed the man in no uncertain terms that he should sling his hook. And that Italian stood at the door of his café and watched me on to the bus that night, and every Tuesday night from then on.

But years of Saturday morning theory classes, of practising in winter-cold rooms, or on warm summer nights when other kids in the street were out playing rounders, eventually took their toll. I hated music, I told my folks. I was stopping lessons and never going back.

Then came the Beatles. I remember that first hit single. 'Love Me Do'. It got to Number 17 in the chart in October 1962, and it changed my life. I can only imagine my parents' consternation when, six months after giving up the piano, I sold my kilt and my train set to buy a guitar, and was playing it till my fingers bled.

And it's amazing how like minds are drawn to one another. By midway through 1963 I was playing in a group. All of us at the same secondary school, and just fifteen years old. A couple of the boys I had known from primary school, completely unaware of their musical talents. The others were friends of Maurie.

Maurie was one of those two childhood friends. Luke Sharp was the other (I know! I don't know what his parents were thinking).

They could hardly have come from more different backgrounds. Maurie's father was a successful businessman. His great-grandfather had arrived in Glasgow at the turn of the century in a wave of Jewish immigration from the continent. His family settled in the Gorbals, establishing a thriving business in the rag trade, and within two generations had gone from running barefoot in the street to buying a detached home in the wealthy south-side suburb of Williamwood.

Luke's parents were Jehovah's Witnesses, and when I think back on it now it seems a miracle to me that he was ever able to join the group. He was one of those individuals blessed with an extraordinary ear for music. He could listen to anything once, then just sit down at the piano and play it. He had been sent to piano lessons so that he could play the Kingdom songs sung by the Jehovah's Witnesses at their meetings. Although, in truth, he didn't need lessons. And when he wasn't playing or practising, most evenings and weekends he would be dragged round the doors by his parents. Something, I was to learn, that he hated with a vengeance.

It was only at school that he could play the music he liked. And he haunted the music department, playing jazz and blues, and astounding the head of music by being able to perform some of Bach's most complex fugues by ear.

It is also worth mentioning that Luke was little short of a genius. He had been top of his year three years running and, had he completed his final year, would certainly have been Dux. Today they would probably claim he was autistic.

I first heard him playing one lunch hour. A Scott Joplin ragtime piece. I'd never heard anything like it. An amazing left-hand rhythm punctuated by a complex, jangling, right-hand melody. It drew me along the corridor to the practice room at the end, where he sat playing. I watched, mesmerized by his fingers dancing across the keys. When he had finished, he turned, startled, to see me standing in the doorway.

'I never knew you played the piano,' I said.

He smiled. 'You've never been to the Kingdom Hall.'

I had no idea what he meant then, but on an impulse I said, 'Want to be in a group?'

I've heard it said that a face can light up. Well, Luke's positively shone.

'Yes.' He had no hesitation. Then, 'What do you play?'

'Guitar.'

'Sing?'

I pulled a face. 'Not very well.'

He laughed. 'Me neither. Why don't we ask Maurie?'

'Maurie? Maurie Cohen?' I couldn't believe he meant the plump Jewish boy who'd been in our class all through primary.

'He's got an amazing voice,' Luke said. 'He just auditioned for Scottish Opera, and they want him to train with them.'

'Then he won't want to sing with us.'

'He might. His parents won't let him do the Scottish Opera thing. They think it'll distract him from his studies. And they have plans for him, you know?'

Maurie just about bit our hands off when we asked him.

And he was much more interested in singing pop than opera, anyway. He thought his parents would be more inclined to indulge him if they saw it as a hobby rather than a career path. And in the end, it was his father who bought most of our equipment.

Our first practice was scheduled a week later in one of the music department rehearsal rooms after school. Me on acoustic guitar, Luke on piano, and Maurie on vocal. We had a list of songs that we'd been learning. Maurie had all the words scribbled down in a notepad. But he turned up with a boy I didn't know, though I'd seen him around the playground and the corridors. A lad from the downmarket end of Thornliebank. He was kind of tall, and good-looking, with a mop of curly brown hair.

'This is Dave Jackson,' Maurie said. 'Good guitarist, but he wants to play bass.' He turned to the boy, who stood sheepishly clutching his guitar in its soft carry-case. 'Tell them why, Dave.' He grinned. 'Go on.'

Dave looked embarrassed. He said, 'I read somewhere that it's the low frequency of the bass guitar that makes the girls scream.'

We all burst out laughing.

Except for Luke, who said, 'Well, no, it's entirely possible that the speed and pressure of a low frequency could have that kind of effect. Although it's not the sound that has the frequency, it's the means of making it that does. Sound is a pressure wave through the air –'

And we all threw things at him. A duster, bits of chalk, Maurie's notepad.

Our laughter was interrupted by the arrival of a good-looking boy with thick, dark hair that tumbled over his forehead, like he was a Beatle himself. Even in his school uniform you could tell that he was powerfully built. And you knew at a glance that he was the kind of boy that the girls would just follow around like little puppy dogs. He was hefting a bass drum, and he set it down in the middle of the room.

'I've got a snare drum, hi-hat, stands and pedals at the end of the hall if you want to come and give me a hand.'

I didn't know him at all. But Maurie said, 'This is Jeff.'

Jeff, it turned out, had never played the drums in his life, but had borrowed a basic kit so that he could be in the band with Maurie. Jeff had come from a different feeder primary, but the south-side Jewish community was a small one, and it turned out that he and Maurie had been best friends all through childhood, gone to shul together and even shared their bar mitzvah.

After he had figured out how to put all the bits and pieces of the skeleton drum kit together, Jeff sat down and gave it a thrashing while we stood and watched. Impressive for a first go.

When he finished, he looked at us with gleaming eyes. 'My dad says if I'm any good, he'll buy me a kit.'

And so we had our first rehearsal that day. 'Big Girls Don't Cry' by the Four Seasons; 'Crying in the Rain' by the Everly

Brothers; Del Shannon's 'Hey Little Girl'; 'Return to Sender' by Elvis Presley; and a whole bunch of songs from the Beatles' *Please Please Me* album that had been released in March that year.

I wish I had a tape of that first session, to hear what we sounded like. We must have been pretty awful. But it seemed great to us at the time. I was John Lennon, and Maurie definitely fancied himself as Elvis. We discovered very quickly that you don't have to have a great voice to sing harmonies, and right from that first day we established ourselves as a vocal group, more than anything else. Serendipity, I suppose, but our voices just blended.

As for Jeff, we had to keep telling him to play more quietly. A waste of breath, as we discovered during the next year and a half, as he regularly broke drumsticks. But by the end of that first practice he had decided that a drummer he was going to be. And a full kit wasn't long in coming thereafter.

II

Within eighteen months we were fully electric, with individual amps and a PA system, and performing a lot of Tamla Motown stuff for dancing. I had a Fender, and Dave was playing a Höfner violin bass, just like McCartney's. The music department loaned Luke their Farfisa organ. We were gigging at dances all over the city, and had grown a reputation for being the best group on the south side. We called ourselves The Shuffle, after the Bob & Earl song 'Harlem Shuffle'.

I had no idea, then, that 1965 was going to be our seminal year, although not in a good way.

It was a year that began with the death of Winston Churchill in January. I have to confess that his passing meant very little to me but, having lived through the war, my mum and dad were glued to his funeral on TV. My mum was in tears. 'You have no idea what those speeches meant to us in 1940,' she said, 'when we half expected to see German tanks rolling down our street at any moment.'

And she was right. I had no idea then. It was only listening to that voice in later years, and hearing the gravelly determination that we would fight them on the beaches, that I realized just how influential those speeches must have been.

But I was preoccupied with other things. The *Beatles for Sale* album had come out the previous month. We knew there was a new single due out that spring, and there were rumours that they were making another film.

And in February I met the girl I would marry five years later.

It was a Saturday afternoon, and we were setting up and rehearsing for a dance that night in the Clarkston tennis club. Jeff had gone through a string of girlfriends, attracted by his looks and his entirely unconscious wit. But they never lasted long once they got to know him. Until Veronica.

Veronica was a tall, classy-looking girl with long, straight, dark hair, and legs in knee-high boots and a miniskirt that just drew your eye. And held it. It was clear that she saw something in Jeff that the other girls hadn't, but what amazed the rest of us was just how she dominated him. Jeff was a happy-go-lucky, simple sort of lad, but he had a stubborn streak in him like marbled gneiss. With Veronica, though, he was pure putty. She moulded him any way she wanted, and he followed her around like the little lapdog that she made of him. She was smarter than him, too. When Jeff made us laugh, he rarely knew why. Veronica made us laugh because she was clever and knew how to.

That afternoon, she brought a friend along to rehearsal. Jenny Macfarlane. The minute I set eyes on her I knew I wanted her to be my girl. I had been out with quite a few lassies in my time, adolescent fumblings in darkened cinemas, or in the back of the van after a gig. But none had set my pulse racing like Jenny Macfarlane. She was a pretty girl. Petite. With short-cut dark hair, wearing jeans and boots and a jacket she'd got out of the Army & Navy Store. Almost butch, except that there was nothing remotely masculine about her. She had full, ruby lips that needed no lipstick, and just a hint of brown eyeshadow on lids above striking blue eyes.

I'd have sat her down, right there and then, taken my guitar and played her 'I've Just Seen a Face'. Except it wasn't released until later that year. But I might have written it myself, just for her.

Instead I spent most of the afternoon chatting her up. To the irritation of the rest of the group, who wanted to get on with rehearsals. But I was already a lost cause. And she was in awe that the guitarist of The Shuffle was so clearly besotted by her.

That night she stood at the front of the stage just watching me through the entire gig. And for my part, I couldn't keep my eyes off her, or the smile from my face. I could take any amount of this kind of adoration.

At the break we all piled into the back room and drank illicit beer, and I sat on the floor next to Jenny, ignoring the grumblings of the group that I was less than focused, and enjoying the warmth of her body next to me.

We were halfway through the second set when the first brick came through the window. Screams cut above the sound of the music, and a wave of bodies rippled back from the front of the hall. We stopped playing and heard someone shout, 'It's the Cumbie!'

Glasgow had a fearsome reputation in the sixties for gangs and gang warfare. There were gangs with names like the Tongs and the Bundy, the Toon, and the Toi, and CODY, which was an acronym for Come on Die Young. I remember once seeing graffiti on a wall: *Even the deaf have heard of the Bundy.* The affluent suburbs, too, had their gangs. And we possessed our very own Busby Cumbie.

We all rushed to pull back the curtains and look out. And there they were, twenty or more of them, running amok on the pristine grass of the bowling green, hacking at its manicured surface with axes and knives, hurling rocks and bricks at the clubhouse. Blood-curdling screams and laughter filled the air.

The organizers of the dance turned out the lights and locked the doors, which seemed to me like madness. If the

Cumbie had torched the place we'd all have been trapped inside. I fought my way through the crowd to find Jenny and put protective arms around her. I could feel her trembling against me.

'Don't worry,' I told her. 'The cops'll be here any minute.'

But all she said was, 'I'm going to be late.'

In fact it was nearly fifteen minutes before we heard the sirens, and the boys out on the bowling green melted away, dark shadow clouds vaporizing in the night.

Everyone was reluctant to leave after that, including Jenny. She told me she was scared to walk home alone. And even more scared of what her father was going to say when she got there. So I left the boys to pack up the gear and told her I would walk her home.

She lived in Stamperland, which was just over a mile away, and we set off in the dark, keeping a wary eye on the empty streets around us, frost sparkling on the tarmac in intermittent moonlight. Up through Clarkston Toll, and over the railway bridge where I remembered an ice-cream van once crashing through the barrier and careening down the embankment on to the line. We were scavenging for sweeties for days afterwards.

The road was better lit here, but there was little traffic around, and nobody on foot. I put my arm around her, our breath billowing together in the freezing night air, and asked her what school she went to. I was astonished to learn we both went to Eastwood Secondary.

'Amazing I've never seen you before,' I said. 'I'd have remembered if I had.'

She smiled coyly. 'Well, I've seen you. Often. Passed you in the corridor loads of times, but you never noticed.'

'Well, I will now.'

'Of course, I'm a year behind you.'

Which meant that she was only sixteen. She looked older. But I think girls at that age are older than boys, anyway. Mentally. So maybe the age gap kind of evened us up.

We were approaching the bend in the road at Stamperland Church when we saw them. Five or six boys heading our way, their collective breath gathering ominously around their heads like a storm warning. There were still a couple of hundred yards between us, so I took Jenny's hand and casually led her across the road. Williamwood Golf Course lay brooding in darkness beyond the fence. The boys crossed to the same side, and the gap between us narrowed. I could hear their voices. Swearing and laughing. They sounded drunk. Jenny's hand tightened around mine.

'Come on,' I said, and I led her across the road again.

Once more the group crossed to our side. I was beginning to panic when I glanced back and saw the last red bus from Mearnskirk coming from the Clarkston direction and heading into town on the other side of the road. Belisha beacons spilled their orange light across the painted stripes of the zebra crossing at the shops on the corner. Pulling Jenny along behind me, I ran out across it, in front of the bus. I heard a squeal of brakes in the night, and the shouts of the boys just twenty yards away.

We ran around the far side of the bus, out of sight of the youths, and jumped on board as it began to gather speed again, swinging ourselves up and on to the platform by the pole. I heard the conductor shouting, 'Hoy! You can't get on the bus while it's moving.' But I didn't care.

The boys came into view again as we passed them running into the middle of the road. They gave up the chase almost as soon as it had started, realizing they would never catch us. I waved two fingers at them from the safety of the platform and shouted, 'Fuck you!'

And then the bus suddenly started slowing, and my heart speeded up.

Jenny swung out from the platform to see why we were stopping. 'Roadworks,' she said. 'The road's down to one lane.'

'Shit!'

The gang realized at the same moment as we did that the bus was going to stop, and they began sprinting down the road towards us.

'Come on!' I grabbed Jenny by the arm, pulling her off the bus, and we ran across the street into Randolph Drive, pell-mell down the hill, arms windmilling as we tried to keep our balance on the frosted pavement and still maintain our speed. I knew they were after us, but I daren't even look behind. It was enough to hear the menace in their voices ringing out in the night. But there was no way we were going to outrun them.

We turned the bend in the road and Jenny gasped, 'In here!' She pushed open a wooden gate in the high wall that ran all along one side of the street, and we ducked into the densely shadowed foliage of a garden that fell away almost beneath our feet to a house in the street below.

I pushed the gate shut, and we moved down through the garden, following the line of a weed-covered path that dog-legged between overgrown flower beds. And there we took cover behind a length of frosted laurel hedge.

I could see in fleeting glimpses of moonlight that the gardens of all the houses below us rose steeply to the walled side of Randolph Drive, and that each one had a gate leading out into the street. Our pursuers, when they came round the bend and saw the empty street, would realize that we had gone into one of the gardens. But not which one.

We held our breath and listened as the chasing footfalls came to a stop and gasping voices consulted. Querulous voices raised in disagreement. Should they continue the chase or give up? And what were they going to do if they didn't? Search every garden?

I turned to find Jenny looking at me, and to my amazement she was fighting a smile. Which brought a smile to my face. And led to both of us trying to stifle a sudden desire to laugh. Hands over our mouths. Nerves, I suppose.

At any event, the decision of the Cumbie boys was to give up. But their parting shot wiped the smile from my face.

A raised voice, ugly in its timbre and intent, rang out in the dark. 'We know who you are, ya smart bastard. Yer fuckin' deid!'

Good enough reason on its own, I suppose, to get out of town, though that wouldn't happen for another six weeks or so.

With the voices of the gang boys receding into the night, Jenny turned to me and surprised me by touching my face with tender fingers. And on an impulse I kissed her. Just a brief, sweet kiss on the lips, but it cemented something between us.

We made our way, then, down through the garden in the darkness, creeping around the side of the bungalow at street level, and out through the front gate into Nethervale Avenue. It was another ten minutes before I got Jenny home. Or almost. We met her father striding down the street in his coat and hat, intent on walking all the way to Clarkston if he had to, to find his little girl.

'My dad,' she whispered when we first saw him approaching, and I dropped her hand fast.

His face looked as if it had been chiselled out of ice straight from the deep freeze. He glared at me and took Jenny's hand.

'The dance got broken up by a gang, and Jack brought me home,' she said.

But he didn't seem grateful. 'There'll be no more dances,' he said. His eyes fell on me once more. 'And you'll not be seeing Jack again, either.'

The way he said my name, it was almost like he'd spat away a bad taste from his mouth. He turned and pulled her with him back along the street. She cast an apologetic glance over her shoulder, and I turned wearily to make the perilous journey home, sticking to the darker side streets, and hiding in gardens if I saw anyone or heard voices. I wouldn't have survived a second encounter with the Busby Cumbie.

III

There is nothing more desirous, somehow, than the forbidden fruit. It always tastes so much sweeter. And so Jenny and I became secretly inseparable. Secret, that is, from her folks. She came to all our gigs, or at least the ones from which she could get home at the time appointed by her father.

When the group wasn't playing we would go to the pictures, usually the Toledo at Muirend, a faux-Moorish palace in the suburban heartland of industrial Glasgow. It's not there any more. Demolished, apart from the Moorish facade, and turned into flats. We saw the Cliff Richard film *Summer Holiday*, and maybe that's something else that put the idea of running away into my head. Then the John Wayne movie *Hatari*. I was almost glad it was so bad. It was a good excuse to spend most of it necking in the back row.

I guess we were both still virgins then, although I was desperate to remedy that situation as soon as possible. But I wasn't welcome at Jenny's house, and there was no chance of it happening at mine. I didn't have a car, and the back of the group van was not a very appealing prospect, especially on a cold winter's night. And besides, I wasn't sure how far Jenny would go, and I wasn't confident enough to push it. Until the night of the school dance.

The Shuffle was booked to play that night, and it was exciting for us – the first time we had played at a school dance for an audience of our peers. The hall was huge. Used for assemblies and indoor games, and school plays performed at regular intervals by a particularly active drama club. And, of course, school dances, which were usually old-fashioned affairs with the 'Dashing White Sergeant' and 'Drops of Brandy'.

Jeff had already left school by then. Failing all but one of his 'O' Grades, he had quit at the end of the fourth year and got himself a job as a trainee car salesman with Anderson's of Newton Mearns, a big sprawling Rootes dealership that sat on the south-west corner of Mearns Cross. It was Jeff who owned the group van, a beat-up old Commer, and drove us to all our gigs. By way of compensation he did none of the gear humping, and before and after bookings he sat up in the front of the van, smoking, while we loaded and unloaded.

The rest of us had gone back for a fifth year to sit our Highers, but the fact that Jeff was out there working made him seem older than us, more mature. Although nothing could have been further from the truth.

But Jeff enjoyed coming back to the school. Lording it over us. We were mere schoolkids, and he adopted a worldly air of superiority. We all smoked in those days, except for Luke. The new Player's No. 6, small and rough and cheap in their blue and white striped packs. But Jeff had arrived that night with something a little different. Pot. Or marijuana, to give it its proper name. Or dope, as it's known these days. Jeff called it 'grass' because that's what the American kids called it. But it wasn't. It was cannabis resin. A little chunk of it wrapped in silver paper, dark and pungent.

It was the first time any of us had taken anything stronger than beer. We went round to the sheds at the back of the school before the dance and gathered in a huddle as Jeff 'cooked' the resin in its silver paper, held over the flame of a match. Then he crumbled it into some loose tobacco in a cigarette paper and rolled it into a joint. You heard all sorts of things in those days about how 'reefers' could make you lose your mind, and we were all a bit nervous. Jeff said he'd smoked it often, and I thought that wasn't a particularly great recommendation.

Luke declined, and watched in consternation as the rest of us passed the joint around, and were reduced within minutes to helpless giggling idiots. I can't ever remember having been so hopelessly amused by nothing at all.

Fortunately, the worst effects had worn off by the time we took to the stage, and we were just feeling mellow and relaxed.

We had a forty-five-minute break at the interval, and I begged Jeff to give me a piece of resin. I wanted to smoke with Jenny. And I suppose that somewhere in the back of my mind was the thought that the pot might lead us to more than the heavy petting that we'd indulged in up until then.

There were lots of kids milling around outside, so we went to the boiler room where I knew we wouldn't be disturbed. I had a big furry coat in those days, which my mother had bought me in Copeland's department store in Sauchiehall Street. It wasn't real fur, of course, just some kind of coarse, shredded polyester that melted if you burned it with your cigarette. But it went down to my knees, had a big collar, and was as warm as anything in the winter.

I laid it down on the concrete floor and we squatted on it, and I fumbled my way through the cooking ritual, then managed to spill both the crumbled resin and the loose tobacco into the lining.

Which was when the door burst open, and the janitor stood there in his dark blue uniform, glaring at us in the light of the single yellow bulb that lit the room, and foiling my plans to lose my virginity.

'What the hell's going on here?'

We both scrambled to our feet.

'Nothing,' I said.

But he sniffed the air, and there was a knowing look on his face. 'You kids have been smoking pot, haven't you?'

'No, sir,' Jenny said truthfully.

He nodded towards my coat on the floor, the contents of the joint along with a cigarette paper and a piece of silver foil scattered over the lining. 'What's that, then?'

'Just a cigarette,' I said, stooping to pick up the coat.

But the edge in his raised voice stopped me short. 'Leave it!'

He made us stand back as he crouched down to fold the coat carefully over on itself, so that the remains of the unsmoked joint were gathered inside. He stood up again, holding the coat to his chest. 'I know you two,' he said. 'You'll be hearing about this in the morning.' He jerked his thumb towards the door. 'Out!'

'What about my coat?'

He gave me a dangerous look. 'You'll get it back tomorrow, son.'

I don't remember much about the second half of the dance, and I know I never slept a wink that night. And it was with a sick feeling in my gut that I walked to school the next day. A dull, cold day with a low, pewtery sky drizzling on a colourless world.

The summons to the headmaster's room came before ten o'clock. I walked the length of the lower-ground corridor with legs like jelly, only to find a pale Jenny sitting in the outer office. I sat beside her without a word, ignoring the frequent, curious glances of the school secretary, and we waited for what seemed like an eternity but was probably just a few minutes. Jenny's hand reached for mine in the gap between the chairs, unseen by the gimlet-eyed secretary. And when she found it, she gave it the smallest of squeezes. I felt an almost disabling wave of gratitude and affection for that tiny gesture of support, and it steeled me to face the dark moments to come.

And come they did.

The door to the headmaster's room opened and he stood glaring at us for a moment. He was a thickset man with thinning grey hair oiled back over a broad skull. He had a grey overtrimmed moustache that was almost Hitleresque, and wore a grey tweed suit. In fact, everything about him was grey, even his complexion and his colourless, washed-out eyes. The sole exception was the nicotine that stained the fingers of his right hand. He was known by everyone at the school, teachers and pupils alike, simply as Willie.

He flicked his head back towards his room. 'In here. Both of you.' He closed the door behind us and left us standing as he went to his desk. He turned, holding up a white envelope. 'I imagine if I handed this over to the police, they'd find that it contained grains of an illegal Class B drug called cannabis.' He looked at me. 'Collected from the lining of your coat, Mackay. A very serious offence, possession of cannabis.'

'It was entirely my fault, sir. Jenny had no idea what was in the cigarette.'

His eyes flickered towards her and back again. 'Is that the truth, Mackay?'

'Yes, sir. It was all my idea.'

'Not sure I believe you, sonny.' He swivelled his eyes back to Jenny and he sighed deeply. 'On the other hand, Miss Macfarlane here has an exemplary record. Academically bright. Destined for university. It would be a shame to spoil her future because of a moment of stupidity.' Eyes back on me. 'And bad judgement in her choice of boyfriend.' He turned again to Jenny. 'So you can go, young lady. But I want you back here in the morning with a letter from your father explaining the circumstances in which you were found in the boiler room with Jack Mackay.'

I glanced at Jenny, and saw that she had turned a ghostly shade of pale.

'Go!'

As she turned, she caught my eye for a fleeting moment, then was gone, leaving me standing to face Willie alone. If he was going to take the tawse to me, I was determined to refuse it. He tilted his head, and the slightest of smiles crept over his lips. 'Jack Mackay. Jack the Lad. Ye of the unexplained absences and the poor exam results. Ye of the big coat and the long hair, guitar player in a trashy pop group. Setter of such a bad example to the whole school. You think I haven't seen you in the corridor, sonny? Doing your cock o' the walk. Well, you cocked it up royally this time, boy.' He paused to let that sink in for a moment. Then he waved the envelope at me. 'If I were to report this to the police, it would be a stain on the rest of your life.' He dropped the envelope on the desk. 'So be grateful I'm not that vindictive.' He let that hang for a very long moment. 'Have you anything to say for yourself?'

I shrugged. 'I didn't think my hair was that long, sir.'

I saw his expression harden, like setting concrete. He strode across his room to a coat stand, where I noticed my coat hanging for the first time. He grabbed it and threw it at me. 'Take your big furry coat, and your long hair, and go home, Mackay. And don't come back. Ever.'

*

I found Luke in the art department. He was sitting on a stool at one of the high wooden benches reading the latest copy of *Mad* magazine. The place was deserted. He looked up and cocked an eyebrow at my big furry coat.

'Willie'll go ape if he sees you wearing that,' he said.

But I suppose something in my face must have told him that all was not well.

He frowned. 'What's wrong?'

'I just got expelled.'

It took him a moment to realize I wasn't joking. Then his eyes opened wide. 'Why?'

'Long story.'

'Bloody hell, Jack. What are you going to tell your folks?'

'I'm not.' In the time it had taken me to walk from Willie's office to the pottery room I had already decided what I was going to do. And facing my parents with the news that I'd been expelled wasn't on the agenda. 'I'm going to London.'

'What?'

'There's nothing for me here, Luke. Might as well go and see if I can't make something of myself in the Big Smoke.'

Luke slipped off his stool and stood up, taking me by the shoulders. 'You're not thinking straight, man.' He stared at me with those big, pale green eyes of his, fair locks tumbling in golden curls over the frown on his forehead.

'I'm thinking as straight as I've ever done,' I said. 'I'm going. And I'm going tonight.'

He gazed at me for a moment longer, and I could see the workings of his mind behind troubled eyes.

Then he said, 'Not without me, you're not.'

I was totally taken aback. 'Why? Why would you want to do that? You're the smartest of all of us.'

He turned away, and I saw him clench his fists at his sides.

'Because I'm sick of fighting with my folks. You've no idea how hard it's been, Jack. Kicking against their disapproval. Every practice, every gig, is a fight. I leave the house in a rage. And when I get back, I never know if they'll let me in or not.'

I looked at him in astonishment. 'Why didn't you say? Why didn't you tell us?'

He turned, eyes full of rage. 'Same reason I never told anyone about the misery of all those years being presented to strangers on doorsteps, so they wouldn't slam the door in my parents' face. Evenings and weekends, walking the streets in all weathers, getting laughed at, or abused, physically assaulted sometimes. All in the name of Jehovah. Clutching my little Bible and smiling for those poor people who hadn't yet seen the light. No point in telling anyone, Jack. Because nothing I said or did was going to change it.'

His unexpected burst of emotion seemed suddenly to drain him, and I saw the slump of his shoulders and the pain behind his eyes, before he recovered his spirit and drew himself up to his full height again.

'So if you're really going. If you really are. Then I'm going with you.'

IV

What had started as a grain of an idea in my head as I made that long, depressing walk along the corridor and upstairs to the art department began to take on a momentum of its own. And when we met up with Maurie and Dave at lunchtime, it snowballed.

They listened in wide-eyed silence to me and Luke as we told them what it was we intended to do, and why.

Then Maurie said, 'What about the group?'

I shrugged. 'What about it?'

'Well, you're going to need a singer.'

Luke said, 'Your parents'd kill you.'

'My parents'll kill me, anyway. They've got my whole life mapped out for me. Law degree, solicitor's practice. Doesn't matter what *I* want to do. I'm coming, too.'

Quite involuntarily we looked at Dave.

A big grin spread itself across his face. 'You're still gonnae need me tae make the girls scream.'

And no one questioned why he might want to run away from home. We'd all seen the bruises.

That was four out of five.

Luke said, 'What about Jeff?'

And Maurie's face set. 'I'm not going without him.'

The new cars at Anderson's were all kept indoors, in the big glass-walled showroom. The second-hand cars sat out front.

Two rows of them, with big price stickers on the windows. Jeff had told us that it was his job first thing each winter's morning to start every one of them.

'Really teaches you how to start a car,' he'd said. 'Any car, in any temperature.'

He seemed proud of the achievement, and it was clear it meant more to him than passing any school exam.

We found Jeff in the cinder yard behind the workshops, doing a stocktake. He was amazed to see us, then listened in astonished silence as I told him what we were planning.

'So what do you think?' I asked him.

'About what?'

'Coming with us, of course.'

He thought for a long moment. 'What about Veronica?'

A tiny gasp of irritation caught the back of my throat. 'What about her?'

'She'll not come with us.'

'No one expects the girls tae come,' Dave said.

He and Luke were the only ones who didn't have girlfriends.

'I'll be leaving Jenny behind,' I said. And for the first time I pictured how that would be.

'You don't understand,' Jeff said earnestly. 'It's different with me and Veronica.'

'Look,' I said, losing patience. 'You don't have to come. It's your choice. But if you don't, then Maurie won't either.'

Jeff glanced at Maurie. 'Really?'

Maurie shrugged, embarrassed now. Jeff seemed genuinely touched. Suddenly it had become a choice between Maurie and Veronica. And there was only ever going to be one outcome.

'The Commer'll not make it to London,' he said. And immediately all our plans seemed to fall away like sand beneath our feet. But Jeff just grinned. 'That's all you wanted me for, wasn't it? My van.'

I shifted a little uncomfortably. Perhaps there was more than a grain of truth in that. But Jeff was oblivious.

'It's not a problem. I can get us something better.'

V

I left a note for my folks on my pillow. I can't remember now exactly what it was I wrote. Something stupid, about going in search of fame and fortune, and that they shouldn't worry. We were all going, so we'd be fine. Safety in numbers.

You don't think at that age how devastating the discovery of such a note would be to your parents. You don't have the experience, to put yourself in their shoes and imagine how it would feel. Only with time, and children of your own, does the full realization hit you. How thoughtless we were. So hopelessly self-obsessed.

Jeff and Maurie were waiting for me at the end of the road in a green Ford Thames 15cwt van. It looked a little smaller than the Commer, but apart from a few scrapes and bashes it appeared to be in good condition.

'Where did you get it?' I said as I climbed up on to the engine cowling between them.

Jeff grinned at me from behind the wheel. 'Borrowed it. Purrs like a baby, doesn't she?' He flicked his head over his shoulder. 'Maurie and me've loaded all the gear. And we stuck an old settee in the back. All the comforts of home.'

'What did Veronica say?'

A shadow crossed his face, like a cloud blotting out the sun. 'Don't even ask.'

Maurie said, 'She'll get over it. And so will you.'

But Jeff's head snapped round, and it was the first time I'd ever heard him raise his voice to Maurie. 'I told you! It's different with me and Veronica.'

He crunched the column shift into gear, and we lurched off down the road. I barely had time to glance back at the pebble-harled suburban semi where I had spent my entire life up until that moment. And my stomach lurched as I thought about my folks finding my letter.

Luke was waiting for us at Clarkston Toll, a tall, languid, good-looking boy in jeans and a donkey jacket, a holdall at his feet. He threw it into the back of the van first, then climbed in after it.

'Where's the organ?' Jeff called back at him.

'It belongs to the school.'

'You'd only have been borrowing it.'

'I think they might have called it theft,' Luke retorted before slamming the door shut.

Jeff glanced at Maurie and me. 'Jobbies!' he mouthed.

It was the word he always used for 'shit', straight from the primary-school playground. A euphemism he had never grown out of.

The problem came when we arrived outside Dave's house in Crosslees Drive. The light was fading fast, and we were anxious to be away in case any of the notes we had left were found before we were gone. We sat for several minutes at the gate, engine idling impatiently, Jeff tapping nervously on the wheel.

'Jobbies!' he kept muttering. 'Where the hell is he?'

The house was dilapidated from years of neglect in those days, like a bad tooth in an otherwise pleasant smile. The front garden was overgrown, and there was an old boat rotting on the path.

Honking the horn was out of the question, and no one was going to go to the door.

Luke glanced at his watch, and his voice came to us from the back of the van. 'Don't panic yet, he's only a few minutes late.'

'Is that earth minutes?' Maurie said dryly.

Then suddenly Dave's front door flew open and Dave appeared, wearing jeans and hiking boots, and a green waterproof army jacket. He had a rucksack on his back, full of God knew what, with tin mugs dangling from canvas ties. He pulled the door shut behind him and sprinted through the long grass of the front lawn, to vault over the wall, catching his trailing foot and going sprawling on the pavement.

'Jesus!' Maurie cursed under his breath, and he and Luke

jumped out to pick Dave up and bundle him into the back of the van.

Jeff turned his head over his shoulder. 'That's what I call a quiet exit.'

'Go! Just go!' Dave shouted at him.

Jeff gunned the motor and we lurched off down the street.

There was one last stop before we finally got on the road. The boys just wanted to be gone, but I insisted. 'If we don't do it, you might as well stop the van and let me out right now,' I said.

So we made the detour. Via Stamperland.

It was dark by the time we pulled up outside Jenny's house and Jeff cut the engine. I had phoned her before I left the house and had heard her distress when I told her what we were planning. I'd promised to come and say goodbye. My heart was in my mouth as I hurried up the path.

She must have been watching for me, because the door opened before I got to the top of the steps, and she slipped out into the darkness of the porch, pulling the door to behind her.

'Jack, this is madness!' she whispered.

I just took her and held her, feeling the beat of her heart and the warmth of her body, and all the uncertainty of my life welling up inside me. But it was too late for second thoughts now.

'I'll send for you,' I said, knowing that I wouldn't. 'Just as soon as we're settled and we get things sorted.'

She untangled herself from my arms and stood back, looking at me. 'Do you think I'm daft, Jack? If you go, you're gone. I'll never see you again.'

'Don't say that.'

'Why? Because you don't want to hear the truth? Because you're living out some fantasy and you don't want to know that there'll be consequences?'

I didn't know what to say. I had never heard her so forthright before.

'We'll be fine,' I said lamely.

'No, you won't. It'll be a bloody disaster. You're just kids. You haven't thought this through.'

'Sometimes you've just got to do stuff. You can overthink things.'

'Says the voice of experience.'

I could hear the sarcasm in her voice.

From somewhere inside the house we heard her father calling, 'Who's that?'

'Just a friend,' she called back. Then she turned to me, her voice a whisper in the dark. 'Call me, Jack, please. First stop on the road. Let me know you're alright.'

I pulled her back into my arms and kissed her with a sort of passionate desperation. This was all so much harder than I had ever stopped to imagine. 'I will,' I said.

'Promise!'

'I promise.'

And I was gone.

2015

CHAPTER FOUR

I

His automatic weapon tracked from side to side as the soldier stepped carefully through the rubble of the bombed-out building. Wisps of smoke drifted across a devastated landscape, and Jack could hear the rattle of distant gunfire and men crying out. An enemy combatant swung suddenly into view from behind a broken-down wall. The soldier reacted before his adversary could release shots in his direction. The sound of gunfire was almost deafening as the string of bullets from the soldier's gun blew his enemy apart. There were body pieces and blood everywhere.

Another soldier appeared, dropping down from the shattered ceiling. Jack was beginning to recognize the enemy by the colour of the uniform and shape of the helmet. The soldier whose point of view he was sharing fired two, three, four times, and the other man flew backwards to slump, bleeding and dead, against a bullet-scarred wall.

'Jesus, Rick! This is horrible.'

'Shhhh.' Ricky's concentration was absolute.

He was barefoot in his pyjamas, crouched on the edge of a settee in the darkened living room and hunched over his controller. The fifty-inch TV screen filled Jack and Ricky's vision, and became the world they were sharing. Jack could almost smell the cordite and the smoke, and the ugly odour of death. There was some kind of count going on. A score accumulating. But Jack couldn't take it any more. He crossed the room and switched off the TV.

'Jesus Christ, Grampa! What are you doing?'

Jack pulled the curtains open and sunlight streamed in to almost blind his grandson. 'I'm surprised the sunlight doesn't burn you, Rick,' he said. 'You should be in your coffin by now.'

Ricky dropped his controller on to the settee beside him. 'Very funny.'

'To be honest, I didn't really expect to find you up at this time.'

It was almost midday.

'I'm not. I haven't been to bed.'

'Have you been playing that bloody game all night?'

Ricky shrugged. 'So?'

'You've spent the whole night killing people?'

'No, I stopped to have breakfast with Mum and Dad before they left.'

'For God's sake, son, do you not see what you're doing?'

'What am I doing, Grampa?'

'You're killing for fun.'

'It's just a game.'

'A game where you kill people and count up the score. That's fun?'

'It takes skill! I've got one of the highest registered scores on the internet. And anyway, it's not real.'

'It might as well be. It's totally desensitizing. Makes you think it's alright to kill other human beings. So how are you going to tell the difference if you're ever faced with the real thing?'

'I'm not daft, Grampa. I'm clever enough to know the difference between a game and reality. And, anyway, what would you know about killing people?' The contempt in his voice for his grandfather was clear.

'Nothing, fortunately.' Jack sighed and sat down in one of the armchairs. 'Seriously, Rick. You can't go on like this. Sitting playing computer games in the dark. You said it yourself. You're not daft. You've got an honours degree in maths and computing, for heaven's sake. You need to get out and get a job.'

Ricky blew contemptuous air through his teeth, and Jack started to get angry.

'So you're just going to be a burden on society for the rest of your life?'

He saw Ricky's hackles rise.

'I'm not one of those benefits scroungers. I've never claimed a penny in my life.'

'Aye, only because your folks indulge you. Most people on benefits don't have a choice in the matter. They don't have honours degrees in anything.'

'No, they're just work-shy scroungers and layabouts. Picking up cheques from the government and going and getting their free shopping from the food bank.'

Jack shook his head in disgust. 'Where'd you hear that? Your father?'

Ricky pressed his lips together and declined to reply, which in itself answered his grandfather's question.

'You know nothing, son. Sitting here in my house, with your big TV screen and your computer games, spoiled rotten by pampering parents who fill your head full of nonsense. I'm ashamed of my own daughter. My father, and his before him, must be turning in their graves.'

Ricky's plump face glowed beetroot red beneath his black curls. 'And what would you know about anything? Failed at everything you ever did, my dad says. Failed student, failed musician, and forty years behind the counter at a bank. I suppose you must have learned a lot about the world from the other side of a glass screen.'

Sometimes words said in anger carry hurt beyond real intention, and Ricky was just being defensive, Jack knew. But words meant to cause pain very often do so because they express a truth that the conventions of politeness avoid. Jack had spent a lifetime avoiding what he knew only too well. But, still, it was almost painful beyond hurt to have it thrown in his face by his own grandson.

If Ricky had any remorse he wasn't showing it. He turned surly instead. Perhaps as a way of concealing his regret.

'And why do you keep calling me *Rick*? It's *Ricky*!'

Jack had always called his grandson Rick. It seemed fonder, somehow.

'Anyway, what are you doing here? You know my folks are out all day.'

Jack took a few moments to calm himself. 'I didn't come to see your parents.'

The hint of a frown gathered faintly around Ricky's brows. He glanced at his grandfather, but was reluctant now to meet his eye.

Jack said, 'Maybe you heard about the time I ran away when I was a kid? Me and the rest of the boys in my group.'

Ricky sighed. 'Once or twice.' He lifted his games controller from the seat beside him and pretended to be fiddling with it. 'Probably the only interesting thing you ever did in your life.'

'Aye, well, I was five years younger than you when I did it. And you still haven't done anything interesting.'

Time to hurt back. And the jibe didn't miss its mark. He saw Ricky's lips pale as he drew them in. But the boy said nothing. Jack let a silence hang between them for a while, like the motes of dust suspended in the sunlight falling through the window.

Finally he said, 'So, anyway, we're doing it again.'

Ricky flicked sullen eyes in his direction. 'Doing what?'

'Running away to London. Those of us who are left, that is.'

Ricky forgot his sulk and his eyes opened wider. 'Running away? At your age? Why would you do that?'

Jack shrugged. 'Unfinished business, son.' Then he hesitated. 'Only thing is . . . we've no transport.'

Suddenly Ricky realized why his grandfather was there. He breathed his annoyance. 'No!' he said firmly. 'You're not borrowing my car.'

And the way he was so possessive about ownership of it made Jack wonder if he realized just how lucky he was to have parents who not only tolerated his lethargy, but who spoiled him by buying him his own wheels. Not a new car, admittedly. A second-hand Nissan Micra. But wheels nonetheless.

'I don't want to borrow it.'

Which momentarily took the wind out of the boy's sails.

'I want to borrow you to drive it for us.'

Ricky's eyes opened wider. 'You're having a laugh, right?'

'No, I'm serious. Just for a few days. A week at the most. We'll pay you for the petrol.'

'No. Way.' A long pause. 'And anyway, my folks would never let me.'

'You're twenty-two years old, Ricky.'

'You don't know my dad.'

'Oh, I think I do.'

'He'd never let me in a million years. Particularly if it was a favour to you.'

Jack pursed his lips, containing his anger.

'So there's no point in even asking. He wouldn't hear of it.'

Which was Ricky's way of deflecting personal responsibility.

Jack sighed. He hadn't wanted to do this. 'I think he would

be even less pleased to hear about those websites you visit when they're both asleep.'

Ricky blushed to the roots of his hair. 'I don't know what you're talking about.'

Jack shook his head. 'Look, son, I might be old, but I'm not daft. I was working with computers before you were born. And you don't spend nearly two years sharing the same house with someone without knowing the kind of websites they frequent. You were careful enough around your folks. But I was just some stupid old man. Invisible. What would I know?' Jack let that sink in. 'All those videos of naked women with . . . well, how can I put it delicately? A little something extra?'

If it was possible, Ricky's colour deepened. 'I was just surfing, that's all!' he said, but his voice was trembling with embarrassment and uncertainty, and he added lamely, 'I was curious.'

Jack spread his hands in front of him, and made a face of resignation. 'I know that, Rick. Young men . . . well, they have to explore a little before they know what it is that suits them. And I'm not saying that's what suits you. In fact, I'm not here to judge you at all. All I'm saying is, I'm not sure your dad would be so understanding.' He waited a beat before turning the knife. 'Or your mother.'

Ricky closed his eyes. 'I'm not! I mean . . . I'm not like that.'

'Of course you're not.'

Jack almost felt sorry for him. The boy was clinically obese. He never set foot over the door, except for his Friday afternoon visits to his grampa. When was he ever going to get a girl who wasn't made of pixels, whether she had something extra or not? He saw the slump of his grandson's shoulders.

'When?'

'Tonight.'

Ricky took a deep breath. 'We're not telling my dad. Or my mum. Alright? They'd only stop me from doing it. We'll just go.'

Jack nodded. 'We can leave them a note on your pillow, son. And don't worry about it, they'll blame me. Everyone always does.'

II

When he got back from the medical supplies store in Shawlands, Jack put a holdall on his bed and began filling it with enough socks and underwear to last him a week. He figured a couple of days to get there, a couple of days to get back, and three days in London to do whatever it was Maurie had to do.

And yet he couldn't shake off the feeling that somehow he was packing for the last time, and that it didn't really matter what he put in the holdall, he was never going to need it. All in stark contrast to the thoughtless optimism with which he had packed his bag fifty years ago, almost to the day. Then, the future had stretched ahead into unforeseeable distance, full of optimism and possibility. The notion of running out of socks had never even occurred to him.

When he had finished, he dropped his bag by the front door and wandered back into the living room. The school across the way was closed up for the day, its pupils long since gone home. When he had first moved into the flats the sound of children playing during breaks in their classes had seemed like music. But the siren call of youth had served, in the end, only to reinforce how far behind him his own childhood lay, and how close he was to the rocks of old age on which he would inevitably founder and die.

He picked up the photograph of Jenny and remembered how they had said goodbye that night. And here he was, all these years later, embarking on the same fruitless journey. One that could only, he suspected, end badly. And he recalled the words of his old history teacher. *The only thing we learn from history is that we never learn from history.*

He stood the photo frame back on the bookcase and gazed out through the trees across the lawns beyond. He remembered, the day he had moved in, thinking, 'This is the view I'll take with me to my grave.' That this was what it had all narrowed down to. Four walls and a landscape. And he had found himself infused, then and now, with an almost overwhelming sense of regret – for many of the things he had done, but most of all for those he had not.

His thoughts were interrupted by the arrival of Ricky's Micra in the car park below. The boy swung it through a three-point turn, then glanced up towards Jack's window as he sat idling on the tarmac. Jack gave him a small wave and wondered what on earth he was leading his grandson into. But as he took his walking stick from the stand in the hall and lifted his holdall, he thought that anything would be better for him than sitting in a darkened room playing computer games.

And as for himself? What the hell? After sixty-seven years it was time to start living.

He hurried down the stairs and out into the car park. Ricky looked pale and nervous behind the window of the driver's door. Jack glanced back towards the top floor of the flats, and saw Fiona watching him from her window.

But by the time he had thrown his bag into the boot and turned to wave, she was gone. And the empty space she'd left behind her seemed big enough to swallow him.

Just as fifty years before, they sat outside Dave's house with the engine running, Ricky drumming his fingers nervously on the wheel, exactly as Jeff had done. But five minutes after the appointed time, there was still no sign of Dave.

Finally Jack said, 'Turn her off, son. I think we'd better go in and look for him.'

The house had undergone several facelifts in the half-century that had passed. The front garden wasn't much, but the grass was neatly cut, and there were rose bushes in the flower beds. Gone was the rotten old boat on the drive, to be replaced by a Vauxhall Corsa. A new garage built on to the side of the house had a bedroom extension above it.

As they approached the front door, they heard voices raised

in anger coming from inside. The door itself was an elaborate construction of wrought iron and glass, a pretentious adornment to the mean little semi that it opened into.

'Maybe we'd be better waiting in the car,' Ricky whispered nervously.

Jack cast him a look. 'Not so brave without a semi-automatic in your hands, eh?'

He knocked on the door, but the sound of his knuckles on the glass was overwhelmed by the shouting on the other side of it. He tried the handle and pushed the door open. As it swung into the hall it interrupted the squalid scene of domestic disharmony that was unravelling there.

Dave's daughter-in-law stood at the foot of the stairs, shouting at the two men in her life to '*Stop!*'

Dave had been a big man in his day, but Donnie was bigger. He had the lapels of his father's coat grasped in huge fists. Dave was almost lifted off his feet and banged up against the wall. Donnie's face was inches from his father's as he shouted at him, spittle gathering on wet lips. Jack could see a large bruise on Dave's cheekbone, below the eye. A small canvas rucksack leaned against the wall by the front door.

It was as if someone had pressed a pause button and frozen the action, and then all heads turned towards the door. The silence that accompanied the moment seemed endless.

Until broken by Donnie. 'What the fuck do you want?'

Jack's voice sounded oddly calm and, as a result, carried a strangely threatening note. 'I want you to let your father go, and treat him with a little respect.'

Almost in spite of himself, Donnie released his father's lapels and turned his anger on Jack. 'Respect? He's a drunk and a thief, and gets all the respect he deserves. And anyway, it's none of your fucking business.'

'Yes, it is.'

Steel in Jack's voice now as Ricky moved almost imperceptibly to put his grandfather between Donnie and himself and watch the unfolding scene from over his shoulder.

'What is it with you people? I stood in this very house more than fifty years ago and watched your grandfather punch and kick his own son. And I stood by and did nothing about it, because I was too young and too scared. All these years on, and nothing's changed. Except it's the son beating up the father. That violent gene must have skipped a generation, because Dave's the gentlest man I ever knew. And he doesn't deserve this.'

Donnie's face turned ugly as he pulled a wad of banknotes from his pocket, all scrunched up in his big fist, and waved it at Jack. 'Aye, well, your gentle fucking pal was stealing from his own family.'

'Only so I could get oot yer hair once and for all!' Dave said.

Donnie turned on him again, spittle flying from his mouth. 'It's *my* money!'

'And this is *his* house,' Jack said. 'And I'll bet you don't pay him a penny in rent. So maybe he's owed it.'

'Come on,' Dave said. 'Let's just go.'

And he tried to squeeze past Donnie to get his rucksack. But his son grabbed his coat and pushed him up against the wall again.

'You're going nowhere, you old drunk!'

The sound of smashing glass stunned them all into silence, broken only by Donnie's wife's startled little squeal. Pieces of glass showered across the hall carpet. Jack stood with his walking stick still raised. The brass owl's head had shattered the glazed door with a single, sharp strike.

'Let him go!' His voice rang out in the stillness that followed. Commanding. Imperative.

And Donnie let go of his father, as if the old man were suddenly burning hot in his hands.

'I did nothing to stop his father. And maybe you think I'm too old to stop you. But you'd be making a mistake if you did.' He swung his walking stick to smash the brass head of it into the wall, gouging a deep hole in the plaster and sending white dust into the still air of the hall. 'That'd make a hell of a mess of your skull.'

Donnie's wife said in a shaky voice, her hands raised as if to calm them, 'Now there's no need for this, boys.'

Jack ignored her. 'Give him the money.'

For several long moments Jack could see that Donnie was weighing up his options. In the end he thrust the money at his father.

And Jack half turned to Ricky. 'Get his bag.'

Ricky looked like a rabbit caught in the headlights, wide-eyed and startled. But he leaned over quickly to retrieve Dave's rucksack. Dave joined them in the doorway and the three of them retreated down the path towards the waiting Micra.

They heard Donnie's voice roaring behind them, 'Don't even think about coming back here, you old bastard. You'll not get over the door.'

Jack swivelled and saw Donnie almost recoil, as if from a blow. '*Dave's* door,' he said. 'Not yours. And maybe you'd better think about getting a place of your own. Because I'm sure Dave won't want to see you here when he gets back.'

'Aye, exactly right,' Dave called from the safety of the gate.

As they got into the car, Ricky glanced at his grandfather and said, 'I thought you didn't believe in violence.'

Jack said nothing, but he sat shaking silently in the passenger seat. And feeling alive for the first time in a very long time.

III

They parked on Battlefield Road, opposite the infirmary, on the hill that climbs from the Rest to the Langside roundabout. Beyond the roundabout itself the elegant columns of a Greek Thomson church that was now a restaurant were lit up as evening leached the last daylight from an overcast sky. Yellow lights burned in all the windows of the old infirmary; wards like legs extended from the main building to oriel windows looking south.

'Who are we meeting here?' Ricky asked.

'We're no' meeting anyone,' Dave said. 'We've come tae get him. He's no' too well, so we're gonnae have tae gie him a hand.'

Ricky looked worried. 'What do you mean, "not too well"?'

Jack said, 'He's got terminal cancer, Rick. And they've attached him to all sorts of monitors after a heart attack.'

Ricky's concern turned to horror. 'And they're just going to let him walk out?'

Jack and Dave exchanged glances. 'Not exactly,' Jack said. 'Not that they've any right to keep him there, mind. But we're going to have to . . .' he searched for the right word, '. . . assist him to leave.' He paused. 'Though not exactly "we".' Another pause. 'You.'

'What?' Ricky's horror morphed to alarm.

Jack eased himself out of the car, ignoring Ricky's protests, and retrieved his holdall from the boot. He placed it on the passenger seat and took out a large, white doctor's coat. 'Biggest I could get,' he said. 'Triple X. But you should just about be able to button it up.'

'Me?'

Dave laughed from the back seat. 'Dr Mullins. It's got a ring tae it.'

Jack pulled a stethoscope from his bag. 'This is probably a bit of a cliché, but it'll make a good prop.'

'I'm absolutely not doing this,' Ricky said.

Jack gave him a look. 'You absolutely are, Rick.' Then he smiled. 'But don't worry. Me and Dave'll distract the nurses. You're going to need a wheelchair, though.'

Ricky's eyes opened wide. 'Where are we going to get a wheelchair?'

'The hospital, of course.'

'You mean, steal one?'

Jack laughed. 'Of course not. We're only going to borrow it. Hospitals lend mobility equipment to patients all the time. And there's a whole bunch of them right outside the ward. Folding variety.' He pushed the coat and stethoscope at Ricky. 'Now put these on.'

'I'm too young to be a doctor.'

'You look old enough to be a junior. And anyway, who'd know?'

'What if we get caught?'

But Jack just shook his head. He was feeling reckless. 'Well, strictly speaking, we're not relatives, so we've got no rights here. But what are they going to do to us, son? Shoot us? I don't think so.'

The coronary care unit was busier than it had been on their earlier visits. There were more visitors, and Jack was pleased to see that the duty nurse was not one of those he had offended the previous night. He needed her to be susceptible to his charms.

They hesitated at the double doors leading to Maurie's ward, where there were half a dozen wheelchairs folded and stacked against the wall. Ricky's face was pink with both exertion and nerves. But he hadn't turned a single head during their walk through the hospital. He made a very convincing doctor, Jack thought.

'You wait here,' he told him. 'Until you see that we've got the nurse distracted. Then just stroll in like you own the place. No one's going to question you. Maurie's is the last door on the left. He'll be all disconnected from his tubes and wires and waiting for you. When you've got him out, we'll be right behind you.'

Ricky looked like he was about to throw up.

Jack and Dave walked casually through the ward. But before they got to Maurie's room, Dave caught his friend's arm, and they drew briefly to a halt.

Dave lowered his voice. 'Just wanted to say . . . about Donnie and everything . . .'

Jack saw what looked suspiciously like tears gathering in Dave's eyes. But grown Scotsmen didn't show their emotions, and he wasn't about to let them spill. He just shrugged and swallowed. 'You know . . . thanks.'

Jack nodded, but there was nothing more to be said.

They carried on to the door of Maurie's private room, and there they almost bumped into an oddly unsavoury, thickset man with short-cropped black hair, hurrying out. He didn't acknowledge them but stuck his hands deep in his pockets, head sunk into his shoulders, as he strode off towards the exit. He left the scent of cheap aftershave wafting in his wake.

Maurie was sitting on the bed beside a holdall bag. He was wearing a coat and hat, both of which seemed several sizes too big for him. Seeing him out of bed like this made Jack realize just how diminished he really was. And for a moment he was struck by the folly of what they were doing.

'Who was that?' Dave said, flicking his head towards the door.

But Maurie just shook his. 'No one. Are we all set?'

Jack looked at the bank of monitors beside the bed. Where the previous night green and red lights had winked and bleeped, and a heart monitor had registered on a green phosphor screen, nothing was illuminated. The equipment looked dead. Wires and sensors lay strewn around it on the floor.

'Won't that have set off an alarm or something?'

'It's disconnected from the mains.' Maurie sounded tetchy. 'Just get me out of here.'

Jack said, 'My grandson'll be here to get you in just a minute. We'll keep the nurse busy.' He hesitated, taking in Maurie's chalk-white complexion, and the deep, dark smudges beneath his eyes. 'Are you okay?'

'As okay as any dying man can be. Go!'

The duty nurse was talking to a middle-aged couple about the condition of their elderly mother, which suited Jack and Dave's purposes very well. They stood, waiting to speak to her, masking her view towards the door of Maurie's room, and Jack gestured to Ricky waiting out in the hall that he should make his move now. As Ricky pushed the wheelchair quickly across the floor of the ward, the nurse turned towards Jack.

'How can I help you?'

Jack fished a pill box with a clear plastic lid from his coat pocket. It was divided into six compartments, each with its own coloured pills.

He said, 'I know you're not a doctor or anything. But since this is a heart ward, I thought I could ask you.' He gave her his best smile. 'These are the pills I'm on following my own little episode, and I'm off tomorrow on a wee trip. Only, I've lost my list of instructions telling me which to take when, and there's no time to see my doctor before I go.'

'Pretty colours, though, aren't they?' Dave said.

The nurse gave him an odd look.

'You wouldnae know just how dangerous they are.'

The nurse frowned. 'Dangerous?'

'Aye, my old man was on these things after his heart attack, and they might have kept his ticker goin', but they destroyed his kidneys.'

'Polypharmacy,' Jack said. 'That's what you've got to be careful of, isn't that right?'

'I'm afraid you'll have to speak to your doctor about your prescription, Mr . . .'

'Aye, I thought you'd say that.' Jack put on his best worried look now. 'I mean, I think I remember the order I'm supposed to take them in, when and how many. But I wouldn't swear to it. I thought you might know. There's just no time to ask the doc, you see.'

He felt Dave dunting him, and glanced over his shoulder to see Ricky wheeling Maurie out of the ward.

'Anyway, thanks for your help, nurse. You can always come to my funeral.'

Her eyes opened wide, and he grinned.

'Just kidding.' And he turned to follow Dave out into the hall.

Ricky had a good twenty yards' start on them and wasn't hanging about. They almost had to run to catch him up.

But as they did, Maurie started shouting, 'Stop! Stop!' and a panicked Ricky pulled up sharply.

Dave reached them first, then Jack, both of them breathless.

'What the hell is it?' Jack gasped.

'I need to go,' Maurie said

Jack looked up to see the men's toilet sign above the door to their right. He cursed under his breath. 'Can't it wait?'

'No, it can't. Just help me out of the chair. I can do this on my own.'

The three of them helped Maurie to his feet and stood fretting in the corridor by the wheelchair as the toilet door swung shut behind him. Visitors and nurses, and the occasional doctor, drifted by as they waited. And waited.

'Jesus Christ!' Dave whispered eventually through clenched teeth. 'What's he doing in there?'

Jack sighed. 'I'll go and find out.'

He discovered Maurie on his knees in a cubicle, his arms around the bowl of the toilet as if he were embracing it, retching and vomiting between huge gulps of air.

'For God's sake, man, what's wrong with you?'

Maurie gasped, 'I'll be alright in a minute.' And he threw up again. When he'd caught his breath, he said, 'It's the chemo.'

'I thought you were stopping it.'

'I just have.' This time he dry-retched. 'I think that's all for the moment. Help me up.'

Jack helped him to his feet and fumbled in a pocket to retrieve a hanky to wipe the saliva and sick from his old friend's lips and chin. 'It's not too late to give this up, Maurie. We can still take you back.'

Maurie turned sad brown eyes on him, so large now in his shrunken face, and Jack saw the determination that still burned in them. 'Not a chance!'

Back out in the hall, Maurie slumped almost semi-conscious into the wheelchair, and they set off again towards the lifts, anxious to be out of there just as quickly as they could. But as the lift doors closed behind them, they heard a nurse's shrill cry from the far end of the corridor.

'Mr Cohen! For God's sake, where's Mr Cohen?'

It seemed to take the lift an eternity to descend to the ground floor, and the palpable silence in it was thick enough to slice. Not one of them dared to meet the others' eyes. When, finally, the doors slid open it was only to reveal the acres of lobby that had to be crossed before they could escape into the night, and a uniformed security man standing by the doorway.

Jack tried to swallow as his tongue stuck to the roof of a very dry mouth. 'Don't rush it,' he said under his breath. 'Just take your time.'

But Ricky was off as if the flag had just been raised on pole position at a Grand Prix. Jack and Dave struggled to keep up with him.

They were halfway across the hall when a wall-mounted phone beside the security guard rang, and he lifted the receiver. He listened for a moment, then his eyes raked the lobby as he spoke, settling on Ricky and the wheelchair before he hung up. Jack saw a tiny trickle of sweat run down Ricky's neck from behind his ear.

The guard glanced at his watch, then raised a hand to stop them. 'Excuse me, doctor,' he said.

For a moment Jack thought Ricky was going to faint, but from somewhere he managed a mumbled, 'Yes?'

'You got the time on you? My watch seems to have given up the ghost.'

Ricky's relief almost robbed him of the ability to stand up, and he very nearly staggered as he let go of one handle of the wheelchair to look at his watch. 'Quarter to eight,' he said.

'Thanks, doc.' The security man held the door open for them. 'Better wrap up warm, it's bloody cold out there.'

By the time they got to the top of the hill they were all wishing they had been able to find a parking space at the bottom of it. It took all three of them to get Maurie up the steep incline, past the Langside Library and the shops below the tenement flats that climbed the rest of the way to the roundabout.

When they reached the car, Ricky said, 'I can't let go. There are no brakes on this thing.'

Jack tutted. 'I thought you were supposed to be the genius, son. Turn it sideways.'

'Oh. Aye.' Ricky seemed chastened.

He unlocked the car, and the three of them helped Maurie into the back seat.

Then Ricky said, 'What are we going to do with the wheel-chair? Even folded up we're not going to get it into the boot.'

And they turned in time to see its front wheels swivel, setting it on a course back down the hill.

Dave cackled. 'Aye, well, that solves the problem.'

'Jesus!' Ricky started after it. But it was gathering pace quickly, and he realized almost immediately that he was neither fit enough nor fast enough to catch it.

The three of them stood by the car, watching as the empty wheelchair went careening down the hill, bouncing jauntily off parked cars and walls as if it were revelling in undreamed-of speed and freedom. Until it smacked into a pillar box on the corner of Sinclair Drive and came skidding to a halt on its side, half wrapped around the pole of a *Give Way* sign. Just as two uniformed police officers on foot patrol turned the corner.

'Holy shit!' Dave said, which was their cue to get into the Micra as quickly as they could. Like schoolboys fleeing the scene of the crime.

Ricky fumbled with the keys and started her up, pulling out into the traffic without indicating or looking. A large van blasted its horn at them.

'Nothing like an inconspicuous escape,' Jack muttered, turning a dark look towards his grandson.

But Ricky was oblivious. He accelerated away, across the roundabout and down Langside Avenue towards Shawlands Cross, tiny beads of cold sweat gathering across his forehead.

Without taking his eyes from the road he said quietly, 'I'll never forgive you for this, Grampa. Never!'

IV

Ricky took the road through East Kilbride on to the dual carriageway that linked up with the M74. The southbound lanes of the motorway were quiet, and by ten they were long past Crawford and heading into the bleak, rolling wastes of South Lanarkshire. Darkness had crept up on them like a mist, sombre and silent, like the mood in the car itself.

The adrenaline-pumping moments at the infirmary were behind them, and now that they were on the road the cold reality of this madness on which they had embarked sat among them like a fifth presence. White lines caught in the headlights passed beneath them with hypnotic regularity, and the constant whining pitch of the little car's motor filled their collective consciousness.

Maurie was asleep in the back, his head fallen on to Dave's shoulder. Dave sat upright, with glassy eyes, his rucksack resting on his knees.

Jack glanced back at him, struck by a sudden thought. 'What have you got in the rucksack, Dave?'

Dave folded his arms possessively around it. 'Nothing.'

'It must have something in it.'

'Just my toilet bag and some underwear.'

'Seemed kind of heavy for a toilet bag and underwear.'

Jack had lifted the rucksack off the back seat while they were manoeuvring Maurie into the car. The weight of it had registered then, but he had forgotten until now.

Dave shrugged, silently defensive.

'Have you got booze in there?'

'No.' His denial came too quickly.

Ricky glanced across at his grandfather. 'What if he has?'

Jack said grimly, 'Dave has a wee problem.'

'Pfffff.' He heard the air escape from Ricky's lips. 'That's all we need.'

Jack turned round in his seat to fix Dave in his gaze. 'You promised.'

Dave was uncomfortable, but unapologetic. 'It's only a few beers.'

Jack grabbed for the bag. 'Give me it.'

Dave turned it away from him. 'No.'

'For God's sake!' Ricky said, trying to keep his focus on the road.

Jack lunged back over his seat, reaching for the rucksack, this time seizing it and prising it from Dave's grasp. He swung it into the front of the car.

'Aw, Jack, come on! That's not fair.'

Jack opened the rucksack on his knees and found the six-pack of beer wrapped in a nightshirt. He rolled down the window and checked in the wing mirror before chucking the cans out into the night, one by one. He saw them explode as they hit the road, bursts of phosphorescent foam glowing briefly pink in the rear sidelights of the car.

He heard Dave groaning in the dark.

When all the cans were gone and Jack had closed the window, Dave's voice came leaden and bitter from behind him. 'See what I said tae you at the hospital, aboot Donnie and that? I take it all back.'

The thick silence that settled in the aftermath of the moment was invaded by a buzz of electronic music punctuated by the repeating vocal refrain: *Turn down for what.*

'What on earth's that?' Jack said.

'My phone.' Ricky's voice came back at him out of the dark. 'It's a cool ringtone. From a single by DJ Snake and Lil Jon. It's in my jacket pocket. You could get it out for me.'

Jack delved into Ricky's pocket and felt the phone vibrating in his hand as he pulled it out.

'It should say who's calling.'

Jack looked at the display and felt a mixer start up in his stomach. 'It's your dad.'

'Oh shit. What time is it?'

'Just after ten. Where did you say you were going tonight?'

'To the pictures.'

'So you'd be mid-movie right now. Why would he be calling?'

'He must have found the note. Don't answer it.'

'Don't worry, I wasn't about to.'

They sat in tense silence until the phone stopped shouting *turn down for what* at them. Then the silence deepened as they waited expectantly for the tone which would announce that Ricky's father had left a message. It came after nearly thirty interminable seconds. Ricky snatched the phone from his grandfather. Flicking his eyes between the road and the screen, he activated the message to play on speaker.

Malcolm's voice was tight with tension. 'Ricky, you silly bloody idiot! What do you think you're doing? How could you let that old fart talk you into doing something this stupid?'

Jack bristled.

They could almost hear Ricky's father trying to control his breathing. 'But it's alright, son. I don't blame you. There'll be hell to pay right enough, but it's your grandfather who'll be paying it.'

'See?' Jack said, glancing at his grandson. 'Told you I'd get the blame.'

Ricky's face was whale-blubber white, but his eyes were fixed on the road. 'And so you should. It's all your fault.'

His father's voice crackled over the messaging service. 'I'm on the road right now. And you know I'll catch up with you eventually. So pull into the first service station you come to, and call me back.'

'Don't you dare!' Jack said.

Ricky swallowed with difficulty. 'What are we going to do?'

Jack thought about it. 'Well, he's right. The Mondeo's going to outrun the Micra in time. But we've got an hour's head start. We'll just keep going. Down the M6 till we can turn off the motorway and go cross-country to Leeds. We can pick up the M1 south from there.'

Dave's voice came chuckling out of the back. He had forgotten his beer for the moment. 'Just like we did back then, eh?'

Jack glanced across at Ricky and saw the tension in his grandson's hands, knuckles almost glowing white in the dark, and he had a sickening sense of déjà vu.

1965

CHAPTER FIVE

I

'Jobbies!'

No one was paying much attention to Jeff, or the road. We were, all of us, lost in our own thoughts. Coming to terms with just what it was we had done, and were doing, and the realization that there was no going back. These were dark moments of doubt and regret, yet at the same time seductive and exciting. Like those first pioneers who had crossed the North American continent, we were setting out on a journey without the least idea of where it would take us and when, or if, we would ever be back. It was a journey into our collective future. A voyage into the unknown.

'What's wrong?' I said. I was still perched uncomfortably on the engine cowling, Maurie in the passenger seat, and Luke and Dave on the settee in the back. I hoped I wasn't going to spend the entire trip with a 1703cc engine thrumming away beneath my arse. It makes me shudder now to think that none of us wore seat belts. There weren't any in the van, and in 1965 we simply never gave it a second thought. But if we'd had a collision, or even made an emergency stop, I'd have been head first through that windscreen.

'I've missed the turn-off,' Jeff said. We had come up through Busby and East Kilbride New Town. As a kid I had thought there was something almost futuristic about East Kilbride. Clusters of skyscraper apartments that I could see on the skyline across the fields. There was nothing like that where we lived, and I thought they looked exotic, like a page from a sci-fi comic pasted on the horizon. Of course, I had no idea then what soulless places new towns really were.

'What road should we be on?'

'The A776 to Hamilton, and then on to the A74.'

'Well, what road *are* we on?'

'The A726 to Strathaven,' Jeff said. (Which is pronounced 'Straven', even though there's an 'ath' in it. I've never known why.) 'There's an *AA Book of the Road* in the glove compartment. Get it out and tell me how we get on to the A74.'

I dug a big Reader's Digest AA book out of the glove compartment and by the light of the courtesy lamp flicked through pages of maps until I found us. 'Okay,' I said. 'We go straight through Strathaven and stay on the A726 till we see a turn-off for Lesmahagow. That's the most direct route for getting on to the A74 now.' Which is how I became our navigator for the journey. By accident and default.

We got safely on to the main road south in the end, and ploughed off into the dark of the night. I was aware of the shadows of treeless hills rising up around us, the old van labouring up inclines, and then gaining speed on the descent. Jeff seemed to be doing his best to run over the rabbits that kept darting across our path, as if it were some kind of a game.

There was a long, slow climb up and over Beattock Summit. I could feel the wind up there buffeting the high sides of our van, and saw Jeff fighting the wheel to keep us in our lane. No one spoke much during those first couple of hours. It was a time of reflection, of ugly reality setting in.

Then Dave's voice piped up from the back. 'Gonnae have tae stop for a pee soon.'

It was another fifteen minutes before we saw the lights of a transport café up ahead in the darkness, like an island of light floating in the black of the night. When I think of that night, I wonder what the odds were of our stopping at that café, at that moment. But I have since learned that fate, and Dave's bladder, work in the strangest ways.

Tall, four-headed lamp posts spilled their yellow light on to a wide gravel parking area as we pulled off the road. There were several lorries, drawn up side by side, a van and a couple of private cars. We all climbed stiffly out into the cold wind that swept down from the hills above us, stamping the blood back into sleeping limbs, and went into the smoky warmth of the café. Some lorry drivers who clearly knew one another sat around a couple of Formica-topped tables that were marked with coffee rings and cigarette burns, and sticky with spilled sugar. A couple of other tables were occupied by solitary travellers, and an elderly woman behind the counter asked us in a velvety-rich smoker's voice what we would like. We ordered coffees and Tunnock's Tea Cakes, and took it in turns to use the toilet.

As I waited my turn I noticed a young man leaning against the far end of the counter, sucking on a cigarette and casting an interested eye in our direction. He wore jeans and Cuban-heeled boots, and a chequered shirt with its sleeves carefully folded up to the elbow, revealing tattoos on both forearms. He had the classic Elvis, or Teddy boy, haircut, heavily greased and swept back to a duck's arse, a tall quiff trembling precariously over an exposed brow. A black leather bomber jacket was draped over the back of the chair behind him, and he had an air of such quiet self-confidence that you could only be impressed. He was skinny, and looked half-starved, but I thought he was cool. Especially the way he sucked his cheeks in when he pulled fiercely on his cigarette. He blew rings that hovered in the still air, and I wish now that I had never set eyes on him.

I spotted a public phone on the back wall, and asked the woman with the velvety voice for change so that I could make a call. I left the others gathered around the counter and headed for the phone. It was with an increased pulse rate that I pumped pennies into the slot and dialled. I didn't press the A button until I heard her voice, having been ready to press B immediately and get my money back if her father answered.

'Hi, it's me.' I wasn't sure what kind of response I was going to get.

Jenny's voice immediately dropped to conspiratorial. 'Jack, where are you?'

'Dunno for sure. Somewhere south of Beattock Summit.'

'Your dad's after you.'

'What!' The shock of her words made my face sting.

'He's with Maurie's dad, in Maurie's dad's car. They left about half an hour ago to try and catch up with you.'

I had an absurd, fleeting vision of our two dads sitting in the dark in Maurie's dad's car with not a word to say to one another. Two more different people it would have been hard to imagine. The Jew and the atheist. To my knowledge they had never actually met. But I immediately refocused.

'How did they find out? I mean, it's not that late. They shouldn't have found the notes yet.'

There was an ominous silence on the other end of the line.

'Jenny?'

And she blurted it out. 'It was me, Jack. I told them. Not long after you'd gone.'

'Why, for God's sake?'

'Because it's madness. You've no idea what you're getting yourselves into. I thought maybe they could have stopped you.'

I swallowed a deep breath and raised my eyes to the nicotine-stained ceiling. 'Jesus, Jenny! You shouldn't have done that. Jesus!' Thoughts were darting through my head like swallows on a summer's evening, and I couldn't keep track of any one of them.

'Give it up, Jack. Come home.'

'No!' I almost shouted down the line at her. Then, more quietly, 'Not sure I'm ever going to speak to you again, Jenny.' And I hung up, breathing hard, pulse racing.

If the dads had left half an hour ago, they could only be about an hour behind us, if that. And given the speed of the van, it wouldn't be long before they caught us. And what then? I conjured a horrible picture in my head of an argument at the roadside, and the humiliation of me and Maurie being dragged off by the ears to sit in the back seat of his dad's car before being driven home in disgrace.

Luke and Dave and Maurie had carried their coffees to a table and were seated around it sipping their hot milky drinks and talking in low voices. I pulled up a chair and leaned into the table. They knew straight away from my demeanour that something was wrong.

'Two of the dads are after us in a car.'

'Christ! Whose dads?' Dave said.

'Mine and Maurie's.' I turned to Maurie. 'They're in your dad's car.'

I have never seen anyone change colour so fast. Maurie's normally florid complexion turned grey, then white.

'How did they know we'd gone already?'

I suppose I must have blushed with guilt. 'Jenny told them.'

Dave pushed himself back in his seat, breathing imprecations.

Luke, who'd been listening in silence, suddenly said, 'What about my dad?'

I shrugged. 'She didn't say anything about him.' And I

saw in his face, just fleetingly, what I've always thought was disappointment. I said, 'They're only about an hour behind us.'

It was pure panic I saw in Maurie's eyes. 'What are we going to do?'

'We've got to get off the A74,' I said. 'And stay off it. At least for tonight.' I looked around, suddenly aware that Jeff wasn't with us. 'Where's Jeff?'

Maurie nodded behind me towards the counter, and I thought I detected a hint of jealousy in his voice.

'He's talking to that bloke over there.'

I swivelled in my seat to see Jeff and the Elvis lookalike in animated conversation at the far end of the counter. Some joke passed between them and they both laughed.

I said, 'We've got to get out of here now.' I stood up and hurried across the café to catch Jeff by the arm. 'Excuse me.' I nodded apologetically to Elvis and drew Jeff away. In hushed tones I explained to him why we had to leave.

Jeff's eyes opened wide. 'Jobbies! And they're actually on the road now?'

'Yes.'

He glanced at his watch. 'How did they know?'

I could tell this was going to cause me some grief in the hours to come. 'Long story. But there's no time to waste. We're going to have to get off the main road.'

'Excuse me.' Elvis leaned into our conversation, and the most unexpectedly soft Irish brogue issued from smiling lips.

'Couldn't help overhearing. Jeff here was telling me what you fellas are up to.'

I glared at Jeff, but he was oblivious, and Elvis offered me his hand.

'I'm Dennis, by the way.'

It was a warm, dry hand that gave mine a firm shake. But there was something about his smile that didn't quite reach his amber eyes, and I felt an immediate distrust.

'Sounds like you boys'll have a bit of explaining to do if the old fellas catch up with you.'

The others had gathered behind me now, and Dennis smiled around the anxious faces.

'How long behind you are they?'

'About an hour,' I said reluctantly.

'Well, if you're going off-piste you'll need a plan.'

I had no idea what he was talking about, but I said, 'We've got good maps.'

'Excellent.' Dennis nodded in smiling approval. 'But a map's not a plan. Tell you what. I've been hanging about here for a while now looking to catch a ride. Figured I wasn't going to make it home tonight. But if you boys want to give me a lift, I can offer you a bed for the night. Or, at least, a floor.' He grinned. 'And your dads'll never find you.'

'Where?' I could tell from Luke's voice that he was as wary as I was.

'I'm renting a wee farm worker's cottage down in the Lake District. Me and the missus. She's got a job in the local dairy, and I've just been up in Glasgow looking for work.'

He looked at his watch, and I saw that the tattoo on his left forearm was a snake curled around a dagger.

'If we leave now we should reach Penrith before the old fellas catch you, then we'll be off the main road and they'll never find you in a million years.'

Jeff had no hesitation. 'Brilliant, that's what we'll do.'

I glanced at Luke, who gave an imperceptible shrug of the shoulders. Dave and Maurie looked uncertain.

I said, 'Maybe we should talk about this.'

Dennis lit another cigarette. 'Be my guest.'

'Just between us,' I said, and I walked off to the table where we had been seated earlier. The others followed.

'What's the problem?' Jeff jerked his thumb back towards Dennis. 'That's a really gen bloke. And we're not going to get another offer like that tonight.'

'I don't like him,' I said. 'We can navigate ourselves "off-piste" for tonight.'

'I'm with Jack,' Luke said, and we looked at Dave and Maurie. Their joint indecision was paralysing.

'This is just rude,' Jeff said. 'We're insulting the bloke now. And we don't have time to argue about it. It's my van. I say we go with him.' He looked at each of us in turn, almost daring us to say no. And when no one came up with a better plan, he turned and waved to Dennis. 'We're on.'

Dennis smiled and lifted his bomber jacket. 'Good call, boys. You'll not regret it.'

But I had a bad feeling that we might.

II

To my chagrin it was still my fate to sit up on the engine cowling. Maurie had moved into the back to share the settee with Luke and Dave, and had been replaced in the front by the cool Dennis who, as if to underscore his image, chain-smoked an American brand of menthol cigarettes called Kool.

There had been a strange, unspoken shift in the hierarchical structure of our little group. I had been the prime mover in the decision to run away, along with Luke, and up until then had been silently accepted, if not actually acknowledged, as the leader. But now I had been displaced by Dennis. He was three or four years older than us, and beside him we just seemed like the schoolkids we were. And Jeff, the only one of us not still at school, had become his lieutenant. I felt control of our situation slipping away from us, but was powerless to do anything about it.

The A74 took us on a tortuous tour of the southern uplands of Scotland before levelling off into the flood plains of the Solway Firth and the River Esk. I saw a signpost caught fleetingly in our headlights for a place called Metal Bridge, and shortly after that we saw a sign at the side of the road for *ENGLAND*, and I left Scotland for the first time in my life. Odd how straight away it felt different, as if I had passed into a foreign land. And those differences were immediately apparent in the change from stone-built to brick-built houses and farm buildings. I felt the chill of uncertainty creep over me. I was well out of my comfort zone now.

Carlisle was like a ghost town, alien and strange. Empty streets simmering in darkness beneath feeble street lamps. We stopped at an all-night filling station for petrol, and drove out of town on the A6.

The tension in the van was very nearly tangible. No one actually voiced the thought, but it seemed likely now that Maurie's dad and mine could not be very far behind. I could see Jeff constantly checking his side mirrors and tensing every time we were overtaken.

The only one of us completely at ease with the situation was Dennis. He lit another Kool as we passed a road sign for Penrith. It was just ten miles away.

'Won't be long now,' he said.

I could hear him grin in the dark, and saw his smoke rings flattening out against the windscreen in the lights of an on-coming vehicle.

And then we were off the A6, heading west towards Keswick on the A594, and it was like a huge weight had lifted off us all. We had made the turn-off before the dads caught up, and now we were home free, as if the invisible umbilical that had somehow kept us attached to everyone and everything we had known since birth had finally, irrevocably, been severed. We were into the uncharted territory of our new lives.

Dave, it turned out, had cans of stout planked in his rucksack. He passed them around, and we smoked our Player's No. 6 and speculated about how much longer it would take us to get to London, and what we were going to do when we got there.

The road wound its way through undulating, open country peppered with darker areas of forest, and a three-quarter moon shone its colourless light across the land. We passed through tiny villages, houses huddled in darkness, and became aware of the land starting to rise up around us again as we drove into the Cumbrian mountains.

Moonlight cascaded across black water below us as we drove down into a larger town beyond the village of Threlkeld. Its street lamps twinkled in the night, light pollution masking the great canopy of the cosmos whose jewelled sky had, until then, sparkled above our flight path.

'This is Keswick,' Dennis said. 'And Derwent Water.

Jeff changed down the gears as we descended into the town, past slate stone villas sitting proud above steep gardens, and a red-sandstone police station on the bend at the foot of the hill.

As we turned into the main street Dennis said, 'Stop here.'

Jeff pulled up sharply. Dennis swung the door open and jumped down on to the pavement. Cigarette smoke from the van billowed out and cold air rushed in.

'Going to call the missus, just to let her know I'll be arriving with a few fellas. If you're lucky, she might do you a fry-up.'

He grinned and pulled open the door of the red telephone box that stood on the corner, swinging himself into the light inside and fishing in his pocket for some coins.

I pulled the passenger door shut and said, 'We don't need him any more, and we've got him almost home. We could just drive off.'

Jeff swung himself round in the driver's seat and glared at me. 'Are you mad? The bloke's just saved our hide. And do you really want to spend the night in the van?'

'I don't like him,' I said.

'Neither do I.' Luke's voice came from the back, and I felt bolstered by his support.

But Dave said, 'He seems alright to me.'

And Jeff clamped his hands firmly on the wheel. 'Well, I'm driving, and I'm not leaving him here. End of argument.'

And it was.

Dennis climbed back in, bringing the chill of the cold night air with him. 'It's all set. My good lady's cracking eggs into the pan as we speak. Bet you fellas are hungry.'

'Sure are,' Dave piped up from the back.

Luke said nothing, and Maurie, who had been ominously non-committal about the whole thing, remained silent.

Jeff glared at me. 'I could eat a scabby dug,' he said, and crunched the column shift back into gear.

The van lurched off through Keswick, gathering speed until we emerged from its leafy suburbs on to a road signposted to Braithwaite. We were there in a matter of minutes, slowing to wind our way through narrow streets crowded by stone cottages, then out again into vivid moonlight that washed across a valley floor of fallow fields and phosphorescent streams.

Tree-covered hills folded in around us. We passed a cottage called Sour Riggs crouched behind high hedges, and the entrance to a place called Ladstock Hall. But we couldn't see the house itself.

'Take a right just up ahead here,' Dennis told Jeff. His earlier, relaxed demeanour had gone, and he seemed alert now, a little on edge, sitting forward in his seat and peering ahead through the windscreen.

Jeff had to slow almost to a halt to make the turn into what was little more than a lane. I saw a wooden signpost pointing the way to Thornthwaite Church.

'You live in a church?' I said sceptically.

Dennis glanced at me. It was clear he knew I didn't like him.

But still he smiled. 'Haha, no. Irreligious, me. The missus, too. Haven't been in a church for years.' He paused. 'The cottage is just beyond it.'

Jeff had reduced the speed of the van to little more than walking pace to guide it between the hedgerows, the bowed heads of thousands of daffodils smothering overgrown verges and glowing virulent yellow in the headlights. We came round the bend at the foot of the slope and saw the church brooding darkly behind a high stone wall and surrounded by the headstones of the dead, big and small, and canted at odd angles. A farm gate closed off access to a muddy track from a small parking area, and a car sat, half-reversed into a path that disappeared into dark pasture beyond a small, fast-running stream.

Jeff stood on the brakes, surprised by the unexpected car, then blinded as its headlights came on full beam.

Dennis was out of the door before any of us could even

speak, and shadows moved through the lights like ghosts in the night. Men with stout poles that they started banging along the side of the van. Fists thumped on the back doors and a voice shouted, 'Open up!'

We were trapped. There was no way forward, and it would have been impossible to back up at any speed. The driver's door opened, and a grinning Dennis leaned in to turn the key in the ignition and pull it out. The engine spluttered to a stop and the lights dimmed imperceptibly.

'Jaisus,' he said. 'What a bunch of losers you kids are.' Then, 'Everybody out.'

And we knew there would be no arguing with him.

Jeff and I jumped down from the front, and the others opened the back doors to climb out. All five of us were herded into the glare of the headlights from the two vehicles, and I saw that our attackers were only four in number. But they were older than us, and bigger, and armed. Resistance just wasn't an option.

Suddenly Maurie broke free of the circle of light and started running back up the lane. I craned round the van to watch as one of our assailants went after him, catching up with him quickly and bringing him to the ground with a whack across the back of his thighs. I heard Maurie cry out in pain and then, as he was dragged back into the light, saw tears of fear and humiliation staining the dirt on his face.

Jeff became almost incandescent with rage. 'You bastard!' he screamed, and leapt at Dennis.

But he didn't even get close. A baton swung through the headlights and I heard the crack of it on his skull, dropping him to his knees.

'Stupid runaway kids,' Dennis said, his smiles and pretence of geniality long since lost to his true colours. 'Bet you've got every penny you possess on you. And anything and everything of any value.' He strutted across the tarmac in front of us. 'So you can just empty your pockets on to the ground and step back. Everything, mind. We'll search you.' And he nodded to one of his accomplices. 'Go check out their bags.'

Maurie helped Jeff back to his feet, and Dennis brought his face to within inches of the drummer's. 'Should have listened to your mate here, sonny.' And he flicked an unpleasant look at me.

But I wasn't feeling particularly vindicated just then. I could see the blood trickling down Jeff's neck from his head wound, and was too angry and scared.

One by one we laid out the contents of our pockets on the tarmac. Wallets and keys, cigarettes, lighters, loose change. One of Dennis's henchmen scooped it all up and began assessing the haul. We must have had nearly a hundred quid between us, which for a bunch of schoolkids was a lot of money back then. But Dennis seemed less than pleased with his booty.

He glared at us in the headlights. 'You hiding something?'

'What would we have to hide?' I said. 'There's only one of us not still at school. That's all our savings.'

The one who had gone to rifle through our bags came back empty-handed. 'Just clothes and toiletries and a few cans of beer wrapped inside a *Playboy* magazine,' he said. He had a broad North of England accent.

The mention of the *Playboy* magazine drew all our eyes towards Dave, and I'd swear he blushed, although it was hard to tell in that light.

Dennis sneered. 'Hardly worth the bloody trouble.'

'What about all that gear in the back of the van?' the one with the accent said. 'Drums and guitars and shit.'

But to my relief Dennis shook his head. 'Too big. We'd need to take the van as well. And we'd only get pennies for the stuff.' He leaned in towards us, leering. 'If you've got any sense you'll get into that van and head back up the road. It's way past your bedtime. Your mammies'll be wondering where you are.' Then he grinned. 'If you can ever find the keys, that is.' And he turned and hurled the ignition keys through the darkness, over the wall and into the cemetery. 'Happy hunting. Or should that be haunting?' Which brought guffaws of laughter from his mates. 'And you'll not be needing this.' He held up Jeff's driving licence and tore it into little pieces before casting them into the night.

They jumped into their car and its engine kicked and revved. With a squeal of tyres it kangarooed out of its place of semi-concealment, accelerated past us to squeeze by the van, two wheels gouging deep ruts in the verge, and sped off into the dark.

We stood then without moving or speaking, hearing the sound of the car slowly vanishing into the night, watching its lights track back along the road we had travelled just ten minutes earlier, until both sight and sound of it were lost to us.

Jeff sat down suddenly in the middle of the road and put his fingers to his neck, bringing them away smeared with blood, startling and red. 'Aw jobbies.'

Maurie said, 'I've got some first-aid stuff in my bag.' And he ran round the van to get it.

Dave's voice, laden with sarcasm, injected itself into the gulf of silence he left us with. 'Thanks, Jobby Jeff! *That's a really gen bloke. I'm not leaving him here.*'

Jeff's head swung slowly round to turn dangerous eyes on Dave. 'Fuck off,' was his only comeback. But then, 'And don't call me Jobby Jeff!'

'Fighting among ourselves is not going to do us any good,' Luke said. 'We've got to figure out what to do. We're not going to get very far without any money.'

Maurie returned to more silence and knelt beside Jeff to wipe the blood from his wound and slather it with antiseptic cream, before crudely covering it with a sticking plaster. We watched despondently, each of us nursing his own private despair.

Until Dave said quietly, 'They didn't get *all* the money.'

Every head turned towards him, and he opened his jacket to start pulling his shirt out of his trousers, revealing a canvas money belt strapped around his waist.

'Got it as a Christmas pressie a few years ago and never used it. Till noo. Thought it might be a good way of carrying my cash.' He unzipped one of its many compartments and pulled out a wad of notes. He held them up. 'Twenty quid. Should get us somewhere.'

And suddenly our predicament didn't seem quite so bleak.

'More than enough to get us back home,' Maurie said, provoking a chorus of unanimous dissent.

Luke said, 'No fucking way am I going back.' His determination to see this thing through was resolute.

It took me a moment to realize why I was so shocked, before I understood. It was the first time I had ever heard Luke swearing.

'So what *are* we going to do?' Maurie's voice was almost plaintive.

I said, 'Well, the first thing we need to do is find those keys.'

'How are we going to do that in the dark?' Jeff winced as he placed his hand over the gash on his head.

'I haven't the faintest idea,' I said. 'But I'm sure you'll figure it out.'

'Me?'

'Aye,' Dave said. 'We wouldn't be in this mess if you hadn't made us give that bloke a lift.'

I stooped to pick up the lighters that the thieves had left lying on the ground. They had taken our cigarettes, so we hardly needed the lighters any more. But I chucked them at Jeff. 'You'll get some light off these till they run out.'

He snatched them up and scrambled to his feet. 'And what are the rest of you going to do?'

'Get some sleep,' Luke said, and he headed off to climb back into the van.

Jeff looked nervously towards the pool of darkness that engulfed the church and the cemetery beyond the wall. 'That's a Christian cemetery?'

I glanced at the sign, which read *Church of St Mary the Virgin*.

'So?'

'So, I'm Jewish.'

'What's that got to do with anything?'

'The spirits might not like a Jew poking about a Christian burial place.'

'Oh, for God's sake!'

'Exactly!' Jeff glanced at Maurie. 'Will you help me?'

But Maurie just raised his hands. 'You're on your own this time, pal.'

To his credit, Jeff accepted his fate, punishment for his role in talking us into taking Dennis on board, and I almost felt sorry for him as he tentatively pushed open the gate to the churchyard. A tangled arch nurtured over decades from the intertwined branches of two trees led to the church itself. Beyond and around it the cemetery lay in deep pools of darkness cast by the shadows of trees in the intermittent moonlight. I was glad it was Jeff going in there in the dark, and not me.

I returned to the van and curled up in my big furry coat in the front passenger seat. The others had made themselves comfortable in the back. But sleep was not quick in coming. It had been a long day, and although we were all tired, the adrenaline was still pumping. It hardly seemed credible that this was the same day that had begun with Jenny and me being summoned to Willie's office. Already that seemed like a lifetime ago.

Dave's hushed voice came out of the darkness. 'Why does Jobby Jeff always have to say that fucking word?'

'What word?' Luke said.

'*Jobbies*. I hate that word.'

Which was met with silence.

Then, 'Are you asking me?' Maurie's voice came out of the dark.

'You're his pal.' Dave made a noise of snorted disgusted. 'I mean, every time he says it I get this picture of brown, stinky sausages dropping oot a dug's arse.'

Maurie said, 'It's to stop him swearing.'

'Why does he want to stop swearing?'

'He told me he was shocked when he started work at Anderson's. He'd always thought it was just us, you know, kids that swore. I mean, you don't hear your folks swearing, do you? Then he's in among all these adults. Grown men. And they're all swearing like troopers. So he thought he would try and stop.'

I raised my head from my coat. 'What about you, Luke? I never heard you swear before tonight.'

'Oh, I decided years ago that I wasn't going to swear.' Luke's was the sweet voice of reason illuminating the night.

'Seemed to me that if you had to swear it demonstrated a lack of vocabulary.'

There was a further silence as we all absorbed this.

Until Luke added, 'Mind you, there's times when nothing else'll fucking do.'

And we all roared and laughed, and heard Jobby Jeff's plaintive voice calling from somewhere beyond the cemetery wall.

'What's so funny?'

III

I woke up freezing cold as the first sunlight of an early-spring morning slanted through the trees and crept slowly into the front of the van. I was stiff and sore from sleeping in a bizarrely twisted position in the front passenger seat. But slept I had, without stirring all night. I stretched and peered into the gloom behind me to see Dave and Maurie on the settee, locked in what was almost an embrace, and wished I had a camera to capture the moment. There was no sign of Luke.

I glanced across to the driver's side and saw Jeff curled up in a foetal position, wrapped up in his own jacket, his head tucked inside it for warmth. I hadn't heard him getting in. The inside walls of the van were running with condensation.

I didn't have the heart to wake anybody, so I climbed stiffly out on to the tarmac. I stood, then, at the side of the road and released a stream of hot urine on to the daffodils, watching steam rising into the sunlight. The scrape of a footfall in the lane turned my head and I saw Luke walking down from the road, hands pushed deep into his pockets. He nodded and stood beside me to unzip his fly and empty his bladder, too. Sunlight sparkled in the twin streams.

'We're not going to get far on twenty quid,' he said. 'Not with five of us to feed. And the Thames is a thirsty beast.'

I zipped up again. 'So what do you think we should do?'

But he just shook his head. 'I haven't the first idea.'

I pushed open the farm gate and slithered down the bank to the stream that bubbled past the church, first dousing my hands in it, then slunging my face with ice-cold water. The shock of it brought blood stinging to my cheeks.

I looked back up at Luke, who stood watching me. 'I wonder if Jeff found the keys?'

Luke pursed his lips. 'He didn't.'

'How do you know?'

'I was still awake when he got back in the van. He didn't look for long. To be fair, he was never going to find them in the dark.'

I shook my head in despair. 'Maybe we're going to have to go home after all.'

Luke was unfazed. 'You go if you want, but I'm not.'

And I knew that if Luke wasn't, then neither was I.

I scrambled up the bank as Maurie and Dave jumped down from the back of the van. They both emptied their bladders and then joined us beside the stream.

Dave glared at Maurie. 'He had a stonking bloody hard-on during the night.'

Luke and I both laughed.

I said, 'How do you know that?'

Dave was indignant. 'Cos it was sticking into my back, that's how.'

Maurie blushed. 'That wasn't my fault.'

'Well, it certainly wasn't mine!' Dave was not amused.

Luke controlled his laughter. 'Nocturnal erections, otherwise known as nocturnal penile tumescence, Dave. We all have them. Three to five times a night, usually during REM sleep. Doesn't mean Maurie's in love with you. You must have woken up with one yourself a few times.'

Maurie growled, 'Or when he's got his face stuck in that *Playboy* magazine.'

Dave punched the fleshy part of his upper arm. 'Shut up!'

Maurie clutched his arm. 'Hey! That hurt!'

I changed the subject. 'So did either of you bright sparks get any ideas during the night about what we're going to do?'

Which brought an abrupt end to the juvenile banter. The lack of any serious suggestion was ominous, the four of us standing there with our hands thrust in our pockets feeling the early warmth of the sun make inroads into the legacy of cold left by the night.

Then Maurie said, 'Do you think we could make it to Leeds?'

He had the oddest look in his eyes that I would remember many years later. But at the time I thought nothing of it. The rest of us gawped at him in disbelief.

'Leeds?' Dave said. 'Why would we want to go there?'

At first Maurie seemed reluctant to tell us. But in the end he said, 'My cousin's there.'

I frowned. 'Is that the lassie that ran off with her boyfriend?'

He nodded.

'I thought no one knew where they'd gone.'

Maurie said, 'They went to Leeds. That's where he's from. Andy McNeil. I'm the only one that knows. She called me, and made me swear not to tell anyone. You know, we were close when we were kids, so she trusted me. Then she wrote to me. Sent me her address and a phone number. I packed her letter to bring with me before we left, just in case my folks found it.' He was struck by a sudden thought. 'Shit, I hope those bastards didn't take it.'

He rushed back to the van and disappeared inside, only to emerge a few moments later clutching a dog-eared blue envelope.

'Got it.' As he reached us again he took the letter out and looked at the untidy handwriting scrawled across the page in pencil. 'Always had a feeling that things weren't going quite right for her.'

He glanced up. And that same expression flickered briefly across his face, like a passing shadow.

'What would be the point?' Dave said.

'Of what?'

'Going tae see your cousin.'

Maurie turned on him. 'A roof over our heads, food in our bellies. And maybe they can lend us money and help us get back on the road.'

I sensed Maurie's anger. He had just broken his promise to his cousin for our common good, and maybe he felt the idea deserved a better reception.

I did, too. 'I think it's a brilliant idea. And in the absence of a better one, I say we go to Leeds.'

'Me, too.' Luke nodded his agreement

Dave shrugged. 'Suppose so.' And, as an afterthought, 'What about Jobby Jeff?'

'He doesn't get a say.' I was adamant about that. 'We wouldn't be in this mess if he hadn't insisted on giving Dennis a lift.'

'Good.' Luke rubbed his hands together with renewed enthusiasm. 'All we have to do now is find the keys for the van and we'll be on our way. Someone better wake up Jobby Jeff.'

IV

We searched among the gravestones for more than half an hour without success. Great gnarled pines sent long shadows through grass that hadn't yet been cut after the winter. It gave me a strange feeling to be searching like that among the dead, where people had been laid to rest for eternity. I felt like we were disturbing their peace. Thomas Bowe of Swinside Farm. Henry Herbert Jay and his wife, Jessie. Joseph Tickell of Thornthwaite, who died on 7th March 1901, at the age of seventy. It didn't seem right to be tramping over their graves, stupid boys on a fool's errand, naive and unworldly, taken for suckers on their first night away from home.

In the end it was Luke who solved our problem. We were simply searching randomly. Until he called on us to stop. We all raised expectant heads as he stooped to pick up a stone from the path, and weighed it in his palm.

'This is probably close to the weight of the keys,' he said. 'I'll go out there and throw it from where Dennis was standing. I think I remember roughly what direction he threw them. You lot watch out for where it lands, and we'll concentrate our search there.'

We watched as he went back out into the turning area, positioning himself where he thought Dennis had been standing, and then throwing the stone just as hard as Dennis had thrown the keys. We watched where it landed, which was quite a bit further in than any of us had been looking. We found the keys nestling in the grass within three feet of the stone in less than two minutes.

Another ten minutes and we were on the road, following the signposts back to Keswick, where we stopped at a café and bought tea and bacon butties. I consulted the Reader's Digest *AA Book of the Road*, and plotted a course. And then we were off, heading south out of Keswick on the A591 to Windermere and Kendal.

The first few miles passed in sombre silence, until someone in the back said, 'It's different with me and Veronica.'

And we all burst out laughing.

Except for Jeff, who looked both puzzled and aggrieved. 'What?' he said. 'What!'

Which only made us laugh even harder.

Spirits soared then, and we started singing daft rugby songs with vulgar lyrics. It is astonishing how youthful ignorance can put adversity so easily aside to breed baseless optimism. Older, wiser heads might have embarked on this leg of the journey with a little more caution. But when you are seventeen, with the road powering past beneath you, and the sun shining in your eyes, you never imagine for one moment that things could ever go anything but well.

The road wound through mountain passes, tree-covered escarpments rising steeply from deep, dark lakes reflecting mountains like mirrors. Thirlmere, Windermere. If I hadn't known better I'd have sworn that the Scottish West Highlands had been transplanted right here in the north-west of England.

It was a stunning day. Chilly still, but without a cloud in the sky. It didn't take us long to reach the crossroads town of Kendal and then on to the A65 cross-country to Leeds itself.

CHAPTER SIX

I

Two things happened on that drive to change our mood. The first was a change in the weather. From that clear, cold, sunny start, the day turned slowly grey. Dark clouds overtook us from the west, low and laden with rain that began to fall around lunchtime. The second was a change of landscape.

From the lakes and mountains of the north-west, we had reached to the rolling farmland and picturesque stone villages of the Yorkshire Dales. But now, as we approached Leeds itself, the darkening sky turned sulphurous yellow, the mills that ringed the city pumping coal smoke into air already thick with it. Stone villages and affluent suburbs gave way to decaying brick terraces. As we drove into it, the city seemed to fold itself around us, drawing us into its crumbling industrial heart.

This was a city in transition, in the process of slum clearance and new build. A city characterized by the chimneys of the mills that pricked the blackening sky, a legacy of nineteenth-century industrialization which, within a quarter of a century, would be decimated by eleven years of Thatcher government.

Years that destroyed the industrial base of a nation and sowed the seeds of future financial meltdown.

I had grown up in another industrial city, but Leeds had little of Glasgow's Victorian grandeur, or the splendid architectural inheritance of the Tobacco Lords. Perhaps it was the rain, and the poisonous sky, but it felt mean as we approached it that afternoon, a city in decline. On another day, in bright sunshine, Leeds might have offered a very different impression of itself. Sunlight so colours our view of the world. But that afternoon it spoke to us only of grim urban deprivation. Our optimism of earlier in the day was crushed by its minacious sky and the creeping return of a brutal sense of reality.

We parked the van in a side street on the south-western edge of the city, bought some cigarettes, and went into a pub crowded with factory workers at the end of their shift. We found seats in an alcove near the back and sent Jeff to get us halves of lager, since he looked older than the rest of us. We sat and smoked, making our own contribution to the pall of pollution that hung in the place, kippering our clothes and stinging our eyes. Maurie used the phone at the bar to call his cousin.

While he was gone, Luke picked up her letter from the table and read it out loud.

Dear Mo,

Wanted you to have my address and number. Just in case. Andy's not exactly who I thought he was when we met in Glasgow. Funny how you think you know folk when you really don't. But things are okay. I'm trying to get a job. That would help. I'd like to feel more independent. Anyway, take care. If anything happens, tell my mum and dad I love them, in spite of everything.

Love,

Raitch

'Raitch?' Dave said.

'Rachel.' Jeff rubbed his chin thoughtfully. 'Lovely-looking girl. Used to fancy her myself.'

'Before Veronica stole your heart?' I cocked an eyebrow in his direction.

He gave me a withering look, then flicked his head towards the letter. 'She doesn't sound very happy.'

Luke whistled, and we all turned to look at him. His eyes were still fixed on the crumpled sheet of blue notepaper in his hands.

'Just seen the address.' He looked up. 'Quarry Hill Flats.'

I frowned. 'What, you mean you know it?'

Luke raised his eyes from the letter. 'It's pretty famous. Or should I say infamous?'

'How would you know?' Dave took a long pull at his beer.

'We got several classes from Mr Eccleston on twentieth-century social housing. Part of my history of architecture course.'

I pulled a face. 'You mean, you were actually awake through that stuff?'

Luke smiled. 'It was interesting. Quarry Hill Flats was the centrepiece of it.'

'Why?'

'Because it's the largest housing estate of its kind in the world. I don't remember the exact details, but I think they took their inspiration for it from some complex in Vienna. A new kind of approach to social housing, old Mr Eccleston said it was. They cleared an area of inner-city slums in the Quarry Hills area in the thirties, right in the centre of Leeds, and built this . . .' he searched perhaps for the word that Mr Eccleston had used, '. . . Stalinesque monstrosity. Almost completely enclosed, with huge archways leading into it. He showed us plans and photographs of it. Massive, seven- and eight-storey blocks, a thousand flats for three thousand people. Sort of teardrop shaped, the whole complex, which is kind of ironic, given the way it's turned out.'

'What do you mean?' I was curious about this social housing experiment where Maurie's cousin had ended up.

'Well, it's become a bit of a nightmare of a place, Jack. Falling apart, really. Physically and socially. Problem families, vandalism, gangs.'

'Jees,' Dave said. 'And that's where Maurie's cousin lives?'

Luke nodded. 'So it seems.'

A troubled-looking Maurie came back and slumped down into his seat. We all turned expectant eyes on him, but he was lost in some glassy-eyed distance.

Jeff couldn't contain himself. 'What did she say?'

Maurie came out of his reverie, as if aware of the rest of us for the first time. 'She said not to come before about ten thirty tonight.'

I leaned forward. 'And?'

'And nothing. That's it. But she did say not to bring the van into the complex.' He hesitated. 'She thought it might not be safe.'

Dave laid his hands on the table and spread his fingers. 'Great!'

Luke said, 'Why do we have to wait till ten thirty?'

'She'd rather Andy wasn't there when we came. She thinks he'll be out till about midnight.'

'Aw jobbies,' Jeff said. 'That means she'll want rid of us before then. So much for a roof over our heads. It'll be another night in the van.'

But my eyes were fixed on Maurie. That sense of troubled preoccupation hadn't gone away.

'What's wrong?'

He glanced up at me, and then away again quickly, reluctant to meet my eye. 'She says she can lay her hands on some money. But she wants to go with us.'

You could have touched the silence that settled among us, as if it had taken form.

Jeff was the first to voice our misgivings. 'We can't take a girl with us, Maurie.'

'Why not?' Maurie turned angry eyes on his friend.

'Because we're five blokes, and . . . well, it wouldn't work, that's all.'

He looked around the table for support, which was there in our faces, but no one said anything.

'Why does she want to go with us, Maurie?' I asked.

'Because she's in trouble, Jack.' He hesitated, then sighed. 'Something to do with drugs. And Andy. She wouldn't be any more specific than that.' He looked around the assembled faces, then said fiercely, 'I'm not going without her.'

'And if we don't want to take her?' Luke said.

'Then you'll go your way and I'll go mine.'

Which really wasn't an option, since Maurie was our singer and frontman, and there was no way we would find work in London without him.

Jeff said, 'How much money?'

Maurie frowned at him. 'What?'

'How much money can she get?'

Maurie shrugged. 'Don't know. More than enough to get us to London. That's all she said. I couldn't talk her into going back to Glasgow.'

'Okay,' I said, 'we might as well be democratic about it and put it to a vote.' I raised my right hand. 'I say we take her.'

I looked at the others, and one by one they raised reluctant hands, all except for Jeff. Maurie glared at him, but there was more hurt than anger in his eyes.

Until, finally, Jeff said, 'Oh, alright.'

And it was settled. But none of us was happy with this completely unforeseen turn of events.

II

It was dark and raining heavily when we drove down Eastgate towards the roundabout at the foot of the hill, shortly after ten o'clock.

'Jees,' Jeff said, his voice hushed as he peered past the wipers and the rain towards the dominating seven-storey sweep of concrete that characterized the front end of Quarry Hill. It curved round St Peter's Street, beyond the roundabout, and filled the view at the end of the road. We all crowded towards the front of the van to get a view of it. I had never seen anything on that scale in my life. It bore no relation, architecturally, to anything else around it. It was as if some giant spaceship had simply landed on the hill, vast and incongruous, and couldn't take off again.

'It looks like a prison,' Dave said.

And I thought yes, that was it. It was exactly as you might have imagined some grim Soviet prison block where political prisoners were sent in their thousands for daring to think. All it lacked was the razor wire and the sweeping criss-cross of security searchlights.

'That must be Oastler House,' Maurie said. 'Rachel said the whole complex is made up of about a dozen different blocks or "houses", as they call them. She said to enter through the arch at Oastler, and they're in Moynihan, which is the big block that runs the length of the north side.'

Jeff swung left into Vicar Lane, and we entered a maze of narrow backstreets lined by three- and four-storey red-brick factories and warehouses. He found parking in Edward Street, and cut the engine and lights. We all sat listening to the tick, tick of the cooling engine, reluctant to go out into the rain that we could hear battering on the roof.

Finally, a little before ten thirty, the rain eased a bit and we slipped out into the dark. The city was pretty much deserted. We could hear the rumble of light traffic on the main thoroughfares of Eastgate and St Peter's Street, and New York Road beyond, but there wasn't a soul in sight as we turned left into Lady Lane and hurried in the darkness down the hill towards Oastler. The Kingston Unity Friendly Society building loomed over us on our right, and on the left stood Circle House and the darkened window of Harold's hairdressers.

We ran across the roundabout in a huddle and on to the concourse that led to the huge archway in the centre of the towering arc that was Oastler House. Lights burned beyond balconies in random patterns across all seven floors, and our footsteps echoed back at us in the dark from the curved walls of the arch as we passed through it. We emerged on the far side into another world. A world unto itself, enclosed and private, the city behind us shut out and lost beyond the dominating blocks of flats that ringed its perimeter. Even in the dark you could see the neglect and decay. Stained concrete, cracked and crazed. Street lamps whose bulbs had died, leaving pools of darkness around them. Weeds poking up through fissures in the tarmac. Football fields and kiddies' play areas sad in their tawdry, shadowed emptiness.

Away to our right I saw an old red-brick building that had somehow been subsumed into the development, and the raised circle of an enormous gas storage tank.

'This way.' Maurie led us off to the left, blocks of flats rising up all around us.

We followed the curve of Oastler to Neilson, and another arch that offered a tempting escape back into the outside world. But we still had business within. There were vehicles parked along the front of the buildings, and further blocks were separated by cluttered open areas abandoned to the creeping advance of nature in the process of reclaiming them.

There was no one around. No movement, no sign of life, except for lit windows punctuating black spaces. I know now, of course, that good, working people lived ordinary lives in these blocks. Were born, and lived and died here. Played, fought, laughed, made love, as well as the best of a deteriorating environment. But to us, in the dark and the rain that night in 1965, it seemed alien and hostile.

Maurie found the entrance to Rachel's stairway near the far end of Moynihan and we escaped the rain into a scarred and gloomy stairwell that smelled of urine. The lift was only big enough to take two, and so we decided to climb the stairs to the third floor. The smell of urine gave way to the perfume of stale cooking, cabbage and onion, and drains – a low, unpleasant note that seemed to permeate the entire building.

We passed along a dimly lit corridor to Rachel's door near the far end. Her flat was on the interior side of the development.

Some idiot with a can of spray paint had left his signature along most of the length of the wall.

Maurie knocked on the door, and after a brief wait we heard a girl's voice come from the other side of it.

'Who is it?'

'It's Maurie.'

The door opened, and she almost flew into his arms. He was as much taken aback as we were. She buried her face in his chest, her arms reaching around his substantial girth to squeeze the breath out of him.

'Oh, Mo, I'm so glad you're here.'

Her voice was muffled, almost lost in the damp of his jacket, and it wasn't until she stepped back that I really saw her face for the first time.

There are many ways to describe a moment like that. Most of them mired in cliché. I could say that time stood still. Or that my heart pushed up into my throat and very nearly choked me. And in their own way these things would be true. I had butterflies in my stomach, and my mouth was so dry I could barely separate my tongue from the roof of my mouth. So I could be forgiven a little hyperbole.

When I first met Jenny Macfarlane, there had been an instant and powerful attraction. I had wanted her to be my girl. But at the risk of sounding like Jeff and his Veronica, this was different. I knew, beyond any shadow of doubt, that *this* girl would mean more to me than any other in my life. I knew it then, and I know it still today, fifty years on. But in the words of the song from a 1969 Rolling Stones album, *Let it Bleed*, you can't always get what you want.

Of course, I didn't know that then.

Her face was thin, and very pale, as if she hadn't eaten much, or had suffered a recent illness. But her eyes were huge. The deepest, warmest brown, a mirror of the chestnut hair that fell in unruly ropes over her shoulders. She just made you want to protect her. From all the darknesses of the world. She wore a long-sleeved, close-fitting white smock over bell-bottomed jeans and brown boots. She was a skinny girl, but not skeletal. She carried flesh on her bones in the right places, and there was something almost classy about her. Elegant. She wore not a trace of make-up, and didn't need to. Her lips were dark and quite full, in contrast to her long, thin nose, and her jawline was so well defined it was almost elfin.

Her relief at seeing Maurie was tangible, and her emotion welled up to moisten those big brown eyes, so that they soaked up and reflected almost every ounce of light in this whole dismal place.

We all stood back a little, feeling like intruders, embarrassed and unwilling witnesses to a very personal moment. She hardly noticed us.

Then she glanced nervously along the corridor before ushering us inside. 'Come in. Quick. You don't want to be seen out here.'

We shuffled into the flat after Rachel and Maurie like sheep, and she closed the door carefully behind us. Through an open door on the left I saw an unmade bed, street light from the window falling across a tangle of sweat-stained sheets. From the hall she led us into the living room, where glass doors opened on to a cluttered balcony that looked out into the very heart of the Quarry Hill development. It seemed that half the flat had spilled out on to the balcony, bags of rubbish, broken bits of furniture, the detritus of a life in disarray, all piled up like debris washed ashore after a storm. The balcony itself gave on to a joyless view of other apartments, lights burning in countless windows, other people's lives spooling out behind glass like so many private movies. Short ones, long ones, sad ones, happy ones.

But there was nothing happy about this apartment. It was a car crash of a place. We had to wade through an accumulation of old clothes, the flotsam and jetsam of lives in chaos, just to get out of the hall. There was a foul smell in the flat, and rising above it the unpleasant odour of paraffin. I saw an old paraffin heater sitting in the corner of the room, and thought that probably explained the tracks of black condensation that stained the walls and windows.

The mouldy remains of half-eaten meals littered a Formica-topped table.

'Jesus!' Maurie voiced all of our thoughts in a single oath. 'How can you live like this, Raitch?'

I saw tears well up in her eyes again.

'It's not my choice, Mo. It really isn't. It's not my home, it's Andy's. And whichever of his friends decide they're going to crash for the night. There can be eight or ten people sleeping over, some nights. You have to step over bodies just to get to the loo.'

Maurie shook his head in confusion. 'So why do you stay?'

'Like I said, I don't have a choice. If I tried to get away Andy would come after me. I'm not his girlfriend, I'm his property. And where would I go? What would I do? I don't have any money.'

Jeff said, 'You told Maurie you could get your hands on some cash, Raitch.'

She glanced at Jeff, and I could tell immediately that she didn't like him. One look was all it took to convey a whole history that the rest of us knew nothing about.

'I know where it is. I just can't get at it.'

'What do you mean?' Maurie said.

Without a word she led us back out through the hall and into the bedroom I had glimpsed on the way in. The smell in here was sour. Body odour and feet. On a bedside table there was a candle and, laid out on a dirty handkerchief, a syringe, a small round metal container, a strip of stained blue rubber about fifteen inches long and other, unidentifiable bits and pieces. Although I had never witnessed anything like them, I knew instinctively these were the accoutrements of the heroin addict. It was startling to see them laid out like that, as if they were everyday things in everyday use. And in truth, they probably were. But I was distracted by Rachel dropping to her knees at the side of the bed and reaching under it to slide out a small trunk secured by a large padlock.

'This is where he keeps his stuff. And his cash.'

'His stuff?' I said.

And she looked at me, I think, for the very first time. There was a moment, I am sure of it, that mirrored for Rachel the moment when I first set eyes on her. I can still see and feel it clearly in my mind, although I wonder now if it wasn't exaggerated in my imagination, and imbued in later years with the memory that I have of it today.

'The stuff he sells,' she said.

'Drugs?' Maurie seemed shocked.

She nodded. 'H.'

'He's a dealer?'

'And user.' Her brave face crumpled just a little before she caught herself. 'He's started making me take it, too.'

She pulled up her sleeve to reveal the bruises and scabbing around the injection sites in the crook of her arm. The stunned silence in the room seemed to affect her more than anything else. As if serving, somehow, to bring home to her just how far she had fallen. We were her peers. Middle-class kids from a south-side Glasgow suburb, staring at her with the same horror she would have felt herself in other circumstances.

Silent tears brimmed on her lower lids, before spilling over to run down her cheeks. 'Please, Mo. Get me out of here.' Though for some reason, it was me she looked at.

But it was Jeff who took the initiative. Not the brightest, but always practical. 'Are there any tools in the flat?'

She wiped her cheeks dry with her palms as she stood up. 'Andy keeps stuff in a box under the sink.'

We followed her through to the kitchen.

In the cardboard box there was a stout screwdriver, a set of spanners wrapped in cloth, a claw hammer, a rusted file with a pointed end, a bicycle pump and some corroded tins of chrome cleaner. Jeff grabbed the box and carried it back through to the bedroom.

Maurie turned to Rachel. 'Get packed, Raitch. Minimum that you need. You got a bag?'

She nodded. 'Andy's got an old sports bag in the back room.'

'Then pack now.'

The imperative in Maurie's voice infused us all with a sense of urgency. None of us wanted to be here when Andy got back. I hurried through to help Jeff try to break open the trunk.

'We'll never bust this padlock,' he said. 'Best we can hope for is to break the clasp.'

His instrument of choice was the file. It was about twelve inches long and solid iron. He insinuated it between the clasp and the body of the trunk and braced his legs against the trunk itself to try to lever it free. The side of the trunk buckled with the force of it, but the clasp remained firmly attached.

I sat on the trunk and added my heel and the strength of one leg, to try to gain more leverage. The scream of metal under stress filled the room, and there was some movement of the rivets that attached the clasp to the trunk. Enough for me to be able to force the head of the screwdriver between the two and hammer it down. The panel welded to the clasp buckled, and with two of us now exerting leverage at different points, the whole thing bent outwards, protesting all the time, until finally it gave. Jeff fell backwards and the padlock dropped to the floor.

I threw back the lid of the trunk. Me and Jeff, and Dave and Luke, all crowded round to look inside. If we had expected it to be crammed full of heroin we were disappointed. It was almost empty, except for a single, clear plastic bag sealed with sticky tape and filled with a white powdered substance. It was about the size of a two-pound bag of sugar. The bottom of the trunk was littered with small resealable plastic sachets, all empty. There was a small set of scales, a spectacles case that opened to reveal several unused syringes, and a black cloth bag with a string threaded through the open end of it, gathered and tied in a bow. I untied it and pulled the bag open to lift out two wads of banknotes. Fives, tens and twenties.

'Jees!' Dave's voice came in a breath that seemed to fill the room. 'Must be a couple of hundred quid in there if there's a penny.'

I weighed them in my hand. It was certainly a lot of money.

'We can't take that,' Luke said suddenly, and we all looked at him.

'Why not?' Jeff said.

'Because it's stealing.'

I stood up. 'Luke, this isn't honestly earned money. The guy sells drugs. He trades in people's misery. It's not theft, it's liberation.'

But Luke shook his head. 'It's still stealing.'

I felt frustration well up inside me. I needed to provide him with a logic for taking it. 'Okay,' I said. 'Andy and Rachel are a couple, right? They share their lives. So, by rights half of this should be hers.' I threw one of the bundles back into the trunk. 'We'll only take her half.'

'Hey!' Jeff protested.

But I never took my eyes off Luke. 'It's more than enough to get us to London, Jeff. What do you say, Luke?'

I could see the internal struggle going on behind his eyes. Whatever else those years of being dragged around the doors had done, they had instilled in him an unshakeable sense of morality, of right and wrong.

He nodded and said quietly, 'Okay.'

Maurie and Rachel appeared in the doorway. She was wearing a black leather jacket now, and he was carrying her holdall.

'We ready to go?'

'We are.' I thrust the notes at Dave. 'Better stash this in your money belt.'

Luke leaned into the trunk and lifted out the plastic bag of white powder. 'Not leaving him with this, though.' And he pushed past the rest of us to get to the toilet, where he burst open the bag and emptied its contents down the pan.

Rachel's voice was hushed and filled with fear. 'Oh my God, he'll kill us. He really will. He'll kill us.'

Luke flushed the toilet.

We were all in the hall when the front door opened. A thickset youth wearing ox-blood Doc Martens and black drainpipe jeans lifted his head to look at us in astonishment. He had a chequered shirt beneath a navy-blue donkey jacket, like coalmen wore, with leather patches across the shoulders and on the elbows. He sported an American army-style crew cut, and had a scar that ran from the corner of one eye, through top and bottom lip, to his chin. His eyes were a dangerous blue, one of them substantially paler than the other, and he was as surprised to see us as we were to see him.

There was a moment of tense stand-off as we all assessed the situation.

His eyes found Rachel's. 'What the fuck's going on, Raitch?'

Incongruously, I was aware that he didn't have a northern accent. It was a London twang, like you heard on *Steptoe and Son*. But he didn't wait for an answer. His right hand went around behind him, to pull a long-bladed knife from beneath his jacket. He held it out to one side, away from his body, tense and ready to fight.

The rest of us were frozen by fear. There might have been five of us, but he was the one with the knife. And whoever came up against him first was going to feel the cold, deadly penetration of its blade.

'Put the fuckin' chib away, pal,' Dave said in his broadest Glasgow accent. 'And you might just come oot o' this alive.'

I flicked a quick glance in his direction. I knew Dave to be the gentle giant that he was, and I had never heard him speak this way before. He was trading on his home city's unenviable reputation for gang warfare and violence, and the attendant sense of menace inherent in the Glasgow accent. It had its effect.

Doc Martens let a little of his tension go, and he took half a step back. 'So what's happening?'

Rachel's voice was trembling. 'Just some of Andy's friends down from Glasgow, Johnno. No need for aggro.'

I saw his eyes pass quickly over each of us in turn, making a rapid appraisal, before his gaze turned towards the bedroom door, and I knew he must have seen the open trunk. It was pure instinct that made me reach for Rachel's holdall and take it from Maurie. If one of us didn't take the initiative, then Johnno would, and he was still the one with the knife.

'Brought him some good stuff,' I said, and Johnno's eyes dropped for a moment to the bag.

I swung it at his head as hard as I could, surprised by the weight of it, swivelling on the ball of my foot and very nearly losing my balance. The bag connected full-on with the side of Johnno's head and smacked it hard against the wall. I saw blood burst from his mouth and his eyes tip back in his head. His knife slipped from his fingers as he dropped to his knees and fell forward.

'Bloody hell!' I looked at Rachel. 'What have you got in here?'

Frightened eyes darted from the bag to meet mine. She shrugged. 'Nothing, really. Shoes mostly.'

'Shoes?' Maurie glared at her. 'That's the *minimum that you need?*'

'Let's get the hell ootie this bloody place!' Dave stepped over Johnno's groaning and semi-conscious body curled up on the floor.

And one by one we followed him down the corridor, moving as fast and as quietly as we could towards the stairwell.

We got as far as the first landing, the echo of our footsteps following us down, when we heard voices and stopped in time to see three youths coming round the bend on the landing below us. They stopped, too, looking up in surprise through the gloom and graffiti, and there was the briefest hiatus. Then the tallest of them, a pale, good-looking boy with blond hair greased back in a quiff, bellowed Rachel's name. The force of it in the confined space of the stairwell was almost shocking.

'It's not what you think, Andy.' Rachel's voice seemed feeble by comparison, like the plaintive cry of a seagull against the roar of a storm.

But Andy's eyes had found and fixed themselves on Maurie. 'You?'

And I saw knives glinting suddenly in the light that came up the stairwell from below. We turned to run back up the way we had come.

'Keep going,' Rachel said breathlessly. 'All the way to the top. We can get on to the roof.'

Then what? I thought.

And almost as if she had heard me, she whispered in the dark, 'We can get down another stairwell.'

As we ran up to the next floor I could hear raised voices

shouting below, Andy's rising above the others. 'Don't worry. They're not going anywhere. I want to check the flat first. Guard the stairs.'

Then the echo of footsteps running along the hall. I replayed Luke pouring the bag of heroin down the toilet, and I knew then that Rachel's worst fears would almost certainly be realized.

Andy *would* kill us if he caught us.

Four floors later, lungs bursting, we staggered up the final flight of steps to the door that opened on to the roof. It wouldn't budge.

'Jesus, it's locked!' Dave's voice exploded in the dark.

There was no light here and we could barely see a thing. Jeff and I put our shoulders to it. On the third attempt, we heard the splintering of wood and the door flew open.

We spilled out on to the huge, open expanse of flat curving roof. A combination of fear and oxygen-starved muscles very nearly stole away the ability of my legs to hold me up. I staggered, gasping for breath, and felt the cold rain mingling with the sweat on my face. I became aware of the almost eerie, yellow-misted cityscape that stretched off to the north, the occasional car or lorry passing seven floors below us on New York Road. On the other side, the lights of Quarry Hill twinkled in suffocating silence. For several minutes it was all we could do to catch our breath, and it took a blood-curdling yell rising up through the dark from the stairwell below to get us on the move again.

The roof was peppered with obstacles. Chimney cowlings, the openings to stairwells, square blocks housing lift gear for each stair. Rachel led the way, running between them, arms pumping, head thrust back, and I realized that I was still carrying her bag.

We were running west, I think, towards Eastgate, even though that sounds contradictory. As we got towards the end of it, the roof dropped down a floor, and we had to turn back to the last stairwell. To our great, collective relief the door was not locked, and we went charging noisily down the stairs. For some reason there were no lights here, and the presence of each and every one of us was felt and heard rather than seen. Heaving lungs and breath catching in throats were the sounds that accompanied us through almost the entire descent.

By the time we got to the second floor there were lights again, and on the first-floor landing we stopped, trying hard to hold our breath and listen for any sounds coming from below. With luck, Andy and his friends would have no idea which of seven or eight stairwells we might have come down. But we didn't want to run the risk that somehow they might be waiting for us below.

Luke volunteered to check. We watched him from the top step as he moved carefully, quietly down to the next landing and then disappeared from view. We heard nothing for so long that I was starting to fear the worst.

Dave put that fear into words. 'Something's happened to him.'

But then, almost immediately, we heard his short, sharp whistle, our signal that it was all clear, and we hurried down after him. It was only when we reached the last few steps that I realized Rachel was clinging to my arm. When we reached the lobby I looked at her, and she became suddenly self-conscious, letting go of me as if my sleeve might burn her.

As if she needed to find something to say, to cover the moment, she muttered, 'Thanks for carrying my bag. I'll take it now, if you want.'

But I held it away from her. 'It's okay. We need you to show us how to get out of here.'

Maurie came back from the door that led out into the complex. 'Yeh, which way, Raitch? I can't see anybody out there.'

She gave me a small, uncertain smile, and hurried with Maurie back to the door. She leaned out, glancing both ways, then turned to look at our anxious assembled faces. Our lives, it seemed, were now dependent on this scared and unreliable teenage girl who had been injecting herself with a Class A drug.

'To our right,' she said, 'and then out through the Neilson arch.'

It was still raining, and a mist was rising now from the ground all about us, cold and damp and forming haloes around the street lamps. But even as we ducked into the Neilson arch, and the world outside was framed by its curve beyond the darkness, angry voices rang out behind us, and we heard footsteps running down the road that ran the length of Moynihan. They were only two or three hundred yards away.

I felt almost gripped by panic, sensing the anger in their voices, and the intent in those sprinting feet. Rachel darted out across the deserted New York Road, and we followed her blindly along an alleyway that ran down the side of the green-tiled City of Mabgate Inn, where we were swallowed by darkness.

I could hear the sound of rushing water, and skinned the palms of my hands as we dropped down from a moss-covered wall into what seemed like a river below. Although we landed on solid ground, the roar of water was deafening now, catching what little light there was down here as it gushed past our feet. As my eyes accustomed themselves to the gloom, I could see brick warehouses with dark, arched windows rising up around us, and the crumbling Victorian stonework of walls that led off into the blackness of a tunnel ahead.

'What is this place?' I heard Maurie's voice struggling to make itself heard above the rush of water.

'It's a stream that they made into a canal.' Rachel's voice came back in the dark. 'The Meanwood Beck. There's walkways along either side. It'll take us into the Mabgate tunnel.'

'And where will that take us?' I could hear Dave's panic. He didn't like the dark.

'Right under the city, for about half a mile. Until it reaches the river. But we won't go that far. There's several culverts that'll take us back up on the other side of Eastgate.'

'You've been down here before?' There was incredulity in Jeff's voice.

'No. But it was Andy's planned escape route if we were ever raided by the cops.' She took her holdall from me and crouched down to unzip it. 'He kept essentials in this bag in case he had to run for it. I chucked most of the stuff out except for this.'

She drew out a long-shafted metal torch, and I realized what it was in the bag that had done most of the damage to Johnno's head.

We heard voices then, whispered calls reverberating not far off in the dark, and we knew that Andy and his friends were close by.

Rachel stood up quickly. 'This way.'

And we followed her into the tunnel.

Only when we had been completely enveloped by the utterly dense, velvety blackness of it did she switch on the torch, and its beam played out ahead of us in the misted underground distance. The dark shapes of what could only have been rats scuttled off up ahead, then stopped to turn and look back at us, tiny eyes glowing like pinpoints of light in the shadows.

Broad walkways on either side of black water in spate ran beneath the low arch of the brick tunnel, and we had to stoop as we ran. I glanced back as the tunnel curved round to the right, and the lights of the city behind us vanished from view. It seemed unlikely that Andy and his pals would pursue us into it without light. But his voice did. A voice filled with hate and anger, bellowing above the thundering of the water.

'You fucking bitch! You're dead! Fucking dead when I get you!'

I caught a momentary glimpse of her scared rabbit's eyes as she glanced back over her shoulder, and I felt again that strangely powerful urge to protect her, no matter what.

We pressed forward into the darkness for eight or ten minutes before Rachel suddenly stopped. She turned the beam of her torch into a crudely constructed side tunnel that narrowed as it twisted off and up. 'I think this is one of the culverts.'

'You're not sure?' Jeff seemed ready to blame her entirely for our predicament.

And I suppose, in a way, she was. But I was quick to defend her. 'She's never been down here before. How could she be sure?'

Luke took the torch from her. 'I'm taller than the rest of you. I'll lead the way. If I can get through, everyone can.'

'What about fat Mo?' Dave said, and I saw him grinning in the peripheral light of the torch. 'He's no' as tall as you, but he's twice as wide.'

'Fuck off.' Maurie glowered at him.

We set off up the side passage in single file, Luke leading with the torch, the rest of us in touching contact with the one in front. I felt Rachel reach for my hand, finding it in the dark, and I let her take it and held it as we climbed more steeply and the passage narrowed. We waded through water rushing down from street level, soaking into shoes and socks, and the roof sloped down so that we had to bend almost double.

Then suddenly we emerged into a wash of yellow sodium street light, and we straightened stiff backs and breathed fresh air to fuel our relief. We were in a narrow, overgrown culvert beneath a tall brick building on one side, and an overgrown stone wall below a railing on the other. But it was easy enough to climb up and over the railing to drop into the cobbled lane on the far side of it.

Rachel stood gasping and looking around anxiously. 'Okay, I know where we are. And we're ahead of Andy,' she said. 'But he's bound to check it out. Where did you park the van?'

'Edward Street,' Jeff said.

Rachel nodded. 'Then we're just a couple of streets away.' And she set off at a loping run without another word.

We exchanged glances and set off after her.

She took us into Bridge Street, then cut up into Templar Place, before we found ourselves back in Lady Lane and immediately got our bearings. Edward Street was less than fifty yards away.

The van seemed like a haven of safety, and it was an enormous relief to reach it. For once, I got the passenger seat, with Rachel perched up on the engine cowling. The others all squeezed on to the settee in the back. Jeff started the motor and the headlights picked out reflections on the wet cobbles as we turned into Lady Lane and headed down towards the Eastgate roundabout.

We were almost there, cruising cautiously and keeping a wary eye on the streets around us, when Andy and three others came running out of Bridge Street and into the middle of Lady Lane. Pale faces were caught full in our headlights.

'Jobbies,' Jeff muttered. He dropped a gear and accelerated straight at them.

Rachel screamed and braced her feet on the metal dash, but at the last moment the drug dealer and his friends leapt out of the way. I could hear their raised voices swearing at us in the dark, and someone thumped the side of the van as we passed.

Jeff swung left on the roundabout, following the curve of Oastler House north, before turning right into New York Road and accelerating past the length of Moynihan, from where we had just escaped. No one spoke as we watched the serried ranks of balconies pass by on our right, misted windows rising up seven and eight storeys to cast diffuse yellow light into a thickening fog.

From there, York Road ran almost straight through the city, heading east. The rain got worse, and Jeff eased back on the speed, headlights raking the misted night as we cruised through what felt now like a ghost town. We passed only occasional vehicles, and there was nobody about on foot.

I checked the time. What had seemed like an eternity had, in fact, been little more than an hour. It was twenty minutes to midnight.

III

I juggled the AA book of maps on my knees by the intermittent light of passing street lamps, trying to get our bearings.

'We're on the A64,' I said, 'heading sort of north-east.' I

looked at Rachel. 'You got any idea where that's going to take us?'

She shrugged. 'Not a clue. I've hardly been over the door since I've been here.'

Suddenly Jeff said, 'I think we're being followed.'

I craned my neck to try to catch a glimpse in the wing mirror of the car that was on our tail. But all I saw were headlights. Luke clambered over the settee and the piles of gear to look through the back windows.

'It's a Cortina,' he said. 'White. Pretty bashed-up-looking.'

'Oh shit.' Rachel was even paler than when I'd first seen her. 'That's Andy's car.'

'How in God's name did he manage tae find us?' Dave said.

'His car wouldn't have been parked far away,' Rachel said. 'They must have gambled on which way we went.'

'Lucky bloody gamble.' Maurie's muttered oath was almost inaudible but summed up our collective sense that the only luck we'd had since leaving home was the bad kind.

'I don't think they'll try anything in the middle of a main road,' I said with a great deal more confidence than I felt. There was, after all, virtually no other traffic on it. 'We're never going to outrun him, that's for sure. Just don't let him get past us.'

'How am I supposed to do that?' I could hear the panic in Jeff's voice.

Then Luke called from the back, 'He doesn't seem to be trying to catch up or overtake us. He's just kind of hanging back there.'

'Hanging back for what?' Jeff could hardly keep his eyes on the road for looking in the mirror.

'Waiting for something. I don't know. The right moment to get past us, maybe.'

I looked again at the map and said, 'Just follow the signs for Tadcaster, and that'll keep us on the main road.'

Jeff began banging his palms up and down on the wheel. 'Jobbies, jobbies, jobbies. You shouldn't have poured that stuff down the toilet, Luke.'

But Rachel said quietly, 'It's not about the H, or the money. It's about me. I told you. He thinks of me as his property. And if he can't have me back, then he'll kill me.'

'We're not going to let him do that,' Maurie said.

'Oh, aye?' Dave's voice was loaded with scepticism. 'Who's this *we*, kemo sabe?'

For ten, maybe fifteen minutes, the Cortina followed at a discreet distance. We were out in suburbia now, residential streets branching off left and right. We took a left at a roundabout and followed the ring road for half a mile, before turning right at the next, sticking to the A64 and the signposts for Tadcaster.

The housing around us became more sparse, and up ahead I saw that the street lamps came to an abrupt end, leaving only darkness beyond them. Fear sat among us like another passenger. It could only be a matter of time before Andy made his move.

To make things worse, the rain began falling harder. Jeff was hunched over the wheel, staring through the wipers, trying to focus on the road ahead.

'Here he comes!' Luke shouted from the back.

I could see the approaching headlights in the wing mirror. I saw Jeff tensing, and at the last moment he swung the wheel hard right and crossed the centre line into the other lane. The Cortina swerved to avoid us, and I saw its lights veer left and right across empty spring fields, as the driver tried to keep it on the road.

We were on the wrong side of the road now, and the Cortina tried to accelerate through on our inside. Jeff swung left, and there was a deafening bang as the side of the van made contact with the front wing of the car. The Cortina braked, and fell back, lurching violently.

Jeff hung on to the wheel, grimly trying to bring the Thames back under control without braking. But we all knew that he couldn't keep this up. The Cortina came screaming up again on our outside.

And I shouted, 'Left, Jeff! Go left here.'

There was a narrow country road, cutting off at an angle just ahead. A signpost to a place called Thorner. Jeff braked fiercely, then pulled hard to the left, and we slid more than turned off, the back of the van snaking behind us, before Jeff regained control.

The Cortina overshot the turn, and I saw its brake lights as we turned. Its wheels had lost their grip on the wet surface and the car was sliding sideways down the middle of the road. Then I lost sight of it behind the hedgerows.

We were now on Thorner Lane. But there was no sign of Thorner itself. Just a long, straight road that disappeared beyond the reach of our headlights. Jeff accelerated to a dangerous speed.

And Luke's voice came from behind us. 'They're back again.'

I could see the lights of the Cortina in the mirror. It was still a long way behind us, but there was never any doubt that it would catch us up. This, though, was a much narrower road, and if Jeff stuck to the middle of it, then there was no way for the Cortina to overtake.

Which is when I saw the lights of a car coming in the opposite direction.

I glanced at Jeff. His teeth were clenched, his jaw set and his focus dead ahead. He made no attempt to slow down.

'Jeff,' I almost shouted at him. 'You'll never get past him at this speed.'

His face was lit up by the lights of the oncoming car. Rachel put her feet up on the dash again to brace herself, and the driver of the approaching vehicle flashed his lights several times

'Jeff!' I almost screamed at him, but it still made no impression. Now I could see the faces of the driver and his passenger ahead of us. 'Jesus! They're cops!'

At the last moment Jeff pulled the van to the left and the oncoming police car swung to our right, mounting the verge and losing control as we passed it. We all turned to look out the back to see what had happened. The police car slewed to a stop, side-on in the middle of the road, and the braking Cortina slid sideways into it. It all seemed to happen in slow motion. By the time the Cortina hit the police car it couldn't have been going at any more than five or ten miles an hour – not enough for anyone to get hurt – but I could imagine only too well the panic in one car and the fury in the other.

I looked over at Jeff again, and saw what I could have sworn was a smile on his lips. There was madness in his eyes.

'You're insane,' I shouted at him. 'Aff your bloody heid!'

He kept his foot to the floor, and through a copse of black trees we saw the lights of Thorner twinkling in the darkness ahead.

'We need to get off the road.' Luke's voice was very close behind us, and I turned to see the fear blanched in his face. 'The cops'll be coming after us now.'

Jeff eased off on the accelerator as we drove into the village. A long street of old honeycomb-yellow stone cottages and newer brick-built houses lost among rolling wooded country. There was blossom on some of the trees, caught pink and white in our headlights, along with the spring green of an enormous weeping willow. Yet more trees stood winter stark and glistening against the blackness beyond them. We passed the stone gables and bay windows of the Mexborough Arms, set back behind an empty car park, and at the foot of the hill I saw the bell tower of the village church standing square at the corner of a sharp bend in the road. We were still going too fast to take it comfortably.

'Slow down, Jeff.'

He ignored the low imperative in my voice.

And so I shouted now. 'For God's sake, slow down!'

I don't know where his head was, but it was only at the last moment that he seemed to realize he wasn't going to make it and stood on the brakes. The wheels locked and simply slid on the wet tarmac, as if on ice, and we sailed almost gracefully, turning as we went, to plough straight into the church gates.

The noise was ear-splitting. A deafening bang followed by the screaming of metal on metal. Then a strange, almost eerie silence. The engine had stalled, and the only sound was the hiss of steam escaping from a fractured radiator. Nobody spoke. I looked at Jeff and saw that he had cracked his head on the door column. Blood was trickling down his forehead. Rachel was almost on top of me, but miraculously neither of us was hurt. The back of the van was a chaos of bodies and equipment.

'You okay back there?' I don't know why I was whispering.

But Dave whispered back. 'No, we're not. I'm gonnae kill that eejit!'

'We've got to go!' It was the urgency in Luke's voice that shook us out of our state of shock. 'Take only what you can carry.'

He pushed the back doors open, and I felt cold, damp air flooding in. The three in the back jumped down on to the road. I could see lights coming on in houses all around us.

Jeff still seemed dazed. 'What about my drums? My dad'll kill me.'

'You're already dead, Jeff.'

I climbed out of the van and ran round the back to get my bag and my guitar in its hard black carry-case. Heavy, but I wasn't leaving it behind. Dave grabbed his, too.

Luke went and pulled Jeff down from the driver's side. 'Come on, man, we've got to get out of here.'

And as startled residents, so rudely awakened from their sleep, started to emerge from doorways and paths, the six of us ran back up the road in the rain towards the pub. Several voices called after us, but we never looked back.

At the Mexburgh Arms a road turned off to the right and there was a sign for Thorner Station.

Luke said, 'If we can get to the station, then we can follow the track out of here without touching the road.'

The distant sound of a police siren drifted through the damp night, hastening our progress away from the main street. The road curved to the right beyond the pub, past a bowling green that lay mired in shadow. On the other side of the street a collection of stone-built farm buildings clustered in the dark. Past them, on the rise, stood the low silhouette of Thorner Victory Hall, and Station Lane cut off to the right. The sweet scent of warm manure filled the night air as we ran silently past Manor Farm towards the arch of a stone bridge and a railway cutting that ran beneath it.

The lane then rose steeply upwards to the station itself, which stood in darkness at the top of the embankment. The gate to the platform was padlocked, and all the windows of the brick station house were boarded up. There was a weathered poster pasted to the wall. *Station Closed due to Beeching Cuts.*

I said, 'Maybe we can lie low here for a few hours out of the rain, then head off before it gets light.'

'Well, we're no' gonnie meet any trains, that's for sure,' Dave said.

I climbed over the gate, and the others passed their bags and guitars across to me before climbing over themselves. By what little ambient light leaked through the trees from the village, we could see that the platform was littered with debris. The rails themselves had already been lifted, and were laid along the side of the track awaiting collection. There was a sad sense of abandonment about the place, haunted by the imaginary ghosts of all the passengers who must once have passed this way, the distant echo of forgotten steam trains lost in the mists of railway history. An old timetable pasted to the wall listed all the stations from Leeds to Wetherby. Scholes, Thorner, Bardsey, Collingham Bridge . . .

Dave and Maurie kicked open the door of the waiting room and we all trooped inside out of the rain. There was a damp, fusty smell in here, the odour of neglect. All the fittings had been stripped out of it, the ticket office window boarded up from the other side, the floor strewn with rubble and covered in a layer of dust.

I laid down my bag, leaned my guitar against the wall and slid down it to sit on the floor, drawing breath for the first time and feeling a pall of depression settle over me as the adrenaline that had fuelled us in these last few hours ebbed away.

It had been almost blind black when we arrived, but now a break in the clouds let a little moonlight through to race across the land, and we cast shadows for the first time over the dusty floor as light fell in through the open door.

Rachel stood, hesitant and painfully alone somehow, in the middle of the room as we all found our spots and settled down to while away the next few hours.

I slipped my arms out of my big furry coat, holding it open, and said, 'It's big enough to share.'

She didn't need a second invitation and I felt, more than saw, Maurie glaring at me across the room. She sat down beside me, and I put the coat around both our shoulders. I liked how she leaned into me, her head resting against my shoulder, and I slipped an arm around her waist to pull her closer.

I was almost overwhelmed just by the softness and warmth of her body. She smelled earthy, musky, and I felt the first stirrings of desire. I laid my cheek on top of her head and closed my eyes, waves of fatigue surging through me.

Then out of the silence that had settled in the waiting room, Jeff suddenly said, 'What's the Beeching cuts?'

For a moment, no one responded.

Then Luke lit a cigarette, his face briefly illuminated by the flame of his lighter, and he said, 'Beeching's a guy commissioned by the government to make the railways pay.'

'What, you mean, they're losing money? Any train I've ever been on is standing room only.' Dave's face, too, was momentarily illuminated as he lit a No. 6.

'They're losing millions,' Luke said. 'So Dr Beeching's solution is to cut all the branch lines that are turning in a loss. Like this one, presumably.'

'How'd you know all that?' Jeff said.

I heard the amusement in Luke's voice. 'Modern studies, Jeff. Our history teacher takes the classes. You've had him too, I think, Jack.'

'What? Mr Shed?'

'Yeah. You should hear him on Beeching. Thinks the guy's an idiot.'

'Why?' Maurie this time.

I saw him lighting his cigarette from the end of Jeff's, and the smell of cigarette smoke in this cold, empty place was oddly comforting. Like the conversation we were having that failed to address any of the real issues that confronted us.

'Because he says that Beeching's ruining the best rail network in the world. Reckons by the time he's had his way and closed half of it down we'll probably end up with the worst.'

'Well, he's had his way here,' I said. And for a moment I had the strangest sense of witnessing the end of something. An era, maybe. A turning point in the history of our country. The dreams of a nation described by an abandoned railway station and torn-up rails. A track from the past leading to nowhere in an uncertain future. A track that we would follow ourselves sometime in the next few hours without any idea of where it would take us.

'I suppose we'll be in big trouble now,' Jeff said. A reality check.

I lifted my head from Rachel's. 'Because of running the cops off the road?'

'Well . . . that, too.'

'What else?

Silence.

'What else, Jeff?' Luke said.

'Well, I'd always figured we'd get the van back before anyone noticed it was missing. You know, get ourselves sorted in London, then I'd drive it back up to Glasgow.'

The tension in the waiting room positively crackled in the dark.

'You stole it?' I couldn't believe what I was hearing.

'I borrowed it. It was a trade-in at the garage. I'm responsible for stocktaking, so it wouldn't have been missed for weeks.'

'Jesus!'

Another first. I'd never heard Luke blaspheme before.

'So now we're car thieves as well. Thanks, Jeff.'

I closed my eyes and tried to picture the scene at the gate of the church. Residents gathered around the wreck of the van. The blue flashing lights of one or more police cars. All our gear abandoned in the back of it. The crackle of a police radio. Perhaps the registration number of the Thames being radioed back to base. How long before they discovered it was stolen? Hours? Days? Weeks? We were in more trouble now than I could ever have imagined.

I laid my cheek again on Rachel's head and breathed in the scent of her. For some reason it lifted my depression.

CHAPTER SEVEN

I

I must have dozed off, because when I came to I realized that everyone else was asleep. The one-time waiting room itself seemed to be breathing, filled with the soft sounds of sleep. Someone was snoring, but I couldn't tell who.

My left arm, extended around Rachel's waist to draw her closer, had gone to sleep as well. I could feel pins and needles in my hand, but I was reluctant to move in case I disturbed her. The gentle purr of her breathing was muffled by my chest where she had turned her head to rest against me. I reached across to feel the shape of it through soft hair, and stroked her, filled with a strange tenderness. I wondered what it was about her that had this effect on me, but I guess there is no way to ever understand these things.

She stirred, and I felt her head turning up, so that she was looking at me. I could barely see her. My voice was the faintest whisper in the night.

'Why did you come to Leeds with him?'

I sensed her tension.

'I made a mistake.'

'Quite a mistake.'

I felt her nodding.

'Sometimes you can't see the real person for the person they want you to see. Andy was . . . well, he made me laugh. He was funny, and quite charming in his own way. He treated me with respect. I felt wanted.'

Her head lifted again, as if she desperately wanted to meet my eyes. But I couldn't really see hers.

'You can't know how good it is to feel wanted, when you never have been your whole life.'

I finally moved my arm out from behind her and stretched it to get the blood flowing. 'Who didn't want you?'

'My parents for a start.'

'I'm sure that's not true.'

'Oh, it is. Ask Mo. They wanted a boy. Someone to take on the family business. But there were birth complications and, after me, they couldn't have any more kids. I always felt kind of resented. All I was good for was marrying and having kids to carry on the Jewish line.' She pulled herself more upright. 'You got a fag?'

I lit one, then another from mine, and handed it to her.

'Not that they ever treated me badly. I got everything I ever wanted. Just to shut me up, really, while they got on with their own lives.' I heard her ironic little laugh. 'Poor little rich kid.' She paused. 'I was so unhappy, Jack. Andy rode into my life like a knight in shining armour. He was older than me. Had money, a car. Dead corny, I know, but he swept me off my feet.'

'I remember Maurie telling us about how you ran away with him.'

A tiny laugh shook her. 'Must have been the talk of the steamie.'

'So when did you know you'd made a mistake?'

'Almost immediately. You saw what Quarry Hills is like. And the flat. It was pretty much that way when we got there. From a posh villa in Whitecraigs to a tip of a council flat in Leeds. Could hardly have fallen further. And Andy . . . well, it was like he just became someone else. The real Andy. The one he'd been hiding behind all that crap.'

'But he still wanted you.'

'Oh yes. But he didn't just want me. He wanted to possess me. I was his trophy bird. He'd fly off in a jealous rage if anyone so much as looked at me. He wouldn't let me out on my own. I always had to be with him, or left behind at the flat. It was a nightmare. And it was pointless trying to make a difference, clean up the place, build the nest. He would only come and shit in it again.'

All of her tension had returned, and I could feel her body shaking, as if she were shivering from the cold. I tried to draw her closer to me under the coat, but she pulled away and stood up, her face glowing red for a moment as she dragged on her cigarette.

'There's got to be a loo in here somewhere.'

'I doubt if there'll be running water,' I said.

But all she said was, 'I'll go see if I can find it.'

I watched the faintest shadow she cast soaked up by the dark, and heard the shuffle of her footsteps as she moved away across the waiting room. A door scraped open, and she disappeared off into the station house.

Silence returned, except for the communal breathing of the sleeping runaways. I thought briefly that I heard voices somewhere in the distance, and the revving of an engine. I listened hard. But it's amazing how invasive and deafening silence can be. Whatever I thought I had heard, I didn't hear it again.

It was impossible to know how long I waited for Rachel to return. I might even have drifted off again, just for a moment. But in the end I began to worry.

I got stiffly to my feet and stretched aching limbs, listening in the dark to see if I had disturbed any of the others before tiptoeing across the waiting room to find the door that she had opened. I almost bumped into it, and felt my way into what must once have been the original stationmaster's house. It was pitch in here, as if someone had placed a soft, black blindfold over my eyes. I felt my way around the walls until I found another open door, and as I stepped out into a narrow hallway my eyes immediately detected light. The faintest flickering line of it, coming from under a door at the end of the hall. The air seemed infused with a strange, sweet, vinegary smell, cloying, and it caught in my throat. For just a moment my confusion was disorientating, before sudden realization dawned on me.

I strode down the hall and threw open the door. The small

toilet was filled with the yellow light of a candle whose flame dipped and dived in the sudden movement of air. She had already cooked her heroin in a small round metal container and was drawing it up into her syringe through a cotton filter. A half-empty sachet of white powder was set on the lid of the toilet seat, next to some burned tinfoil and a cotton swab. The case that she used to carry her gear lay open beside it.

She had removed her jacket and rolled back her sleeve, a length of black rubber tubing already tied around her upper arm.

Her head whipped round in surprise, dark eyes full of fear and need and deceit.

'You fool!' My voice thundered in the confined space, and I swept all the paraphernalia of her habit off the toilet seat. I grabbed the syringe and threw it on the floor, stamping on it until it was shattered and useless, and tipped her cooked H into the dust.

The sound of her scream erupted even before the echo of my voice had died, and she flew at me in a rage. I felt the force of flailing fists hammering at my face and my chest. I tried, and failed, to catch her wrists, and in the end simply threw my arms around her and pulled her hard against me so that she had no room to move. She fought and kicked and shouted, and I heard the footsteps of the others running through the station, voices raised and calling our names.

By the time they reached us, Rachel was reduced to a sobbing wreck, still held firmly against me, but no longer fighting it. Maurie's face in the doorway flickered pale in the candle-light, eyes wide. The faces of the others pressed in around him. I nodded towards the floor, the shattered syringe, the scattered paraphernalia of a user's habit, and I saw his eyes close in despair. When they lifted again to meet mine I saw the question in them. What could he do?

My almost imperceptible shake of the head said there was nothing. I saw Luke's hand on his shoulder, pulling him away, and the four of them were absorbed into darkness.

I held Rachel like that for a long time, feeling her tremble almost uncontrollably.

Then her voice came, sobbing and muffled. 'I don't want to take it. I don't. But you have no idea how bad it feels when I can't.'

'It'll pass,' I said, and immediately felt her push against me.

Her face turned up, eyes burning with anger. 'How would you know? What would you know about any of this? I hate you!'

And still I held her. 'I'll help you.'

'How?'

'I'll help you get through it.'

'There is no getting through it, there's only hell.'

'Then I'll go to hell with you!' I shouted at her. 'But I'll bring you back again.'

She swallowed hard and stared at me, eyes filled with many emotions. Confusion, pain, distrust. And something else. Something almost animal. And suddenly her face rose to meet mine. Mouth against mouth. A kiss so full of primal passion that I swear I very nearly lost consciousness. Her tongue forced its way past my teeth, then she bit my lower lip and sucked it into her mouth before just as suddenly she broke away. And we both stood breathless, staring at each other. I still wasn't sure if what she felt was loathing or lust.

But that was the first time that Rachel and I kissed, and it is a moment I will take with me to the grave.

II

She spent most of the remaining hours we passed in that place coiled around me like a limpet beneath my coat, sometimes shivering violently, and at other times just trembling. She was frequently in tears, and I had no real idea of what kind of pain she was going through.

Once, she untangled herself from me to go out on to the platform and I heard her throwing up. I went out after her, and found her standing right on the edge of it, arms wrapped around herself for warmth, shaking uncontrollably. The rain had stopped, and the sky above was broken now, moonlight flashing through silver-edged clouds in fits and starts. But it was cold, and in the colourless moonlight she had the bloodless face of a ghost. I put my arms around her and enveloped her in my coat, lending her my warmth to try to stop the shivering.

'What does it feel like?' I whispered. 'What does it give you that makes you keep coming back?'

For a long time she was silent, and I didn't know if she was thinking about it or just ignoring me.

Then in a tiny voice she said, 'Oblivion. It takes you down to a place where nothing else matters, Jack. Feels so good, like an end to pain.' A pause. 'But when you come back up the pain's still there, just waiting for you. The world seems even shittier than before, and you can't wait to escape from it again.'

I tried to imagine what that must be like. And I said, 'I guess life's really all about pain, isn't it? That's what feeling is. Any feeling. Even good feelings can be painful in their own way. And pain, pure pain, is just the most heightened feeling of all.' I felt her head lift, and looked down to see her big brown eyes staring up at me. I chuckled. 'Never knew I was a philosopher, did you? Neither did I.'

A smile brought a little animation back to her face.

'If you don't feel anything, Raitch, you might as well be dead. I don't pretend to know what a heroin high is like, and I never want to. But what you describe seems to me like dying a little. I'd rather be alive and deal with the pain.'

She nodded and laid her head against my chest. 'Me, too. But once you start along that road, Jack . . . It's a gentle slope on the way down, but Everest climbing back up.'

'So let me be your Sherpa.'

Which made her laugh, and I think it was the first time I ever heard her do that.

The moment was broken by the sound of a car engine turning over at low rev and slowly approaching through the night. Then came the sound of acceleration, and headlights tipping up into the sky, before levelling off and shining among the wet branches of the trees that grew along the near embankment. The car had pulled up outside the station.

We ran quickly inside to waken the others, but they were already on their feet. The sound of a car door opening seemed inordinately loud in the still of the night.

Jeff peered out through a gap in the boards that blanked out one of the windows. 'Jobbies, it's the cops!'

His whisper conveyed his panic, and there were no words required to choreograph our flight. Splinters of light came through all the gaps in the boarding, like cracks in the dark, as someone on the outside shone a torch on the building. In hurried silence we collected our stuff and moved quickly out on to the platform. The sound of footsteps on gravel accompanied the beam of the torch as it flashed around the gate off to our right, and we jumped down on to the track and began running north, across the bridge we had seen from Station Lane. Houses and pasture shimmered below us on either side of the embankment, a stream bubbling in reflected moonlight, and I felt how totally exposed we were before we reached the shadowed shelter of the trees.

I didn't look back until the track began to curve away to the left, and I saw the beams of two torches playing around the station platform before disappearing inside the building itself. Of course, we had left traces. Cigarette ends. The scattered remains of Rachel's abortive attempt to reclaim oblivion. They would know we had been there, but not how long since we had left, nor which direction we had taken. It only remained for us to put as much distance as possible between them and ourselves before daybreak.

And so we pressed on. It was not easy to make good speed walking on uneven ballast, which was all that remained of the track after the lifting of the rails and sleepers. Nature was already reclaiming it, with weeds and grasses poking up between the stones, and growth from the embankments on either side encroaching on what had once been clear and well-maintained track.

We were, intermittently, raised up above the land, or plunged into the shadow of steep embankments rising up into the night. Sometimes exposed to the world, and at other times lost beneath overhanging branches, wading through long grass and briars.

There was not much to be said as we trudged through the darkness, tired and dispirited, each of us wondering perhaps how it had all come to this. How quickly we had transitioned from predictable suburban existence, school and group, exams and dances, to the chaos of the last thirty-odd hours. How easily we had completely lost control of our lives. And I suppose that only now were we starting to come to terms with how lost and foolish and naive we really were.

Dawn arrived almost without us noticing. A grey light that gradually brought definition to the world around us, before the first shallow rays of angled sunlight played through the branches of the trees. The birdsong was very nearly deafening.

Tangled, tree-covered embankments rose steeply on either side, and ahead we saw the tall arches of a bridge that carried a road across the old line perhaps thirty feet above us. A car passed unseen across it, behind high brick walls. Sunlight fell in broken patches all around us, and I felt the chill of the night slowly start to dissipate.

I had no idea how far we had come, but Luke suggested it was perhaps time to get off the track and back on to the road, and there was not one of us who was going to take issue with him.

It was a hard climb, with bags and guitars, up the sodden, overgrown embankment, brambles and branches catching and tugging at our clothes. But the reward was sunshine and smooth tarmac beneath our feet. I glanced at Rachel. Her pallor was almost deathly, and she seemed to have shrunk during the course of the night, her eyes even larger in her skull.

'You alright?' I asked her in a low voice.

She nodded, but she didn't look it.

We walked, then, for fifteen or twenty minutes along the narrow country road that the bridge had carried across the railway until we reached the main A58 road to Wetherby. It was another ten minutes before we successfully flagged down a farmer in a tractor pulling an empty animal trailer. Luke did an amazing job of persuading him that our van had broken down on the road and that we needed to get to the nearest town to phone for help. All those years, I thought, spent on doorsteps with his parents, smiling and feigning vulnerability, drawing the pity or sympathy of otherwise hostile householders.

The farmer chuckled and said, 'Well, if you don't mind squatting down in the straw and shit in the trailer, I'm going to the market at Wetherby, and I can take you that far.'

And so that's what we did. A kind of final indignity. But in truth, by then we were past caring.

III

In a café in Wetherby we got egg rolls and mugs of steaming hot tea, and began to feel almost human again. I watched Rachel eat hungrily, as if she had not fed herself properly in weeks. She caught me looking at her, then quickly averted her eyes, embarrassed. We lit cigarettes, and through a fug of smoke drew up our battle plan.

Maurie had crossed the street to a newsagent's shop to bring back a map so that we could see where we were. He stabbed a finger at Wetherby, then traced a line along the B1224 to York.

'Bound to be able to catch a train to London from there,' he said.

Luke nodded. 'It's on the main east-coast line from Edinburgh.' He glanced at Dave. 'We got enough money for that?'

Dave patted his middle. 'More than.' Then he glanced at Jeff. 'But maybe we should be looking for a new drummer. It would save us money.'

'Hey!' Jeff protested

But it was Maurie who shut him up. 'You don't even get a say in this. We were running away from home, that's what we were doing. Being accessories to theft wasn't part of the deal. The least you could have done was tell us.'

Jeff adopted a wounded look. 'We'd never have got on the road at all if I hadn't got us a van.'

And I began to think that maybe that would have been the best outcome of all.

There was a silent stand-off before Jeff said, 'Aw, come on, you're not serious.'

Dave leaned across the table, his voice low and dangerous. 'I'd dump you in a heartbeat, pal.'

It was Rachel who surprised us all. 'Maybe you should just go home, the lot of you.'

Twenty-four hours earlier there would have been an instant chorus of NO! The fact that no one said anything spoke volumes.

I looked at Rachel. 'What about you?'

'I'm going to London.' Her quiet certainty left none of us in doubt that she meant it.

'I'm going with Rachel,' I said.

'Never in doubt for me,' Luke said. 'The day I left home was the first day of the rest of my life. And that doesn't include going back. Ever.'

'Well, I'm going with you guys.' Maurie looked at his cousin. 'Someone's got to look out for Rachel.'

She glared at him. 'I can look after myself.'

'Oh, really? You haven't done such a great job of it so far.'

I felt a spike of anger and pushed my hand into Maurie's chest, shoving him back in his seat. 'Lay off her.'

Luke intervened. 'Okay, enough! Enough! We're going to London, right?'

There was a silent, huffy acknowledgement around the table, and Jeff said, 'But not without me.'

It was more a question than a statement, though not one that anyone chose to answer.

Luke said, 'We need to save our money. So we should hitch. But not all together. In ones and twos. It's not that far. About fifteen miles. We should make it by lunchtime and we can all meet up at the station.'

'I'll go with Rachel,' Maurie said, and he looked at me in a way that dared me to contradict him.

Which, of course, I did. 'No, I will.'

He glared. 'Well, maybe we should ask Rachel.'

All eyes turned towards her. She glanced at both of us and I willed her to choose me.

Finally her gaze met mine, conveying a confusion of unspoken messages. 'I'll go with Jack.'

And Dave said, 'Aye, and if Jeff's the last there, we'll just get the train without him.'

It was no surprise, then, that Jeff somehow contrived to be first.

Rachel and I got a lift almost immediately. I made myself inconspicuous as she stood at the side of the road. A white delivery van driven by a young man in his twenties pulled up within the first few minutes. He looked seriously disappointed when I appeared behind Rachel to climb up into the front beside her. But by then it was too late. Grudgingly he slid my guitar into the back of the van and took us all the way to Station Road in York, dropping us right in front of the historic, yellow-brick station building.

However, he'd had to stop to make several deliveries en route, and Jeff was standing under the clock waiting for us when we got there. He had cadged a lift on a motorbike, riding pillion without a helmet, and his hair looked like he'd been pulled through a hedge backwards. He was pleased as punch to have got there ahead of us.

By ten thirty we were all assembled in the station. By eleven we had six one-way, off-peak tickets to London and were standing on the platform waiting for our train. Within half an hour we had a second-class compartment to ourselves. We were oddly subdued as, finally, the Deltic, Class 55, diesel-powered train pulled out of the station on its two-and-a-half-hour journey to the capital.

At long, long last we were on our way to the Big Smoke, and not one of us had a word to say about it.

2015

CHAPTER EIGHT

I

It was Jack's idea to retrace their footsteps of all those years before, as if in doing so they might find something they had lost on the way.

The night before, Ricky had left the M6 shortly after Carlisle, then navigated them cross-country using the GPS on his iPhone. They had found a lay-by with toilets somewhere in the Northumberland National Park, and pulled in to spend the night.

Maurie had slept most of the way, and only got out of the car once they stopped for the night. He threw up and emptied his bladder, took his painkillers and was asleep again in minutes.

Dave was still barely on speaking terms with Jack for lobbing his cans of beer out of the car on the motorway. He had hunched himself up in his coat and turned his face to the window, a small patch of condensation forming where his slow, laboured breath burst against it.

Ricky, too, was in a huff with his grandfather, reclining his seat as far as possible, then closing his eyes.

Which had left Jack as the sole occupant of the car for whom sleep would simply not come. He listened to the snorts and grunts of his sleeping companions in the back, and the gentle snoring of his grandson in the seat beside him. The night folded itself around them, the foggy constellation of the Milky Way as visible as he had ever seen it above the tops of the trees. Like smoke. And as it always did, any contemplation of the vastness of the universe made him feel infinitely small.

Just like fifty years before, he had found his mind full of doubts about the wisdom of what they were doing. And full of trepidation about what lay ahead. But these were such tiny concerns in the grand scheme of things, that come daybreak they burned off with the rising of the sun, like morning mist.

He had wakened the others at first light to slunge sleepy faces in icy water, and the GPS had taken them down the A66, then the A1, before turning them off on to the A64 towards Leeds.

It was only as they passed a sign on their right to Thorner that Jack suddenly sat up. 'Hey, remember that place!'

'What?' Dave lifted his eyes from some sightless reverie.

Jack turned in his seat, looking back as they passed it. 'Thorner Lane. That's where we very nearly had the head-on with the police car.'

Maurie seemed to wake up fully for the first time. 'Where we crashed the van?'

'Where Jeff crashed the van,' Dave corrected him.

'Yeah, in Thorner itself,' Jack said. 'Stop, Rick. Let's go back.'

Ricky slowed up and the car behind peeped its horn. He glanced in the mirror. 'What for?'

'Just turn round and I'll tell you.'

Ricky sighed and turned into a lay-by at the opening to a field. When the road was clear he made a U-turn, and they headed back towards the turn-off to Thorner while Jack provided his grandson with a potted version of what had happened that night. Ricky listened with a growing sense of astonishment, his mouth gaping as his eyes widened on the road ahead.

Thorner Lane ran long and straight with fallow fields stretching away into the hazy morning on either side. It was all that Jack could recall about the road. It had been so dark, and wet, that the only remaining memory he had of it was the black, shiny ribbon of tarmac stretching off to infinity, and Rachel sitting on the engine cowling beside him, her feet up on the dash.

Thorner itself was just coming to life, people setting off on their commute to Leeds. A coach was parked opposite the Mexborough Arms, a knot of elderly men standing on the pavement, shuffling and stamping their feet in the early chill. At the foot of the hill, the sun caught the honeyed stone of the church tower, and Jack half expected to see their old van, crumpled and broken, where it had ploughed into the gate.

'Go left, Rick,' he said, and they turned down by the side of the pub, past the bowling green and the farm buildings, to where Station Lane cut right, and Thorner Victory Hall stood up on the left. They had only ever been here in the dark, and yet somehow it seemed as if nothing had changed. The railway bridge and cutting were still there. Manor Farm. The sweet smell of manure. Ricky pulled into the side of the road, and Jack and Dave got stiffly out of the car to help Maurie from the back and on to his feet, supporting him on each side as they stood looking up the embankment to where the station had once stood. It was long gone. A modern house built in its place. Although the bridge still existed, the line of the track beyond it had been developed into a small cul-de-sac of private homes.

Jack glanced at Maurie and saw the intensity of sad recollection in his face, a face so grey and pale that it was almost as if he didn't exist. And it occurred to Jack that none of them did. At least, not in this place. Here they were just ghosts haunting their own past, a past long gone and as insubstantial as themselves.

But somewhere up there, where someone had since built a home – lived, raised a family, perhaps died – Rachel had first kissed him. No matter how lost it was now in time and space, nothing could take away the memory of that moment.

And suddenly, Jack realized why he was here. Why he had ever agreed to go with Maurie and Dave back to London. Deep in his sub-conscious, where the thought had refused to coagulate, he had been harbouring the hopeless fantasy that somehow, somewhere he might find her again.

He gripped Maurie's arm a little more tightly and the two old men met each other's eyes. Maurie searched Jack's gaze, almost as if he had divined his friend's thoughts.

Jack said, 'I want to know what happened to her, Maurie. Before you die. You owe me that.'

But Maurie just turned his eyes back towards the embankment where they had huddled, cold and frightened, in the dark all those years before, and said, 'I owe you nothing, Jack.'

II

They drove into Leeds city centre shortly after nine o'clock on that brilliantly sunny spring morning. The GPS took them by circuitous suburban roads, past parks and gardens filled with cherry and apple blossom, into the centre of town. Fifty years ago, the mills had poured their bile into the rivers, and belched their filth into the skies. People had lived and worked and died in serried rows of dilapidated brick terraces, or in the new council housing estates that had promised so much and delivered so little. Or in the failed social housing experiment that was Quarry Hill. It had been a city then on its knees, cowering beneath a leaden sky that rained tears of acid.

Like a bad dream, that Leeds of fifty years before had vanished in the morning light of this spring day in 2015. New roads swept through the heart of it. Shiny, twenty-first-century glass and steel structures rose brightly into a blue sky. Dismal industrial canals, where barges of coal or cotton once plied their trade, were transformed now into arterial waterways for pleasure-seekers. Expensive boats cruising past wine bars and restaurants fashioned from former warehouses. A transformation. A veneer of affluence and success, tarnished only by occasional glimpses of some rotting brick factory in a half-concealed backstreet, cracks opening on to a hidden past that lurked still, despite appearances, somewhere not far beneath the surface. Fleeting memories of the bad dream.

'Edward Street,' Jack told Ricky. 'That's where we parked.'

And Ricky punched it into the GPS.

It seemed to Jack as if buildings had been demolished to make way for a car park along the north side of Edward Street. But it had been so dark in 1965, the gap might have been there then, too. A bomb site perhaps, damage inflicted during a wartime air raid. The official car park was full, but they found a space on the street, and Ricky helped them get Maurie out on to the pavement. Jack leaned heavily on his stick, supporting Maurie's right arm, and they made slow progress into Lady Lane and down to the roundabout that was now called the City Centre Loop.

They hadn't gone more than ten yards when Maurie stopped. 'Where's it gone?'

And they all looked down the street towards the loop. Fifty years before, the skyline had been dominated by the huge sweep of Oastler House. It was no longer there.

'Where's what gone?' Ricky said.

And as they made their slow progress to the foot of the road, Jack told him about Quarry Hill Flats. But when they got to the roundabout it was clear that the entire complex had gone. Off to the right was a block of flats and the square brown building that housed the West Yorkshire Playhouse. And somewhere beyond it were the BBC and Leeds College of Music. A concourse of concrete and glass rose up on the far side of the loop, where Oastler had once stood, and wide steps led up to a walkway that ran east beyond a line of tall, spring-green trees, leading to a vast edifice that dominated the skyline perhaps even more than the flats had done before it. On its roof, a strange structure of silver columns and spheres rose to a spike that pierced the bluest of morning skies.

Jack had the disorientating sense of having just landed on another planet.

They stood under the monkey-puzzle trees at the foot of the hill, and Ricky tapped the screen of his iPhone.

'Here we are,' he said. 'Quarry Hill Flats. Demolished in 1978 due to social problems and poor maintenance.' He looked up. 'That huge building there is called Quarry House. Home to the headquarters of NHS England, and the Department for Work and Pensions.' He chuckled. 'Apparently, it's nicknamed the Kremlin.'

'Aye,' said Dave, 'so they just replaced one Stalinesque monstrosity wi' another.'

'Let's get some breakfast,' Jack said.

They found a French-style café on Eastgate and ordered coffees and croissants, sitting at a tubular steel and glass table in the window.

But Maurie refused to eat anything. 'I'll just throw it up,' he said.

Faces streamed past in the sunshine on the other side of the glass, and Jack had a very powerful sense that he and the others were not even visible to them. Phantoms from another century haunting a future world. Maurie looked so ill that Jack began to wonder if his old friend would actually make it to London. All he had ordered was a glass of water to wash down his heart pills and painkillers.

Ricky's phone rang, as it had done several times already that morning. Jack watched his grandson's face as he looked at the display.

'It's Dad again.'

On an impulse Jack reached out and took the phone from him. 'Here. I'll talk to him.'

He touched the green answer icon and put the phone to his ear before Ricky could stop him. And he spoke before his son-in-law could get a word in.

'Look, Malcolm. Just stop bloody bothering us, will you? We'll be back in a few days. And none of this is Rick's fault. You can blame me. I twisted his arm to give us a lift to London. I've only borrowed him for a few days, and I'll bring him back safe and sound. So, in the meantime, will you please just FUCK OFF!' He hung up and thrust the phone back at Ricky. 'Sorry for my French.'

Heads in the café turned towards them, and Ricky blushed with embarrassment.

'I need to go to the loo,' Maurie said suddenly.

Jack looked at him and saw that he was the colour of ash. 'You take him, Rick.'

'Me?'

'Aye, you. We're going to have to share this around.'

'I need to go now!' There was urgency in Maurie's voice.

Ricky sighed heavily before heaving himself out of his seat to help Maurie to the door of the toilet at the back of the café. Jack turned and watched as his nephew squeezed into the little toilet with the old man. Although he shut the door behind them, there wasn't anyone in the café that didn't hear Maurie retching. And when they came out again Ricky was, if anything, more ashen than the old man. He glared at his grandfather.

Ricky and his elderly companions made their way back up Eastgate, past the Red Sea Restaurant and Cash Converters, to an alleyway that led back through into Edward Street. They were halfway along the street before they realized that the Micra was gone.

There was a moment of disorientation when Ricky said, 'The car's not there!' Panic rising in his voice.

And Jack said, 'No, we must have parked it further along.' Even though he didn't think they had.

'No, it was here,' Ricky said.

The space between the white lines seemed painfully empty, and none of them could quite believe it.

'We've made a mistake. We must have,' Dave said. 'We're in the wrong street.'

But it was Maurie who shook his head. 'We're not.' He looked grim, and infinitely weary. 'All my stuff was in it. Wallet, the lot.'

'Mine, too,' Dave said, realization dawning suddenly that if the car wasn't there, then someone had stolen it – and all their things with it.

'I've only got a tenner in my wallet, and some loose change.' Jack fished it from his back pocket and opened it up.

'At least you've got a credit card.' Dave jabbed a finger at it.

Jack pulled a face. 'Way past its limit.'

A long, mournful wail cut into their exchange, and they turned to look at Ricky. He was very nearly in tears.

'My car's been stolen,' he shouted. 'And all you can talk about is the tenner you've got in your wallet and a stupid bloody credit card that doesn't work. My car has gone! It's gone! My car, my bag, my Nintendo, everything. My dad is so going to kill me.'

'What do we dae?' Dave said.

And Jack saw him looking lost and old somehow for the first time. He shrugged. 'Report it to the police.' He turned to Ricky. 'Have you got the log book on you, son?'

Ricky bit his lower lip and shook his head. 'No.'

'But you know the registration number, right?'

'Er . . .' He blinked rapidly, trying to think. Then he grimaced and shook his head. 'I don't, Grampa. I never had any reason to memorize it.'

Jack slumped down on to one of a row of yellow posts that

separated the street from the car park. He thought about it. 'Well, your dad's going to have the paperwork from when he bought it. So he'll have the number.'

'I'm not calling my dad!' Ricky was emphatic.

'You don't have to call him, son. Just send him an email. Use your phone to take a photo of the place where the car was parked, and email your dad with the details. He can contact the cops.'

Ricky was almost hopping on one foot with agitation. 'I can't.'

Dave said, 'Yer grampa's right, sonny. Yer pa's the only one who can sort this oot.'

'As long as you report the theft, the insurance'll cover it,' Maurie said suddenly. 'And your old man can do that for you, okay? No need for us to hang about here any longer than we have to.'

Dave cocked an eyebrow at him in surprise. 'Where are we going?'

'London, of course.'

'How?' Jack shook his head. 'We've no wheels, Maurie. No money.'

Maurie said, 'I'll make a phone call. Have some money wired to us.'

'Wired?' Jack said. 'Do they still do that?'

Maurie waved a dismissive hand. 'I don't know. However it's done, it shouldn't be too difficult.'

The peep of a horn startled them, and they turned to see a minibus pulled up outside the Wing Lee Hong Kong Chinese supermarket opposite. The driver jumped out and slid open the side door. He was a middle-aged man, wearing turned-up jeans and a knitted jumper. He had a florid face that warned of high blood pressure, and a bird's nest of wiry hair arranged around a bald crown.

'Sorry I'm so late, gents,' he said. 'The traffic's right bad this morning, and I've still got a few calls to make, but we should get you there on time.'

For a moment none of them knew what to say.

Then Jack improvised. 'Where are we going?'

'Well, you'll be meeting the coach at Bramley. But you'll get a bite to eat first with the old folk at the lunch club in the community centre. That's where you'll get picked up.' He looked at Ricky. 'You looking after them, young fella?'

'Aye, he is,' Jack said, and he nodded the others towards the van.

Ricky glared at him and hissed under his breath, 'What now?'

'You heard the man. Going to get something to eat, son,' Jack said, and grinned. 'Better take that photo before we go.'

He and Dave helped Maurie across the road and into the van while Ricky rattled off several quick pictures of the empty parking space where his Micra had been, then hurried over to join them.

The driver smiled. 'Doing a bit of sightseeing are you, son?'

Ricky didn't trust himself to speak and just nodded.

'Funny sort of thing to show the folks back home. A parking space in Leeds.' And he chuckled. 'Alright, gents. Everyone safely aboard?' He slid the door shut, then rounded the van to climb back into the driver's seat. 'Hope you don't mind, but I've a whole load of stuff in the back there to drop off at the Farsley Food Bank. Shouldn't take too long.'

III

Farsley was an old mill town halfway between Leeds and Bradford, subsumed now into the Leeds metropolitan area. It seemed to comprise a main street that ran steeply up a hill to a church at the top of it, with roads like spokes going off left and right to factories and former mills and micro housing estates.

'It's a bloody shame,' the driver said as they drove up the hill. 'There's folk in Farsley worked hard all their lives, till them bankers went and ruined the economy. Bloody gamblers, that's all they are. And it's honest working folk like what live here that are paying the price of it. Nearly ten per cent unemployed, if you even believe the figures.' He snorted his disgust. 'Those that have jobs don't even earn enough to pay their bills. And these bastards are still picking up their bonuses!'

'So who employs you, then?' Jack asked.

'Oh, I work the night shift at a factory in Bradford. This is just volunteer work.' He half turned. 'You've got to do your bit, don't you? Because the bloody government won't. One of the richest bloody countries in the world, we are, and we've got more than three and a half million children living in poverty. One in four! And nearly half of those in severe poverty. Never been a gap this big between rich and poor since the First World War. Bloody disgrace!'

Jack said, 'When I left school in the sixties, unemployment was one per cent.' He shook his head. 'Hard to believe it now. Jobs were so thick on the ground, if you didn't like the one you were in you could quit, walk round the corner and get another.'

Dave chuckled. 'I remember old what's-his-name, Harold Macmillan, saying we'd never had it sae good. And we thought, bloody Tory!' He made a sound that was halfway between a snort and a laugh. 'If only we'd known. But the auld bugger was right.'

They turned left off the main street into Old Road, climbed to a turn before a row of old brick terraced houses, and then drove into the car park of the Farsley Community Church.

'Used to be the Methodist church,' said the driver. 'And there's still a working chapel inside. The hall's given over now to the food bank.' He pulled up by a tall wooden entrance porch built on to the blackened stone church, and turned to Ricky. 'You can give me a hand in with these boxes, young fella, if you don't mind.'

Ricky looked like he minded very much.

But Jack said, 'He'll be only too delighted to help, won't you, Rick?'

He saw Ricky's jaw clench, but the young man said nothing.

He climbed out of the van and went round the back to help the driver unload.

Jack turned to the other two. 'Wonder who we're supposed to be.'

Dave smiled. 'Does it matter? As long as we dinnae let on that we're no' who he thinks we are, the least we'll get is a free lunch.'

'I guess so.' Jack looked up at the big old church. 'Never seen a food bank myself. Fancy taking a look?'

Maurie said, 'On you go. Life's depressing enough.'

Jack and Dave followed Ricky and the driver up the stairs and into the main hall. Beneath a polished wooden ceiling sunlight streamed in through tall, arched windows to fall across tables laid out around the perimeter. Tinned and packaged foods were organized into blue plastic crates, and groups of people, some with children, shuffled from table to table filling their bags with the necessities of life.

Jack and Dave stood by the door watching. There was some discreet banter going on among the volunteers, but the recipients themselves moved around the tables in sombre silence, with just the occasional whispered exchange over a pack of rice or a bag of sugar. It dawned, then, on Jack that what he was witnessing was humiliation. People stripped of all dignity and forced to come here to feed themselves or their children. And he immediately felt a sense of prurience.

He turned at the sound of their driver's voice, low and breathless, as if imparting a secret. 'Crying shame, in't it? You know, more than a million people had to use food banks in this country last year. And a lot of these folk have got jobs. They just don't earn enough to feed their families.'

Jack glanced beyond him towards Ricky, and saw the young man's discomfort.

'Most people don't realize it, but the biggest cause of folk needing to use food banks is delays in benefit payments. They just don't have any bloody money at all. Second biggest cause is low income.' He shook his head. 'Low income! Can you imagine? How is it even legal to pay people less money than they need to live?' He lowered his voice even further. 'And this?' He nodded towards the lines of tables. 'This is just the last step in a kind of ritual humiliation.'

Jack noticed that the driver used the very word that had come to his mind.

'If you were to believe the papers, you'd think anyone could just trot along here and help themselves. They can't. They have to be assessed by care professionals. Social workers, doctors, police officers. And if it's decided they're in crisis, they get vouchers to exchange for food.' He looked at Jack and Dave, and cocked his eyebrow in disgust. 'Hard to believe this is 2015.'

As they shuffled out, Jack caught his grandson's arm on the stairs, and leaned in to whisper. 'Bloody scroungers, eh? Just topping up their weekly shopping at our expense.'

IV

Ricky sat in the back of the minibus working his iPhone with his thumbs, emailing his father and sending him the photograph of the empty parking space. The road from Farsley took them through suburban housing schemes and new industrial estates, round ring roads and loops. When they reached Bramley they passed countless *For Sale* and *To Let* signs on houses and shops. The roads were patched and potholed, and their minibus bumped and lurched, making it almost impossible for Ricky to hit the correct keys.

At the Halifax Building Society they turned right by a row of ugly, square, brick-built shops roughly assembled into a poor man's shopping centre. A long street of red-brick semi-detached villas fell steeply away towards a Leeds skyline that shimmered against a blue sky in a hazy distance of spring heat and pollution. An area of waste ground grew unkempt, yellow-sprinkled with dandelions. On the other side of the road stood the Bramley Community Centre, with its freshly blue-painted facade and a narrow strip of parking behind a broken stone wall.

Their driver pulled the minibus into the parking area and slapped his steering wheel with satisfaction. 'There we are. Bang on time, gentlemen. The coach should arrive any minute now. Then after lunch you can join them for the rest of the journey.'

'Where's the coach coming from?' Jack asked innocently. Although what he really wanted to know was where it was going.

The driver obliged on both counts. 'Didn't they tell you? The north-east. Newcastle. You're the last lot to get picked up before they hit the M1 for London.'

Jack and Dave exchanged looks, and Maurie nodded gravely. Ricky shut his eyes and kept his sigh to an almost inaudible puff of air.

The driver helped them down on to the tarmac. 'You don't have much luggage with you for a three-day trip.' He paused and frowned. 'In fact, you don't seem to have any at all.'

Jack said, 'My son was heading down to London this week. So he took our stuff on ahead. Saved us carrying it.'

'Very wise. In here, gents.' And the driver led them into the hall of the community centre.

It was arranged with rows of tables covered with paper cloths and set with plates, cutlery and china teacups. A row of windows along the front of the building laid sunlight across them in broken, zigzag slabs.

Ricky leaned in to whisper in his grandfather's ear. 'I've never heard anyone lie so easily.'

Jack searched his face as if looking for a sign, any sign, that his grandson was learning anything from his experience. He said, 'It's called survival, son. You'll find out about that if you ever join the rest of us in the real world.'

'This is the OAP lunch club,' said the driver, 'run by Bramley Elderly Action. The only square meal some of these folk get, and often the only company they have from one week to the next. There are a few regulars here today, but mostly it'll be folk from your tour. Why don't you sit beside Mr Maltby? He's an interesting old fella. Ninety plus, I think.'

Mr Maltby sat at a table near the back. There were others, sitting together in groups of two or three, but Mr Maltby was on his own, and had chosen a place in the full glare of sunlight from the window. He seemed burned out by it, like an over-exposed photograph, so that he appeared almost spectral.

His dark suit was shabby and shiny. It must once have fitted, but he had clearly shrunk, and it was now several sizes too big for him. His shirt was buttoned to the neck, but hung loose around it. He wore no tie, and his hands were folded together on the table in front of him. Gnarled, arthritic hands with huge knuckles and deformed fingers. His fingernails were too long and the skin on the backs of his hands was bruised and stained with the brown spots of age.

He had a strong face, airbrushed by the light from the window so that his skin seemed quite smooth and almost shiny. His ears and nose were enormous, as if the rest of his face had contracted around them, and only a few wisps of silvered hair clung stubbornly to his scalp. A drop of clear mucus hanging from the end of his nose glistened in the sunlight.

'Here, young man,' the driver pulled out a chair next to Mr Maltby. 'You can have the honour of sitting next to him.'

Ricky looked as if the last thing in the world he wanted to do was sit beside Mr Maltby, and he drew his chair into the table with a bad grace, immediately pulling a face and putting a hand to his nose. Mr Maltby, it seemed, was disseminating the perfume of old age. Jack glared at his grandson and very deliberately took the seat on the other side. Dave and Maurie sat opposite.

Jack reached over to shake the old man's hand. 'Pleased to meet you, Mr Maltby. I'm Jack, and these are my friends Dave and Maurie.' He nodded towards Ricky. 'And my grandson, Rick.'

'Ricky,' Ricky corrected him.

Jack was surprised by the strength of Mr Maltby's handshake. 'Knew a Ricky once,' the old man said. 'Private Richard Tyson, he were. But everyone knew him as Ricky. Worked in the hat department at Harrods in London before the war. Absolutely bloody useless, 'n all.' His green eyes shone with mischief, his voice strong and lucid in spite of his years.

'You were in the war, then?' Jack said.

'Aye, I were that. Last two years of it, anyroad. They wouldn't let me go and fight the bloody Hun till I were eighteen.'

'What did ye dae? Were you front line?' Dave eyed him with curiosity. None of his generation had fought in any war.

The old man chuckled. 'No, we were beyond the front line. The no-man's-land between them and us. Wi' a radio and a pair of bloody binoculars. It were our job to radio back the position of the enemy so our boys could drop their shells in the right place. Safest spot to be, really. In the middle. Nobody dropped their bombs there. But it were bloody noisy, I can tell you.' A distant memory flickered across his face in a fleeting smile. 'Ricky, the hat boy, he couldn't deal wi' it. Shat himself the first time we took him out, then started screaming when the shells was flying over our heads. Me and Tommy had to sit on him to shut him up.' His laugh crinkled his eyes, then faded into some sad recollection that never found voice.

They knew the coach had arrived when the pensioners' party from Newcastle flooded noisily into the hall, gaggles of women and groups of men finding their seats at separate tables as if there were some unspoken ban on integration of the sexes. Almost immediately, volunteers started serving up the soup, a thick vegetable concoction of lentils and barley.

Jack supped his, and dipped in some bread. Then he said mischievously, 'Our Ricky here's a bit of a soldier, Mr Maltby.'

The old man looked at Ricky, surprised, and cast an appraising eye over him. 'Really? You don't look very fit, son.'

Ricky blushed.

'That's because he's an armchair soldier, Mr Maltby. TV screens and remote controllers. It's all a game to him.'

Mr Maltby shook his head gravely. 'War's no game, son. It's a bloody tragedy. Just be grateful you've never had to do it for real, and I pray you never will.'

Ricky glared at his grandfather in wordless fury, and they finished their soup in silence.

The main course was roast beef in gravy with Yorkshire pudding and mashed potato. As he ate, old Mr Maltby wiped away a dribble of gravy from his chin with the back of his hand. Miraculously, the drop of mucus still clung to the end of his nose.

Then out of the blue he said, 'Poor bastard.'

'Who?' Maurie said.

'Ricky.'

Jack frowned. 'My Ricky?'

'No, Harrods Ricky.'

And when it seemed as though he wasn't going to elucidate, Jack said, 'What happened to him?'

Mr Maltby sat with his fork raised halfway to his mouth, roast beef dripping gravy back on to his plate, and he appeared to drift off in space and time to a place only he could see and hear. Then he lowered his fork back to his plate.

'I killed him,' he said.

And although the babble of voices raised in chatter and laughter rose up like mist all around them, there was a strange pall of silence at their end of the table that none of it could penetrate.

Finally, Dave said, 'How dae ye mean?'

Jack could see emotion welling up inside the old man. A tremble of his lower lip, the shaking of his hands as he gripped the edge of the table.

'You don't have to tell us if you don't want to, Mr Maltby.'

If he heard, he gave no sign of it. He said, 'We hadn't slept for two days. Ricky had learned not to scream or we would sit on him again, but he were still bloody useless. Finally the shelling had stopped, and there were a right unnatural sort of silence on the battlefield. So we took the chance to try and snatch some sleep.' He shook his head. 'It were raining, and there was debris everywhere. You know, abandoned jeeps and busted gun emplacements, and more than a few bodies. And Ricky, the stupid bloody bastard, crawls under this burned-out tank without telling anyone. Just so he'd be out of the rain. Well, the rest of us wake up with him screaming again. Took us a minute to find him in the dark. And there he is, pinned under the tank. The bloody thing's sinking into the mud.'

'Jees!' Maurie's voice punctuated the story and prompted a dramatic pause.

Old Mr Maltby sat lost in his memories, the pain of them only too visible in his eyes.

Finally, he said, 'Of course, we tried to pull him out. No good. And we tried digging under him, but there were no space. It were just impossible. And the damn thing just keeps sinking. Slow as you like. But crushing him to death, a fraction of an inch at a time.'

He lifted his head and looked around the faces of Jack and Dave and Maurie and Ricky. And he seemed suddenly to return to the present. 'What would you have done? I mean, he's screaming. Not just wi' fear now. But in agony. And not a damn thing any of us could do.'

'What *did* you do?' Ricky's face was milk white, eyes like saucers, gazing in horror at the old man.

'I took out me gun, lad. I put it to his head and I shot him.'

The horror of the moment sat among them like the ghost of the Harrods hat salesman himself.

'The look in his eyes in that moment before I pulled the trigger –' Mr Maltby's voice choked itself off. And there was a moment before he found it again. 'It's a look that's lived wi' me every moment of every day since.' He swallowed, and Jack saw tears tremble then spill from bloodshot rims. 'Went through that whole bloody war without killing a single soul, except for Ricky Tyson. And he were on our side.'

Dessert was some kind of cake in pink custard, which made Jack think of school dinners in the sixties.

The tears had dried up on Mr Maltby's face by now, although that mucus drip still clung stubbornly to his nose. Almost as if he couldn't stand it any longer, Ricky took out a clean handkerchief, placed his hand on Mr Maltby's back and wiped his nose for him.

'There,' he said. 'That's better.'

Old Mr Maltby turned and gazed at him, a curious look in his eyes. 'I'm sorry, Ricky,' he said. 'I'd have done anything to get you out from under that bloody thing. We tried. We did.' And his eyes filled up again. 'I hope . . . I hope, son, that one day you'll be able to forgive me.'

Ricky looked stricken, and for several long moments seemed at a loss for what to say. Then, in a small voice, he said, 'Nothing to forgive, Mr Maltby.'

And the old man pressed Ricky's hand between his two. 'Thank you, son. You don't know how much that's appreciated.'

He paused. 'You might have been a great hat salesman, but you were a bloody awful soldier.'

The coach driver counted them all on to the bus after the meal was over. 'You must be the Leeds lot,' he said to Jack, and cast his eyes over the group of them. 'A couple missing.'

'Last-minute cancellations,' Dave told him, with a surreptitious glance at Jack.

The driver looked at Ricky. 'And who are you, son?'

Ricky took Maurie's arm. 'Mr Cohen's nurse,' he said boldly. 'He wouldn't be able to make the trip without me.'

'Fair enough.' The driver nodded them up the steps. 'Plenty of seats up the back.'

Ricky helped Maurie all the way to the back of the coach, and they found themselves seats in the back two rows.

'Quick thinking, Ricky.' Dave put his hand on Ricky's shoulder. 'Very convincing. Especially since you were a doctor yesterday.' And he laughed.

Ricky sighed theatrically, rolling his eyes, and Jack said, 'Aye, the boy's learning.'

Five minutes later the coach pulled away and trundled down the hill towards Leeds. From the ring road they got on to the M621, and finally the M1 itself. Jack sat by the window, gazing out into the afternoon sunshine as urban landscape gave way to suburbs and finally open country.

He wondered about the group whose places they had taken on the coach and what on earth had happened to them. They must have realized long ago that they had missed their pick-up and were going to miss out, too, on their three days of sight-seeing in London. He had a momentary pang of conscience, then pushed it aside. Neither Jack nor the others had set out to deceive anyone. It had been a simple case of mistaken identity which had worked in their favour. They were owed a bit of good fortune.

He checked his watch. It would be a three-and-a-half-hour drive, he reckoned. Maybe four, with stops. They would be in London by this evening.

1965

CHAPTER NINE

I

We watched in wonder, and not a little disappointment, as the train made its final approach to King's Cross Station in London. The last few miles gave on to the backs of dilapidated terraces, mean and blackened by smoke, ugly high-rise flats, and factories pumping their poison into a cold grey sky. London had not earned its moniker of the Big Smoke for no reason.

The end of the platform was lost in smoke and light. Great metal arches with glass panels in the roof letting drab afternoon light fall in daubs all along its length, and we shuffled with the other passengers past rows of half-lit wooden luggage trolleys, to pass through the gate and on to a crowded concourse.

London! We were finally there.

The clock tower between the arches in the station's grand facade dominated King's Cross and displayed a time of five twenty. Traffic choked the artery that was Euston Road, belching fumes into the late afternoon.

A mini-skirted girl wearing knee-high white boots and a

black and white striped top walked by with such confidence that she must have known that every eye was on her. Mine certainly were!

Everything, it seemed, was 'mini' that year. Even the cars. Jeff got excited when he spotted a Mini Cooper S.

People dressed differently, especially the young. Clothes-conscious teenagers parading all the latest Carnaby Street couture, Mary Quant and Beatle haircuts, fashions of the Swinging Sixties that wouldn't reach the provinces for a year or more. I felt like some poor country cousin arriving in the big city for a day out, grey and dated, a refugee from the sepia world of the fifties. Conspicuously old-fashioned.

The thing that struck me most that first day, an impression that only increased with time, was the sense of arriving in a foreign country, a land of wealth and privilege. I would learn, of course, that there was dreadful poverty and deprivation in some of the housing estates and run-down boroughs around the capital, but in the city itself affluence moved in pools and eddies all around you. In such stark contrast to the industrial deprivation of the places we had come from. Glasgow. Leeds. The streets of London were not, as in legend, paved with gold, but money walked the pavements and motored the roads.

Rachel grabbed my hand. 'Come on, let's explore.'

'Wait!' I held her back. 'We should take the Underground somewhere. I've never even been on the subway in Glasgow.'

'Why would you?' Dave said. 'It just goes round in a silly wee circle.'

So we all piled into King's Cross tube station and spent several minutes consulting the big Underground map, before deciding to take the blue line to Piccadilly Circus. For no other reason than that it was a name which we had all heard.

We went down into the bowels of the city, where incoming trains dispelled hot air to rush up stairwells and corridors. A couple of boys stood busking, music echoing all the way along tiled passageways. Acoustic guitars strumming, and voices bent to mangled imitation of the Everly Brothers. I clocked the coins that passers-by threw into an open guitar case on the floor at their feet.

I don't know if I really expected there to be a circus at Piccadilly, but I was almost disappointed to find that there wasn't. Just a glorified roundabout with a winged statue of Eros set in its centre, red London buses and black hackney cabs circling before heading noisily off to other parts of the city. The roar of the traffic was wearing and relentless, and we had to shout to make ourselves heard above it.

There was nothing for us here, and we headed off along Shaftesbury Avenue. *Robert and Elizabeth*, a musical with June Bronhill and Keith Michell, was playing at the Lyric Theatre. The farce *Boeing-Boeing* at the Apollo. I recognized the name David Tomlinson as an actor I had seen in *Mary Poppins* the previous year, and suddenly felt very close to celebrity and the heart of all things. This, after all, was London. The very centre of the universe.

At the top of the avenue we turned into Charing Cross Road and walked up the hill past Foyles to stop beneath three gold-painted balls hanging outside the door of a pawnbroker's shop.

I saw our reflections in the window. A motley crew of dishevelled teenagers who had slept rough for two nights, and hadn't changed clothes or had a proper wash in nearly forty-eight hours.

'Is this a music shop?' Jeff said.

I jumped focus and saw that the window was full of musical instruments.

Luke said, 'It's a pawn shop. Lends people money in exchange for goods. If they don't come back to claim them, the shop sells them.' He turned to gaze thoughtfully at the array of musical instruments on display. 'I guess musicians must get pretty hard up.'

'That's encouraging,' Maurie said dryly.

But I had an idea. 'What if we exchanged our electric guitars for a couple of acoustics. Then we could busk in the Underground and make some money.'

This was greeted with a few moments of silent contemplation before Jeff said, 'And what would I do?'

'Hold the hat,' Rachel said, and we all laughed.

'I wouldn't have anything to play either,' Luke said.

But I pointed in the window at a tiny two-octave keyboard about fifteen inches long, with a mouthpiece at the top end. 'What about that?'

'A melodica,' Luke said. 'I've read about those. You blow into it, and when you press a key it opens a hole to let the air pass across a reed. Polyphonic, too.'

'Let's see what we can get,' I said, and we all trooped in, with Jeff bringing up the rear.

'Jobbies!' I heard him mutter.

In the event, by adding ten of our precious pounds to the trade, we were able to exchange my electric guitar and Dave's bass for two acoustics, the melodica and a couple of bongo drums to satisfy Jeff.

We were distracted by a crowd gathering around the door of a little record shop twenty yards or so further on. Its window was jammed full of classic album covers. The Beatles, the Stones, the Beach Boys, the Kinks, the Everly Brothers, Buddy Holly, Elvis.

I heard someone saying, 'What's going on?'

And someone replying, 'They're playing the new Beatles single. It's out today.'

We joined the crowd, pushing our way towards the door in time to catch 'Ticket to Ride' for the very first time. Hearing the first play of a new Beatles record was like sharing in a part of history. Our history. A seismic shift from the past and our parents' generation.

'Listen to those drums!' Jeff was in awe.

Ringo's staggered, staccato half-beats drove the song, building around the repeating guitar riff and leading to the punctuated harmony at the end of the line. It was exciting, and I loved it immediately.

But Rachel was listening to the words. 'God, Lennon sounds just like Andy,' she said. 'Like it was all *my* fault, or *hers* in the song. Because, of course, *he* was bringing *her* down, and that's why *she* had to leave. Couldn't possibly have been because *he* was such a shit.'

I looked at her in astonishment and realized for the first time that perhaps the sexes interpreted lyrics differently. I had empathized with his sadness. His girl had left him and made up an excuse for it, blaming him.

'Anyway,' I said. 'It's a great song.'

She shrugged, indifferent. 'I'm hungry.'

In Wardour Street we stumbled on the entrance to the Marquee Club, aware that this was probably the most important venue in the pop music of our generation. The Stones, the Who, the Yardbirds with Eric Clapton, and the Animals had all played here, and we could do no more than dream that someday we might do the same.

But it was Rachel who spotted the newly opened Pizza Express just along the road. The first time any of us had encountered British fast food. Ironic since the cuisine was Italian. It wasn't particularly cheap, but we were inclined to celebrate. We had got to London, we had musical instruments, a little money in our pockets, and a bucketload of self-belief.

We shared three pizzas among us. Hot, soft, bready pizzas with delicious tomato and cheese toppings, all washed down with ice-cold bottles of Coca-Cola, and by the end of the meal there were more than a dozen cigarette ends in the ashtray.

When we had eaten we sauntered off through the falling evening, and I was aware for the first time that it was warmer here. There was a softness in the air that remained in spite of the gathering dusk. The city was alive. People and lights. Diners crowding tables in the windows of expensive restaurants, drinkers spilling out of pubs to head for West End shows.

At the end of Park Lane we arrived at Marble Arch without passing Go or collecting £200, and crossed into Hyde Park, where we set up to busk for the crowds at Speakers' Corner. Jeff squatted on the grass beside an open guitar case and the rest of us gathered around to start playing through our repertoire.

It's not really for me to judge, but I think we were pretty good, in spite of our acoustic constraints. At least, I could see from Rachel's face that she thought so. It was clear that we exceeded any of her expectations, and she stood watching us with a kind of wide-eyed astonishment. She saw me looking at her, and we locked eyes for a moment. I felt as if something were kicking in my stomach trying to get out. Butterflies with hooves.

Pennies and threepenny bits, sixpenny pieces and the occasional shilling showered into our guitar case, and I almost started to believe we could make a living just doing this. We played for half an hour and made almost three quid before two London bobbies wearing tall helmets with silver Brunswick stars moved us on. Jeff gave up some cheek and they told us to scarper, and we went running off across the grass, jumping and whooping and shouting obscenities at the coming night. Until we settled ourselves on the bank of the Serpentine, lying on our backs in the grass and watching the sky overhead clear itself as darkness drew a veil over the park.

With the arrival of night, and the first chill breath of damp air rising from the water, the euphoria of just being there began to fade, and a more sombre reality settled itself on us like down after a pillow fight.

'Where are we going to sleep tonight?' Luke said.

Nobody knew.

'There's bound to be cheap hotels somewhere, or a youth hostel or something,' Jeff suggested.

But I was the one who quickly dispelled dreams of a soft bed for the night. 'We can't afford it. Even somewhere cheap would go through our cash in no time.'

'So what do you suggest, smart arse?' Maurie cocked an eyebrow in my direction.

'We passed an eatery earlier. The Serpentine Restaurant, I think. Overlooking the lake. Weird thing with glass pyramids on the roof. It'll be closed by now.'

Jeff's voice was derisive in the dark. 'Well, if it's closed, what use is that to us?'

'It had kind of open terraces under concrete eaves. It would give us shelter for the night.'

'Mmmmh, concrete pillows,' Rachel said. 'Just what I've always dreamed of. You boys really know how to show a girl a good time.'

I said, 'Just for one night. Maybe we can get ourselves sorted out with something better tomorrow.'

II

It must have been after midnight by the time we got ourselves settled among the shadows on the terrace of the Serpentine Restaurant. Coats laid on concrete, underwear balled up inside shirts for pillows. Rachel and I shared my coat but sat awake for a long time, smoking in the dark and listening to the heavy breathing of the others as one by one they drifted off. It was an extraordinary journey that had brought us here, and I had never for one minute expected to meet someone like Rachel on the way.

Moonlight dappled the water, and its silvery reflection shimmered under the eaves of the restaurant. I stole a glance at her as she gazed out across the lake.

'How are you feeling?'

She shrugged. 'Okay.' But she didn't really look it.

I took her hand. It was ice cold, and I could feel her trembling. 'Is it still bad?'

She pressed her lips together as if trying to stop herself from speaking. 'I'm alright. Last night was worse. Give me another fag.'

I lit one and passed it to her. She sucked on it savagely and drew the smoke deep into her lungs.

'What did you dream of?' I said.

She gave me an odd look. 'What? Last night?'

I smiled. 'When you were young. What was your dream? What did you want to do with your life? Who did you want to be?'

Her smile was wry as she lifted her eyes towards the stars. 'To be famous. A star of the silver screen. To be someone people looked at and envied. To be rich. To be in love with a beautiful man who loved me back.'

'Didn't want much, then.'

She laughed. 'I was just a kid. You know what it's like when you're just a wee lassie.'

'No!' It was my turn to laugh. 'I was always a wee laddie. No matter how much my mother would have liked to dress me up in a skirt and tie my hair in pigtails.'

'You don't have any brothers or sisters, then?'

'No. Just after I was born my dad got TB and spent two years in the sanatorium at Peesweep. I suppose he was lucky to survive it in those days, but I don't think he could have any more kids afterwards. And I'm sure my mum wanted a wee girl.'

Rachel said, 'We should have swapped parents.'

'Hmmm,' I said doubtfully. 'Not sure I would have been very happy about the circumcision.'

She laughed. 'Don't be such a baby. Actually, I've never seen one without a foreskin.'

'And, of course, you're such an expert.'

She smiled.

And I said, 'Andy wasn't Jewish, then?'

'No.'

'And you and he . . .'

She turned to look at me, amusement twinkling in her big dark eyes. 'He and me what?'

'You know . . .'

Now she laughed. 'Of course we did.'

I nodded and didn't like to think about it, or the irrational jealousy it stirred inside me.

'What about you?'

I looked at her. 'What about me?

'Do you have a girlfriend?'

'Sort of.'

'Well, either you do or you don't.'

I shrugged my shoulders in the dark. 'Well, I did before we ran away.'

'And were you and she . . .?'

'She and me what?'

'You know.'

I grinned, in spite of my embarrassment. 'No, we weren't.'

Suddenly I felt her whole body turn towards me. 'You're a virgin!'

'I'm not!' My denial was too hot and too fast.

'Ohhh, Jack.' She stroked my cheek with the back of her hand, and it felt cold on my hot face. 'My very own little virgin.'

'I'm not,' I said again. With less force this time, but no more conviction.

'We'll see.'

And I turned to meet her eyes. They almost glowed in the dark. Darker than the night itself. Gathering, as they always seemed to, every bit of light to reflect somewhere in their hidden depths. And I wondered what she had meant by that. While I am sure I knew really, such was my insecurity when it came to girls that I was always riddled with uncertainty.

But in that moment I was emboldened by her words, and kissed her for the second time. A very different kiss from the one the previous night. A soft kiss full of tenderness, and I felt her tongue in my mouth, sending little electric messages to my loins where an erection quickly burgeoned to push hard against my trousers.

Stupidly, Luke's words from two days before came into my head. *Penile tumescence*. I almost laughed.

She pulled back and looked at me quizzically. 'What?'

I grinned, feeling sheepish, and told her. About Maurie and Dave and the nocturnal erection, and Luke's description of it as 'penile tumescence'. We stifled our giggles like children in the dark. And suddenly she reached her hand over to slip it between my legs, taking me completely by surprise.

'I think the colloquial "hard-on" is more appropriate in your case.'

I gazed at her, my stomach flipping over, enjoying the way her hand stayed there, squeezing me. And I said, 'Only, in my case, it's down to the Rachel effect, rather than REM sleep.'

She laughed. 'You damn well better not go to sleep on me!'

So I kissed her again, and we got kind of lost in it for what seemed like a very long time. When, finally, we came up for air, she looked at me for even longer.

'I like you, Jack Mackay,' she said.

I didn't know what to say. *I like you, too*, seemed like such a lame response that I didn't say anything.

Then she said, 'What about your dream?'

I thought for a moment. 'I suppose I'm living it. Well, the fantasy version of it, anyway. To play in a group. Make music. It's all I really want to do with my life now.'

How could I have known then that failure of ambition is like a long, lingering death, and that disappointment with your life never goes away? It only grows stronger with the passage of time, as the clock ticks off the remaining days of your life, and any residual hope slips like sand through arthritic fingers.

She touched my lips with the tip of a finger. 'You're talented,' she said softly. 'I could tell that straight away tonight.' She kissed me. 'It's arousing. Talent. You know that?' Then she smiled and said, 'We should sleep.'

So we lay down together, covering ourselves as far as possible with my coat. The concrete beneath us was unyieldingly hard, and I spooned in behind her, pressing myself against the softness of her bottom, allowing my hand to slip over and cup one of her breasts. I was half expecting her to move it away, but she didn't. And I was both aroused and comforted, and asleep within minutes.

CHAPTER TEN

I

We were awake early, with first light and the dawn chorus. All of us stiff and cold and bruised by the concrete, deathly pale, with dark, penumbrous smudges beneath bloodshot eyes. Our third day living rough, and we were starting, I thought, to look like down-and-outs.

We found underground public toilets in Knightsbridge at Hyde Park Corner and were at least able to wash and brush our teeth. I changed into precious pairs of fresh socks and underpants and wondered what we were going to do for laundry when the time came.

We took the Underground from Hyde Park Corner to Leicester Square. Rachel and I got separated among the rush-hour crowds in the carriage and I became aware of Maurie pushing up behind me. His mouth was very close to my ear and I felt his breath hot on my neck.

'I'm watching you, Jack.'

There was something dangerous in his voice. Threatening. I turned my head to look at him, and his face was very close.

'What are you talking about?'

'She's my cousin. She's not for you.'

I felt anger prickle across my shoulders, and pushed my face at him so that our foreheads were almost touching, like young stags locking horns. My voice was low and just as threatening.

'None of your fucking business, Maurie!'

We glared at each other until the doors opened at Green Park. People got off, and more got on, and Rachel found me again and took my hand. But those big eyes of hers missed nothing.

She looked at me. 'What's wrong?'

I just shook my head. 'Not a thing.'

It was a grey, overcast morning, cooler than the day before, and our spirits had dipped along with the weather as reality began to set in. Just off the square, in Bear Street, we found a greasy-spoon café and refuelled ourselves on egg, bacon and sausage, washed down with hot, milky tea. Almost immediately the world looked a more promising place. Grudgingly, the woman behind the counter loaned us her Yellow Pages, and we began surfing it for music agencies and recording studios. Luke wrote out a tidy list and we headed back to the tube station to consult the big map and work out an itinerary.

There was a brief debate about whether we should split up to save time and money, but we decided that we should stick together in case anyone asked us to play for them. How naive were we?

We made the long trek out to Fulham Broadway and a tiny recording studio, tucked away in an industrial unit off the King's Road, behind Warr's Harley-Davidson franchise and an old art bronze foundry. Motorbikes were stacked side by side all the way along the street.

A lean, unsympathetic young man with long, greasy hair and a thinning pate told us his hourly rate for two-track demos. He eyed us sceptically through smoke that rose from the cigarette clamped permanently between wet lips, and told us that we would need to bring our own gear, and that setting-up time would be included in the hourly rate. But we had already lost interest. We had no gear, and couldn't afford to hire any. Besides which, the hourly rate itself was beyond our means.

Outside, in the King's Road, Luke stabbed a nicotine-stained finger at his notes and suggested that we try some of the agencies closer to town.

So we set off on a fruitless search for an agency that would sign us. A search that took us out to Belsize Park in the north, Shoreditch in the east, and the Roger Morris Agency in Oxford Street. Everywhere it was the same story. We would need demo tapes. No one wanted to hear us play. We said we would gig anywhere. Pubs, hotels, dances . . . funerals – which didn't even raise a smile. When we were asked for a contact address and phone number, of course we didn't have one.

By the end of the morning we were tired and disheartened and sitting in the waiting room of an agency in the Strand.

A secretary popped her head round the door of her office and said, 'Sorry, boys. The boss won't entertain you without a demo tape.' She gave us her sweetest smile and almost closed the door on a young man on his way out. 'Oh, sorry, John,' she said.

He had collar-length brown hair, and wore jeans and a leather jacket. He grinned and winked as he passed. 'It's tough lads, eh? You write your own stuff?'

I shook my head. 'No, just covers.'

'Then you're wasting your time, boys. No one's interested. My advice is go away and write. And, you know, if you can't write, forget it.' He cocked an eyebrow and pulled a face. 'See you around.'

He skipped off through swing doors and down the stairs.

Rachel's voice was hushed in disbelief. 'You know who that was?'

'He looked a bit familiar,' Jeff said.

'That was John Lennon.'

'Nah.'

It wasn't possible that I had just spoken to John Lennon, and hadn't even realized it.

But Luke was nodding slowly. 'I think it was, you know. People look different in the flesh. And that was definitely a Liverpool accent.'

'It was John Lennon, I'm telling you,' Rachel insisted.

Many years later, when such things were possible, I tried to find out on the internet where Lennon might have been that day. It turned out the Beatles were in London filming *Help!*, out at Twickenham Film Studios, in the spring of 1965. So it

at the neck, with no tie. His aftershave smelled expensive, and he had a smile to match. It was the first time that we set eyes on Dr Cliff Robert, and it is a moment I will never forget.

'I'll sort this out,' he said confidently to the porters. 'No need to cause a scene.'

'If you say so, sir.'

The two of them retreated reluctantly towards the door, and the young man turned to us.

'Who's the head man here?'

There were several moments of confusion. Nothing had ever been discussed or acknowledged in regard to who should speak for the group, but all heads turned towards me and the man drew his own conclusion. He held out a hand to shake mine, and I took it uncertainly.

'Cliff Robert,' he said. 'And you are . . .?'

'Jack Mackay.'

'Ah. Scottish, I'd say from the accent.'

It was an accent that seemed gauche and broad compared to his creamy public-school drawl.

'Does the group have a name?'

'The Shuffle,' I said.

But he didn't appear impressed. 'Interesting sound. I like your vocals. But that's for another time, maybe. Right now, how would you boys,' he inclined his head towards Rachel, 'and girl, like to make a few pounds?'

I glanced around the faces of my friends and saw the same trepidation in them as I felt myself. 'Doing what?'

'Oh, nothing very much, and it won't take more than half an hour or so of your time. We have a documentary crew round the back of the hotel here setting up to do a bit of filming. We just need a few strategically placed bodies to prevent vehicles or pedestrians from interrupting once we're turning over.' He looked at us expectantly, showing beautifully white teeth behind pale lips, and a winning smile that crinkled around his blue eyes. 'What do you say?'

III

A narrow, cobbled lane called Savoy Steps climbed the slope off Savoy Hill, squeezed in between the small white-stone Queen's Chapel and a brick wall at the back of the hotel that was covered in builder's scaffolding. A group of young men was clustered around a thickset man with a cumbersome-looking cine camera strapped to his chest. He was young, too, with an unruly mop of wavy brown hair. Various pieces of equipment lay around, and the group seemed to be involved in a debate over the words scrawled on a pile of large white cards, about eighteen inches by twelve, which were stacked up against the wall. Random words, it seemed, without any meaning. The top one read *BASEMENT*. The cameraman was talking to a small skinny guy who looked about sixteen. He had long, curly hair that might have been permed, and wore a dark waistcoat unbuttoned over a long-sleeved shirt. He seemed to me to be in need of a square meal.

'Jees, Bob, I know they're heavy, but they'll get lighter as you drop them.'

You could tell straight away from his accent that the cameraman was American, and I felt an immediate thrill. I had never met an American before.

'That's alright for you, Donn,' the kid said. 'You don't have to hold 'em up there.'

'Maybe you'd like to try the camera on for size, Bob. You can bet your life it's a damned sight heavier.'

The kid with the perm sucked in smoke from his cigarette and threw it away. 'Just kidding, man. Let's do this thing.'

'Okay,' Donn said. He turned to the others. 'Hey, Allen, you and Neuwirth get over there by the sacks and try to look like workmen, willya?'

A large bald man with a beard and glasses, dressed up like he might have been a workie, and a thin guy with a flat cap and a stick detached themselves from the group and stood by a wooden crate on the other side of the lane, lighting cigarettes.

'What's going on exactly?' I asked Cliff Robert.

'They're making a documentary of the UK tour,' he said. 'This is the opening sequence they're shooting here. All those cards have got bits of lyrics from the new single scrawled on them. Bob'll hold them up and drop them one by one as the words come up in the song.'

Jeff said, 'Whose single?'

'Bob's, of course. It's called 'Subterranean Homesick Blues.'

'Daft name for a song,' Rachel said.

'Bob who?' Maurie asked.

Cliff Robert looked at us as if we all had two heads. 'Dylan. He's just arrived for his first tour of Britain.'

I looked again at the skinny guy with the curly hair and the haunted face as he hefted the cards up into the crook of his right arm. And was both amazed and thrilled at the same time. Bob Dylan! We were in the presence of rock royalty.

My jaw went slack. 'Dylan and Lennon both on the same day!'

Cliff Robert frowned. 'Lennon?'

And I told him about our encounter at the agency.

He smiled. 'I doubt very much if that was John Lennon.'

But I didn't have time to be disappointed. Because this really was Bob Dylan.

There were four possible approaches to the corner of Savoy Steps, and we were given our instructions to stand guard at all of them, and politely stop any people or vehicles from coming through while they were filming.

I have seen that video many times in the years since. Allen Ginsberg and Bob Neuwirth hovering in the background pretending to be workers, a bored-looking Dylan standing in the foreground, right of frame, dropping the cards to match the lyrics. Well, almost. He got a little out of sync here and there.

It was a chilly, grey London morning. The video captures that, and Dylan's sullen mood, perfectly. And all these years later I can almost believe that the world itself was black and white that day, and that it wasn't just the film in the camera.

They say it has been acknowledged as the very first modern pop video. And me and Rachel stood together at the entrance to the access tunnel under the Savoy Hotel and watched them shoot it.

Afterwards, Dylan and his entourage headed back into the hotel and one of the men paid us a tenner for our trouble.

'Jesus' jobbies,' Jeff said. 'That's more than I earned in a week at Anderson's.'

We made our way back up the hill to the Strand and stood debating what we should do now. A frustrating morning had ended well, but the future did not look promising.

'So what brings you to London, boys?'

We all turned at the sound of Cliff Robert's voice. He had come up the hill after us.

I was embarrassed to tell him, and shrugged hesitantly. 'We sort of ran away.'

'The whole group,' Jeff added quickly. 'We're looking to be signed up by an agency and get a recording contract.'

Cliff Robert smiled. 'Just like that.'

'We're good.' Luke was defensive.

The older man shrugged. 'I don't doubt it. But the world's full of great groups nobody's ever heard of. You're just another in a long list.'

One of the cabal of men from the Savoy Steps passed us and slapped Cliff Robert on the shoulder. 'Thanks, Doc.'

'My pleasure.'

'Doc?' Maurie said.

Robert smiled. 'I'm a qualified doctor. But medicine's not my passion. Music is.'

'You got a practice?' Rachel asked.

And he smiled again. 'Let's just say I'm freelance.' His smile faded. 'Look, if you boys are any good, and you're serious about making it in this business, I might be able to help.' He looked at our two acoustic guitars. 'Is this all the stuff you have?'

Jeff said quickly, 'Our van got stolen. With all our gear.' And he shifted uncomfortably as the rest of us looked at him.

Dr Robert nodded. 'Well, I know where you can borrow some gear, and find a place to rehearse. But I'd like to hear you before I make any promises. And if you want to make a bit of cash in the meantime, I know someone who's looking for performers.'

'You mean you can get us a gig?' Jeff said.

The good doctor seemed reluctant to elaborate. 'Well, not a gig exactly. And not the kind of performing that you're probably used to. But it's money, and I can offer you a roof over your heads. At least temporarily. If you want to come back to my place I'll explain it to you.' He glanced at his watch. 'I just have a little business to conclude with Donn Pennebaker and I'll be right back. Think it over.'

He headed off along the Strand to the entrance of the hotel. We stood on the corner, with the traffic rushing past us on the street, and the first drops of rain spitting from a frowning sky. For quite a while no one knew what to say.

It was Jeff who sliced through our hesitation. 'I think we should go for it.'

Rachel's scepticism was evident in her voice. 'You really trust that guy?'

'Not as far as I could throw him,' Luke said. 'He says he's a doctor, so what possible connection could he have with the music business?'

I said, 'Well, he was with the Dylan entourage, wasn't he? That's pretty connected, if you ask me.'

Maurie weighed in. 'I don't know about the rest of you, but I wouldn't mind somewhere reasonably civilized to lay my head tonight. And it seems to me that's what's on offer here.'

'Yeah, but what else is on offer?' Rachel looked at me. 'Come on, Jack. The guy's a creep.'

'A connected creep,' I said. 'It's the only offer we've had all day, and probably the only one we're likely to get. There's six of us. If we stick together, what harm can there be in it? We should at least find out exactly what it is that's on offer.'

'I agree,' Maurie said.

'Me, too.' Jeff looked around the faces of the others like a dog hoping someone will throw the ball.

Luke sighed. 'I suppose so.'

'Aye, well, that'll make it five.' It was the first time that we'd heard from Dave all morning.

Rachel just shook her head. 'You boys need your heads examined, you know that?'

And I have often wondered since how different all our lives might have been had we followed her instincts and chosen not to go with Dr Robert that afternoon.

CHAPTER ELEVEN

I

Dr Robert lived in Onslow Gardens in the Royal Borough of Kensington and Chelsea, in a fabulous four-storey townhouse with a basement, attic rooms and a huge roof terrace. It looked out over tree-shaded gardens behind wrought-iron railings, a stone's throw from Old Brompton Road and its rumble of distant traffic.

It was a grand property in yellow brick and white-painted stone, with porticos and balustrades. The streets around it reeked of wealth, lined by expensive cars and flanked by beautifully manicured gardens. There was a sort of reverential hush in those streets, as though it might be considered vulgar to raise your voice. Our silence, though, was induced by open-mouthed awe.

We arrived, all seven of us, in two taxis that Dr Robert paid for, and he led us up steps and through glazed doors into a wide hallway with carpeted stairs sweeping up through a half-landing to the next floor. Everything looked freshly painted. White, glossy woodwork, pale pastel walls, blue and yellow and cream. The hall and stairs were carpeted in a rich, subtly patterned grey. Through open doors I could see into a large kitchen in the back, and a dining room that overlooked a garden where the trees were heavy and fragrant with blossom.

Dr Robert took us up to the next floor. 'I mostly live on this level,' he said. And pointing down a long hallway with doors opening off on both sides, he told us, 'My study's down at the end there. But I spend most of my leisure time in here.'

We passed through a door into a high-ceilinged room that ran from the front of the house to the back. Perhaps two rooms at one time, but opening now one into the other through an arch. The front half was dominated by a vast, ornately carved wood and marble fireplace, around which settees and soft armchairs were gathered on a polished wooden floor as if huddled there for warmth. Bay windows gave on to a view over the park. Shelves on the wall opposite the fireplace groaned, floor to ceiling, with books. The back room was used for dining. A long, polished oval table reflected light from every window, and a gleaming silver tea service stood on an elegant, low mahogany sideboard.

In stark contrast with the old-fashioned gentility of these rooms, the walls were covered by the most extraordinary modern artwork. Large and small canvases, mostly black and white. Squares and circles, cubes and whorls, painted in such a way as to create the illusion of depth. Almost 3D. An image folding in on itself. Another buckling within its frame. Distorted geometry. *Trompe l'oeil*, an expression I had learned during my history of art classes at school. Fooling the eye. They were startling works, really, and quite out of keeping with the rest of the house.

'Do you like them?' Dr Robert was clearly proud of his collection.

No one knew quite what to say.

'All works of a friend of mine. Bridget Riley. She's exhibiting soon in New York. Going to be huge.' He smiled his self-satisfaction. 'And these, my friends, are going to be worth a small fortune one day.' As an afterthought, he added, 'Although I have no intention of selling them.'

He took us up through the rest of the house, waving expansively along corridors to his left and right, following the curve of the polished wooden bannisters from floor to floor. It seemed that most of the other rooms in the house were bedrooms, including several in the attic, which he said had once provided accommodation for the staff.

'Of course, I have no staff,' he said. 'Couldn't afford it, even if I wanted to. I was fortunate to inherit the house from my parents, but it's as much as I can do just to pay for the upkeep of the place.'

On the top floor we went out through French windows on to a wide, square terrace with a low, white-painted stone balustrade around three sides. And from here we had a view across the rooftops of Kensington. A forest of chimneys sprouting from steeply angled slate roofs, in turn broken by countless attic dormers.

'It's wonderful up here of a summer's evening,' the doctor said. 'With the air soft in your face, the perfume of a thousand blooms in your nostrils, and a glass of fine Scotch in your hand.' He turned to smile at us. 'The basement, on the other hand, smells a little damp. But I'm sure you won't mind that.'

The basement was much darker than the rest of the house, limited light slanting in at acute angles through high windows that opened into a sub-pavement alleyway where stone steps climbed up to locked wrought-iron gates. There were three small bedrooms, a toilet and a sitting room down here, and the all-pervasive miasma of damp that seemed to have contaminated curtains, carpet and furniture in equal measure. But the doctor was right. We didn't mind at all. It was a vast improvement on the concrete terrace of the Serpentine Restaurant, or the back of the van.

'Make yourselves at home,' he said. 'There's a girl comes in once a week to change the sheets and do the laundry.' He pulled a face. 'Speaking of which, can I suggest that you get yourselves a change of clothes. Or underwear at the very least. And a bath wouldn't be out of order. There's plenty of hot water.'

He took out his wallet and, to our amazement, counted out a sheaf of notes that he dropped on to the coffee table in the sitting room.

'Consider this an advance on that little performance job I told you about. There are plenty of shops down the Old

Brompton Road. When you've got yourselves freshened up, I'll order some carry-out for this evening and tell you all about it.'

II

We were in the hall, on the way out to do an underwear shopping, when we heard the rattle of a key in the latch, and the front door opened before we got to it. A painfully good-looking young man with a shock of Scandinavian blond hair, tumbling like straw across his forehead, looked startled to see us. He wasn't terribly tall, but you saw at a glance how beautifully proportioned he was. He wore an open-necked shirt with sleeves carefully rolled up, revealing a tattoo of a bluebird on his left forearm. A pair of neatly pressed slacks folded themselves over spotlessly Blanco-ed tennis shoes. He looked like he might have acquired his tan at the same time and place as Dr Robert, but his pale green eyes lacked warmth and he glared at us as if we were aliens.

'Who's this?' His voice cut sharply through our chatter, the question posed directly to our benefactor at the foot of the stairs. It carried more than a hint of hostility.

The doctor said, 'They're a young group from Glasgow, Sy. Going to help out at the Victoria Hall. They'll be staying in the basement in the meantime.'

Sy looked far from pleased. 'I need peace, Cliff, you know that.' His voice was modulated by petulance. 'I'm due on set at six tomorrow, and I've got five pages of dialogue to learn.'

'No one's going to disturb you, Sy.' Dr Robert's voice was calmly soothing, like a psychologist reassuring an agitated patient. 'The boys will be out for the rest of the afternoon, won't you, boys?' He barely looked at us and didn't wait for an answer. 'You'll have the place to yourself. And you can run your lines later with me, if you want.'

But Sy appeared less than mollified by the promise of peace and the offer of help. He flicked a dismissive hand theatrically in the air and pushed past us, fastidiously avoiding contact as if we might somehow be contaminated.

'I just don't need this right now, Cliff. I don't.' And he took the steps two at a time, disappearing round the curve of the staircase beyond the first landing.

Apparently unruffled, Dr Robert said to us, 'I'll see you later, then.'

And we all tumbled out into the street. The door shut behind us and Rachel turned excitedly on the pavement.

'You know who that was?'

'Well, it definitely wasn't John Lennon,' I said.

She made a face. 'It was Simon Flet.'

When we all looked at her blankly, she raised her eyes to the heavens.

'The actor. He was in that movie last year. You know, the one that's been tipped for an Oscar. Shit, what's it called?'

There wasn't one of us could help her. Jenny and I had been to the flicks together a few times, but we hadn't paid much attention to the films. And anyway, I was interested in music, not movies.

'*The Killing Breath*,' she said suddenly. 'It was a psychological thriller. Simon Flet got rave reviews, and every girl in the country fell in love with him. He's totally gorgeous.'

'Well, they'll all be disappointed then, won't they?' Dave said.

Rachel gave him a quizzical look. 'Why?'

Dave grunted. 'Obvious, isn't it?' When no one responded he looked around our curious faces in surprise. 'Well, he's queer, isn't he? And I'll bet that Dr Robert is, tae.'

III

Bridget Riley's op art paintings took on an almost sinister air by candlelight. The flickering flames of a dozen or more candles set around the dining room danced across the geometry of black and white patterns, causing them to shift shape and distort if you let your eyes rest on them for more than a few seconds. Along with the effects of the wine, it was quite unsettling.

I don't think any of us had ever drunk wine before. A warm, rich, heady red with which Dr Robert filled our glasses each time they were in danger of emptying. We all sat around his table, changed and washed, eating Greek food that he'd had delivered from a restaurant in the high street. Another first – at least, for me. I had never tasted anything like it before. Lamb flavoured with mint and cinnamon. Rice wrapped in vine leaves. Slow-cooked beef in a rich gravy that simply fell apart when you poked it with your fork. Tuna like steak, broken into pieces and served in a salad with little cubes of white cheese.

It was the first decent meal we'd had in three days, and we devoured it.

Dr Robert sat languidly in his chair at the head of the table. He wore jeans and an open-necked white shirt, and his tan seemed deeper by candlelight. There had been no sign of Simon Flet when we returned to the house.

We hadn't spoken much, our focus on the food, but the wine had dissipated much of the tension that lingered among us and we began to relax.

The good doctor wiped his lips with a cloth napkin and lit a cigarette before leaning forward and resting his elbows on the table as if about to impart some solemn secret. 'Ever heard of J. P. Walker?' he said, only to be met by blank looks. 'He's from your neck of the woods.'

Then Luke said, 'The psychiatrist?'

Dr Robert nodded. 'Author of *The Two of Us*, international bestseller and direct challenge to all the fundamental precepts of twentieth-century psychiatry.'

None of us had any idea where this was going, and so no one said a word. The doctor smiled.

'JP disputes the very existence of madness, at least as we have come to accept it. He argues that "normal" is just an averaging out of human behaviour, and that no such thing truly exists. And so what we define as insanity is just another form of behaviour that should, by rights, come within the very broad spectrum of normality.'

'I've read something about this,' Luke said. 'J. P. Walker believes that the treatment of mental illness with drugs, or worse, is wrong because the "illness" as defined by psychiatrists doesn't actually exist.'

Dr Robert nodded a smiling acknowledgement in Luke's direction. 'You have a bit of a savant among you, boys.' He interlocked his fingers on the table in front of him. 'That's broadly correct. Dr Walker believes that what the profession defines as schizophrenia is a form of behaviour conditioned by conflict in the family and can be treated by a kind of regression during which the patient is taken back to infancy, or even earlier, and rebuilt to be what society would accept as "normal". A sort of second chance at growing up.'

I was wondering why on earth he was telling us this, when he looked at me and smiled, almost as if he had heard the thought spoken aloud.

'You're probably wondering what this has to do with anything.'

I was glad of the smoke and the flickering light that hid my blushes. And I had the oddest sense of having been violated, the fingers of his mind reaching in to grasp my innermost thoughts.

'Dr Walker is the one who will be employing you. And you should feel honoured. The man is famous on both sides of the Atlantic. He has set up a project in the East End of London to put his theories to the test. Along with colleagues, he has taken possession of a former community complex known as the Victoria Hall, in Bethnal Green. He lives there with a number of patients who would otherwise be confined in mental institutions. Under his tutelage, they are free and equal members of the hall's twenty-five or so residents, which include psychiatrists and psychologists. And, trust me, you'd be hard pushed to tell the difference.'

I could hear music now, but had no recollection of Dr Robert putting any on, and no idea where it was coming from. The strange thing was that, although I knew it was music, I couldn't have told you what kind of music. Classical, pop, rock 'n' roll, jazz. It was just music, and it seemed amazing to me.

'The Victoria Hall experiment has already gained quite a reputation. There's a lot of media interest, and a number of what you might call celebrities drop by to consult with JP or just hang out.' He grinned. 'Names and faces you probably wouldn't believe.'

He stubbed out his cigarette and lit another. It gave me the urge to have one myself, and although I managed to get a cigarette out of the packet, I somehow couldn't seem to hold it between my fingers. It kept moving as if it were alive. I looked up and saw Rachel turning her head towards the window. It left a kind of coloured trail that traced the movement of her head, and I felt a tiny seed of anxiety start to burgeon deep inside me.

'Anyway, our friend JP is looking for performance artists

who will improvise dramas for the residents at his direction. Nothing too structured, but designed to provoke discussion.' He blew smoke towards the ceiling and it seemed to me to take shape in the form of a dragon breathing fire. 'There's a local pop group in Bethnal Green who use the hall for practising. They leave their stuff set up there. I'm sure JP can persuade them to let you use their gear to practise for yourselves. And then we can get an idea of just how good you are. Or not.'

Finally, I managed to get the cigarette to my mouth. But when I turned the sparking wheel on the lighter, the flame that leapt out of it reached the ceiling. I looked up as it flattened itself against the plaster, and spread out like water to cover the entire surface.

I heard Dave say, 'What the fuck?' And when I turned he was staring, wild-eyed, at one of Bridget Riley's paintings on the wall.

I felt Rachel's hand slip into mine, and for a moment all my anxiety slipped away. She was smiling. Serene and beautiful. Her hair was glowing, silver and gold, red and green, and as she reached out to touch my face I saw each movement of her arm as a sequence of images, each fading as the next formed, a slow-motion trail of fingers and flesh, and then the touch of her fingertips on my skin like needles.

And still Dr Robert's voice penetrated my consciousness.

'Johnny . . . that's what they call him. Johnny Walker. Get it? Johnny uses LSD in some of his treatments. He takes the trip with them, so that he can share what can often be a psychotic experience, and guide them through it. Of course, some people like to use it for purely recreational purposes. Some big names are into that these days, boys. Bet you didn't know the Beatles are dropping acid. I've heard some of the stuff they're writing. Man, it's just taking them to the next level. And they're not the only ones.' He sat back and smiled. 'Just about everyone comes to me when they want to go tripping. You know what LSD is, boys?'

I heard Luke's voice come from somewhere. 'Lysergic acid diethylamide. Commonly known as acid.'

'Ah, our savant again. Our know-it-all. But absolutely right. A semi-synthetic psychedelic drug that can alter thinking processes, visual and aural awareness, leading to sometimes intense spiritual experiences.' He grinned. 'So how is it for you, boys?'

And I realized, with a sudden and very intense clarity, that Dr Robert had somehow slipped acid into our meal. All my anxiety returned in a rush, and Rachel's hand in mine felt like it was crushing me. I turned to see her wolf's head snarling in my face.

But Luke's voice somehow cut through all of it. Clear, controlled and reassuring.

'You shouldn't have done that, Dr Robert. Not without their permission. I have read that LSD is the only thing, apart from cancer, that can actually split your genes and change your personality.'

I glanced across the table and saw that Luke's wine glass

was untouched. He had not drunk a drop. So it had been in the wine, and he was quite unaffected.

Dr Robert said, 'There is some debate about that. But, anyway, no need to worry. It was the tiniest dose, and it will wear off very quickly.' He looked around the table, eyes shining. 'This is the sixties, boys. You need to experience it all. You can't do it second-hand. Not if you want to compete with the rest.'

By the time we went down to the basement for the night, we were also coming down from the trip. Angry and excited at the same time. I was quite shaken. I had not enjoyed the strange visual distortions produced by the acid, and still felt a residual sense of anxiety.

Luke, of all of us, was the most furious and wanted us to pack up our stuff and leave immediately. 'He had no right. No right at all!'

But we weren't going to go down that road. Both Maurie and Dave were unsure of the experience and hesitant about trying it again. But their hesitation, I knew, meant that they would.

I knew I wouldn't. The heightened sense of awareness that came from smoking dope was different. You felt in control of that. But an acid trip seemed random, and utterly dependent on your mood to determine whether it would be a good or bad journey on the road to paradise or psychosis.

I caught Rachel eyeing me with strangely dilated pupils, a faintly knowing smile curling the corners of her mouth, and I wondered what kind of experience it had been for her.

For Jeff, however, there was no doubt. 'Man, that was AMAZING,' he said. 'Did you see them? Did you?'

'See what?' Maurie said.

'The rainbows. Coming right out of the wall. I swear to God, I've never seen colours like it. It was just beautiful.' He looked around all our vacant faces. 'Didn't you see them?'

'It was all in your head, Jeff,' Luke told him. 'Everyone experienced something different.'

And Jeff seemed disappointed by that.

Luke picked up his bag. 'I think we should all get a decent night's sleep and talk about this in the morning.'

I had thought there was going to be some argument about who was going to get which room. There were only three: a single and two doubles. But it seemed the others had already discussed it and made a decision to which neither Rachel nor I had been privy. Rachel, Maurie said, was to get the single at the end of the hall. He would share with Jeff, and Luke and Dave would share the other. I was to get the settee.

'That's not fair!' I said.

'No one cares what you think,' Maurie said. 'It's been decided.'

I glanced at Rachel and she just shrugged, lifted her bag and headed off along the hall.

Luke hung back when the others had gone. He kept his voice down. 'I don't like this, Jack.'

But I wasn't in the mood to hear it. 'Well, let's take a nice democratic vote on it in the morning. I might even tell you we're having it. Unlike some people.'

'Jack –'

'Fuck off, Luke.' I kicked off my shoes and dropped on to the settee, pulling my coat over me and burying my head among the cushions. 'And switch off the light.'

He stood for a while without moving, then I heard him cross the room to the hall, and the light went out.

IV

I don't know how long I'd been asleep when I felt her fingers on my neck, cool and trembling. I awoke with a start and sat up suddenly, almost cracking my head on the underside of her chin.

She giggled in the dark. 'What are you trying to do? Knock me out?'

I caught hold of her arms and pulled her down on to the settee. And somehow, without being able to see her, I found her lips. It was a hungry kiss, full of lust and impatience, and I don't think I have ever been so awake so fast in my life. 'Do you want me to come through?' I whispered.

'No. The bed's far too small.'

I was disappointed. 'The settee's even worse.'

She giggled again in the dark, and I would have given anything to see the light in those big, full-moon eyes. 'It's our first time, Jack. We deserve something a little better.'

My mouth was so dry I had difficulty swallowing. 'First time?'

I heard her smile. 'Well, not for me. For you. For us.' And then a deep sigh. 'We're in a house full of bedrooms that nobody's using.'

'The doc'll kick us out, if he catches us.'

'Maybe. And maybe it'll be worth it.'

I discarded my coat and stood up, feeling for and finding her hand. 'Come on, then.'

And we both had trouble stifling our giggles as we snuck out of the basement flat and started up the stairs. Maybe it was a residue of our acid trip, but I think more likely it was nerves.

Light from street lamps outside laid down long, elongated rectangles through the glazing in the door, and our shadows danced along the hall like cartoon silhouettes as we ran barefoot along it, the deep-pile carpet soft under our feet. The curving sweep of the stairs took us up to the first floor. A night light burned dully somewhere at the end of the hall. This was the floor where Dr Robert said he spent his time. One of these rooms would surely be his bedroom. The living room stood in darkness, but I saw a pencil line of light beneath the door of his study and heard the hushed sound of distant voices.

Rachel pulled my hand and we moved quickly to the next flight of stairs. In a whispered exchange, we decided to go all the way to the attic. After all, as far as 'class' was concerned, our parents were far more likely to have been employed by Cliff Robert's folks than be their peers. So it seemed appropriate that we should make love where the maid might once have slept. But before we climbed that final, narrow flight to the servants' quarters, she pulled me back.

'Stop!' There was an imperative in her whisper. 'Wouldn't it be more fun to do it in the master's bed?'

'What? In Robert's own bed?' I couldn't keep the incredulity out of my voice.

'No, silly! Not his. Not exactly. But one of the pukka guest rooms. One with a nice big, soft bed and feather pillows and a quilt to wrap ourselves up in.'

We checked out three rooms on the top floor before finding a large bedroom at the front of the house with a four-poster bed. Neither of us could believe it. A real four-poster! I had never seen one in the flesh before. It was the sort of thing you saw in period dramas on TV, or at the flicks. It was covered with a canopy and had drapes at the four corners. And judging by the way it creaked when we threw ourselves on it, it could have been a genuine antique. It almost sucked us down into its bosom, with the soft-sprung mattress positively enveloping us.

The curtains were open, and light from the street flooded in. Somewhere above the rooftops I could see an almost full moon rising into a diamond-studded sky. But we were driven now. Pulling clothes off each other, discarding them carelessly on the floor. And then I felt her skin on mine, smooth and cool, like a thousand tiny electric shocks. I am not sure I have ever felt quite so hopelessly aroused – so lost in lust and the moment – that my brain seemed to have given up on all rational thought.

Over the years I have read many accounts of young men and women losing their virginity. For the most part they seem to have been fumbling, frustrating encounters that ended prematurely, often in pain and blood. Perhaps it was Rachel's experience that saved us from that.

Because of the complete disconnect between me and my brain, she was in total control. In as much as our passion would allow. And she almost forced me to wait, and savour. To linger over our kisses, holding my head to her breasts, urging me to bite, then pulling my head away when there was too much pain, before drawing me to her again to salve teeth marks with my lips and tongue.

All my primitive sexual instincts wanted me simply to be inside her. But she made me wait for that, teaching me instead that we could give and receive as much pleasure with our mouths. Things I would never have known, or thought to do. But which, ultimately, led to the most heightened moment of release when finally I was inside her, feeling her grip me with her muscles as my hips rose and fell to the most ancient rhythm known to mankind.

I can't imagine what kind of noise we must have made, but we were unrestrained in giving voice to our passion, and neither of us cared.

When it was over, we lay breathless and sweating, wrapped

in each other's arms, a tangle of legs. Kissing and whispering words that came without thought.

'I love you.' Had I really said that? It sounded like me, but I had no idea where it came from. After all, what could I possibly know about love? I was barely seventeen and had just lost my virginity to a girl I'd known for two days.

She said, 'Shhhh,' and held my head and kissed me. 'Time enough for that.'

But we had no time even to register the opening of the door before the room was flooded with hard, cold electric light. I turned over quickly on the bed, naked, exposed and feeling horribly vulnerable. Dr Robert stood in the doorway looking at us. We were on top of the bed and so had no way of covering our nakedness. Rachel didn't seem to care. She just lay there, brazenly returning his stare. I wanted to say something, but couldn't think of any words.

There was the slightest lascivious smile about his mouth as he ran his eyes over us and appeared to consider the situation. In the end, all he said was, 'Enjoy,' and pulled the door shut.

CHAPTER TWELVE

I

We were picked up the next morning in a Volkswagen minibus driven by a young man with incredibly long hair. Dr Robert sat up front and we all piled into the rear. As we headed down to the Old Brompton Road he leaned back over his seat. 'Just popping up to Abbey Road to collect some demo tapes, then we'll head out to Bethnal Green and you can meet Johnny.'

Abbey Road, it turned out, was a tree-lined suburban avenue north-west of Regent's Park. Just beyond a zebra crossing our driver pulled off, inching through a sizeable crowd of teenagers standing outside black wrought-iron gates. The gates opened, allowing him into a small parking area outside a white-painted villa. Steps led up to the front door. Above it, a white-glazed panel bore the legend *Abbey Road Studios*.

Dr Robert jumped down on to the tarmac and leaned back in, grinning at us. 'This is where the Beatles record, you know.' And then he laughed at the expressions on our faces. 'It's a bit of a Tardis inside.'

He ran up the steps and into what looked just like a large

suburban villa. Anything less like a recording studio would be hard to imagine, at least from the outside. But when I think back on it now, that zebra crossing we passed must have been the one that appeared in 1969 on the cover of the second-to-last Beatles' album, *Abbey Road*, the four Beatles crossing in single file, Paul's barefoot appearance giving rise to all kinds of rumours, including one that he was dead.

Dr Robert re-emerged clutching several tape boxes, and we headed south to Circus Road, then east towards Wellington Road.

As we crossed Cavendish Avenue, Dr Robert said, 'McCartney's in the process of buying a house here at number seven. Less than ten minutes' walk from the studio. Forty grand, he told me it's going to set him back, and probably as much again for the renovations.'

Rachel said, with a kind of hushed awe, 'You know Paul McCartney?'

His smile was a smug affirmation of our naivety. 'I know lots of people.'

It took us another half-hour to get out to Bethnal Green. The Victoria Hall was to be found, appropriately enough, in Albert Square, and stood in a small patch of neglected gardens surrounded by high-rise council flats. It was a curiously impressive building of black and red brick, built on four levels, with tall arched windows on the first floor and a roof terrace with commanding views of the surrounding area south of the gardens towards the railway. The first leaves were appearing on winter-dead creeper that was gradually spreading its tendrils across the walls, and a green sheen shimmered around towering trees in early bud in the neighbouring gardens. Large, white-lettered graffiti on the wall urged *NUTTERS OUT!* While another scrawl proclaimed *SHIT RULES*.

Dr Robert said, 'The Victoria Hall experiment is not very popular with the locals.'

He led us through the main doors and upstairs to the hall itself. Early-spring sunlight lay in patches across its wooden floor. A drum kit and amplifiers were set up on a low stage at one end, electric guitar and bass leaning against a single manual Vox Continental organ with its distinctive red top, and white sharps on black keys.

At the other end, a door led into what the doctor described as the common room. 'Everyone eats here,' he said.

I noticed a small kitchen opening off one side. There was no one around, but I could hear voices drifting through the building. Someone was singing. Two, or maybe three, voices were involved in some kind of animated conversation. The air was heavy with the sour perfume of body odour, and something else. Something distinctly unpleasant. I noticed huge coloured candles sitting in pools of molten wax all around the floor and on almost every laying surface.

Dr Robert went into the kitchen to put the kettle on. 'Make yourself at home,' he said. 'Or take a wander around. JP should be down shortly, once he's finished his morning consultations.'

Maurie and Jeff went off to examine the group equipment at the far end of the hall, and Luke sat himself down at the table to light a cigarette. He looked distinctly unhappy.

'Want to take a look around?' I asked Rachel.

'Sure,' she said.

And we headed off hand in hand to explore the building.

I had found it almost impossible to keep the smile from my face, or my eyes from hers, all morning. From time to time she had caught me looking at her, and laughed, shaking her head.

'You're like a love-struck puppy dog,' she whispered in my ear in the VW.

And I suppose that's exactly what I was. No doubt, either, who the pack leader was. In contrast to Luke, I couldn't have been happier. The crap of the last few days had receded into obscure corners of my memory, and my whole being was filled and consumed by the presence of Rachel in my life.

We wandered along dark corridors, doors opening off into offices or bedrooms. On one landing, the walls were covered with crudely painted figures, and the place was stinking.

I screwed up my nose. 'What *is* that smell?'

Rachel sniffed the wall and recoiled as if she'd been struck in the face. 'Jesus! That's not paint, it's shit!'

We hurried away in search of fresh air, up narrow stairways, through burned-out pools of light from unexpected windows on dusty landings, until we emerged, blinking, into full sunlight on the roof. A low wall surrounded its black bitumen surface. There were some tattered deckchairs set out around a half-rotten slatted wooden table, and the roof was littered with plastic cups, discarded food wrappings and a thousand cigarette ends.

A figure in a cream robe sat cross-legged on the wall looking out over the garden, upturned hands resting open in his lap, thumbs and middle fingers lightly touching. We couldn't see who it was until he turned at the sound of our voices. Simon Flet. I felt Rachel's hand tightening around mine at the excitement of seeing him. Her reaction stirred feelings of jealousy deep inside me, in spite of Dave's assertions that he was 'queer'.

He was less than pleased to see us. 'What do you want?' His voice was terse, verging on hostile. 'I came up here for some peace and quiet, if you don't mind.'

Rachel said, 'Sorry to interrupt.'

He glared at us. 'You're those kids that Cliff brought to the house. I hope you're not staying long. You're not wanted.'

And he turned away again to resume his meditation. Although what kind of inner peace could ever be attained by such a troubled personality I could not imagine. Rachel pulled a face at me, and it was clear that her infatuation with celebrity had been short-lived. We went back downstairs to the common room and the mugs of hot tea that sat awaiting us on the table.

We arrived almost at the same moment as J. P. Walker. He shuffled in after us, hands sunk deep in his pockets, apparently unaware that there was even anyone there.

'Johnny, these are the kids I told you about on the phone last night,' Dr Robert said.

JP emerged from his private reverie as if someone had just turned on a light in a dark room. His face became immediately animated and his smile was oddly seductive. He stepped forward to shake all our hands.

'Pleased to meet you, boys.' Then, as he spotted Rachel, 'Oh, and girl.'

He wore only a pair of jeans ripped at the knee, and an open-necked, collarless white shirt hanging out at the waist. He was barefoot, a slight man in his middle thirties, with long, thinning brown hair, and the most hypnotic hazel eyes I think I have ever seen. If he looked directly at you, you felt trapped and held by their gaze. It was quite disconcerting. His personality completely overshadowed his modest stature. But there was something about the familiarity of his soft-spoken Glasgow accent that was strangely comforting and removed any sense of intimidation.

Dr Robert said, 'Look, I've got to go. You can get the tube back, boys, whenever you're done here. Central Line to Holborn, Piccadilly to South Ken.' He grinned. 'Have fun.' And he was gone.

JP beamed at us. 'Cliff's probably told you all about us, and what it is I'm looking for.'

'Some kind of improvised theatre,' I said.

He turned smiling eyes of surprise on me. 'Scottish?'

I nodded. 'From Glasgow.'

'Never! I grew up in Shawlands.'

'That's where my dad was born.'

He shook his head. 'What a small bloody world it is. You know, I might have taken up a musical career myself if things had been a little different. Got to Grade Eight on piano at the Ommer School of Music.'

It was my turn to be astonished. 'You're kidding! I went to the Ommer School. In Dixon Avenue.'

'You're not serious!' Those hypnotic eyes opened wide to completely encompass me. He shook my hand again, grasping it in both of his. 'The Ommer School. Man, those sisters were some girls! And it's good to hear the sound of home. I've been away far too long. We'll have to chew the cud sometime, you and me.' He stood back then to survey us all, and his smile faded a little. 'Cliff says you've run away from home.'

We all nodded, and exchanged sheepish glances.

'Do your folks know where you are?'

'No,' I said.

'Well, the least you need to do is call them and let them know you're safe. Promise me you'll do that.'

I glanced at Rachel. 'We will.'

'Why did you do it?'

'Do what?'

'Run away.'

'It's a long story.'

'Listening is what I do for a living.' He grinned.

And we all sat around the table then and told him the whole

sordid tale. My being expelled from school, deciding to run away as a group, being robbed on the first night, and rescuing Rachel from her boyfriend the next.

He listened in grave silence. When we had finished, he said, 'Well, you're getting your education, anyway. Ambition is all very well, but you know, boys, you get nothing for nothing in this world, and people are not always what they seem. You're lucky you landed here, and if things work out I'll be happy to have you help at the hall for as long as you like.'

His eyes raked around the table like searchlights on a dark night, casting a piercing light into hidden places. But then he brought his own darkness to the conversation.

'Word to the wise, though. Your benefactor . . . Dr Robert. He has his virtues, and his uses. But if you take my advice, you'll keep your distance.' Then he smiled again, just as suddenly. 'You can put on a wee show for us tonight. I'll brief you on that later. Meantime, you'd better stay for lunch.'

II

Lunch was weird. One by one the patients and doctors began assembling in the common room. And Dr Robert was right, it was almost impossible to tell which was which. They were universally dishevelled, most of the men with long hair or beards, or both, shabbily dressed and often unwashed. I noticed fingernails bitten to the quick, and others that were long, broken and dirty.

According to a rota pinned on the wall, they took it in turns to prepare the food, but a glance into the kitchen revealed that the rules of hygiene were not necessarily being observed. We were hungry, but we didn't eat much that day.

There was almost an equal number of men and women, ranging in age, I'd say, from early twenties to somewhere in their fifties. Some introduced themselves, some didn't. Some gawped at us with naked curiosity, others ignored us.

Much of the conversation around the table seemed to me to be gibberish, and I was afraid to catch the eye of Rachel or any of the others in case I would start laughing. Which is shocking, when I think back on it now. These were poor souls, most of them, and we should have been counting our blessings.

One middle-aged man held an animated conversation with no one that we could see, gesticulating wildly, voice rising and falling as if in argument. 'Now mathematicians have been debating this for centuries,' he argued. 'Temperance, that's the symbol. Temperance, whether reading in the house or not. And I don't care what you say, but it's the way of the world. It is. Yes, it is. It is. It is.'

Like the needle stuck in a record, he repeated this assertion until it became almost unbearable. And yet nobody else even seemed to hear him. A large man with a full black beard caught my eye, and smiled and winked, and I wondered if he was one of the doctors.

JP himself sat at the end of the table, locked away in some distant inner thoughts, and paid no attention whatsoever to what was going on around him. We might all have been invisible to him, or he to us.

After lunch the residents began clearing the table and washing the dishes and we went into the hall to examine the equipment on the stage. It was good gear. Whoever was financing this group from Bethnal Green had spared no expense.

The hum and crackle of valve-driven amplifiers filled the hall as we powered up, tuning the guitars and shouting at Jeff to shut up as he tried out the kit. In all my years of playing music, drummers were always the noisiest, most annoying and inattentive members of any band. And when they had no kit in front of them, their fingers would tap on any surface to hand, incessantly, as if some inner urge to communicate drove them to beat out a constant, demented tattoo. I can remember being at Jeff's house for dinner with his family when the meal was repeatedly punctuated by Jeff's father, whose almost unconscious admonition to 'Stop tapping, Jeff' was nearly as irritating as the tapping itself.

When we were finally set up and ready, we launched into the set that we would normally perform for the first half of a dance gig. Just to get ourselves back in the groove. The acoustics in the Victoria Hall were good, and we were fresh and full of energy, just because we hadn't played in a while.

In groups of twos and threes the residents of J. P. Walker's experiment in the democracy of madness trooped into the hall and stood listening to us. There is something universal about the communicative power of music. It cuts through all barriers of language and culture, of sanity and lunacy. And we connected that first day with almost everyone at the hall. Someone began dancing, and very soon all of them were. Crazy, wild dancing that transcended the music. And it was exciting to watch. To know that you were doing this to people and that, whatever their mood or depression, whatever their physical or mental problems, they had left them at the door along with their inhibitions. Music made them, and us, free. And one.

JP himself stood watching with interest, a tiny smile playing about pale lips, and I caught the admiration in Rachel's eyes. They were fixed on me and filled with an intensity that released something deeply primal inside me. And I remembered her telling me that she found nothing more arousing than talent.

We had just finished 'Roll over Beethoven', and were counting in to 'She was Just Seventeen', when the most bloodcurdling scream cut us off mid-count. The door into the hall burst open and a middle-aged woman stood there, stark naked and yelling at the top of her voice. Yells interspersed with lung-bursting sobs, then fresh screams.

She was a woman in her forties, breasts like empty sacks, her flesh carried on a small frame like a baby's jumpsuit that was two sizes too big. Her body was smeared with some thick, dark substance, and it didn't take long for the smell of it to tell us what it was. She was covered in her own shit.

'Where's my bottle?' she screamed. 'I want my bottle! Johnny says I've got to have my bottle.'

And she started running around the hall, scattering everyone in her path. No one wanted to go near her. The run turned into a skip, and she began singing some toneless, unrecognizable tune.

I glanced at JP but he made no attempt to intervene. He watched disinterestedly for a moment, then turned to disappear into the common room.

The smell was beginning to fill the hall, and Rachel took refuge on the stage beside us. But the woman stopped right below us, staring at us with wild eyes.

'Why did you stop? Why did you fucking stop?' Her voice was like tearing paper. 'I want to dance. Play! Play!'

I glanced at Jeff and nodded. Anything to get her away from us. He struck his sticks together four times, and we launched into 'I Saw Her Standing There', wishing in fact that she wasn't standing there at all. But she didn't move away. She began writhing and twisting on the spot in the most grotesque and violently malodorous dance I have ever seen. It was all I could do to stop from throwing up.

Then suddenly one of the men who had been at the table during lunch came running out of the common room. A big man, completely bald, all his head hair concentrated in a mass of black beard, and matted curls covering his chest and neck. His arms were spread wide, holding out a large grey blanket which he wrapped around the dancing woman as he reached her, completely engulfing her. I could see in his face his repulsion at the smell. And yet still he held her – against all her kicking, thrashing, screaming protests – until gradually she began to lose impetus, surrendering finally to the hold of his arms, whimpering and sobbing.

A woman emerged from the common room with a baby's bottle filled with milk and handed it to the bearded man, who immediately thrust the teat between the shit-smeared lips of the woman in his grasp. She began sucking on it with a passion, and allowed herself to be led away, distracted and consumed by the feeding process. The remaining residents moved aside, like a parting of the Red Sea, to let them past, then several went running around the hall opening all the windows.

A small, bald man walked up to the front of the stage and grinned at us, revealing two missing front teeth, one top, one bottom. 'That's Alice,' he said. 'The star of the show.' He took a pull on his cigarette, then pushed the tip of it into the cavity in his lower teeth so that it stuck there and moved with his mouth when he spoke. 'She's about six months now.'

'What show?' I said, confused.

'The Victoria Hall show. Johnny's prize patient. Stripped back to the womb, and growing again to childhood.' He closed his lips around the cigarette and sucked in smoke. 'Gets all the fucking attention!' He turned and stomped across the hall back to the common room.

Not for the first time, I had been unable to discern whether this was a doctor or a patient. A distinction, I was to learn, as fine as that between madness and sanity.

I turned to look at the others, and saw in their faces the trepidation that I felt. None of us was sure that this was a gig we really wanted.

III

The hall was so big and dark that the few candles carried by shadowy figures barely made an impression. Joss sticks burned in unseen corners, filling the air with a sweet, pungent scent. I was aware of bodies all around us, forming a large, loose circle. Four of us moved slowly around its interior circumference. Me and Maurie and Luke and Dave. And Rachel. She had insisted on being a part of it.

She'd had a bad afternoon, slowly succumbing to the shakes and an insidious itching that had her scratching her arms and scalp. There was nothing I could do to comfort her, and in the end JP led her away mid-briefing, an arm around her shoulder, his voice soft and filled with reassurance. When he brought her back half an hour later, she had been calm, almost serene, and I was torn between jealousy and relief, wondering if he had given her medication, or whether it was the power of his personality that had triumphed over her craving.

Now she was back to normal, if any of this could have been described as normal.

Suddenly, a rectangle of yellow light fell from the door of the common room, cutting through the crowd and extending to the back of the hall. A man stumbled through it. A silhouette.

And although we couldn't see his face, we could feel his confusion.

It was our cue to surround him, the wider circle closing around us as we did so. We were close enough in the dark now to touch and smell him, and I pushed him as instructed into Luke's arms. Luke immediately spun him round, passing him on to Maurie, Dave, Rachel and then me. Round and round our tight little circle. His body relaxing into trust, growing heavier as it did, his momentum preventing him from falling. Faster and faster, as we ourselves moved round the bodies that encircled us. Until a crack like a gunshot was our signal to stand back.

Both inner and outer circles moved out from the centre, like rings of water from a pebble tossed in a pond. And the man dropped to the floor, crouching on his knees. The bearers of the candles moved in to create a circle of light around him, and he got unsteadily to his feet, dizzy and confused after all his spinning.

Another figure stepped into the circle, a sweep of white robe swirling around him as he turned to reveal himself in the flickering light. A young man, face powdered white, his lipsticked mouth a slash of red. He wore a felt hat with a toy parrot affixed to the top of it. Although I knew it was Jeff, I would never have recognized him. He cut a dramatic, half-comic, half-scary figure.

I could see the light of fear in the eyes of the man in the centre of the circle as Jeff drew a pistol from beneath his robes and pointed it straight at his head. The man raised his hands, as if somehow he believed they could stop the bullets.

'No!' he shouted. 'No! No!'

But Jeff held his arm straight and steady, a slow smile spreading itself across his face. He was enjoying this. Then, very slowly, he began to lower the gun, still at the end of a ramrod-straight arm, until the barrel of it was pointing directly at the man's crotch.

He was very nearly hysterical now. Screaming at Jeff. Urging him not to shoot. Hands grasping his crotch as he bent himself almost double.

Then, *Bang! Bang! Bang!* Jeff fired three times, and the man's scream ripped through the darkness like a knife through flesh. He collapsed, whimpering, to the floor, clutching his private parts, rolling back and forth, moaning and weeping.

Almost immediately, several figures detached themselves from the crowd and stepped forward to lift him to his feet, hurrying him away through the yellow glow of the common room as the lights in the hall itself snapped on to leave us blinking in their sudden glare, pale startled faces all around, like floating Chinese lanterns.

JP stood by the door, a solitary figure whose lone clap resounded around the rafters. 'Bravo! Bravo!' he shouted. Then, 'Time to eat.'

As at lunch, we ate very little. But there was wine on the table, a seemingly unending supply of it, and we drank to lose ourselves. It had been the strangest of days.

The coloured candles in their pools of melted wax burned all around the common room, sending the shadows of the diners dancing across the walls. A pile of albums played on a Dansette record player on the sideboard, and the sounds of the Beatles and the Beach Boys, the Kinks and the King thickened the smoke-filled air. The man at the centre of the evening's little drama seemed perfectly recovered from the shots to his crotch, and he ate and drank hungrily. Jeff had washed and changed, but a residue of lipstick left his mouth unnaturally red, and he looked strangely feminine.

Rachel and I flanked JP, but it was Rachel who had the courage to ask what I had only wondered.

She was blunt and to the point. 'What was all that about tonight?'

JP's smile, it seemed, always reached his eyes, and he appeared genuinely amused. He kept his voice low, beneath the hubbub around the table, and said, 'Richard suffers from what I can only describe as castration anxiety. Several months of psychotherapy have made very little progress. So tonight was an experiment of last resort. A kind of shock therapy to make him confront the illusory nature of his anxiety. Not to put too fine a point on it, Jeff blew his balls off. Or so he thought, or feared. Now he'll have to deal with the fact that his testicles are still intact, and that his fears are groundless.' He nodded acknowledgement to the possibility of failure. 'Only time will tell if it has worked or not.' He looked at each of us in turn. 'That's what the Victoria Hall experiment is all about.

Taking an unconventional, non-pharmaceutical approach to problems that conventionally would be treated with drugs.'

His eyes sparkled, and I felt his excitement.

When the food was finished more wine was opened, joints were rolled and passed around the table. The residual excitement of the earlier drama was gradually dispelled, and the mood became more mellow. I noticed for the first time that there was no sign of Alice, or the big, bald, bearded man who had pulled her away.

'Tell us a story, Johnny,' one of the women implored. 'Tell us a story.'

'I've told enough stories to last a lifetime,' JP said. 'Someone else's turn.'

An expectant silence settled itself around the table, and for a time it seemed as if no one was going to step up to the mark.

Then a dapper man in a white shirt and slacks pushed round tortoiseshell glasses back up the bridge of his nose and leaned into the table. 'I'll tell you a story.'

He had a lazy, North American drawl, and the streaks of steely silver through Brillo-pad hair made me think that he could be in his forties or fifties, which seemed very old to me then.

He pulled on one side of his short, wiry moustache. 'This was when Johnnie and I were on that speaking tour of the States last year.'

All eyes turned towards him, and he seemed momentarily discomfited by the spotlight. But he quickly regained his composure.

'Everyone knows what a hard time they gave us. The Institute of American Psychiatrists weren't just sceptical. They were abusive. They were rude. They took every opportunity to criticize us in the press, to debunk our research and our papers. They sent hecklers to all our speaking engagements. It was like trying to bring enlightenment to the Dark Ages. After all, these people still believed in electric shock therapy and lobotomies. They were like witch doctors.'

His passion was clear, and I glanced at JP to see how he was reacting. But he was giving little away, lounging back in his chair, one bare foot up on the table, and a tiny enigmatic smile playing about his lips as he pulled on his joint.

'Anyway, we were somewhere in the Midwest. Ohio or someplace, I don't really remember. And they laid this ambush for us. A kind of challenge they knew that Johnny would have to accept but could never win.

'They were waiting for us after the event that night. A group of psychiatrists from a local mental institution. Throwing themselves on our mercy, they said. But it was no coincidence that the press was waiting for us when we got there. The problem they claimed they were seeking Johnny's help with was a young woman in a deeply psychotic state. She was locked up in a padded cell for her own safety. Refused to wear any clothes, and hadn't spoken, quite literally, to anyone for more than six months. They had tried all sorts of shit with her and nothing worked. She was catatonic.

'So we looked at her through the glass in the door. And she's sitting there, cross-legged on the floor, staring at the wall. Someone says she hasn't moved from that position since she performed her last toilet. And Johnny says, "Let me in." So they do. When the door closes behind him, he starts taking off his clothes. "What the fuck!" they say, and I have to stop them going in to pull him out again.

'Johnny puts all his clothes in a neat pile in one corner and goes and sits cross-legged on the floor beside her. He doesn't say a thing. Doesn't even look at her. Just sits there. Half an hour goes past. Forty minutes. Then after about three-quarters of an hour, I see her half turn her head to look at him. He continues to ignore her. By the time we're an hour in she's staring at him. Then suddenly she reaches out and touches his face and says, "What's wrong?" Within fifteen minutes they are telling each other their life stories.'

The storyteller grinned in the candlelight.

'Totally backfired on them. Press the next day was full of how Johnny had brought this woman out of catatonia in an hour, when the local psychiatrists had failed to get through to her in six months.'

There was a ripple of delighted applause around the table.

JP tipped himself even further back in his chair and said, 'I was only after her body.'

Which provoked a roar of laughter. As it died away, so did his smile.

'Trouble is, most psychiatrists like the sound of their own voices too much. It's what the patient has to say that's important. Listening is the virtue.'

And I thought how true that was. Not just of psychiatrists and their patients. But of everyone, in any relationship. And it wasn't too long before I wished it was a lesson I had put into practice sooner myself.

We never got back to South Kensington that night. We were drunk on wine and high on dope. And by the time we realized the hour, the last tube train had already gone. So everyone went off to find himself a spot to curl up and sleep for the night. Rachel and I were about to make our way up to the roof when Maurie insinuated himself between us.

'I want a word with Jack,' he said.

I hesitated, sensing the danger in his voice, then nodded to Rachel. She sighed theatrically and went to wait for me in the common room. Maurie's voice was low and tight, and his fingers held me by the fleshy part of my upper arm, bruising me, I was sure.

'I told you, Jack. She's not for you.'

I looked into his eyes for a long time, trying to find some reason in them for this obsessive protection of his cousin. But all I saw was hostility. 'Yeah, you did.'

We stared each other out for a very long moment before I pulled my arm free and went off into the common room to find Rachel and take her up to the roof.

The weather had changed during the course of this spring day, a shift of season, and the night air was positively balmy up there. Like a summer's evening. You could smell the blossom and the scent of leaves bursting out of their buds, and from somewhere the perfume of lilac, sweet and cloying. It was a fragrance I had always associated with the arrival of summer, burgeoning invisibly from the lilac tree that grew outside my bedroom window at home.

We lay back in the deckchairs, gazing up at the sky, and I forced myself to stop thinking about Maurie.

'What did he give you?' I said.

'Who?'

'JP. This afternoon when you got the shakes.'

I sensed her hesitation in the dark, her reluctance to tell me.

'I don't know,' she said finally. 'But whatever it was I felt better after it.' More hesitation. Then, 'I think he might be an addict.'

I sat up, startled. 'What makes you say that?'

'The needle marks on his left arm.' Maybe she felt my disappointment, because after a moment she added, 'But who knows? Maybe he's just diabetic.'

I lay back again in the deckchair and gazed at the cosmos, lost in its vastness, my mind drawn to all those pinpoints of light like a moth to a million flames. 'You ever wonder what's out there?'

I turned to see her shake her head.

'I never do. What's out there . . . well, we'll probably never know. And chances are we wouldn't understand it even if we did. I only ever worry about what's in here.' She put a hand on her breast, and turned her head to meet my eye.

'And what's in there?'

'A day or two ago I couldn't have told you.'

'And now?'

Her smile was pale and washed with moonlight. 'You,' she said. 'You're in there. Filling the big empty void that used to be me. Filling it up with something better. Something good.'

While I might have whispered 'I love you' in the throes of passion the night before, I knew now in my heart that I meant it. Whatever it was, whatever it did to me, however long it would last, I knew it was what I felt. I eased myself out of the deckchair and took her hand. She stood up, then, and we kissed. And the big furry coat my old headmaster had thrown at me that day in his office got laid out on the bitumen. Our bed for the night, and the cushioning beneath us as we made love again, this time under the stars, as if all of eternity had existed to create only this moment.

CHAPTER THIRTEEN

I

It's funny how the bizarre nature of that first experience at the Victoria Hall became not only familiar, but routine. In the next month or so we fell into a pattern of time spent between Dr Robert's house in Kensington and the dafties at Bethnal Green. I use the word 'daftie' in that fond, Scottish way that is not meant to offend. Because, in fact, all of us very quickly ceased to think of the residents of the hall as dafties at all. The norm became extended to include what had, at first, seemed outrageously abnormal.

However, smearing yourself and the walls with shit was never going to be acceptable, and everyone at the hall was hugely relieved when JP gave Alice the gift of paint. Using her shit to draw on the walls was, he said, her way of giving expression to her inner self. Literally. But paint very quickly became an acceptable substitute, and across the course of those weeks we saw a marked change in her. Paint became her new medium of communication. JP had acquired from somewhere a huge roll of newsprint, and Alice would tear off great lengths of it to hang from the walls all around the hall and paint. Fantastical, colourful creations with their own narratives. Figures in distress, making love, fighting. Jesus. God. The Virgin Mary.

The hall received frequent visitors – actors, pop stars, writers, artists – and Dr Robert seemed to know them all. He was everybody's friend. And we were treated as equals by residents and visitors alike. More than once I found myself sitting in conversation with people I had only previously seen on television, or the big screen. As if I were one of them. I saw Richard Burton one time. And Audrey Hepburn another. And had a very stoned conversation with Brian Jones. Gradually I came to see that, for all their fame and celebrity, they were just like us, with all the same fears and insecurities. Knowing that, oddly, had the effect of decreasing mine, and I found myself growing in confidence and maturity.

A BBC documentary crew came and filmed at the hall for several days. I never saw the film they made, but I suppose that somewhere in the vaults of the corporation there still remain some dusty old reels of film, recording for posterity a little of the flavour of that time we spent at Bethnal Green.

The group played often for both residents and visitors, always drawing applause and getting people on their feet to dance. JP himself never danced, but would often stand by the door, watching the dancers with a curious smile on his face.

He asked me once if I didn't perceive dancing as being a little strange.

I said I didn't.

And he said, 'What if you couldn't hear the music?'

I didn't see how that was possible. My head was always filled with the stuff.

He smiled that enigmatic smile of his and said, 'Nietzsche once observed that those who were seen dancing were thought to be insane by those who could not hear the music. It's a fun thought, don't you think?'

And I don't believe I have ever seen dancers in quite the same way since.

Dr Robert promised he would set up a recording session so that we could make demo tapes. Not at Abbey Road, but at a tiny four-track studio above the Marquee Club in Soho where, he said, he knew one of the engineers. But he also said we had to start writing our own songs, just as the young man who might have been John Lennon advised us on our first day in London.

So Luke and I spent hours in the basement flat at Onslow Gardens with an acoustic guitar and the melodica trying to write songs. I suppose that was probably the first time in my life that I really bumped up against my own limitations. We both did. Luke had an extraordinary talent, and I was reasonably accomplished on the guitar, but it was one thing to copy others, another to be original. Writing songs was the hardest thing either of us had ever attempted. It required something else. Something more. Something deeper. And the more we tried, the more aware we became that we simply didn't have it.

Strangely, it was Dave who came up with the best song during those frustrating, sometimes fiery sessions, when we took our lack of talent out on each other, as if the fault might lie outside rather than inside of us. He turned up one afternoon with lyrics scribbled on a sheet of paper. It was the story of our running away. Unsurprisingly, he'd called it 'Runaway'. They were simple, narrative lyrics, quite unlike the derivative love-and-loss stories that Luke and I had been playing with.

I never had a lot of friends, truth is I didn't want them.
Was a lonely kid in my own little world, all I did was suck my thumb.

The whole song was built around three chords. G, C and D, with a repeating chorus of *Run, Run, Runaway, Run-Runaway*.

I can just about remember now how the melody went. But the song itself was never finished, and never recorded, so I have nothing to bring it back, except for the haziest recollection of sun slanting down from high windows in a smoke-filled room, and the all-pervasive smell of damp.

I took JP's advice and contacted my parents. I didn't have the courage to telephone, so I wrote them a short letter to say that I was okay. That we were all okay, and that I would be in touch when things had settled down. It was hard to find the right words, and so it was the briefest of notes. Cruel, when they must have been so hungry for news. I had no real sense then of what I was putting them through. Only with the passage of time, and graduating to parenthood myself, was I able to imagine their pain, and realize how selfish and thoughtless I had been.

I just lost myself in Rachel during those weeks. Immersing myself in my obsession for her, burying my head in the sands of our relationship and ignoring the real world that one day I knew I was going to have to face. We made love often, sometimes several times a day. The bedroom with the four-poster bed became ours by default. Dr Robert never mentioned the night that he found us there, but each week when the girl came to clean we would find that our sheets had been changed.

We often lay for hours at night just talking, learning everything there was to know about each other. Childhood adventures, teachers at school, first kisses. Rows with parents. Best friends, worst enemies. Hopes, dreams, jealousies, fantasies. For the first time I felt that I was actually absorbing another person into the very fabric of myself. I got to know every physical and mental contour of this girl who had so bewitched me. We each began to anticipate what the other would say before we said it, and then laughed when we did, both knowing that the other already understood. For perhaps the only time in my life I didn't feel alone in the universe.

Conversely, my relationship with Maurie was deteriorating almost daily. He could scarcely bring himself to speak to me. Rachel and I made no secret of our relationship, or the fact that we were sleeping together in that upstairs room, and it all came to a head one evening when I interrupted an argument between Maurie and Rachel in Dr Robert's sitting room. I don't know where the others were, but I had gone upstairs looking for Rachel. And when I found that she wasn't in our room, I came back down to hear raised voices. Rachel's was shrill and distressed, Maurie's little more than a low growl.

As I walked into the room Maurie was snapping at her, 'Don't you dare tell him!'

'Tell who what?'

They were both startled by my unexpected arrival, perhaps wondering just how much I'd heard. Which was almost nothing.

Rachel stared for a long hard moment at her cousin. 'Doesn't matter,' she said, and she turned and ran out of the room, brushing past me as she hurried into the hall.

I heard her footsteps on the stairs. 'What the hell's going on, Maurie?'

He turned on me, almost puce with anger. 'I told you to stay away from her.'

His anger fired mine. 'And I told you, it's none of your fucking business.'

'She's my cousin!'

'So bloody what? That doesn't give you the right to tell her who she can and can't be with. She's her own person. Entitled to make her own decisions without reference to you.'

He took a step towards me, his whole body conveying barely restrained violence. 'Stay away from her.'

'Why the hell should I?'

'Because you're not Jewish!' He almost shouted it.

I could hardly have been more startled if he had physically hit me.

'What?' I could hardly believe it. Religion had never been an issue – at least, not one that I had been aware of. 'Oh, don't be such a Yid,' I said, knowing that would hurt him.

His simmering anger burst into full-blown fury. He came at me. Grabbing me by the collar and pushing me back towards the doorway. Almost full into Simon Flet, who was just emerging from the darkness of the hall.

His anger stopped us in our tracks. 'What the hell do you think you boys are playing at?' It was extraordinary how bad temper could turn such a handsome face ugly. 'This is not some pub where you can go about brawling and swearing. And who told you that you could come into Cliff's private apartments when he's not here?'

Neither of us knew what to say and we stood, chastened, like naughty schoolboys.

'Really! If you're going to be here at all – and I hope that won't be for very much longer – then stay down in the basement, unless otherwise invited.' He turned and glared at me. 'And *you* might like to rethink your sleeping arrangements. This is not a brothel.'

I am sure I blushed. And I glanced nervously at Maurie, whose face was like stone.

'Now get out!'

I didn't dare go upstairs immediately, so I went back down to the basement with Maurie. He went straight to his room, and I sat nursing my resentment on the settee. I waited half an hour before creeping back up to our second-floor room to find Rachel standing by the window, staring out over the rooftops, arms folded across her chest.

She neither turned nor waited for me to speak, pre-empting my question with a curt, 'Don't even ask.'

And we never spoke about it again.

II

Sometimes, when Simon wasn't there, all six of us would sit in the evenings with Dr Robert in that first-floor living room watching TV and smoking dope. One time we saw J. P. Walker on a late-night current affairs programme talking about the Victoria Hall experiment, and it felt odd to be watching someone we knew up there on the television screen. It probably increased our illusion of being at the centre of things. And an illusion it was. For we were going nowhere fast. Treading water in a deep, dark pond that would eventually suck us down and drown us.

That was also the night, I'm sure, when Dr Robert told us that JP's personal life was a mess. How he'd sacrificed his marriage on the altar of his career, losing his wife and family to separation and then divorce.

'He's a wreck of a man, really,' he said. 'How he manages

to work through other people's problems when he can't even deal with his own, I'll never know.' He was half sitting, half lying in a leather armchair, legs extended, sucking on a joint. 'He's on medication for depression.' He grinned. 'I should know. I write his prescriptions.'

Which seemed to me a breach of medical ethics and his Hippocratic oath. I think that was when I finally decided that I really didn't like Dr Robert.

But the most worrying thing during those weeks was the sense that we were losing Jeff. From that first night, when Jeff had seen rainbows coming out of the walls, he was lost to LSD. I think maybe Maurie and Dave took it again a few times, but Jeff couldn't get enough of it. And Dr Robert, it seemed, made sure he had all he wanted. It released something in Jeff, some inner sense of himself that he'd never been aware of before. He had always been the poor performer at school, the runt of the intellectual litter. I suppose that nowadays the therapists would say he had low self-esteem, and that his extrovert, often brash, behaviour was a compensation for that. Well, with acid, he didn't require compensation. He'd found something beautiful, he said. A part of himself that he never knew existed.

But it changed him. And not in a good way. He no longer felt a part of the group, either to us or himself. He frequently failed to turn up for practice at the hall and spent more and more time with Dr Robert. They would often go out together in taxis, or on the tube. It wasn't that he was secretive about where they went, he just believed it was none of our business.

And increasingly Dr Robert appeared to be exerting an almost Svengali-like influence on him.

We had a council of war one day. Me and Luke, and Dave and Maurie. We were losing Jeff, and we knew it couldn't go on like this. Maurie was taking it the hardest. They had been so close all through their childhood years, sharing everything. Hopes, dreams, ambitions, thoughts. For Maurie it was almost as if Jeff had died. And although Maurie and I were still barely speaking, Rachel told me that he was becoming increasingly depressed. While he and Jeff shared a room, it seemed that the two of them hardly ever talked any more.

But as far as the group was concerned, we were losing our drummer, and so it was agreed that Maurie should speak to Jeff that night, raise our concerns with him, and try to bring him back into the fold.

The four of us, and Rachel, sat about in the basement flat smoking nervously, waiting for Jeff to get home. We had returned from Bethnal Green late in the afternoon and there was no sign of him. He had left no word of where he was, and Dr Robert was not around to ask.

It was almost nine before he finally appeared, and I guess he must have sensed the atmosphere the moment he came in. He hesitated, almost imperceptibly, by the door when he came down to the flat, glancing around the room with a kind of dead-eyed disinterest. Even from where I was sitting I could see how dilated his pupils were.

'Hey, guys,' he said, and went straight through to the bedroom.

We sat in silence for several moments, none of us wanting to look at Maurie. Finally he eased himself out of his chair and I saw how pale he was. Apprehension filled his eyes. He followed with heavy steps in Jeff's wake.

I suppose we had always known it would not turn out well, but the moment had come when we couldn't let it go any longer. There was an elephant in the room and the time had arrived to acknowledge it. Though none of us had anticipated just how badly it would go.

At first we heard only a murmur of conversation. Then Maurie's voice raised in anger, though we couldn't hear what it was he said.

Then silence. Followed almost immediately by more raised voices.

And finally, clear as a bell, Jeff shouting, 'You're just jealous!'

'Jealous?' Maurie sounded both hurt and angry. 'What have I got to be jealous of?'

A loud crash brought us all to our feet. We exchanged glances, but nobody moved.

The door to the bedroom flew open and we heard Jeff screaming, 'You're just a stupid little bunch of fucking wankers. No talent, no future. Grow up, go home!' And he stalked from the hall into the sitting room. He stood and glared at us in turn, the strangest look in his eyes, before turning and slamming out on to the stairs and running up to the first floor.

It was a long time before Maurie came out into the smoke-laden silence of that basement living room. He didn't say anything. Just dropped himself into his seat and lit another cigarette. But I would swear to this day that there were tears in his eyes.

The other thing that became only too apparent during those weeks was that Dr Robert and Simon Flet were lovers.

When he wasn't on set, Flet spent all his time at the house, often prowling the stairs and hallways, reciting mumbled lines of dialogue and growling at any of us that he came across. He was a thoroughly objectionable individual, and I never met anyone who had a good word to say about him. But that he and Dr Robert were obsessed by each other was obvious to everyone.

They shared a bedroom and breakfasted together in the kitchen, spending evenings, when Flet was free, smoking and drinking up on the roof terrace. They went to film premiers and West End shows together, and often dined out, returning in the small hours, tipsy and giggling and barely able to contain themselves until they got to the bedroom.

Flet never made any pretence of the fact that he hated our presence in the house. He was openly rude to us, individually and collectively, and it was apparent that he was deeply jealous of his lover's relationship with Jeff. A relationship that was not clear to anyone, least of all us.

I knew that there was a showdown looming when I heard them arguing one day. I was coming down the stairs from the top floor, and as I approached the first-floor landing I could hear their voices coming from the doctor's study.

'I won't put up with it any longer, Cliff. I won't. They're horrible. Unwashed. Rude. Scottish! I don't know why you insist on keeping them here.'

Dr Robert laughed. 'Scottish? Is that a pejorative term, these days?'

'They're uncouth. Common as dirt. They contaminate this house with their language and their music, and that boy and girl fucking every night up on the top floor. Honest to God, why do you put up with it?'

Dr Robert's voice was soothing, persuasive. 'They have their uses, Sy. And when their usefulness runs its course, they'll be gone. I promise you.' A pause. 'Come here . . .'

Flet's petulant voice came back at him. 'You can't win me over like that.'

I could hear the amusement in Dr Robert's voice. 'Oh yes I can.'

I didn't like to imagine what they were doing, and tiptoed across the landing to hurry silently down the stairs, wondering just what our 'usefulness' was, and how long it might be before it ran its course.

But everything else was pre-empted by the bomb that Rachel dropped suddenly and unexpectedly into the mix. Its detonation destroyed us, ruining the rest of my life, and was probably the single most influential factor in precipitating the tragedy to come.

CHAPTER FOURTEEN

I

We hadn't made love that night, and I had not questioned it. She had been moody and distant for some days, and I had assumed it was just her time of the month. But as we lay in bed, in the dark, side by side, not even touching, I sensed something more. Something much bigger. And because I couldn't see it, the presence it created was almost frightening.

It grew in my mind until it took over my entire consciousness. I became aware of her slow, impatient breathing. I knew she was not asleep, but neither did I feel her to be there in our bed. Not really. She was somewhere a long way away, and I had never felt so separated from her in all our weeks together.

For the longest time I lay looking at the light from outside lying across the ceiling, divided and subdivided by the frames of the windows. Until I could stand it no longer. I rolled my head to one side on the pillow. She was staring straight up with her eyes wide open, gathering as they always did all the light that there was in the room. I could see it reflected somewhere deep in their inaccessible darkness.

'What's wrong?'

There was neither a flicker of her eyelids, nor any indication in her face that she had heard me. And she made no reply for so long that I began to believe that she hadn't. I was about to ask again when she said, 'I'm pregnant.'

And I felt the bottom fall out of my world.

I sat up immediately. 'You can't be!'

'I am.' Her voice was flat and emotionless.

'But we take precautions.'

'No. I take precautions. You take it for granted.'

We had never used condoms. She told me that first night that she had a diaphragm. I had no idea what that was, but she said I didn't have to worry about it. And I never had.

'Then, how . . .?'

'I have no idea. Nothing is a hundred per cent safe.'

I had heard of women trapping their men by deliberately getting themselves pregnant. But I didn't believe that of Rachel for one second. She had no need to trap me. I was unequivocally hers. And we were just seventeen. Having babies wasn't even a distant shadow of desire on our horizon. Neither of us would have wanted that. We were little more than children ourselves.

At first I simply couldn't believe it. There had to be some mistake.

'Are you sure?' Then clutching at straws, 'Are you sure it's mine?' I withered under the gaze she turned on me.

'Yes, and yes.' That flat, toneless voice again.

'Have you seen a doctor?'

'Yes.'

'Who?'

'Dr Robert arranged it privately.'

I was stabbed by a spike of jealousy. 'You mean you told him before you told me?'

'There was nothing to tell. I didn't know until I had the test.'

I reached over to switch on the bedside lamp. And by its harsh yellow light, I saw that her face was bloodless. She lay like a ghost beside me on the bed and wouldn't meet my eye.

'Jesus!' I dropped my face into my hands. 'Jesus! What are we going to do?'

I saw my whole life vanishing like smoke in the wind. Everything I had dreamed of doing, of being. And fatherhood had never figured on that list, nor any of the responsibilities that went with it. A job, a flat, a weekly rental. A mortgage if I was lucky. Nights spent stuck at home, building my life around TV schedules. I had watched it happen to my parents. Two weeks on a cold beach somewhere in the summer, a lumpy bed in a cheap guesthouse, and a baby that kept you up half the night. It was my worst nightmare.

'What do you want to do?' she said.

'I don't know.' My voice rose involuntarily, out of my control. Panic, I suppose. 'How the hell should I know? Jesus Christ, why weren't you more careful?'

'Why weren't you?' I heard the hurt in her voice.

'Because you said you were taking care of it.' I turned to look at her. 'You don't really want to have a baby, do you?'

'I didn't want to get pregnant, if that's what you mean.'

'Fuck!' My voice resounded around the room, and the silence that followed it was deafening.

I fell back, staring up at the ceiling again, and felt the movement of her head as she turned to look at me for the first time. I let my head fall to the side to meet her gaze, and what I saw there was so painful I almost cried out. I suppose, when I think about it now, it must simply have been a reflection of what she saw in me. My fear, my selfishness, my total lack of concern for her or the baby she had conceived. Our baby. And I think I saw her disappointment, too. The realization that I was not, and never would be, the man she had hoped for. All the illusions we had constructed around each other, falling away like so much scaffolding to reveal the ugly reality of the buildings beneath. Just two kids hooked on each other, on having sex and a good time. And one of us, at least, neither ready nor willing to give up his dreams.

I was a mess of emotions, unable to think clearly. And so I clutched at what she said next like a drowning man grabbing for a piece of driftwood.

'I could get rid of it.'

I was so naive, I hadn't the least idea what she was talking about. But they were words that brought the first crack of light to the darkness of my nightmare.

'What do you mean?'

'There are ways to abort a baby, if you catch it early enough.'

'Abortion?' I had heard of it, of course, although I wasn't at all clear what it involved. But one thing I did know. 'It's illegal, isn't it?'

She sucked in her lower lip, biting down on it, and nodded.

I was confused. 'Well, how's that possible, then?'

'There are women who will do it. For money.'

All the light in her eyes was reflected in the tears that gathered in them. I know now that what she wanted with all of her heart was for me to say no. That I couldn't possibly put her through some backstreet abortion, that the idea of killing our baby was reprehensible to me and not even a consideration. Every hope, or dream, or illusion she'd ever had about me hung right there, in that room, in that moment. And all I could see was a way out for me. A way to get my life back. Blind and selfish.

I can find all sorts of excuses now for how I was then. Young. Ignorant. Naive. Insensitive. Incapable of seeing the big picture. Lacking the maturity and empathy to understand how it must have been for Rachel. But that's all they are. Excuses. She saw me in that moment for what I was, and I guess in that moment, too, she stopped loving me. And how I wish with every ounce of my being that I could reel back time and change it. Change me. Change the words that next came out of my mouth.

'How much would it cost?'

II

We never discussed it again, and the only person I confided in was Luke. He was more shocked by the idea of an abortion than he was by the news that Rachel was pregnant.

We were in the basement flat, just the two of us, and he immediately closed the door to the stairs. He lowered his voice, and I have rarely seen such intensity in his eyes.

'You can't do it, Jack. You can't let her have an abortion.'

'It wasn't my idea.'

Already my guilt was leading me to blame her. I was in denial, and Luke knew it. He took me by the shoulders, and for a moment I thought he was going to physically shake me.

'You can't do it.' He pronounced each word like a separate sentence. 'Jack, you'll regret it for the rest of your life.'

I pulled away from him. 'I don't need your judgement. I need your support.'

'I'm not judging you, Jack. I'm telling you. It's not too late, you can stop this.'

I didn't know it then, but things were already in train. The first I learned about it was when Dr Robert took me aside after breakfast one morning. Rachel had been avoiding me for days. Maurie had leapt to the conclusion that we had split up, and was happier than I had seen him in weeks. Almost gloating, glibly unaware of what had created the rift between us.

But it wasn't just me that Rachel was avoiding. It was everyone. She had gone back to sleeping in the single bedroom in the basement flat, while I had stayed upstairs in the big room, sprawling sleeplessly in the big empty four-poster, hoping against hope that one night the door would open and she would slip in beside me to tell me she still loved me, and that everything was going to be alright.

The others had already trooped out to the waiting VW minibus when Dr Robert called me into a downstairs lounge. It was a room I had never been in before. A room overcrowded with antique furniture, every shelf and surface playing host to framed photographs of what must have been the doctor's family. His parents. Brothers and sisters, or perhaps cousins, since he was the only one who seemed to have inherited. Aunts and uncles. Grandparents. Black and white images of dead people, locked away in this forgotten room that was never used.

He closed the door carefully behind us. Through the window behind him I could see the VW waiting for me in the street.

'Rachel tells me you want her to get an abortion.'

My hackles rose immediately. 'I never said that.'

He sighed impatiently. 'Well, do you or don't you?'

It was decision time, and still I couldn't bring myself to say it. Perhaps I was figuring that if I just went with the flow I wouldn't have to blame myself. I shrugged, paralysed by indecision.

Irritation crept into his voice. 'Look, I can fix it, or we can drop it. Up to you. I know someone who knows a woman in Stepney. A former nurse. She'll do a good professional job. But it'll cost.'

'How much?'

'A lot.'

'I don't have any money.'

He shook his head. 'No, you don't.' He sighed again. 'I'll lend you it. But you're going to have to pay me back.'

'How?'

'There are always ways you can earn it. We can talk about that later.'

I felt like I was standing on the edge of a precipice. One step forward and I would fall, irretrievably, into the big black hole of regret. And yet stepping back just didn't seem like an option. I reached out, clutching at straws, desperately searching for some way to avoid the decision.

'How safe is it?'

'Safe?' Dr Robert very nearly laughed. 'There's no such thing as safe. Women die in childbirth. Everything in life has risk, Jack. Everything we do. Abortion is no different. Are there risks? Yes. Is it riskier than going full term? Yes. But these are the choices we make.'

The driver of the minibus peeped his horn, and I felt something like panic rising in my chest.

'Well?'

I drew a deep breath and nodded. The die was cast.

III

The morning that we took the taxi to that crumbling red-brick terraced house at 23A Ruskin Avenue will probably rate as the worst and most shameful of my life. Several days of fine, warm weather had seen the trees of West London spring into full leaf. The air was balmy, warm and laden with the scent of early summer. The fact that the sun rose into the clearest of blue skies seemed only to mock our misery. A bruised and weeping sky on a bleak, cold day would have provided a much more appropriate backdrop for what I can only see now as an act of murder and betrayal. I was the perpetrator, and Rachel and our baby the victims.

Dr Robert had given me the money in a brown envelope that I had stuffed into an inside pocket. Everyone else had gone to Bethnal Green, and I had made a point of avoiding them before they went, so that I wouldn't have to find an excuse for not going with them.

Rachel was waiting for me in the hall when I came downstairs, caught in the sunlight from the door, diminished somehow, and vulnerable. All I wanted to do was take her in my arms, and waken with her in the four-poster bed to the realization that it had all just been some awful dream.

She was carrying a small holdall and wouldn't meet my eye.

I said, 'Do you have the address?'

She nodded, and the taxi sounded its horn out in the street.

And that's how we left, without a word, on that fine, sunny morning to take a taxi across town and kill our child.

Ruskin Avenue was one street back from a small square around a fenced-off area of gardens. These terraced homes must once have been quite grand but were now divided, and sometimes sub-divided, into flats and studios. Number 23A had a nicely kept lozenge of garden at the front and steps up to a door with only two names on it. Griffin was the one we wanted, and I pressed the bell-push with a slightly trembling finger.

A voice barked out of a loudspeaker. 'Yes?'

'It's Richard. We've come about the cat.'

It sounded so ridiculous that in almost any other circumstance we might have laughed.

'Upstairs.'

A buzzer sounded and the door unlocked. I pushed it open and we entered a dark, dusty hall that smelled of stale cooking and body odour. An old people's smell. It reminded me of visits to my grandmother as a child. I followed Rachel up to the next landing. We had not uttered a single word during the thirty-five-minute drive from west to east, sharing the bench seat in the back of the taxi, but with a gulf between us wider than could ever be measured in feet and inches.

Miss Griffin was a lady in her fifties. I was surprised when she opened her door to us on the first landing. I'm not sure what I had been expecting. Someone witchlike, I think. Thin, with bony, clawlike hands and sunken cheeks and the reek of death about her. Instead, she had a round face and a pleasant smile and there was the smell of baking coming from her kitchen.

'Come in, come in, my dears,' she said. She took off her pinny and draped it over the back of an armchair in a small comfortable lounge with a window looking out over a garden at the back. Sunlight came dappled through the leaves of a large chestnut tree, like daubs of yellow paint. A large TV sat on a cabinet in the corner. A radio on the sideboard was tuned to the BBC Light Programme, playing *Housewives' Choice*. A woman's bright, Home Counties voice read out requests and chattered like one of the birds in the tree outside the window, introducing records that were as anodyne as the paper pasted on the walls of this incongruously cheerful little room.

Miss Griffin took Rachel by the hand. 'Now, you don't need to worry about a thing, my love. I've done this many times, and I have medical training. Nothing invasive here. No needles or coat hangers poked up the uterus.'

She smiled, as if somehow this was reassuring. But all she did was conjure in my mind a picture of some dark dungeon filled with implements of torture. God knows what it did to Rachel.

'The drugs I use are perfectly safe. You'll spontaneously miscarry within the next twenty-four hours. You might experience some discomfort, and it'll be a little messy.' She laughed. 'But we women are used to that, aren't we, my dear?'

For the first time that day my eyes met Rachel's, and all

I could see in them was abject terror. I wanted to be sick. I wanted to scream, 'Stop!' But still I said nothing.

In truth, what I really wanted was for it to be over. I find it hard to believe now that it was me. That I was that person. That selfish, cowardly bastard who let the girl he loved go through with this. But it *was* me, and I *did*. And I will carry the shame of it with me to my grave.

Miss Griffin opened the door to the hall and said to Rachel, 'The room on the right at the end, my love. Just make yourself comfortable. I'll be with you in a minute.'

I saw her disappear into the gloom. The sun from the window at the back didn't extend into the hall, and so I barely saw her face as she glanced back, black eyes like saucers in the palest of faces. Miss Griffin shut the door carefully and turned to me. Smiling still, no judgement in her eyes. How often had she dealt with couples just like us?

'You have the money?'

I handed her the envelope that Dr Robert had given me and she opened it up to count diligently the notes inside it. There was something about the care that she took over it, and the mercenary look in her eyes, that must have found a reflection in mine. For when she looked up, satisfied that it was all there, her smile faded on seeing my face.

'Don't judge *me*!' she said, in an ugly little whisper.

And she turned and left the room.

I stood for a long time, my face stinging with the shock of her words, before I turned and walked slowly to the window, hands in pockets, to stare out into a world filled with sunlight, in total contrast to the darkness in my heart. I paid a terrible price that day for what I thought of as my freedom. But the true cost was in allowing Rachel to pay it for me.

Miss Griffin, her smile restored but strained now, finally ushered Rachel out of the darkness and back into the living room. That brave little girl whom we had wrested from the clutches of her drug dealer in Leeds looked crushed. Her face was stained with tears, her eyes red with the spilling of them, and she absolutely could not bring herself to meet my gaze.

'When you get her home, leave her be for a day.'

The coldness with which Miss Griffin looked at me almost froze my soul. But there was something else in her gaze, something that I have never been able to identify, which left me unsettled then, and still to this day. A look that has haunted my worst nightmares and darkest hours. Almost as if God himself had peered through a crack in the brittle shell of my mortality to pass his judgement upon me ahead of the grave.

The taxi ride home was painful. Rachel gazed from her window with unseeing eyes, her silent misery filling the cab until I could bear it no longer.

'I'm sorry,' I said finally. My voice barely a whisper.

But she couldn't hear me above the rattle and roar of the taxi and turned cold eyes in my direction. 'What?'

'Rachel, I'm *so* sorry.' And when she didn't respond, 'I wish –'

'What do you wish, Jack?'

'I wish . . . I wish I hadn't let you do it.'

The oddest little smile soured her face, and cynicism stretched her voice thin. 'A bit late now.'

IV

Dr Robert was waiting for us when we got back. He was sitting in the breakfast room with a pot of coffee, smoking and reading the newspaper. I could see him through the open door as soon as we came into the hall. He folded his newspaper, stood up and came through to greet us. He ignored me, all his attention and concern focused on Rachel.

'How did it go?'

She just gave the tiniest of shrugs.

'I've had a room prepared for you up in the attic. It's your room, Rachel.' He glanced at me with cold eyes, then turned them back to Rachel. 'I'll stay home for the next twenty-four hours. If you need me at any time . . .' He looked at me again. 'I've moved your stuff down to the basement. Rachel's old room. The four-poster's out of bounds.'

Like a punishment. Although, in truth, I would not have wanted now to sleep in the room where Rachel and I had conducted most of our relationship. The bed in which we had conceived the child we had just destroyed.

But neither did I relish the little single room in the damp, dark basement where I knew that sooner or later I was going to have to face the disapproval of the others.

Dr Robert led Rachel up the stairs, and she disappeared round the curve of the landing without a backward glance, leaving me to stand in the sunlit hall, with my guilt and regret, feeling lonelier than I had ever felt in my life.

I was in my room in the basement when I heard the others return late that afternoon. But I couldn't face them, and sat miserable and depressed on the edge of my bed. Their voices came to me from along the hall, sounds of laughter and wise-cracking. After a while they subsided, and I heard someone going back up the stairs.

Ten, perhaps fifteen minutes passed before there were steps on the stairs again, and I heard raised voices in the living room. It sounded like an argument, though I couldn't make out what it was they were saying.

Then Maurie's voice raised above the others, shrill and filled with rage. 'Where the fuck is he?'

I heard his footsteps in the hall and stood up as the door burst open. His face was livid, dark eyes burning. He looked at me for the briefest moment. 'You bastard!' The words exploded from his lips in a breath, and he flew at me across the room.

The whole weight of his body knocked me over and we both landed on the bed before falling to the floor, Maurie on top, forcing all the breath from my lungs.

'You fucking bastard!' Spittle gathered around his lips, and his fist smashed into my face.

I felt teeth cut into my cheek and blood bursting into my mouth. A second blow broke my nose, and tears and blood blinded me. I made no attempt to defend myself. If this was the worst punishment I would receive for my sins, then I was getting off lightly. Of course, I know now that the punishment didn't stop there. The punishment has never stopped.

I think that Maurie might very well have killed me if Luke and Dave hadn't pulled him off. I don't know where Jeff was, but the two of them dragged Maurie away, still kicking and shouting, and somehow I managed to get to my knees. The blood was streaming from my nose and mouth, dripping from my chin on to the carpet.

I spat out a tooth, and looked at Maurie through my tears. 'I'm sorry,' I said.

An echo of the words I had uttered in the taxi. Too few and too late. My voice was hoarse and barely audible. Maurie was breathing hard, and shook himself free of Luke and Dave's hands, and stood staring at me with hate in his eyes.

'I'm so, so sorry.' And I sat back on the floor then, dropping my face into my hands, and cried like a baby.

I didn't see Rachel all the next day. I stayed at the house while the others went to Bethnal Green, harbouring perhaps the faint hope that she might come looking for me, and that I would be there for her if she did.

Dr Robert insisted on treating my mouth and facial injuries. He reset my broken nose and held it in place with some kind of strong white Elastoplast that he stretched across the bridge of it. I didn't see him for the rest of the day, although I knew that he was somewhere in the house, probably in his study.

He had given me paracetamol, but I didn't take it. Somehow I wanted to feel the pain, to punish myself. My face and mouth hurt like hell, and my head was bursting. I couldn't bring myself to eat, and sat alone in the basement flat smoking for most of the day.

When Rachel finally appeared the next morning, she seemed frail, a washed-out shadow of herself. The life, and the light, had gone from those dark eyes, and it was so painful to look at her that I could barely bring myself to do it.

She came down to the basement, searching for some of her stuff, and I half expected her to pack her bags and leave. She didn't once glance in my direction, although she said hi to the rest of the guys.

When she had collected her things, she looked at Maurie. 'I need to talk to you,' she said.

Maurie nodded, and the two of them disappeared back up into the house. Just in that moment before she left the room, her eyes flickered almost involuntarily in my direction and I saw the shock in them.

Then she was gone.

Dave lay back on the settee, his acoustic in his lap, idly picking at some riff he was working on, a cigarette burning in the corner of his mouth. Luke sat on the edge of one of the armchairs, leaning forward on his knees, staring off into space. I have no idea where he was or what he was thinking, but we all knew by now that the dream was over. None of us felt inclined to speak.

Except for Jeff, who sat at the table rolling himself a joint. He looked at me and shook his head. 'Ya stupid big jobby,' he said.

When Maurie returned about twenty minutes later it was with the news that Dr Robert had offered Rachel a job cleaning and tidying the house in exchange for her room. 'I don't know how long she'll stay,' he said. Then he looked at me. 'But apparently you guys owe Cliff some money.'

I lowered my head and felt the disapproval in the room. 'She doesn't have to do that,' I said. 'I'll pay him back.'

'Oh yeah, how you going to do that?'

When I glanced up again I saw the oddest look in Maurie's eyes. Anger, yes. Contempt, yes. But something else. Something it took me a moment to identify. Pity. Which is not what I had been expecting. And I have always thought that no matter how angry he had been at me, in the cold light of day he regretted what he had done to his friend.

'I don't know. I'll work something out.'

'And you're so good at that, Jack, aren't you? Working things out so that someone else has to pay.' The moment of regret seemed to have gone.

'It wasn't my idea. The abortion. I'd never even have thought of it.' I don't know why I was trying to defend myself.

'No,' Maurie said, anger brimming in his eyes again. 'And she wouldn't either. Except that you were too selfish to see her through the pregnancy. And she knew it.'

And there was nothing I could say. Because that was the truth, and everyone else knew it, too.

I couldn't sleep again that night, lying sweating, covered with just a sheet, light from the street outside shining through the barred fanlight high up in the wall, and falling in a zigzag pattern across my troubled bed.

Sometime around 3 a.m., I got up and slipped on my jeans and a T-shirt, and tiptoed silently through the basement flat. I could hear the sound of heavy breathing coming from the other bedrooms, and eased open the door to the landing and the stairs up to the house.

The whole house simmered in darkness, except where light fell through windows in unexpected angles and shapes. I followed my own shadow, ascending two flights of stairs, and then climbed the narrow staircase to the attic.

Rachel's was the only door that was closed. When it wouldn't open I knocked softly. I waited, but there was no response. I knocked again, a little harder.

'Who is it?' Her voice sounded small and frightened.

'It's Jack. Rachel, I've got to talk to you.'

A long pause.

'Rachel?'

'There's nothing to say, Jack.'

'There's everything to say.'

'No.'

Another pause.

'It's over, Jack. And nothing you can say is ever going to change that.'

2015

CHAPTER FIFTEEN

I

Forty miles from London, the coach from Leeds pulled off into Toddington Services, and their driver drew up in an empty slot in the lorry park. For several minutes he spoke animatedly to someone on his mobile phone before reaching for the microphone. They were taking a short comfort break, he told his passengers, and they might like to take the chance to grab some food or coffee. There was a Costa Express and a Burger King, and an M&S Simply Food if anyone wanted to buy sandwiches for later.

Jack shook Ricky awake, and the young man blinked in confusion. It was obvious that for a moment he had no idea where he was. Then the fog cleared and reality crystallized. And with clarity came depression, his brain flooded with the recollection of everything that had happened in the last twenty-four hours. His life had turned to crap in the space of a day. He glanced ruefully at his grandfather, who smiled at him.

'Come on, Rick. Time to get yourself a pee and a coffee.' He paused. 'And you can take Maurie to the loo.'

Ricky glared at him and got to his feet with difficulty, stretching muscles that had stiffened up in the last three hours. He took Maurie by the elbow and helped him up.

Maurie himself looked dreadful. Worse, if anything. The skin on his face was the texture of clay, but paler and tinged with green. He had taken painkillers earlier, and their effect still dulled his eyes.

Jack watched as his grandson helped the dying man down the aisle of the bus, and remembered how Maurie had flown at him in a rage the day that he learned about Rachel's abortion. How his fists had torn a tooth from Jack's mouth and broken his nose. And he thought how young, stupid and impulsive they had all been.

He had never forgiven Maurie for what he did to him that day, because he had never had to. There was nothing to forgive. Maurie had done nothing to him that he hadn't deserved. What was more surprising was that somehow, somewhere along the way, Maurie had forgiven him. They had gone on to play in a band together until Maurie's final year at university, and Rachel had never been spoken of once. Almost as if she had never existed. But the affection they had once felt for each other was lost. Until that moment, three nights ago, when Jack had sat on Maurie's hospital bed and stared mortality in the face. And something of what there had once been between them was there again, in a look and a touch. A bond of fifty years that had never quite been broken.

They were last off the bus, Dave leading the way. But the

driver rose from his seat as they approached the door and blocked their path. He seemed much bigger out of his seat than in it. The three old men and Ricky looked at him, and there was a brief stand-off.

'Alright,' the driver said. 'Who are you?'

Dave glanced at Jack.

And Jack said, 'The party from Leeds.'

'Are you hell!' The driver glared at them. 'I'm just off the phone to Leeds. The party that were due to join the bus there was found wandering about the city centre. Poor bloody souls wondering what happened to their lift, and asking if the coach had gone yet.'

Jack saw panic in Dave's eyes.

'Run!' Dave shouted, and he shoved the driver in the chest, forcing the big man to step back and sit heavily in his seat.

But the speed of their exit from the coach failed to live up to the urgency in Dave's call to flee. He climbed stiffly down the steps and turned to help Ricky down with Maurie. Jack was forced to stand and wait until the door was clear, embarrassed and avoiding the driver's eyes.

The driver looked at them with a mix of anger, consternation and amusement. He shook his head and waited a full sixty seconds until all four of them had made it on to the tarmac.

Then he stood up and leaned out of the door. 'At that rate you might just make it to the loos by the time the cops arrive.' He started dialling a number on his mobile. 'I'm calling them now. But even if they take their time coming, you boys are going nowhere fast. No way out of here except back on to the motorway.'

They made their way as fast as Maurie's progress would allow, across the car park to the Moto building that housed the shops, restaurants and toilets. They went straight to the men's room, where Jack and Dave stood at the urinal listening to Maurie throwing up in a cubicle, the door open and young Ricky standing over him to stop him from toppling head first into the bowl.

Dave glanced at Jack. 'This is madness, Jack. We shouldnae have done it.'

'Bit late now.' And Rachel's words to him in the taxi came echoing back across half a century. 'Only thing we can do is get there.'

'Then what?'

Jack shrugged and zipped up his fly. 'Whatever Maurie wants.' He glanced over his shoulder and lowered his voice. 'I'll be surprised if he makes it through the week.'

After they had washed their hands, and Maurie's face, and Ricky had wiped the sick from the old man's collar, they went into Costa Coffee and sat at a table.

'Can't even afford a bloody coffee,' Ricky muttered. 'So what are we going to do? Sit here until the police come and get us?'

'No!' Maurie surprised them all with the strength in his voice.

'What, then?' Jack said. 'Like the driver told us, there's no way out of here except by getting back on the road.'

'We'll hitch a lift.'

They all looked at Maurie as if he were mad.

'Maurie, there are four of us,' Jack said. 'And none of us have got the legs for it. I used to look quite good in a kilt, but a miniskirt's out of the question.'

Maurie forgot their woes for a moment and chuckled to himself. 'Raitch would have got us a lift in five minutes.' Then almost as if he only now heard his own voice, he became suddenly self-conscious and glanced at Jack.

Jack's face reddened. 'Aye,' is all he said, and he looked at his hands on the table in front of him.

Dave stood up suddenly. 'Well, if we're gonnae get a lift, we'd better start looking for it before the cops get here.'

They decided that their best chance of cadging a ride would be at the petrol pumps and so made their slow, painful way across the parking lot to the filling station.

'This is crazy,' Ricky kept saying. 'No one's going to give us a lift. *I* wouldn't give us a lift.'

Jack left the others hanging around the pumps, and positioned himself outside the door to the shop where all the motorists came and went to pay for their petrol.

The first person he approached, the driver of a Ford Transit, told him in no uncertain terms where he could go, and Jack lifted two fingers to his back as he returned to his van. Others weren't as rude, but equally firm in refusing them a lift.

The rest watched as Jack stopped half a dozen or more motorists on their way in or out, before he got into a lengthy conversation with a young man in a dark suit. When the man disappeared into the shop to pay, Jack hurried across the forecourt to a blue Volvo Estate. He stopped at the driver's door and peered inside, then turned and waved urgently to his nephew and his two old friends.

'Come on, quick,' he said as they approached, and he held open the rear door for Dave and Maurie. Dave slipped in first, then Ricky helped Maurie and was about to follow him when Jack said, 'Not you. You're driving.' He opened the driver's door for him, then glanced towards the shop before hurrying round to climb in the passenger side.

But Ricky just stood on the forecourt looking bemused. 'Driving?'

'Hurry up and get in,' Jack shouted at him. 'Quick! The key's in the ignition.'

And suddenly it dawned on Ricky what was going on. 'I'm not stealing a car!' he said emphatically.

'We're not stealing it, Rick. We're borrowing it. The young man's got sales business in there. We'll drop it off for him at the next service stop. A minor inconvenience.'

Ricky was incredulous. 'You mean he's agreed to it?'

'Just get in the fucking car!'

Ricky slid reluctantly behind the wheel.

'Go, go!' Jack shouted at him.

And Ricky started the car. He pushed it into first gear and eased it out from beneath the canopy towards the exit signs.

'Why would he agree to lend us his car?'

Jack rolled his eyes. 'Sometimes I wonder if they didn't get their figures wrong when they gave you that IQ test.'

Dave was cackling in the back. 'Haha! Just like Thelma and what's-her-name.'

'You mean we *are* stealing it?' Ricky glanced in the rear-view mirror and saw the young man in the dark suit running after them, shouting and waving his arms. 'Jesus!' He started to slow down.

Jack looked at him, urgency in his voice. 'Better go, son, or we really will be in trouble.'

Ricky breathed his anger and frustration. 'I can't believe I'm doing this!' And he dropped into second gear and accelerated away from the chasing driver.

As they passed their coach, still parked up in the commercial vehicles section, Dave leaned out of the back window and raised his middle finger to the driver whose face, as they sped by, was a mask of astonishment.

II

'Madness! Pure bloody madness!' Ricky's eyes had the startled look of a deer caught in headlights. They flickered constantly between the road and his rear-view mirror. 'I don't know why I let you talk me into any of this. We're going to go to jail, you know that?' He turned his gaze, fired with fear and anger, on his grandfather. 'You've ruined my life.'

There was a time when Jack, too, might have shared Ricky's anxiety. But to his surprise, he found that he really didn't care any more. What did any of it matter? And what could anyone do to him that might be worse than the life of mediocrity he had lived until now? The life he had wasted. If it came to it, he would step up and take all the blame.

'We'll be on the security cameras,' Ricky wailed. 'The cops'll know who we are.'

'They won't have a clue who we are,' Jack said. 'Three old guys and a fat boy borrowing a car and dropping it off at the next services. Not exactly high priority when you compare us to murderers and bank robbers.'

But Ricky wasn't going to be comforted. 'And that poor man.'

'What poor man?' Dave asked.

'The one whose car we're in!'

'Poor, nothing!' Jack said. 'That was a bloody expensive suit he was wearing. And the car's not his, anyway. He's a rep. It's a company car. And like I said, it's not stolen, it's borrowed.'

The next services turned out to be the last on the M1, just thirteen miles from London. Previously Scratchwood, now London Gateway, it had provided a viewpoint eighteen years before when Princess Diana's hearse had followed a route up the M1 to her childhood home at Althorp, where she was buried. Jack remembered watching it on TV. Not normally a sentimental man, he had surprised himself by crying.

Ricky pulled the Volvo into a parking space and turned off the engine. He sat back in the driver's seat and breathed deeply. There was a fine mask of perspiration covering the contours of his face.

Jack said, 'See? Not so hard, was it?'

The look of barely contained fury that Ricky turned on his grandfather was more than even Jack could deal with, and he averted his eyes to escape the accusation in it.

The moment was broken by Dave opening the back door. 'I'm off for a pee. Back in a tick.'

'You've just been,' Maurie said.

Dave grinned. 'Och, that was half an hour ago. You know how it is at oor age.' He slipped out and hurried away across the tarmac to the shops with a strange, crouching gait.

Jack was distracted by a mobile phone lying in an empty cup holder between the two front seats, and he picked it up. 'Look,' he said to Ricky. 'We can just call him and tell him where his car is.'

Ricky made a face. 'How can we call him when we've got his phone?'

'Ah. Good point. That's why you're the one with the high IQ, then.' He thought about it, then switched on the phone and opened its address book to scroll through the names. He stopped at the end of the 'B's. 'This is him here. Adam Burley.'

'How d'you know that?' Maurie asked.

Jack grinned back at him. 'Cos it says "Me" next to the name.' He scrolled down. 'And here's Jessica Burley. Bet that's his wife. Or his mother, or his sister. Any of the above will do.' He tapped to dial and handed the phone to Ricky. 'Here.'

Ricky almost dropped it, juggling it in his hands as if it were red hot. 'What?'

'Just tell her where the car is.'

'Me?'

They heard a voice answering, and Jack nodded encouragement to his grandson.

Ricky bared his teeth and raised the phone to his ear. 'Mrs Burley? I . . . I don't know if you've heard from Adam. But his car was stolen. Well, not stolen. Taken.' Then he corrected himself again. 'Borrowed.' He winced at the voice in his ear. 'Doesn't matter who I am. The thing is, his car's safe and sound, and it's in the car park at London Gateway Services on the M1. We'll leave the keys for him under the driver's mat.' And he hung up quickly, before she could respond.

The look he gave his grandfather would have curdled milk. But he couldn't come up with words adequate to express his feelings. Instead he leaned over to drop the phone into the glove compartment and got out of the car.

'Out!' he said. 'The sooner we get away from this damned car the better.'

He and Jack helped Maurie out of the back seat, then Ricky hid the keys, and they hobbled across the car park to the huddle of box-like buildings that housed the facilities, the metal tip of Jack's walking stick clicking erratically on the asphalt.

Inside, they stood in the middle of the crowded concourse, looking around, feeling more than a little lost. They were so, so near to their goal. But without wheels, they might just as well still have been in Glasgow. People milled around them as if they weren't there, and Jack had that sense of invisibility again. This was no longer his world. At some point, without his even being aware of it, the baton had been passed from one generation to the next. The past and present co-existing in the same space, but barely touching. The world he had known, populated now by others. Ricky's generation, he supposed, and their parents. Although Ricky was as alien here as his grandfather. Too clever, too fat, his knowledge of reality scarcely extending beyond his bedroom and the virtual world of his violent computer games.

The names of all the commercial outlets around them were known to Jack, of course, but familiar only in name. Starbucks. Waitrose. Costa Express. A bewildering array of food and drink, newspapers, magazines, people, children, more people.

'So what now?' Ricky's voice forced him out of his cloud of uncertainty, and he tried to clear his mind. But nothing came to him.

'I've no idea.'

'Well, we're not stealing another car.'

'No.'

Maurie's voice, thin and reedy, cut above the hubbub. Once such a beautiful voice, Jack thought.

'Where's Dave?'

They looked all around, but there was no sign of him. He had been gone for ten minutes or more.

Jack said, 'Better check the toilets.'

There was a constant stream of men coming and going at the urinals. But Dave wasn't among them. Three of the cubicles were occupied. Jack raised his voice. 'Dave, are you in there?'

No reply.

Ricky went off to search the shops and restaurants, while Jack and Maurie stayed in the toilets in case Dave showed up. Maurie leaned back against the wall by the dryer and closed his eyes.

'Are you going to be okay, Maurie?'

Maurie slowly opened his eyes to look at Jack, and nodded. 'As long as I make it through the day tomorrow. There's somewhere we've got to be by tomorrow night.'

'Where?'

'You'll see.'

'Maurie, we're taking an awful lot on trust here.'

Maurie stared at him through his misery. 'It's all I ever asked of you, Jack. That you trust me. Will you do that? Will you?' He paused, then, 'I'm sorry I hit you. I really am. It's been on my mind.'

Jack's smile was wry and touched by sadness. 'Aye, for fifty years.' Then, 'I trust you, Maurie.'

Ricky returned after about ten minutes. He shook his head. 'No sign of him.'

Jack sighed deeply. 'Damn him!' Then a worm of suspicion

wriggled its way to the head of his queue of thoughts. 'Wait a minute.' He strode across the floor of the toilets. 'That end cubicle's been occupied the whole time we've been here.' He rapped on the door with the head of his stick. 'Dave! Dave, are you in there?'

There was a brief hiatus before Dave's muffled voice returned to them. 'Can a man no' get five minutes tae himsel'?'

'What are you doing in there?'

'Whit dae ye think?'

'Are you drinking?'

The silence that followed was laden with guilt before the denial. 'Course not!'

Ricky looked at his grandfather, appalled. 'Where would he get drink?'

Jack banged on the door again with the brass owl's head. 'Open up, Dave. Come on, open the door!'

Another hiatus, then they heard the bolt being pulled back and the door swung in to reveal Dave sitting on the toilet, three cans of beer in plastic wrap cradled in his lap, two empties on the floor and a third in his hand. 'You're just spoilsports, the lot of ye.'

Jack stared at him in astonishment. 'Where did you get those?'

'They were on the floor by my feet in the back of the car. Wasnae gonnae tell you. You'd just have chucked them oot the windae.'

Jack reached in to try to grab the remaining cans, but Dave wrapped his arms around them.

'I've been good for long enough. We're on a wild fuckin' goose chase here, and nae bloody idea why.' He glared across at Maurie, who hadn't moved from his place beside the hand dryer. Then a sly smile crossed his face. 'Anyway, I've earned them.'

'How's that?' Jack wasn't in the mood for forgiveness. Dave had promised to stay sober.

'Oh, just caught sight of a wee notice oot there. Didn't know this was a coach stop, did you? On the road tae London. Another one due in . . .' he glanced at his watch, 'aboot twenty minutes.'

Ricky expressed his feelings in a snort. 'And we're going to buy tickets with what?'

Dave laid his remaining cans carefully on the floor and stood up. With slightly unsteady fingers he pulled his shirt out of his trousers and rolled it up to his chest, revealing a thread-worn canvas money belt around his waist. He grinned. 'Remember that? Saved us once, saved us again.' Now he laughed at the look on Jack's face. 'What's more amazing than the fact that I've still got the bloody thing is that I can get it roon my middle.'

Jack shook his head. 'Aye, it's called the alcohol diet. Keeps you skinny when you don't eat.' He paused. 'How much have you got?'

'Aboot a hundred quid.'

'And when were you thinking of telling us?'

Dave raised his eyebrows indignantly. 'I'm telling you noo, amn't I?'

*

Half an hour later, the rumble of wheels on tarmac vibrated beneath them as their coach accelerated down the M1 towards what they would once have called the Big Smoke.

They sat again at the back of the bus. Dave had only one can of beer left, and Jack had been relieved to find that there was a toilet on-board. But for the moment, Dave was asleep, one side of his nose and mouth squashed up against the glass of the window, a tiny drool of saliva seeping from the near corner of his mouth.

Ricky sat beside his grandfather, his mood little improved. 'So where are we going to sleep tonight?'

Jack shrugged. 'No idea.'

Ricky sighed. 'Great!'

Maurie's clawlike old hand came between them from the seat behind, a slip of paper trembling in big-knuckled fingers. 'Here,' he said to Jack, urging him to take it. 'Call this number.'

Jack unfolded the piece of paper and looked at the number. 'Whose is it?'

Maurie managed the palest of smiles. 'Who do you think, Jack?'

It was a moment or two before realization dawned, and Jack's eyes widened. 'Really?'

Maurie nodded.

Jack handed the number to Ricky. 'Call that number for me, Ricky, son.'

'Who the hell is it you want me to talk to now?

But Jack shook his head. 'Just dial the number. I'll do the talking.'

III

It was evening by the time their bus pulled into Victoria Coach Station, and drew in alongside a long row of buses. Late sunlight slanted in through the pitched-glass roof, casting the shadow of the white-painted iron superstructure that supported it across the tarmac below.

Jack had watched the city unpacking itself before his eyes on the other side of his window. Tall buildings and narrow streets choked with traffic. Pavements jammed with folk on their way home from work. Tree-lined avenues in spring bloom, swallows dipping and diving through the waning sunlight that angled its way between apartment blocks and skyscrapers. And it brought back very vividly that day fifty years before when they had arrived by train at King's Cross and stepped on to the streets of London for the very first time. And there was still an excitement in it.

They were last off the coach, Dave still woozy from beer and sleep. And Maurie, it seemed, losing strength by the minute. Jack and Ricky helped him down the steps to the concourse. It was only when he turned that Jack saw Luke standing there.

It was a strange, heart-stopping moment. He had not set eyes on his friend since the day they parted at Euston Station. There had been no contact between them over the years. No letters, no phone calls. Not really surprising, since neither knew the other's address or telephone number. But, then, neither had made the effort to find out. They might each have died that day, and yet here they were half a century later staring at one another across all the years in between. And Jack knew that he would have recognized Luke anywhere.

He was still tall and lean and boyish. His shock of fair curly hair was now a shock of white curly hair, but just as abundant. His face was deeply creased by the scars of time, but his pale green eyes were just as full of life and gravity as they had been when he was a boy. He gazed at Jack with unglazed affection. And Jack stood looking at him, almost overpowered by the unexpected wave of emotion that broke over him. How extraordinary, he thought, that the feelings developed during those few short adolescent years should have survived all the decades that had passed since. He stepped forward to shake Luke's hand, but at the last moment put his arms around him and hugged him instead, feeling the strength of the other man's hug in return.

When they drew apart, Luke's eyes were shining. 'You haven't changed, Jack.'

Jack laughed. 'And you should have gone to Specsavers. Or are you too vain to wear glasses?'

Luke laughed. But the lines of fondness and affection that creased his face quickly turned to furrows of concern when he looked beyond Jack to the feeble, failing figure of Maurie Cohen. 'Bloody hell!' The oath was whispered under his breath.

Jack glanced back, then lowered his voice. 'He hasn't got long, Luke. Maybe only days. Weeks at the most. I didn't even know he had your number or I'd have called you sooner.' Then he turned towards the others. 'What do you think, boys? It's Peter Pan! How come we're all old farts now and he hasn't aged a day.'

Luke laughed then, and stepped up to shake Dave's hand. 'Still got trouble with your piles, Dave?'

'Oh, aye, they're murder, Luke. Hanging in bunches, noo.'

Then he took Maurie's hand and held it between both of his. His smile faded as he gazed into Maurie's drug-fogged eyes. 'I didn't know, Maurie. You should have told me.'

'And you'd have done what? Waved a wand and made it all go away?' He chuckled. 'You didn't need to know, Luke. But I'll be pissed off if you're not at my funeral.' He placed his other hand over the back of Luke's. 'Need your help before I die, though. We all do.'

'Anything,' Luke said. 'All you have to do is ask. You know that.'

Then, almost as if for the first time, he noticed Ricky, who was hovering awkwardly in the background, as discreetly as his weight would allow.

'My grandson,' Jack said. 'Rick. Sorry. Ricky. Don't ever let on I told you, but I'm proud as hell of him.' And he was embarrassed to meet the look of surprise that Ricky turned in his direction.

Luke shook his hand. 'Then I'm honoured to meet you, Ricky.' He nodded back over his shoulder. 'My car's parked outside. I was going to take you straight back to my place, but you look like you could do with a decent meal. And I know just the place.'

IV

The Merchants Tavern was just off Great Eastern Street in Shoreditch, in a narrow alley of shops and pubs and restaurants beneath yellow-and-red-brick apartments that leaned overhead and seemed to close it off from the darkening sky.

The restaurant itself was in a converted workshop with skylights and exposed ducting, but it had been expensively remodelled with polished mahogany and green leather. Luke had phoned ahead to book a table.

When they were seated, Luke said, 'The chef's a young Scottish lad. Cut his teeth in France under one of the world's top chefs. Opened this place a year or so ago. Fantastic food. Can't be long before he gets himself a Michelin star or two.'

That Luke was in his element here was evident to the others, and it had the effect of making them feel distinctly uncomfortable. Where he was clearly accustomed to fine dining in expensive restaurants, Dave or Jack were more used to Chinese or Indian carry-outs, or pizzas at Dino's. There was a time, perhaps, when Maurie might not have felt like such a fish out of water. But his days of good living had all preceded his eighteen months in Barlinnie. And life had never been the same again.

A voice raised itself from beyond the leather banquettes, in a kitchen open to the restaurant. Chefs in silhouette moved back and forth from pot to pan, and from oven to grill, in a kind of ordered and orchestrated chaos.

'Mr Sharp!' A tall young man in chef's whites detached himself from the others and made his way to their table, grinning broadly. He shook Luke's hand. 'Great to see you again. How you doing?' His east-coast Scottish twang was unmistakeable.

Dave said, 'Jesus Christ, we've been in London half an hour and talked to nothing but Scotsmen!'

The chef's grin widened. 'We're taking over the world.'

Luke said, 'Neil, these are my friends from Glasgow. Wanted to treat them to something a wee bit special. Just a main, I think.'

Neil said, 'I'll do a wee special for you, then. For the table. Slow-cooked rib-eye, thyme-roasted onions and a few girolles thrown in. How's that?'

'Sounds good.' Luke beamed at the others, searching for approval. But the smile faded a little in the face of their blank looks. 'Doesn't it?'

Jack shrugged. 'If you recommend it, that's good enough for me.'

Maurie said, 'I'll not eat, if you don't mind. Just some water for me.'

'Will there be wine with that?' Dave looked hopeful.

Luke nodded. 'We'll order something from the list.'

'I'll get that sorted, then,' Neil said.

But before he could head back to the kitchen Ricky said, 'What's rib-eye? It's not . . . eyes, is it?' There was distinct panic in his voice.

Neil smiled indulgently. 'It's beef.'

'Do you not have a burger, or pizza or something?'

Jack dropped his head into one hand, muffling his voice. 'Oh dear God!'

'Do you not like beef?' Neil asked him.

'Well . . . it's okay, I suppose. I don't like blood running out of it, though.'

Jack thought Neil's patience was worth a star in itself.

The chef said, 'No blood running out of this, I promise you. If it doesn't melt in your mouth, you can have your money back.'

'*My* money back.' Luke grinned. 'My treat.'

And none of them was about to argue with him.

Luke ordered a bottle of red. And with their glasses filled and their rib-eye cooking, a strangely awkward silence descended on the table.

Luke let his eyes drift from face to face. 'So how's everyone been? What have you being doing for the last fifty years?'

Jack's laugh was a little forced. 'Not a lot.'

Luke smiled. 'That must have kept you pretty busy, then.'

Dave blurted, 'I done my City and Guilds in plumbing and bent pipes aroon' my knees for most of them. Bloody wrecked them an' all.' He took a long draught of wine from his glass. 'My knees, that is.'

Luke turned his gaze on Jack. 'You were going to go to university, Jack.'

Jack nodded and looked at his hands on the table in front of him. 'I did. But it wasn't for me, Luke. Ended up with the Bank of Scotland.' He flicked a glance at Ricky and saw that his grandson was assiduously avoiding his eye. He deflected attention away from further elucidation. 'Maurie was the smart one. Got his law degree.'

Luke seemed surprised. 'What did you practise, Maurie? Criminal law?'

'Nooo.' Maurie shook his head. 'Civil. Property. Conveyancing mostly.'

There was more awkward silence then, and it was clear to Jack and Dave that he wasn't going to mention the disbarment or his eighteen months in prison.

'What about you?' Jack said. 'Nice car, nice togs.' He cast his eyes around the tavern. 'Fancy restaurant. You've obviously done well for yourself.'

Luke nodded. 'I have. But it didn't come easy. Or quickly. Truth is, I'd probably have ended up in a shop doorway somewhere if I hadn't met Jan. Saved my life, she did.'

'How?' Dave drained his glass and pushed it towards Luke for a refill.

'By falling in love with me.' He laughed. 'Though God knows why. But, you know, sometimes it takes someone else seeing the worth in you for you to find it in yourself.' He looked around the table. 'No one follow a musical career, then?'

There was a collective shaking of heads, and Luke smiled ruefully.

'Me neither. Designed and printed T-shirts and sold them off a market stall. Jan was teaching, and we rented a place in North London. She got pregnant and we had a wee boy, and we needed some more income. Someone told us about work for babies, you know, doing TV ads and that sort of thing. Wee James was cute as hell, and we got work for him quite easily through an agency. We didn't realize it at first, but the money had to be put into a trust for him. Not that we grudged it, but having been through the process it got us to thinking, why not set up a wee agency of our own, get some more kids on our books? Take a percentage. There was obviously work around. So that's what we did, starting from a back room in the flat.'

He shook his head and took a sip of his wine.

'I would never have guessed that life would take me in that direction. But one thing led to another. We expanded to take adults on to our books. By the time we retired, we had the biggest modelling and acting agency in the UK. The two boys run the business now, and that's our pension.' He looked at the others. 'You guys got kids?'

'Just the one daughter,' Jack said. 'And my grandson, of course.' He paused. 'Wife died a year or two ago.'

A little of the sparkle went out of Luke's eyes. 'I'm sorry to hear that, Jack.'

Dave said, 'My wife left me. And I've got one brute of a son. Good riddance to them both.'

Luke seemed embarrassed, unsure of what to say, and let his eyes stray towards Maurie. But Maurie was preoccupied, his eyes and mind elsewhere.

Jack said, 'Maurie never married.'

The same awkwardness returned to the table, but it was broken almost immediately by the arrival of their food. Ricky poked suspiciously at his meat in its rich, dark gravy, before very reluctantly pushing a little past unreceptive lips. Only for his face to lighten with surprise, eyes opening wide. And he took another, bigger mouthful.

'Wow!' he said. 'This is amazing.'

And Jack allowed himself a small, private smile.

Dave tipped the last of the wine into his glass and said, 'Maybe we'd better get another bottle. I'll pay for it.'

But Luke just smiled and signalled the wine waiter. 'Like I said, it's my shout.'

Wine and food released inhibitions accumulated over five decades, and the four old men were soon talking about that day fifty years before when Jack was expelled from school and they all decided to run away together.

They laughed about the robbery in the Lake District, and Jeff crawling about in the cemetery in the dark, looking for the van keys. They recalled the thrill of their escape with Rachel from the Quarry Hill Flats, pursued in the pitch black through tunnels and drains beneath the city.

Dave said, 'I'll never forget being chased by yon car in the dark and almost running head-on intae the cops. Jees! Jeff was like a madman behind the wheel!'

Ricky ate and listened in wide-eyed silence as his grandfather and his one-time band mates reminisced. Sometimes laughing, sometimes shaking heads in disbelief at long-forgotten moments. Even Maurie joined in.

But by the time their plates were cleaned and the second bottle of wine was empty, they had exhausted the source of their conversation. Memories could only fuel so much talk. The greater part of their individual lives had barely, if ever, touched. And beyond that handful of very intense years shared in their teens they had little else in common.

There was only really one thing left to address. But as if they all knew that these fond moments of precious reunion would be lost for ever once they did, none of them wanted to be the first to raise it.

By way of avoidance, Luke said, 'So what were you doing stuck at a motorway services on the M1?'

Ricky's theatrical sigh made Jack laugh, and he gave Luke a potted version of their entire, eventful trip down from Glasgow.

Luke listened in astonishment. When Jack had finished, and Luke stopped laughing, he said, 'You guys are just as crazy as you were back then.'

'So what's it like, Luke?' Jack said. 'Living in London.'

It's what they had set out to do all those years before, but only Luke had stayed.

Luke scratched his chin thoughtfully. 'It's funny. Since we first arrived here in sixty-five, everything's changed, but nothing has, if you know what I mean. Not really. London exists in that same old bubble. It's still another country. A virtual city state, these days, fuelled by financial services and ignorant of anything that's happening anywhere else in the country. If you live and work here, why would you care what happens elsewhere? Until the bloody Scots threatened to vote for independence and take the oil revenues away! Road signs point to *The North*. And the north is for holidays, or shooting or fishing. No one wants to know about unemployment, or food banks or pensioners in poverty. No one here wants to lift that stone to see what lies beneath.' He shook his head. 'But the truth is, London's been good to me, and I could no more go back to Scotland now than fly in the air. This is my home.'

Which brought a thoughtful silence to the table, and Jack wondered fleetingly how it might have been if he, too, had stayed.

But the moment couldn't be put off any longer.

Luke leaned on the table and examined their faces carefully. 'Why are you here?'

With difficulty, Maurie fished his dog-eared newspaper cutting from the *Herald* out of an inside pocket and pushed it across the table to Luke. Luke read in silence, and they watched as his mouth fell slowly open.

'How did I miss this?' he said. But he didn't expect an answer. He read on, then he looked up. 'Who'd have believed that Flet was still alive all these years?' When finally he'd finished reading, he looked puzzled. 'This is what brought you back to London?'

No one else seemed willing to explain, so Jack said, 'Maurie claims that it wasn't Flet who killed that fella, after all. But he won't say who did. Just that he knows who killed Flet.'

Jack could see a thousand questions forming themselves behind Luke's eyes.

In the end, all Luke said was, 'In that case, why wouldn't you just go to the police?'

All heads turned towards Maurie.

The old lead singer of The Shuffle sighed, as if he carried the weight of the world on his shoulders. 'It's too late for that now. Fifty years too late.' He drew air into his lungs, as if summoning courage. 'Before we left Glasgow I made a rendezvous to meet up with an old friend of ours tomorrow night.'

'Who?' Jack said

But Maurie just shook his head. 'You'll find that out when you get me there.'

'Where?' Luke asked. 'Where do you want us to take you?'

Maurie lifted his chin, thrusting it out almost defiantly. 'The Victoria Hall.'

Jack lay in the dark listening to Ricky's slow, steady breathing and knew he was not asleep. They were in a back room on the second floor of Luke's semi-detached townhouse in Hampstead Heath, Jack in the double bed, Ricky on a fold-down settee. Curtains were drawn on windows that looked down on to a substantial back garden and the heath beyond. Dave and Maurie had rooms on the floor below. Luke's boys had been in large attic rooms he'd had built into the roof, before they grew up and moved out to establish their own lives and their own families. Now Luke rattled around in this big house on his own with his Jan, who had turned out to be a petite, very sweet lady in her early sixties with short-cropped hair the colour of brushed steel. Her strong features reflected a strong character that had been in evidence within moments of meeting her.

She had welcomed Luke's old friends with open arms, diplomatically disguising the shock she must have felt when confronted with the dying Maurie. She made tea, and prepared rooms for them all, and chattered like a bird. But Jack could see that all her talk was just a way of covering her concern, and he caught her frequent glances at Luke, searching perhaps for some kind of reassurance. What did they want? How long would they be staying?

The house was beautifully maintained and impeccably furnished. At current London prices, Jack reckoned, it was probably worth somewhere between £1.5 million and £2 million. As someone who had spent his life counting other people's money, it was clear to him that Luke had more of it than he could possibly imagine.

Depression settled on him like dust from an explosion as he lay in Luke's bed, in Luke's house, replaying the story of Luke's success. Thinking about the woman Luke had met and married, the partnership they had forged from love to raise a happy family and create a successful business. It wasn't that Jack was resentful, or even envious. He begrudged Luke none of it. But the contrast with his own sad story was so painfully stark that all the regrets of his life came flooding back to very nearly drown him. All the missed opportunities and squandered chances. The loss of Rachel. His unrealized dream of becoming a professional musician. Dropping out of university. Settling always for second best, because that was the path of least resistance. Leaving him now, in his late sixties, widowed and alone, treading the boards in the role of a non-speaking extra until it was his turn to exit the stage.

He was almost startled by Ricky's voice coming unexpectedly out of the darkness. 'I always thought,' he said, 'I don't know why . . . but I always thought that, you know, old people were just annoying.'

Jack chuckled, glad to have a focus other than his own self-pity. 'I suppose I *can* be pretty annoying at times.'

'I didn't mean you in particular. Though you can be *more* than annoying. Trust me. I meant old people in general.'

'Of which I am one.'

'Of which you are one.'

'Well, you see, there's the thing right there, Rick. I don't think of myself as old. In my head I'm still the boy I was at seventeen. I just can't do the things I did back then, and I get a shock when I look in the mirror. But I don't see me as you do. In fact, I can look at fellas ten years my junior and think of them as "old boys". I look at attractive young women and delude myself that they might still fancy me. It's just a matter of perspective.'

He heard Ricky sigh. 'Can I finish?'

'Sorry, Rick.'

'What I'm trying to say is that you never think of old people as having been young once. I mean, you know they were, but you just can't picture it. All you see is the grey and the old, and you get fed up hearing how everything was so much better when they were young.'

Jack laughed. 'You'll be saying that yourself, some day.'

'Aye, well, you see, that's hard to imagine, too.'

Jack thought about it. 'You never can. Not when you're young. You think you'll live for ever. You know you'll die sometime. But it's so far away, you can't imagine that either. Then one day you'll look in the mirror, and see forty-year-old Ricky staring back at you. And before you know it, it'll be fifty-year-old Ricky, then sixty-year-old Ricky. And suddenly you'll see the finish ahead of you, like buffers at the end of the line, and you're hurtling towards them and there's no way to stop the train. And everywhere you've been on your journey of life, the people you've loved, the things you've learned and seen, they'll all be gone. In a moment. Just like they'd never been. And all you'll want to do is grab folk by the shoulders and tell them that you've done extraordinary things. Like that old man at the lunch club in Leeds. Just so they'll know you existed. Just so you won't get airbrushed out of history, like you'd never been there in the first place.'

Jack's voice fell away then, and he lay thinking about his own words, thoughts to which he had never before given form. And he heard himself say, 'But then, maybe you haven't. Done extraordinary things, I mean. Maybe you never were and never will be anything special. And no one'll miss you when you're gone, and when you're breathing your last you'll wonder what was the bloody point of any of it.'

There was a long, laden silence.

Then Ricky's voice. 'But you have.'

'Eh?'

'Done extraordinary things, Grampa. I mean, I knew you'd run away to London when you were a kid. It always just seemed boring to me. But listening to you all tonight, around the table, made me realize there was so much more to it than I ever imagined. To you. And them. And all that stuff about a murder? And the killing of that actor? And Rachel? I don't know anything about her. And Jeff. I never even knew there were five of you in the group.'

'Aye, son, there were five us. And Rachel . . .? Rachel was the biggest love and the biggest regret of my life. Then and now. I did wrong by her, Rick, and I lost her.'

There was a long silence then, and Jack began to listen for signs that his grandson had drifted off. He wasn't expecting it when the boy spoke again, several minutes later.

'Grampa?'

'Yes, Rick.'

'What happened to Jeff?'

1965

CHAPTER SIXTEEN

I

In the days that followed Rachel's abortion it was clear to all of us, except for Jeff, that we were falling apart. Not just as a group, but as friends. Although it was the music that had brought us all together in the first place, friendship was the glue that had seen us through the last weeks. And now we were simply coming unstuck. We hadn't practised for more than a week. Maurie barely acknowledged my existence, and I hadn't set eyes on Rachel since she told me through the locked door of her room that we were finished.

But the end itself was precipitated by an entirely unforeseen event.

It was one of those late-spring mornings when the air was at blood temperature, the sun rising over the park, early-morning mist floating above the chimney tops to vaporize in a painfully clear blue sky. The kind of day that lifts your spirits. But in Onslow Gardens, depression hung about Dr Robert's house like a fog.

I didn't know where the others were, and didn't really care. I had descended into a torpor from which I was finding it almost impossible to raise myself. I knew that something had to be done. The status quo was no longer acceptable, but I had no idea how to change it – nor did I have the energy to make it happen even if I did. I was sitting smoking in the breakfast room, watching my cigarette smoke twist in the sunlight that streamed in from the back garden, and nursing a coffee that I had poured and then let go cold.

I turned at the sound of someone in the hall and Dr Robert leaned in the door. He was wearing low-slung jeans with a white belt, and a pale pink shirt with fastidiously rolled-up sleeves.

He smiled. 'You got a minute, Jack?'

'Sure.'

'Some stuff I'd like you to see.'

He went back into the house and it was clear I was supposed to follow. I eased myself reluctantly out of my chair and went into the hall. He was already halfway up the stairs.

He called down, 'I've got a date for that demo recording at the Marquee. And a photoshoot afterwards. So we've got to get the group a visual identity. Haircuts, clothes. I've had some outfits sent over from a friend in Carnaby Street. Big friend of Twiggy's. You know, the model?'

I didn't. But I followed him up the stairs anyway. I should have got suspicious when we went down the hall on the first floor and into his private bedroom.

I had never been in here before, and if I hadn't known better

I'd have thought it was a woman's room. It was filled with the heavy, musky scent of eau de cologne, and through the open door of the en-suite bathroom I could see pink towels abandoned on the floor. The whole room was tastefully decorated in pale pastel blues and pinks – drapes and sheets, walls and ceiling. The carpet was a white shagpile.

A fussy, frilly throw covered a very large bed, pillows piled up at one end, and I noticed a mirror fixed to the ceiling above it. When I think back on it now, I am amazed at how naive I was in not realizing why it was there. An array of coloured shirts and trousers was laid out on top of the bed.

Dr Robert closed the door softly behind him and said, 'Try these on, Jack. For size and for colour. I mean, I think you should all wear the same gear – same colours, but different – like your shirt should match Jeff's trousers, Maurie's trousers matching Luke's shirt. You get the idea.'

I nodded and waited for him to leave so I could try something on. But he just stood watching me, with the strangest look in his eyes.

'On you go,' he said.

And I started to get uncomfortable. 'Not with you watching.'

He laughed. 'Don't be silly. Won't be seeing anything I haven't seen before.'

I suppose I should just have walked out there and then. But I was embarrassed, and still uncertain about my reading of the situation. I stripped off my T-shirt and quickly pulled on one of the shirts. It was peach, with long sleeves, and ruffles down the side with the buttonholes. I hated it immediately.

'Looks good,' Dr Robert said. 'Button it up.'

I did up the buttons and caught a glimpse of myself in a full-length tilting mirror. More than the shirt, or its awful peach colour, I saw how red my face was, coloured by my embarrassment.

'Try it with the blue trousers. They're the latest fashion. Hipsters they're calling them, because they sit on the hips, two or three inches below the waist. Very sexy.'

I didn't know what else to do, so I kicked off my shoes and dropped my jeans, aware all the time of his eyes on me. I avoided looking at him, and pulled on the pair of blue hipsters as fast as I could. But they were tight. So tight I could barely get them up over my thighs.

'They don't fit,' I said. 'They're too tight.'

'Nonsense. That's the fashion, Jack. You need them to be tight. Show the girls what you've got when you're up there onstage. Just like P. J. Proby.' He grinned. 'Without splitting them, of course. Here, let me give you a hand.'

He came round behind me, and grabbed the waistband to pull them half over my hips, until I was squeezed so tightly into the crotch that it was almost painful. He was very close, his aftershave nearly overpowering. His body pressed itself into the back of me, and I felt his hand come across to pull up the zip and then close around the bulge it contained.

I reacted instinctively and without thought, pulling away hard. 'Get off!'

As I turned to face him he took a step towards me, and I swung a bunched fist at his face, connecting with the side of it, feeling his teeth through his cheek. He staggered back, half falling on to the bed, his hand at his mouth, blood on his fingers.

'You little bastard!'

I wriggled out of the hipsters as fast as I could and pulled on my jeans, hopping on one leg, then the other, before falling backwards and dragging them all the way on as I lay on the carpet. I zipped up, grabbed my shoes and scrambled to my feet.

He was on his feet, too, by now. Breathing hard and glaring at me. He snatched a tissue from a box on the bedside cabinet and dabbed his mouth.

'Unsophisticated little shit!' he shouted at me. 'This is the sixties. Time to experiment, little boy. Do things differently.'

My heart was hammering so hard I thought I might be in danger of breaking a rib or two. I ripped off the peach shirt and grabbed my T-shirt. And even through his anger and humiliation I could see him eyeing my body.

'I'm sorry I hit you,' I said. 'But you're going to have to find someone else to experiment with.' And I hurried out of the room.

Even as I ran down the hall, pulling on my T-shirt, I heard him shouting after me from the bedroom.

'You owe me, Jack. Remember? You all owe me.'

I started down the stairs and he raised his voice to a bellow, like an elephant trumpeting its anger.

'Or maybe you'd rather be back on the street where I found you, with nothing more than the clothes you stand up in!'

In the downstairs hall I passed Simon Flet on his way in. He threw me his usual cursory glance of disdain.

And then something in my face must have sounded an alarm, because he stopped and called after me as I ran down the stairs to the basement. 'What's wrong?'

I didn't reply until I got to the foot of the stairs and looked back to see his head turned up towards the first-floor landing. I raised my voice so that he would hear me. 'Nothing.'

He glanced down at me very briefly before turning and taking the stairs to the first floor, two at a time.

I was startled to find Rachel in the basement sitting room, and stopped in my tracks. I am not sure what she was doing there, but she was just as startled to see me. We stood looking at each other during several long moments of uncomfortable silence. Then I saw a slightly quizzical look in those dark, dark eyes and her head canted a little to one side.

'What's wrong?' An echo of Simon Flet.

I didn't tell her. 'Where is everyone?'

She shrugged. 'I have no idea. At the hall probably.'

I lifted my jacket from the back of a chair and pulled it on. And we stood in more awkward silence.

I said, 'See you around, then.'

But I didn't move until she had nodded and turned away,

and I ran back up the stairs to the ground floor. Then out into the glorious May morning, breathing hard and ready to weep, if I could have been sure that no one would see me.

II

I took the tube across town to Bethnal Green. In the weeks since our arrival in London, I had begun to get some kind of sense of the place. But only vaguely. I had spent so much time underground that I had only become familiar with those parts of the capital around the tube stations that I travelled to and from. Like some subterranean creature that pops its head up for a few minutes to get its bearings before plunging back down into the dark.

Like everyone else, I sat on the train lost in private thought, cocooned from the people around me by my very indifference to them.

They were the same thoughts I took with me as I walked through the leafy, littered streets of Bethnal Green in the spring sunshine. Dark, desperate thoughts.

I knew now that it had all been a big mistake. That the streets of London were not paved with gold, but with illusion. That no matter how far you run, the things you are trying to flee are there waiting for you when you arrive. Because you always take them with you.

In my desperation to escape I had done a dreadful thing. I had made a girl pregnant and taken a life. And the verse from

Omar Khayyám that I had learned at school came back to me as my feet beat down on the warm asphalt. I am sure my English teacher, Mr Tolmie, would have been pleased to know that I not only remembered it but fully understood it now, perhaps for the very first time.

The Moving Finger writes; and, having writ,
Moves on: nor all thy Piety nor Wit
Shall lure it back to cancel half a Line,
Nor all thy Tears wash out a Word of it.

But, oh, how I wished it was possible.

There was no sign of the others when I got to the hall. One of the residents was up a ladder outside, nailing a board across a broken window. There was shattered glass all over the pavement, and the main door appeared to have been damaged somehow, split open in places, with jagged shards of wood lying around the entry. I recognized the resident as a man called Joseph.

'What's happened here, Joe?'

He interrupted his hammering and looked down at me. 'Bunch of locals got drunk last night and attacked the hall when they came out of the pub. Threw stones at the windows and tried to break down the door with an axe. We were all locked inside. It was quite terrifying.'

There was no one around in the hall itself. Except for Alice. Thankfully, for once, she was covering her nakedness with a flimsy white gown and dancing around a long strip-painting that hung on the far wall. The paint, still wet where it had been freshly daubed on the paper, glistened in the sunlight that fell through arched windows on the south side. Music boomed out from the Dansette in the common room. The Kinks version of the Martha and the Vandellas hit 'Dancing in the Street'.

'Where are the boys?' I asked her.

'Haven't a clue, darling.' She pirouetted around me, dabbing the air with a long paint brush. 'Dance with me.'

'No thanks, Alice. Is Dr Walker around?'

I needed someone to talk to. Someone to give me a perspective, and I'd always felt a connection with JP, ever since discovering that we had both attended the Ommer School of Music.

'Ahhhh, Johnny, poor Johnny. Chief of the sanity police, punishing me with his cures. Physician, heal thyself.'

'Is he here?'

'Try his office, darling.'

There didn't appear to be anyone around as I made my way through the building, up the dark back stairway, through slashes of light from windows high up in the stairwell, and I wondered where all the residents had gone.

J. P. Walker's office was on the first floor. It was simply furnished with a scarred desk, an office chair, and two worn old leather armchairs with the horsehair bursting through the arms. As I approached its open door I could hear someone softly sobbing. A contained sob, held back and smothered in the chest. Without thinking, I slowed my walk to push up on tiptoes so that I wouldn't be heard.

Daylight flooding in from the office window spilled out through the open door into the darkness of the corridor, and I edged cautiously into the light, craning round the door jamb so that I could see who was crying in JP's office.

I was stung immediately by a sense of shock. JP was sprawled in his office chair, legs stretched out in front of him, face tipped forward so that his forehead was resting in his open palm. The doctor's face was shiny with tears, and deep, dark lines were etched into the grey skin below his eyes.

He was crying like a baby. I had no idea why, and I forgot myself for a moment, standing there and looking at him with unabashed curiosity. He lifted his head suddenly and saw me. For a moment I thought he was going to speak, then he leaned forward to push the door shut in my face.

I walked back along the corridor feeling both guilty and chastised. Guilty because of the prurient pleasure I had taken for a moment in witnessing his misery. Chastised because the door closed in my face had told me more eloquently than words that, whatever the reason for his tears, it was none of my business.

I heard voices in the common room as I came back down the stairs, and went in to find Dave and Luke and Maurie making tea. They seemed surprised, and a little embarrassed to see me.

'You want some tea?' Dave said.

'Sure.'

Luke put a tea bag in a fourth mug, and Maurie said, 'What are you doing here?'

I sat down at the end of the table, in JP's seat, and stared at my hands in front of me. The Kinks had progressed to the final track on Side One and were so tired of waiting. Alice was still dancing and painting out in the hall.

I looked up and said, 'I'm leaving.'

All three looked at me. Clearly surprised.

Maurie said, 'What do you mean?'

'I mean, I'm leaving. Going. Quitting. Departing. Fucking off out of here. I don't know how else to say it.'

Luke passed me a mug of steaming tea, and the others pulled up chairs.

'Is this because of Rachel?' he said.

I shrugged. 'Yes. And no. Well, I mean, she's part of it.' I drew a deep breath. 'Dr Robert tried to . . . I don't know how to say this . . . seduce me this morning.'

There was a dead stillness around the table. I was embarrassed to talk about it, as if somehow it reflected on me. But I'd started. And the rest just came pouring out of me. The whole sordid incident, ending with the punch.

'Jeeeees,' Dave said. 'You actually gubbed him?'

I nodded, and could sense their collective shock. For the longest time nobody spoke. The Kinks were no longer tired of waiting, but the arm had failed to lift at the end of the album and the needle went click, click at every endless revolution of the record.

Then Dave broke the silence, his voice unusually small. 'Happened to me, too.'

We all looked at him.

I said, 'What do you mean?'

He flushed deeply. 'Same thing. Wanting me to try on clothes.' He had difficulty concealing his shame. 'Wish I'd gubbed him, 'n all.'

Suddenly no one was looking at anyone else. Eyes were fixed on hands or cups.

Then Luke said, 'And me.'

He became the focus of our attention, and he blushed, too. It took a moment before we all turned our eyes towards Maurie. He looked grim, but his lips remained firmly pressed together and all he did was nod.

'Fuck's sake!' Dave said. And he turned blazing eyes in my direction. 'You're no' going without me.'

'Or me,' Luke said.

And we all looked at Maurie again.

'Is there a plan?'

But I shook my head. 'No plan. We fucked up. Whatever it was we thought we were going to find here, we haven't. My fault.' I raised my hands. 'Mea culpa.'

And I caught sight of myself in a cracked mirror on the far wall, with my bruised face, the white Elastoplast still stuck across my nose. The picture of failure.

'But I really never meant for any of it to happen. I really didn't.' I glanced at Maurie. 'And I never, ever thought I would lose my friends.' I had to swallow my emotion.

'You haven't.' Luke's voice was stiffened by a kind of steely resolve, and he looked pointedly towards Maurie.

Maurie spoke much more quietly, and still avoided my eye. 'You haven't.'

'Has to be a plan, then,' Dave said.

'I'm going home,' I told them.

Maurie shrugged. 'Then that's the plan.' He paused. 'But I'm not going anywhere without Rachel. Or Jeff.'

'Damn right.' Dave thumped his fist on the table. 'We came thegether, we go thegether.'

I smiled ruefully. 'Runaway home.'

CHAPTER SEVENTEEN

I

It was Luke's idea to wait until the evening before going back to the house to get our things. Dr Robert was throwing a party. We only knew about it because there had been some discussion of whether we would play at it or not. But in the end it was decided that the logistics were too complex. And the rift among us was an added complication.

So we whiled away the rest of the day in town, in cafés and pubs, talking about what we would do when we got back home, how we were going to explain everything to our folks, and what kind of reception we were likely to get. None of us was looking forward to that.

We counted up our cash and ended up at the information desk at Euston Station to calculate the cost of six single fares back to Glasgow, to see if we could afford it. We could, but only just. Maurie was dubious about whether Rachel would come with us. But at the very least, he said, he wanted to get her away from Onslow Gardens. And I harboured the secret hope that if we could persuade her to come back to Glasgow, there might just be some chance of patching up the damage between us.

We got back to the house around nine, when we knew the party would just be starting to get into full swing, and no one would notice us arriving. The place was already jumping. You could hear the music halfway down the street, and we could see partygoers dancing beyond the balustrade up on the roof terrace. Silhouettes against the evening sky. The front door was open, the hall and stairs leading up to the next floor jammed with the young and beautiful people of these Swinging Sixties. The rich and the famous from the world of music and movies, drinks in hand, spilling out from the kitchen and into the breakfast room and downstairs lounge. The Stones version of 'Under the Boardwalk' from their second album was blasting out of the lounge, and I could hear the single 'Zoot Suit' pounding down from the first floor, raw and filled with energy.

We pushed through the bodies in the hall, to the stairs leading down to the basement flat. No one wanted to party down there. It was too gloomy and cold and smelled of damp. Maurie shouted above the noise that he was going to find Rachel, and he headed off into the house.

As I turned to go down the stairs a girl caught my arm. She was beautiful, with long, tangled blonde hair and a skirt so short it barely covered her arse. Her eyes were glazed, pupils dark and dilated, her pale pink lipstick blurred around slightly too-full lips.

She pouted at me. 'Who bust your nose, baby?'

'Long story,' I said, and pulled my arm free.

'Don't you want to fuck me?' she called after me as I hurried down the stairs.

'No!' I shouted above the melee, without looking back.

And I heard her scream, 'Well, fuck you, then!'

The sound of the party was muffled in the basement, but it vibrated through the ceiling. We went off to our separate rooms to gather our things and pack them into the bags we had brought with us. It didn't take us long, and in five minutes we were gathered in the sitting room waiting for Maurie and wondering if Jeff was even in the house. No one had seen him all day.

It was nearly fifteen minutes of anxious waiting before Maurie appeared with a sullen-looking Rachel clutching a holdall. Black eyeliner was smeared and smudged around her eyes.

'She's coming with us,' he said. 'All the way.'

But she didn't look happy, and it was clear she didn't want to go. Somehow Maurie had persuaded her, and I wondered what it was he'd said.

'What aboot Jeff?' Dave asked.

Maurie sighed. 'Rachel says he's dancing up on the roof. We're going to have to go and get him.'

Rachel shrugged. 'I think you'll find he doesn't want to go with you, either. I saw him about half an hour ago. He was high as a kite. He might have dropped a tab.'

'Not going without him.' Maurie's voice was low and determined.

And we all knew that the only chance of saving Jeff from himself was by getting him home.

'Come on, then,' I said. 'Let's go bring him down.'

We left our stuff in the flat and hurried up the stairs to the hall. Dave was ahead of the group, but even before he reached the top of the stairs he stopped suddenly and turned back, colliding with the rest of us.

'Jesus,' he hissed. 'It's fucking Andy!'

'What? Rachel's Andy?' Maurie looked at him in disbelief.

Rachel paled to a sickly green-tinged pallor.

I peered up through the bodies beyond the bannister and saw Andy and two others that I recognized from the stairwell at Quarry Hill. Andy wore a black leather jacket with the collar turned up. His face was carved from concrete. Hard and rough-edged, cancerous and unforgiving. He was pushing through Dr Robert's party guests as if they weren't there. Ignoring their protests, shoving them aside. His henchmen followed in his wake, kicking or punching anyone who got in their way. Drinks were spilled, glasses broken, but beyond the path they scythed through the crowd, revellers in the kitchen or the lounge were oblivious, ears deafened by the music, senses dulled by drink and drugs.

I ducked back out of sight. 'It bloody is!'

'How the hell did he find us?' Dave growled.

And everyone looked at Rachel.

'I never gave him this address.'

Maurie's eyes bulged with disbelief. 'You mean you spoke to him? After everything we went through to get you away from there?'

Defensiveness made her angry. 'It was after I got pregnant . . . and before the abortion –' She broke off, and for the first time met my eye. But only for the most fleeting of moments. 'I was so low. I wanted . . . I needed . . . I don't know what I needed.' Then, more determinedly, 'I wanted a fix, that's what I wanted. And Andy was the only one I knew who could give me that.'

'So you told him where we were?' Maurie slapped his hands on either side of his head. 'I can't believe you, Rachel.'

'I didn't!'

Luke ushered us all out of sight, back down the stairs.

Rachel's voice dropped to a hissed whisper. 'I told him I had this job working with loonies at an experimental residence in the East End. I didn't think for a minute he could track us down to the Victoria Hall.'

'Well, obviously he did!' Dave's face had lost all colour and he was glaring at Rachel. 'Someone there must have given him oor address here.'

'I'm sorry!' But Rachel's apology was aggressive and lacking sincerity. 'I was depressed. Okay? I couldn't see any other way out of it.' She drew a deep breath. 'Anyway, I changed my mind the next day. Never, ever thought he would come looking for me.'

'Fuck!' Maurie's exasperation made me think he was not going to forgive her easily.

'Look,' I said. 'We just need to get Jeff and get out of here. And stay out of Andy's way in the process.'

And so we set off again up the stairs, very carefully. Threading a path through the fabric of the party, and making our way in ones and twos up to the first floor.

There were fewer people here, where Dr Robert had his study and bedroom. The door to the living room was shut. I tried the handle but it was locked.

With all the doors closed in the hall that led to the back of the house, it was dark there. But at the far end of the passage, electric light lay across the floor and angled up the wall opposite the open door of Dr Robert's study. Shadows moved through the light, and we heard raised voices.

'Oh my God, that's Andy!' Rachel's hand flew to her mouth.

I heard Dr Robert shouting, 'Get out! Just get out!'

We crept along the hall until we could see into the room. Andy was on his own, and I glanced over my shoulder, suddenly afraid that his sidekicks might be sneaking up behind us. But there was no one there.

Andy was leaning forward, his hands bunched into fists and planted on Dr Robert's desk. 'Not until you tell me where I can find them. Or I'll kick the shit out of you. And that's no idle threat, friend.'

Dr Robert stood on the other side of his desk, emboldened by its presence between him and the gatecrasher. 'I'm warning you. I'll call the police.'

He lifted the phone and Andy snatched the receiver from his hand, banging it back into its cradle.

'I told you. Do. Not. Fuck. With. Me!'

I hissed at Luke, 'Jesus, just let's get Jeff and go!'

And we turned and ran back along the hall, to push our way up the stairs to the second floor. It wasn't until we reached the upper landing that I realized that Maurie and Rachel weren't with us. But there was no point in turning back. And no time, anyway. None of us had the least idea where Andy's unsavoury friends might be, and the last thing we wanted to do was bump into them.

Dave and I followed Luke into the lounge. The French windows leading to the roof terrace stood open. Rachel had said that the last time she'd seen him, Jeff had been dancing out there.

The roof was thick with dancers, music from loudspeakers fed by a gramophone in the lounge booming out into the fading light of the evening and echoing across the rooftops. The air was heady with the perfume of marijuana, and simmering with unfettered sexuality. The dancers seemed transported, frenzied, bodies rubbing one against the other. Male, female. Male, male. Female, female. It didn't seem to matter. The dance and the music were primitive, tribal, a release of the most basic of human instincts.

For the briefest moment I saw JP dancing like a maniac among all these beautiful people, wild-eyed, transported as far from reality as the patients he treated at the Victoria Hall.

And I recalled seeing him just a few hours earlier, crying like a child in his office.

'There he is.'

I turned at the sound of Luke's voice, and my heart very nearly stopped. Jeff was balanced on the low stone balustrade on the street side of the roof. His feet were drawn together and he held himself very erect, arms straight out on either side, for all the world like a competitor preparing himself for a medal dive in an Olympic competition. No one was paying him any attention, and he seemed oblivious to the presence of the dancers crowding the roof.

'Jeff!' I positively screamed at him.

His head came around. He smiled when he saw us, and we began shoving our way through the bodies to get to him.

'I can fly,' he called over their heads.

'Jesus!' Dave's voice exploded from his lips.

'No, you can't!' Luke shouted.

But Jeff just grinned that big stupid grin of his. 'Yes, I can.'

Before we could get to him, he had flexed his knees and swung his arms straight out in front, as if he thought he was Superman. And he launched himself into space.

I heard the echo of my own voice yelling back at me from the rooftops. And then others. Those nearest the balustrade who saw him go. And the shockwave swept back through the dancers like a tsunami. Those who got to the balustrade first began screaming.

I was still numbed by an overwhelming sense of disbelief.

That what I had just seen could not possibly have happened. I wanted to get to the balustrade and look down to find Jeff smiling in the street below and waving back up at us.

But all such illusions were dispelled in a millisecond when we reached the spot where Jeff had jumped, to be replaced by the most gut-wrenching feeling I have ever experienced in my life, before or since.

Jeff was spreadeagled on the wrought-iron railings below, face up, skewered by half a dozen spikes which had punctured his back and exited through his torso and neck. I could see his eyes wide and staring back at us, and I knew that he was dead. But his body was still twitching, lost in the convulsions of some awful death throes.

I turned away, blinded by tears, and threw up on the bitumen, gasping for air and thinking that my insides were about to drop out of me. I felt Luke's hand on my arm, strong, reassuring.

'We've got to go.'

And I looked up at him to see the shock on his face.

It was chaos all around. Girls screaming, people running inside. I straightened up and Luke pushed me towards the door, Dave at my side, and we somehow managed to force our way through the lounge and into the hall.

People inside still had no idea what had happened, and music blasted up the stairs from below. We had reached the top of the staircase when I saw Andy's friends running up towards us, faces upturned and contorted by the scent of revenge. And all the shock and loss that I felt in the wake of what I had just witnessed converted itself somehow into pure, distilled fury.

I swung round and saw a fire extinguisher fixed to the wall. I cannot even begin to describe the thought processes that led me to rip it from its bracket and slam the release valve into the wall. I was simply incandescent. Foam exploded from the short length of rubber hose that I turned on the thugs as they reached the top of the stairs. Into the face of one, then the other, before I swung the canister full into the chest of the nearer of the two. The force of it sent him cannoning into his friend, and they fell backwards down the staircase.

The screaming and yelling all around me was deafening, drowning out even the pounding of the music that came from the living room and up the stairwell. Those people must have thought I was a madman, and in truth I felt possessed as I ran down the stairs, Luke and Dave right behind me, jumping over the sprawling bodies of the thugs from Leeds who lay in a tangle halfway down.

I heard someone shouting, 'Call the police. For God's sake, someone call the police.'

We got to the first landing and turned into the hallway, very nearly colliding with Simon Flet. I felt his open hand thump into my chest as he pushed me out of the way, and I saw the blood on his face and hands, and the terror in his eyes as he ran past, turning to sprint down the stairs to the ground floor, bellowing at partygoers to get out of his way.

Somehow, control of anything seemed to have slipped from my grasp. Everything was happening quickly and slowly at the same time. As if we were all starring in our own movie spooling in slow motion. I saw Maurie standing at the end of the hall, half in silhouette, half lit in outline by the lamp in Dr Robert's study. He seemed transfixed, and turned towards us, his face a veil of confusion. Luke ran down the hall towards him, and Dave and I followed.

The door to Dr Robert's study stood wide. Dr Robert himself was on the near side of his desk now, and standing over Andy's body. Rachel's one-time boyfriend lay in a twisted heap on the floor, blood pooling around his head. One side of it was split open, and I could see the grey-white of his brain marbled by the red that oozed through it. A large brass paperweight in the shape of an Oscar stood incongruously upright on the floor beside him, like a witness to murder, and yet clearly the murder weapon itself, blood trickling down the contours of the body from its bloody head.

Dr Robert stared down at the dead man at his feet, before looking up to see us standing in the hall.

His voice was little more than a whisper. 'Simon . . . killed him.' His voice rising in pitch now. 'He's killed him!' He gazed down on Andy again. 'I don't even know who this man is.' Then his head snapped up, accusation in his voice. 'What did he want with you?'

And in his moment of helpless confusion, I very nearly felt sorry for him.

It took Luke's cool head to wrest control of the situation.

He grabbed Maurie by the arm, and Maurie turned, stupefied, to look at him.

'We have to go!' Luke said. And when Maurie didn't respond, he yelled in his face. 'Now, Maurie, now!'

And he virtually dragged him along the hall as we ran back towards the stairs.

It took hardly any time for us to get out of the house. People were escaping it like rats from a sewer, and we were simply carried along by the flow. Through the hall, out of the door, down the steps and into the street. All the time to the incongruous accompaniment of the Rolling Stones song 'Pain in My Heart'.

It was almost fully dark now, street lamps casting pools of illumination broken by the flitting shadows of demented moths. Partygoers from the house spilled from the pavement into the road, forming a semicircle around the railing on which Jeff had fallen. We couldn't see beyond them to where his body was skewered on the spikes. But I could hear sobbing, someone screaming, a girl staggering free of the crowd to double over on her knees in the warm night and empty the contents of her stomach all over the tarmac. And I realized it was the girl who had propositioned me in the hall just half an hour before.

Maurie seemed dazed, as though he were concussed.

I took him by the shoulders and shoved my face in his. 'Where's Rachel?'

He looked at me blankly.

'Rachel. Maurie, where is she?'

He simply shook his head. 'Gone.'

'Gone? What do you mean? Gone where?'

'Gone,' he said. Then, almost as if realizing where he was for the first time, he found focus and glared back at me. 'Where's Jeff?' And when I couldn't meet his eye, it was he who grabbed me by the shoulders. 'Jack, where's Jeff?' Sudden fear in his voice. 'Jack?'

He let me go, then, looking around with wild eyes, as if only now aware of the mayhem in the street. I heard the distant sound of a police siren.

Luke said, 'Maurie, we need to go.'

But Maurie wasn't listening. He pushed past us and cleaved his way through the crowd on the pavement with such violence that he knocked one man over, and pushed a girl to her knees. The not so beautiful people parted in the face of his fury to let him through. And we saw, at the same moment he did, the prone form of poor Jeff impaled on the railings, blood dripping to form pools on the wall beneath him. His mouth was gaping and filled by the curl of his tongue, his eyes wide and staring as if in shock.

The most feral and frightening human sound I have ever heard issued from between Maurie's lips, and raised goosebumps all over my arms and shoulders. It was followed by the strangest hush as the anguish in his voice communicated itself to everyone on the street. I shoved my way through to him, turning him by the shoulders to lead him away. He offered no resistance, his face a mask of misery and disbelief.

'He thought he could fly,' I said.

And Maurie's head turned slowly. He looked at me with such incomprehension.

The police siren was very close now. And the Stones were singing something about being afraid of what they'd find.

Luke said, 'Nothing we can do for him, Maurie. We should go. We really should go.'

'What about our stuff?' Dave said.

'Doesn't matter.' Luke's eyes were open so wide with stress, I could see the whites of them all around his irises. 'If we don't want to get caught up in all this, we have to go.'

I nodded, and we almost dragged Maurie away along the street out of the light of the street lamps. Dave tried the gate to the gardens and it opened into darkness. A darkness that swallowed us as we ran off across cut grass that felt soft beneath our feet, through the shadows of trees towards the distant light and the sounds of traffic in Old Brompton Road.

Behind us I heard the wail of the siren as the first police car arrived, its blue light strobing in the night.

II

At this time of night the waiting room at Euston was all but deserted. Out on the concourse passengers stood in desultory groups of twos and threes, smoking, watching the arrivals and departures boards, times and platforms, names of places only ever seen on railway timetables, destinations known only to those who lived there.

Maurie sat between Luke and me in the far corner, leaning forward, elbows on his knees, face buried in his hands. He had wept inconsolably on the tube, and now seemed overtaken by inertia. Almost catatonic, like JP's naked lady in Ohio. Luke had his arm around Maurie's shoulder. He leaned forward and spoke so softly that I could barely hear what he said.

'What happened, Maurie? In Dr Robert's study.'

Whatever he had seen, he was a witness to murder. But he wasn't saying anything. Neither then, nor in all the years since. He gave the slightest shake of his head, before straightening up, to stare straight ahead into the smoky gloom of the waiting room. His face was still shiny wet with tears, but his eyes were dry now. Red and puffy.

'Poor Jeff,' he said. 'Poor Jobby Jeff.'

I closed my eyes and took a deep breath. 'Maurie, you have to tell me what happened to Rachel.'

His head swung slowly round and the pain in his eyes was almost too great for me to bear. I struggled to maintain eye contact.

'I don't have to tell you anything.'

But I wasn't going to give up that easily. 'Where is she?'

'I told you, she's gone.'

I sighed my exasperation. 'Gone where?'

'Just gone, Jack. Away from you. Away from all of us. Just gone. Forget her.'

The door swung open, and Dave came in, breathing smoke from his final cigarette. 'We've missed the last train tae

Glasgow. Next one's no' till the morning. We're gonnae have tae spend the night here.'

'Shit.' I banged my head back against the wall and closed my eyes.

Dave sat down opposite and sucked on his cigarette. And I heard Luke's voice, quiet but filled with determination.

'I'm not going back.'

I opened my eyes wide and turned to look at him. 'How do you mean?'

'I'm staying here.'

'In London?'

He nodded. 'We left nothing behind at Onslow Gardens to identify us. Some dirty linen, a couple of guitars and a melodica. Those goons in the Lake District ripped up Jeff's driver's licence, so they won't even know who he is. You can go back home and just pick up your lives where you left off.' He paused. 'Not me. I'm not going back to *them*. To my parents. To the Kingdom Hall and tramping the streets in all weathers. For better or worse, this is where I'm going to make my life.'

'You've no' got any dosh,' Dave said.

Luke shrugged. 'I've got a few quid. As much as I'll save on my train fare, anyway. I'll survive.'

I looked at him with his wide green, innocent eyes and remembered all the good times we'd had. The laughs. The madness. And I thought about Jeff, and his Veronica. Five of us had run away that fateful night more than a month ago.

Only three of us would be going back. And nothing, nothing would ever be the same again.

III

And so we spent that night in the waiting room at Euston Station, knowing that we wouldn't sleep, and yet drifting off in moments of overwhelming fatigue to dreams of Jeff, and his poor broken body impaled on the railings in Onslow Gardens. I don't know how often I replayed the moment when he launched himself into space, believing he could fly, and searched for something I might have done to stop it. But it always ended in the same, tragic conclusion.

Again, and again, and again.

In moments of waking misery, I saw Rachel's black, black eyes gazing at me out of the darkness, the light in them conveying, in turn, love, hurt and betrayal. And I cursed my cowardice.

Morning brought no relief from the torment. Luke went and bought our tickets for us, and we gathered on the concourse as the station came to life around us. A new day. The first without Jeff. Or Rachel. The sounds of trains revving on their platforms. The hiss of brakes. The monotonous announcement of arrivals and departures reverberating around the rafters.

Luke handed over our tickets and each of us in turn solemnly shook his hand. Because boys, especially boys from big macho Rain Town, didn't hug. At the last, I took his right hand in my left, and pressed a bunch of folded notes into his palm.

'What the hell's this?' He withdrew his hand as if I had burned him, and he looked in confusion at the notes he was holding.

'That's everything we've got among the three of us,' I said.

'I can't take this!'

'Of course you can. What bloody use do we have for it? Can't spend it on the train, and won't need it at the other end.'

He was touched and embarrassed. 'Thanks,' he muttered. Then, very quickly, as if he didn't trust himself to say more, 'See you sometime, then.'

And I saw his eyes filling up just before he turned away to walk briskly across the concourse, shoving his hands deep in his pockets.

2015

CHAPTER EIGHTEEN

I

'And I never saw him again until we stepped off the bus today at Victoria Coach Station.' Jack's voice died in the dark, to be replaced by a very long silence. And he began to think that Ricky had fallen asleep. 'Rick?'

'I'm here, Grampa. Just . . .' His voice was hushed. 'Poor Jeff.'

'Yes. Poor Jeff.'

'You never hugged Luke back then, but you did today.'

Jack couldn't resist a smile that no one would see. 'I did. Times have changed, Rick. Not sure how, or why. Seems we have permission to show our emotions, these days.'

'You could have stayed. I mean, fifty years ago. When Luke did.'

'I could. And maybe if I had, things would have been different. But, you see, I didn't have Luke's courage, Rick. I was afraid. I wanted to go back. I wanted the safety of the womb. The security of the family.'

Ricky could hear the bitterness in his grandfather's voice.

'So I went back to a life shaped by fear.' He turned his head on the pillow, trying to see his grandson in the dark. 'And that's the biggest crime you can commit in life, Rick. To be afraid of living it. It's the only one we've got, and you've got most of yours still ahead of you. So don't waste it, son. Trust me. You don't want to be looking back on it fifty years from now and wishing you'd done things differently. There's nothing more corrosive than regret.'

A further silence settled between them, but neither of them was ready for sleep.

Ricky said, 'What happened when you got home?'

'It was a long five-hour train ride, Rick. Maybe the longest five hours of my life. I'm not sure there was a single word passed between any of us all the way up through England and back into Scotland. It was as if anything we said might be an acknowledgement that Jeff was gone, and that Luke was no longer among us. I think we felt, all of us, diminished. Like we'd lost limbs. It's hard to explain.'

For the first time in many years Jack felt like a cigarette. A fleeting longing for the comfort that sucking smoke into your lungs can bring, the nicotine hit that both stimulates and calms. He had not felt any desire to smoke since giving up more than thirty years before, and was startled by the sudden and unexpected craving.

He said, 'When Luke went off to buy the tickets and we divvied up our remaining cash to give him when he got back, I left the others to make a phone call. A reverse-charge call to my folks.' He remembered the hushed sense of disbelief in his mother's voice when he had said, *It's Jack, Mum. I'm coming home*. 'So my dad was waiting on the platform when the train got into Central Station. Platform One. It's strange, because we never discussed this. But he must have called the other families. They were all there. Maurie's dad, and Luke's. And Jeff's. Not Dave's, though. My dad had to give Dave a lift home.'

Jack hesitated, remembering the moment as clearly as if it had been yesterday. His dad stepping forward to shake his hand. *Well done, son. I'm glad you had the courage to come back.* And Maurie's dad shaking his son's hand and saying almost the same thing. As if it had been discussed and rehearsed. And Luke's dad and Jeff's, standing there, puzzled, fearful. Lost.

'We never did tell Jeff's folks what happened to him. Just that he had stayed in London with Luke. Which was true in a way. And I suppose it was kinder to let them go on believing that their son was alive somewhere, making his way in the world. How could we have told them the truth? It was hard enough to carry it in our own hearts.'

Jack clenched his teeth hard and pressed his lips together to stop the emotion that welled up inside him from spilling over. That would have been embarrassing in front of his grandson.

'The rest of my life you pretty much know all about.'

Another lengthy silence drifted in the dark before Ricky said, 'So, if this actor, Simon Flet, didn't kill Rachel's boyfriend, who did?'

Jack closed his eyes and felt his stomach lurch at the thought that he had refused to even entertain since Maurie had told him that Flet was not the killer.

Rachel never had come home. And Maurie had always refused to say where she'd gone or what had happened to her.

He said, 'I don't know, Rick. Guess we'll find out tomorrow.'

II

Early the next morning, Jack and Luke walked on Hampstead Heath with Luke's black schnauzer, Odin, leaving the others at breakfast with Jan. Wild flowers grew among the long grasses in this gently undulating pasture, and Jack found it hard to believe that they were still in the heart of the city. Beyond the tops of the trees he could see chimneys and skyscrapers in the hazy distance of the cool, grey morning, but it felt like they were miles from anywhere. And a little of the sense of oppression that had descended on him since their arrival in London lifted like a weight off his chest. Suddenly it seemed easier to breathe.

A jogger, in clinging mauve Lycra, passed them on the half-gravel path that cut through the grass, an iPod Nano strapped to her arm, earphones firmly plugged in her ears to shut out the world. She almost certainly did not hear Odin's playful bark or Luke's call of rebuke, which brought the dog smartly to heel.

'Did you ever contact your folks?' Jack asked him.

Luke gazed thoughtfully into the distance. 'Never did.' He turned to Jack. 'Was that cruel of me?'

Jack shrugged. 'No more cruel than what they put you through, I guess.'

'I often wonder how my life would have been if I'd gone back.'

Jack smiled, 'Probably as often as I wonder how mine would have been if I had stayed.'

Luke was lost in a moment of reflective silence. 'I sometimes think I *should* have got in touch. But I didn't, and I don't regret it. Regret is such a waste of energy. You can't undo what's been done. But every new day offers the chance to shape it in the way you want. And that's how I've lived my life, Jack. Looking forward, not back.' He paused. 'Only thing I regret. Only thing I wish I could go back and change is what happened to Jeff. I've wondered so many times how different it might all have been if only we'd got up to the roof sixty seconds earlier.' He looked at Jack again. 'Do you ever think about those days?'

Jack nodded. 'Often.'

'Whatever any of us have or haven't done since, Jack, those were the days of our lives. I don't think I ever felt quite so alive.' He smiled fondly. 'Poor old Jobby Jeff . . .' he chuckled, 'as Dave would have called him. He missed out on so much.'

'It's different with me and Veronica,' Jack said.

And they both laughed.

Odin cocked his head and looked at them, no doubt wondering what was signified by the strange quacking sounds that issued from their mouths.

When their laughter died and their smiles faded, Luke said, 'Your grandson tells me he graduated with honours in maths and computer studies.'

'The boy's a bloody genius, Luke. Don't know where he gets it from. Certainly not me. He'd give you a run for your money any day.' He stooped to pick up a stick and throw it ahead of them for Odin to chase. 'But he's in danger of chucking it all away. I guess he's self-conscious about his weight. Got no real confidence. Locks himself away playing computer games half the night and sleeping most of the day. And his parents are a dead bloody loss.'

Odin returned with the stick, and Jack threw it for him again.

'Nightmare though it's been, I think this trip might actually have been good for him. Although we're both going to get it in the neck when we get home.'

They walked, then, in silence for a time.

Luke seemed lost in thought before he said, 'My boys are just about to commission an IT developer to write software for a custom-made database and accounting system for the agency.' He looked at Jack. 'Is that something Ricky might be able to do?'

Jack smiled. 'That's good of you, Luke. And I appreciate it. But you run a professional business. You need a professional software developer.'

'If he could do it, I'd rather the contract went to friends or family. And we have plenty of space in the house here. He's a nice lad. I think Jan's taken a fancy to him.'

Jack said, 'I twisted the boy's arm to get him to bring us down here. He really didn't want to do it. But, you know, we'd never have made it without him.' He tilted his head towards Luke. 'Why don't you ask him? See what he says. He'll not bullshit you. If he can't do it, he'll tell you.'

Luke grinned. 'Then I'll ask.'

They were almost back at the house when Jack said, 'Luke . . . about tonight.' He avoided looking at him. 'You don't have to come with us, if you don't want to. We've already burned our boats, but none of this has to touch you. And God knows what it is that Maurie's got planned.'

But Luke shook his head. 'You think I'm going to let you old farts go out to the Victoria Hall on your own?' He lifted his head to stare in thoughtful wonder at the sky. 'The Victoria Hall. The very name of the place brings it all back. I've thought about that bunch of people a lot over the years. J. P. Walker. And that crazy woman, what was her name? Alice. Both dead now.'

'Are they?'

'She died sometime in the seventies. You probably wouldn't have heard much about her up there, but she was a minor celebrity in London for a while. *Cured* by JP. Her art became quite fashionable. There were exhibitions, she wrote a book, started making a lot of money.' He paused for a moment of reflection. 'She dropped dead suddenly at a vernissage, a glass of champagne in her hand. An aneurism, apparently.'

'And JP?'

A sadness crossed Luke's face, like the shadow of a cloud as the sun slipped momentarily behind it. 'His philosophy and his writings were à la mode for a few years. But he seemed simply to drop off the radar in the seventies. Overtaken by age and fashion, I suppose. Then I saw his obituary in *The Times*. Must have been mid-eighties. He'd got into a tussle with the American immigration authorities over a conviction for possession of cannabis in the seventies. Sometime before that he'd established a home, and some kind of relationship, in New York City. Came back here for the funeral of his ex-wife, the mother of his children, and they wouldn't let him back into the States. He'd developed a drink problem by that time, too. Full-blown alcoholic, it seems. Anyway, they found him dead in a hotel room in the West End. Massive overdose of barbiturates.'

Jack was shocked. 'He killed himself?'

Luke nodded.

And Jack remembered that day he'd found JP weeping in his office. And the last time he'd seen him. Dancing wildly on the roof of Dr Robert's house in the moments before Jeff jumped to his death. *And those who were seen dancing were thought to be insane by those who could not hear the music.*

Luke stopped and turned earnest eyes on his old friend. 'I'm going with you tonight, Jack. Whatever really happened back then, I was as much a part of it as any of you. And I still am. I want to know what happened, too.'

CHAPTER NINETEEN

I

The last light of the evening had gone by the time they cruised slowly through the backstreets of Bethnal Green in Luke's Mercedes, turning finally into the square that was bounded on its south side by the Victoria Hall, dark and dominating against a sky of low cloud that reflected back the city lights.

Rising up around the other three sides of it were the same blocks of council flats that had been there fifty years before. Face-lifted now, many of them privately owned and lived in by Arabs and Asians, Eastern Europeans, and a handful perhaps of native East Enders.

The gardens were even more overgrown than they had been back in the day, and the Victoria Hall itself was boarded up, graffitied and neglected, abandoned to future demolition and redevelopment.

Luke drew his Merc into the kerb at the front door and looked up at the grim, decaying edifice that had once played host to a brave experiment in the treatment of mental illness. 'Locked up tight. We'll not get in there.'

'Aye, we will,' Maurie's voice came from the back seat, surprisingly strong and filled with resolution. 'There's always a way in. Help me out.'

Ricky and Dave slipped out from each of the back doors, then helped Maurie on to the pavement in front of the hall. Broken glass crunched underfoot, just as it had that final day when Jack came looking for the others to tell them he was going home. Jack came around to join them, and Luke stood hesitantly by the open door of his car.

Maurie managed a smile. 'I don't blame you, Luke. I wouldn't want to leave my Merc here either – if I had one.' He turned towards Ricky. 'That's why the boy here's going to stay with it, park it a street or two away so we don't frighten off our visitor. If you trust him with it, that is.'

'Of course I do,' Luke said.

But Ricky was disappointed. 'I want to come in with you.'

Maurie shook his head. 'It's none of your business, laddie. And nor should it be. You stay with the car and keep it safe.'

Luke chucked him the keys, and Ricky caught them reluctantly.

Maurie looked at his watch. 'Come back about twelve. We should be done by then.'

Jack nodded to his grandson, and Ricky slipped huffily behind the wheel, slamming the driver's door shut and starting the engine. He revved several times, filling the cool night air with the toxic fumes of carbon monoxide, before slipping into gear and driving slowly away, turning at the end of the street to disappear from view.

As the sound of the motor faded, an uncanny silence fell on the square. Lights in windows dotted the darkness around them, but there was no one in the street. Four of the original five members of The Shuffle stood in the shadow of the Victoria Hall. They had neither played together nor stood together on this spot for half a century, and although fifty years had passed and much had changed, the ghost of Jeff still hovered among them, as if he had always been there.

'So how do we get in?' Jack said.

'Service entry,' Maurie said. 'Always was the weak spot.'

He pulled his heavy winter coat around himself, as if he were cold, and Jack thought how he looked drowned by it. Diminished by his disease, a shadow of the man he had once been.

They followed the wall along the front of the building, ignoring the main door, until they reached a rusted wrought-iron gate that blocked the way into a narrow alley leading down the side of the building to a service door accessed through a brick archway. On the other side of a broken-down railing, the gardens lay brooding darkly in their leafy neglect.

Dave tried the handle of the gate, and it swung inwards with a creak of rusting hinges. The alleyway was littered with debris. Bricks and broken glass, bits of a dismembered doll, the ragged remains of a coat, the skeleton of an umbrella, a single, soggy trainer.

Luke drew a torch from his jacket pocket and shone it into darkness, picking out the detritus of decades of abandonment. They stepped carefully through it to a black-painted door beyond the arch. It was padlocked.

'No way in here,' Luke said.

'Aye, there is.' Dave's voice boomed out of the dark. 'Gimme that torch a wee minute.'

And he took the torch from Luke's hand and made his way back along the alley, before turning the light and his attention towards the broken fence. It took him less than two minutes to break one of the palings free of its rusted anchor and return, brandishing it triumphantly.

'Okay, light the lock for me. A wee leaf oot of Jeff's book here.'

He thrust the torch back at Luke, and in the circle of its light slipped the paling through the loop of the padlock and braced himself against the door with his foot. Years of bending pipework, and hefting baths and sinks and toilet bowls, had built muscle in his arms and shoulders that was still there and still strong.

But in the end it wasn't the padlock itself that gave. It was the bracket that fixed the clasp to the door. Wood splintered and cracked in the still of the night and it came away in its entirety, padlock and all.

A flimsy Yale lock then offered no resistance to Dave's boot as he slammed it into the door once, twice, three times. He stood panting triumphantly as it finally gave, and the door swung into the blackness beyond.

He grinned. 'Missed ma vocation, eh?'

Maurie snatched Dave's flat cap from his head and chucked it at him. 'Here, go and hang that up on the gate, so our friend knows where to get in.'

'Ma guid bunnet?' Dave protested.

But Maurie was dismissive. 'No one's going to steal your greasy old cap, Dave.'

The darkness beyond the door was full of must and memories, and an all-pervasive reek of damp and decay. Luke led the way through a rubble-strewn hallway, shining the beam of his torch on the floor ahead, then up the narrow service stairs to the landing, which led to the common room and the hall. Here, faded paint on scarred walls bore the faintest traces of the designs once painted on them in shit by the demented Alice.

No one spoke as they all trooped into what had been the common room. A table stood at its centre, white with plaster dust, lumps of broken ceiling strewn across its surface. It might have been the very table they had all sat around in those long-ago days of madness. Luke righted a couple of toppled chairs before swinging the beam of his torch briefly into the old kitchen. An ancient rusted cooker still stood there, its door open and hanging off a broken hinge. Incongruously, a blackened aluminium cooking pot sat on one of the rings, as if waiting for someone to make their morning porridge.

With the others close behind him, he stepped through into the hall itself. A couple of table-tennis tables were half covered by dust sheets. The wooden floor had been marked out in different colours at some time for badminton and basketball. There were hoops mounted on the walls at either end, and old moth-eaten badminton nets lay in a discarded pile at one side.

'They must have used it as a youth or community centre at some point,' Jack said. He turned to Maurie. 'What now?'

'We wait.'

'When's our visitor due?'

Maurie checked his watch. 'Not for another hour. I wanted to be sure we were here well ahead of time. Who knew how long it might take us to get in?'

II

Back in the common room they dusted down chairs and sat themselves around the table. But Luke was dubious about how long the batteries in his torch might last, and he went in search of the fuse box to see if there was still power in the hall. The others were left in the dark, sitting at the table and listening to his footsteps as he moved around on the landing and up the stairs.

When he returned, he shook his head. 'No juice.'

He went into the kitchen and rummaged around in cupboards and drawers before they heard his 'Aha!' and he returned with a cardboard box of old candles, some of them half burned, others with pristine waxed wicks.

'Anyone got a light?'

No one had, and Luke's smile quickly faded. He laid the

candles on the table and went back into the kitchen, returning a few moments later with a renewed smile on his face and a box of matches clutched in his free hand. But they were damp, and old, and one after the other they sparked and sputtered and shed their phosphor, but failed to ignite. Until the second from last, which fizzed and popped before bringing flame to the splinter of wood. Quickly he lit the first candle, and they all grabbed one, lighting each in turn, and setting them on the floor along the walls, fixed in their own molten wax.

Then they sat at the table again, as they had done all those years before, their shadows dancing around the walls to remembered music. Jack recalled all those faces, pale and drawn, many of them bearded, eyes lit by madness, a fug of cigarette smoke and marijuana hanging over them in a cloud. And JP tipped back in his chair at the head of the table, bare feet crossed in front of him, regaling them with tales of insanity and miracle cures, his charm and charisma the single factor that bound and kept the residents of the hall together.

Dust settled around them, along with their silence, and they waited in the flickering darkness with the ghosts of the past, and Jack could almost imagine that Alice was still dancing out there in the hall, slashing the air with her brush, painting their ordinary lives with extraordinary colours. And for just a moment he believed he could actually hear the distant echo of the Kinks playing on that scratchy old Dansette. They had been so tired of waiting back then.

Jack, too, was tired of waiting. He had spent a lifetime wondering what had become of Rachel, and still Maurie was giving nothing away.

'What the hell was it with you and Rachel?' he said suddenly.

And Maurie's eyes flickered towards him.

Although his focus was on Maurie, Jack could feel the tension among the others around the table, like a fist clenching.

'And don't tell me it's none of my business, or that you don't owe me anything. Not after all these years. Not after everything I've been through to get you here.'

Maurie's expression was bleak. His eyes held Jack's for only an instant before they slipped away to stare off into some long-buried past. Or perhaps towards a dwindling future that promised nothing but pain and death. Whichever, it brought him little comfort, and Jack saw how his hands bunched into fists on the table in front of him, turning his knuckles white. A physical manifestation of what they all felt.

'You always wanted us to go to Leeds, didn't you?' Jack said. 'That's why you had her letter with you. One way or another you'd have talked us into going there and getting her out of that place.' Jack's thoughts raked through old coals and found that there was still a glow among the embers. 'Maybe that's the only reason you came with us in the first place.'

It was a thought he had never entertained before, and hadn't seen coming until now. But he saw how it affected the wreck of a man sitting opposite him. Like a physical blow, bringing a hint of pale colour to a dead-white face. Maurie unbunched his fingers and laid them on the table in front of him.

'I was eleven years old when I found the letter from the Beth Din.' His voice was thin and reedy, and not much more than a whisper, but somehow it filled the room. 'I don't know what my parents had it out for. Maybe the rabbi had asked to see it, I don't know. But my father had left it on his bedside cabinet. I used to sneak into their bedroom sometimes when they were out, to look at the soft porn magazines he kept hidden under the bed. Which is when I saw it.'

He dragged his eyes away from their focus on his hands, and he looked around the faces silently watching him. And in spite of himself he smiled at their consternation.

'The Beth Din's a Jewish court that rules on matters of Judaic law. The letter was marked "Confidential" and addressed to both my parents. The Clerk of the Court was writing to advise them that the Beth Din had established that Maurice Stephen, their adopted son, was of Jewish birth, and that an entry had been made accordingly in the Proceedings Book.'

'You were adopted?' Dave said.

Maurie nodded.

'And you never knew till then?'

'Nope.' A sad smile attempted to animate his face but somehow failed. 'It's quite a feeling when everything you thought you were and knew falls away from beneath your feet. There were only two things in my head. The first was that they had lied to me. My parents. By omission, perhaps, but it was something they should have told me. I had a right to know.' He paused, and they all heard his breath rattling in his windpipe. 'The second was a question. Who the hell was I?'

Jack closed his eyes. There was a sudden clarity in his mind about where this was going, and his thoughts went reeling back through time, like the tumblers in a slot machine, making sense of so much that had made none at the time.

'What did you do?'

'I went through all the deed boxes in my father's study till I found a folder marked "Adoption". And there it all was. A receipt from Renfrew County Council children's department for payment of fees due in the legal adoption of Maurice Stephen Cohen. Five pounds and five shillings. Or five guineas. That's what it cost them to buy me. Cheap at the price, wouldn't you say?'

His bitter little laugh turned into a cough, and it took almost a full minute for him to bring it under control.

Finally he said, 'But there was other stuff. Personal correspondence between my father and a woman who ran a hotel and restaurant in the Gorbals. Smith's Hotel. Though I guess the Smith was probably a corruption of Schmitt. It was famous in the years after the war, a gathering point for the Jewish community. Any Jew arriving in Glasgow would end up there. And Isa Smith was a sort of godmother to the whole community. My mother, my adoptive mother, worked there as a bookkeeper. It was Isa who arranged the adoption.'

His eyes wandered off again to some distant past.

'I knew the place. My mother took me often, and I would eat in the kitchen. There was an older woman who worked there. Always made such a fuss of me. Serving me little treats, kissing me on the forehead. Always with a gift for me on my birthday. Turned out she was my grandmother. My blood grandmother. Her daughter had got herself pregnant. Unmarried. Just a teenager. And in those days it was common for unmarried mothers to give up their babies for adoption. Only she didn't want to. She wanted to keep that baby. Me.'

And for a moment it seemed as if Maurie would be overwhelmed by emotion.

He swallowed hard. 'But she'd never have managed to keep it without the help of her mother. And then the stupid girl gets herself pregnant again, almost immediately. Not even by the same man. And her mother tells her she can't look after two babies, and that the second one will have to be adopted.' He shook his head. 'But before she even got the choice she went and died in childbirth, and there was no way her mother could cope. It was Isa's idea to put us both up for adoption.' He refocused to meet the gaze of his old friends. 'Me and Rachel.'

Luke's voice was hushed. 'She was your half-sister.'

Maurie nodded. 'My adoptive mother and her sister were both older women. Neither of them had been able to conceive. Something genetic, probably. So I went to one, and Rachel to the other. The perfect solution. Kept us both in the same family. Except that my aunt had wanted me, a boy, but drew the short straw and got Rachel.'

'Did Rachel know?' Jack's voice was so quiet as to be almost inaudible. 'I mean, about being adopted.'

'Not until I told her. And then it was our secret. One we swore to keep always. Just the two of us. Our parents never knew that we knew. I had confronted the woman who worked in the kitchen at Smith's. My real grandmother. She couldn't deny me anything. Least of all the truth. And I think, in the end, she wanted me to know. She broke down and told me the whole sordid tale, but made me swear never to tell a soul. Which, apart from Rachel, I haven't until now.'

Maurie's eyes dipped to the table, then rose slowly to seek Jack's. 'She had too much of her mother in her. I was scared –'

'That she was going to sleep with some guy and get herself pregnant.' Jack held his gaze, unblinking.

Maurie swallowed back his emotion again, then spat it out as anger. 'It was only too clear to me. History repeating itself. First that thug Andy . . .' he hesitated, '. . . and then you, Jack. She gave herself too easily. Just like her mother. And you took advantage.' His lip trembled as he sucked in a breath. 'And I was right. Because it happened, didn't it? Just as if it were programmed into her DNA. Got herself pregnant, just like her mother had! And I saw the whole damned cycle repeating itself a generation on. It was only ever going to end badly.'

No one knew what to say, and silence hung among them like a pall of cigarette smoke in a sixties pub.

*

It was some minutes before they heard it. The first scrape of leather on concrete. Footsteps disturbing rubble on the stairs. Slow, cautious steps. Jack glanced at his watch. Whoever it was had arrived early. And the tension in the common room became palpable. A beam of torchlight played out on the landing then snapped into darkness, before a tall, lean figure stepped into the undulating wash of candlelight in the doorway. An elderly man, well into his seventies, Jack thought. He wore an expensive camel coat and shiny black shoes. His strong, handsome face beneath a head of thick white hair swept back from his forehead was still extraordinarily familiar. Even after all this time.

Jack had been half expecting Dr Robert, and so it came as no surprise. What did surprise him was the rude health and powerful build of a man who was anything up to ten years their senior. Evidently life had treated him well.

But if he was still familiar to them, his incomprehension as he looked at the faces gathered around the table was patent.

He frowned. 'Who the hell are you?'

'Don't you remember?' Maurie said.

Dr Robert swung his eyes in Maurie's direction, and his shock at the appearance of the dying man briefly widened them.

'Five lads from Glasgow who lived for well over a month in the basement flat at Onslow Gardens. Who were there the night that a young thug called Andy McNeil was bludgeoned to death by the actor Simon Flet. Must be hard to see those young boys in these old men.'

The doctor's transition from confusion, to fear, to recognition and resignation passed across his face like so many shades of the same colour. But darker each time.

'The Shuffle,' he said.

And Jack wondered how on earth he remembered the name after all these years.

'Jack,' Jack said.

'Luke.'

'Dave.'

Dr Robert's eyes swung back to Maurie, whose smile seemed more like a grimace.

'No. You wouldn't have recognized me in a million years, would you?'

'Maurie,' Dr Robert said, his voice so soft it scarcely penetrated the still of the room.

'Well remembered.'

'What's wrong with you?'

'Just about everything that could be. Sit down, doctor. It was me that emailed you.'

Dr Robert took a step into the room, but didn't sit.

Maurie watched him, unblinking, totally focused. 'Must have scared the shit out of you, my message, eh? Scared to come, scared not to. It was the sting in the tail that caught you, though, wasn't it?' He bared his teeth. 'Just irresistible. I knew it would be.' He paused for effect. 'That I knew who really killed Andy McNeil.'

Dr Robert was impassive, and his voice was stronger now. 'It was Flet.'

Maurie shook his head. 'It wasn't.'

Jack turned towards Dr Robert. 'Then it must have been you.'

And the doctor's eyes flickered in his direction, hostility flashing briefly behind his apprehension.

But Maurie shook his head again. 'No. Not the good doctor, either.' He kept his eyes fixed on the older man. 'But you did kill Simon Flet. Didn't you?'

The blood drained from Dr Robert's tanned face and left him looking jaundiced. But he said nothing.

Maurie leaned forward on the table. 'That scumbag Andy McNeil attacked you that night, didn't he? Ripped your phone out of the wall and came at you round the desk. And you lifted that Oscar paperweight and hit him with it. And who could blame you? A clear case of self-defence. He went down on to his knees clutching his head, blood oozing through his fingers.' He drew a tremulous breath. 'I know, because me and Rachel were out in the hall. We saw it all. And you ran out to go and call the police from another phone somewhere else in the house. Ran right past and didn't even see us.'

He was having trouble breathing now, and took a moment to collect himself before he turned his head to look at the rest of the group.

'It's the only reason I wasn't up on the roof with you when you went looking for Jeff. Rachel thought she could talk sense into Andy. I didn't, and I wasn't about to let her try.'

There was almost a full minute when the only sound in the room was Maurie's stertorous breathing.

Then Luke said, 'So what happened, Maurie?'

'When the doc had gone, we went into the study as Andy got to his feet. He was pretty unsteady, seriously concussed, I'd say. The blood was streaming down his face and he was in a filthy mood. Rachel wanted to help him, but I wouldn't let her. He started shouting at her. Cursing her, calling her every foul-mouthed name he could think of. Told her how he was going to make her pay for running out on him. Lock her up and make her his fuck puppy.' His mouth curled in distaste. 'His words.'

Maurie reached into his coat pocket now to bring out a handkerchief, with an almost uncontrollably shaking hand, and wipe his mouth.

'He was a piece of shit. And that was my sister he was threatening. So I picked up the Oscar and smashed his fucking head in.'

There was not a sound in the room. And as far as Jack could tell, not a soul breathing in the entire universe.

Then Maurie said, 'I can still hear the sound of his skull breaking.'

'*You* killed him?' Doctor Robert was almost breathless with incredulity.

'I killed him. And I'd do it again. A hundred times over.'

'But you weren't there when I got back. Only Simon. Crouching over the body.'

Maurie was having trouble speaking now. 'Do we have any water? I need some water.'

Luke went through to the kitchen and found a cracked mug that he rinsed under the tap, filled and brought back for Maurie to drink from. Maurie tipped his head back as he drank, water cascading from both sides of his mouth to run from his chin on to his chest. His face was the colour and texture of wax. He breathed deeply for a good thirty seconds. Then summoned all his strength to speak again.

'Rachel was hysterical. She knew I'd killed him. I dragged her back out into the corridor.' He let his gaze wander around the table. 'You guys were probably never aware of it, but there are service stairs at the back of the house that go up from the ground floor all the way to the attic. Rachel knew, though. There's a door at the end of the corridor beyond the doctor's study that leads out to them. She took me out there and said we could escape without being seen. But I told her this was my problem now, not hers, and I wasn't leaving without Jeff. But that she should go. When she refused, I screamed at her and slapped her. Hard. And told her if she didn't leave I wouldn't keep her secret any more.' His eyes blazed at us.

Dave said, 'What secret, Maurie? That she was your sister?'

And a tiny, bitter smile twisted his lips. 'No. Not that. And, after all, she went, didn't she? So it was a secret I kept.' He returned his focus to Dr Robert. 'I came back into the hall just as you returned to the study and found Simon there. Obviously he'd gone in looking for you while we were out on the stairs.

He found Andy McNeil lying dead on your study floor and he thought you'd done it. And when you came back to find Andy dead, you thought you'd done it, too.'

For the first time since his arrival, Dr Robert looked his age. Paler and frailer, the certainties of a lifetime suddenly stripped away, to confront him with a truth which had evaded him all these years.

Maurie said, 'You really did think you'd killed him, didn't you? So when Simon looked into your eyes, that's what he saw there. Guilt, fear. The realization that your life as you knew it was about to change irrevocably because of one stupid, thoughtless act. And that foolish young man sacrificed himself for you. For the man he loved, the man he believed loved him, too.'

Maurie was transported back through fifty years, the little life left in him burning fiercely in his eyes.

'He didn't know that his lover was a serial molester of young boys. Or maybe he suspected it, who knows? Who can even begin to guess what was in his mind? But I saw you flinch when he lifted that paperweight, as if you thought he might hit you with it. And I was just as confused as you when he put it down again, standing it upright on the floor next to the body, covered in his fingerprints and began smearing his face and hands with blood. And it dawned on me that he was taking the blame. Taking the fall for you. The stupid man almost knocked me over when he ran out of your study.'

Dr Robert pulled up a chair and sat down heavily, staring at his hands laid flat on the table in front of him. 'I always thought it was me. My whole life. That I'd killed that man. And it took me all that time to figure out why Simon did what he did.'

'Because he loved you,' Luke said.

'And you killed him for it.' Maurie fixed the doctor with a look so filled with hate that Jack recoiled from it, as if it were something physical. 'Half a century later, you killed the man who sacrificed his life for yours.'

Dr Robert looked up, eyes on fire. 'No! Sy was . . .' he searched for the word, '. . . he was an egomaniac. Arrogant. Disruptive on set. He'd been fired from the film he'd been working on that morning. They'd just had enough of him. And his agent had dumped him. So he was in a pretty volatile state of mind. You see, Sy wasn't an actor, he was a *celebrity*. All he was interested in was fame. And what he did that night, taking the blame, it didn't just make him famous. It made him . . . a legend. The man who simply disappeared off the face of the earth.'

He looked round their faces, as if looking for their sympathy.

'You think it was love? Really? So how is it he comes back fifty years later threatening to expose me if I don't stump up? If I don't get him a little apartment somewhere in London with a monthly stipend, so he can live out the rest of his days in anonymous safety, financially secure.'

'Why didn't you just do that?'

'How could I trust him? How? I mean, who knows how he survived all these years, or where? Or what bitter jealousy it was that brought him back. Seeing me reach the pinnacle of my life and career. Honoured by my country. Arise, Sir Cliff. Who the hell knows? But I wasn't about to risk it. To let him spoil it all now. Even if no one believed him, the publicity would have tarnished me. I couldn't allow that.'

He stood up again, suddenly agitated.

'And anyway, the man was already dead. That's what everyone thought. No one to miss him, or regret his passing.'

He paused, gazing beyond them all into some personal hell all of his own.

'I was sure I had removed all possibility of identification when I cut away his tattoo.' He shook his head in frustration. 'But I was wrong. Wrong!'

And he thumped his fist on the table. The noise of it reverberated around the room and out into the hall. The blood had flowed back into his face now, coloured red by a cocktail of mixed emotions.

'I suppose you're going to go to the police.'

Maurie shook his head. 'No.'

Dr Robert's relief was tangible, but it vanished in a moment as Maurie drew a pistol from an inside pocket. Bizarrely, to Jack, it looked like a toy gun he'd had as a kid. But he was under no illusions about it being a toy. It shook so much in Maurie's hand that he had to steady it with his other, both arms extended in front of him, the gun pointing across the table at Dr Robert.

His three friends were on their feet in a moment, chairs toppling backwards to raise dust in the candlelight.

'For Christ's sake, Maurie!' Dave's voice was elevated by alarm.

Maurie's smile was grotesque. 'Amazing the acquaintances you make during eighteen months behind bars. And the things they can get you when you really need them.'

Luke's voice was more controlled, but Jack could hear the tension in it.

'Don't be stupid, Maurie. Nothing to be gained by this. You barely knew Flet. He meant nothing to you.'

Maurie's gaze was fixed on Dr Robert. 'This isn't for Flet,' he said, and suddenly the light of all the candles seemed to flicker more brightly in his eyes. 'This is for Jeff. Poor Jeff who thought he could fly. Poor Jeff, who was my best and only friend all through childhood, who stood up for me against the bullies. Who was always there for me, whatever the problem. Poor Jeff, who never had the life he should have.' His eyes held Dr Robert helpless in their thrall. 'Seduced into taking drugs, and God knows what else, by you, you bastard.'

And he pulled the trigger three times, pumping his bullets straight into Dr Robert's chest, the recoil almost toppling Maurie backwards in his chair.

The noise was deafening in the confined space, and the doctor flew back against the wall, then slowly slid down to the floor leaving a trail of blood glistening on the painted plaster behind him.

The sound of the gunshots seemed to take an eternity to fade, and left them feeling as if their ears had been plugged by cotton wool.

Dr Robert sat on the floor, back against the wall, his eyes wide, mouth hanging open, blood staining his camel coat a dark brown.

Dave gawped at him in horror. 'Jesus Christ, Maurie, you've killed him.'

Maurie lowered his hands to rest them on the table, but still he held the gun. 'It's what I came to do. No knighthood for Dr Robert.'

Luke bent down to check the doctor's pulse. He caught Jack's eye and shook his head, then stood up again.

Maurie said, 'You'd better go. These walls probably contained the sound of the shots, but who knows who else might have heard them?'

Jack frowned, panting hard and still in shock. 'We're not going without you, Maurie.'

'Yes, you are.' Maurie was quite calm now. Even his hands seemed to have stopped shaking. 'I only have a week or two left in me. Maybe not even that. You boys . . . well, you might all have a whole wheen of years left among you. So go and live your lives, and make the most of what you have left of them.'

'Maurie . . .' Luke took a step towards him.

'Go!' Maurie raised the gun to point it at him.

Luke was startled. 'You wouldn't!'

Maurie forced a grin. 'No, I wouldn't.' He turned the gun to press the barrel to his temple. 'But unless you really want to watch me blow my brains out, I suggest you go now.'

Jack said, 'You're really going to do this, aren't you?'

'I am, Jack. Quick and easy. And gone. But . . .' He reached into his pocket with his free hand and drew out a white envelope, which he placed on the table in front of him and pushed towards Jack. 'I figure maybe I owe you this, though part of me says you still don't deserve it. But, well . . . I never promised Rachel I'd take her secret with me to the grave.'

Jack felt a chill of apprehension as he reached for the envelope.

'She never had the abortion, Jack.'

Jack's face stung as if he had been slapped, and he felt Luke and Dave's eyes on him.

'Oh, I know you took her to that woman's place. But in the end she couldn't go through with it. And didn't tell you because she didn't want you to think you *had* to stand by her. Though, in my book, that would have been the decent thing to do. Even though you weren't Jewish. Anyway, the only person she told was me, and she made me promise not to tell.'

Jack's world had stopped turning on its axis. He stood paralysed. 'You mean she had my baby?'

'She did, Jack. Kid doesn't know.' He chuckled. 'Hardly a kid now, though.'

Jack was almost afraid to ask. 'And Rachel?'

Maurie nodded towards the envelope. 'You'll find an address in the envelope. Go there at three tomorrow. Someone will meet you and tell you all about Rachel.'

The envelope trembled in Jack's fingers. It felt as if it held his destiny in it. A coda to a life that had never lived up to his hopes for it. An average life, stultifying in its ordinariness, except for those few extraordinary weeks in 1965. The days of their lives, Luke had called them, and that's what they were.

'Now go!' Maurie's voice echoed out into the hall.

But Jack rounded the table, ignoring the gun.

Maurie panicked. 'What are you doing?'

Jack leaned over and kissed his forehead. 'Thank you, Maurie.' And he saw tears spring into his old friend's eyes.

'For fuck's sake get out of here. I hate farewells.'

The three old men stopped by the door, and looked back at the shrunken figure who had once been their lead singer. But they didn't see the shrivelled old man about to put a bullet in his head. They saw the plump young singer who had once auditioned for Scottish Opera and had the voice of an angel. Maurie. Their friend. And not one of them could bring himself to say goodbye.

They had reached the alley where Dave forced open the service door before they heard the shot.

A single shot, clear and pure, like Maurie's voice had been once.

EPILOGUE

They drove up the hill past suburban semis on their left, and on their right what looked like a city park abandoned to the vagaries of nature behind a wall and fence. Gloomy and neglected. Long grass and tangling briar, dead trees in among the living, stark in their leaflessness.

At first, Ricky had driven Luke's car through the London traffic with meticulous care born of fear. That Luke had trusted him with it was flattering, but he was terrified of bumps or scrapes, and his confidence on strange roads in a strange car was not high. But after half an hour he had begun to relax a little.

The GPS burbled out its instructions. A woman's voice that sounded uncannily like Margaret Thatcher. Ricky preferred to rely on the video screen to map out their progress, and the orange arrow that kept them right. His grandfather sat beside him. Silent. A black hole. Lost in thoughts he was not about to share. Ricky dragged his eyes from the road for a moment to look at him.

'Are you ever going to tell me?'

'No.'

'At least tell me what happened to Maurie. I deserve to know that.'

'You don't want to know.'

'I do.'

'Trust me, Rick, you really don't.'

Ricky fell back into a semi-sulk. Then, as they reached the top of Brunswick Park Road, he said, 'Luke offered me a job.'

'I know.'

'He told you?'

'Yes.' Jack looked at his grandson for the first time. 'Can you do it?'

Ricky snorted derisively. 'Of course I can. He said I could stay with him and Jan. He also said I'd have to get my National Insurance sorted out as a freelance, then we could talk about a contract and terms.'

'It's a great opportunity, Rick. To get away from home. Break the cycle. See a bit of the world.'

Ricky was indignant. 'I've seen more of the world than I ever wanted to in the last few days!'

Jack smiled. 'You're just scratching the surface, son.'

They cruised down the far side of the hill, and the GPS warned them that they were three hundred yards from their destination.

'Thanks, Grampa,' Ricky said suddenly.

Jack cocked an eyebrow, distracted from where they were going by his surprise. 'What for?'

'For making me go on this trip with you.'

Jack laughed, in spite of himself. 'That's not what you were saying three days ago.'

But Ricky's face was a study of reflection. 'I never knew it, but it was like I was in hibernation or something. Just waiting to wake up. It's . . .' he glanced across the car again, '. . . it's been one hell of an experience, Grampa. I just wish you'd tell me what happened last night. I'm a big boy now, honest.'

But Jack was spared from responding by Mrs Thatcher. She said, 'You have reached your destination.'

And Jack looked around, surprised. They had arrived at a small roundabout at the foot of the hill. He was looking for a house. Number 147. But on their left was open parkland behind a mesh fence, and on their left wrought-iron gates on stone pillars leading to an area of mature trees and manicured lawns. He'd missed the sign, but Ricky hadn't.

The boy's voice was hushed. He knew immediately what it meant. 'New Southgate Cemetery and Crematorium,' he read.

And Jack's heart went dead.

He'd had no idea what to expect, or how it might have been to face a Rachel in her mid-sixties all these years later. And maybe somewhere in the darkest recesses of his mind he had known she was already gone. Really gone.

Ricky pulled in to park the Mercedes outside the gate, and they stepped out into the sunshine of this breezy spring afternoon to see a man selling flowers from a cart just inside the cemetery.

Ricky glanced awkwardly at his grandfather. 'She's dead?'

Jack nodded. 'I should have known it was the only way Maurie would have given away her secret.'

Ricky slipped an arm through his. 'Come on, then. You'd better go and say goodbye to her.'

Once inside, the size and extent of this old cemetery became only too painfully clear to them. It was enormous, with paths turning in concentric circles, linked by spokes, and a chapel half hidden by trees at their centre. Undulating land was divided and subdivided into countless plots. A population of the dead so huge that they had built special white-stone walls to accommodate coffins four deep. From the distance they looked like miniature blocks of flats.

Ricky was bewildered. 'How will we ever find her?'

But Jack had spotted the tiny sign planted in the grass. White letters on a black background and an arrow pointing the way: *Hendon Reform Synagogue Cemetery*.

With Ricky on one arm, and his stick in his free hand, he followed the signs round to their left. They passed a grave festooned with colourful plastic butterflies and big-petalled flowers, another hung with a heart. The words at the centre of it read, *I love you, Daddy*. The names here had their origins in many far-flung places. Italy, Greece, Russia, China. A cosmopolitan community of the dead. No prejudice against immigrants here.

The cemetery of the Hendon Reform Synagogue stood opposite the chapel, a small plot of Jews screened off from the sea of

Christian crosses that surrounded them by dilapidated wooden fencing that had collapsed in places.

Jack told Ricky to wait, and went in on his own. A small brick building bore a legend in Hebrew above the door, and one exterior wall was given over to niches where ashes could be stored. Those that were occupied were closed off by grey plaques engraved with gold lettering. *In Loving Memory of John Hans Schuck, dearly loved husband and father, 1919–2002.*

The plot itself was small, on a downhill slope, gravel with cement paths, and it was filled almost to capacity. Plain marble headstones set above concrete plinths.

A middle-aged woman stood on her own halfway down. Lean once, but carrying now a little of the weight that comes with age. She had dark hair drawn back from a strong face, and looked up from the grave she was standing over as Jack approached.

He glanced down at the headstone. *Rachel Stahl. 1949–2013.* So she had never married, or at least had kept her maiden name. And died just two years ago. Jack felt a wave of melancholy weaken his legs and he supported himself heavily on his stick.

When he looked up, he found the woman gazing at him with puzzled curiosity.

'Are you the man Uncle Maurie said would meet me here?'

Jack nodded, not trusting himself to speak.

'You're a friend of his?'

'Since we were boys.'